# HEREWARD
## The Immortals

*Also by James Wilde*

HEREWARD
HEREWARD: THE DEVIL'S ARMY
HEREWARD: END OF DAYS
HEREWARD: WOLVES OF NEW ROME

For more information on James Wilde and his books, see his website at www.manofmercia.co.uk

# HEREWARD
# The Immortals

James Wilde

BANTAM PRESS

LONDON • TORONTO • SYDNEY • AUCKLAND • JOHANNESBURG

TRANSWORLD PUBLISHERS
61–63 Uxbridge Road, London W5 5SA
www.transworldbooks.co.uk

Transworld is part of the Penguin Random House group of companies
whose addresses can be found at global.penguinrandomhouse.com

First published in Great Britain in 2015 by Bantam Press
an imprint of Transworld Publishers



A CIP catalogue record for this book
is available from the British Library.

ISBN 9780593071854

Typeset in 11.5/14pt Sabon by Falcon Oast Graphic Art Ltd.
Printed and bound by Clays Ltd, Bungay, Suffolk.

1 3 5 7 9 10 8 6 4 2

For Elizabeth, Betsy, Joe and Eve

# Foreword

For the warriors, wealthy merchants and nobles who fled the iron rule of King William after the invasion of England in 1066, Constantinople was the shining star in the east. Filled with immense wealth, secure behind its great walls, and accepting of strangers, the city could become, many hoped, a home away from home. Constantinople was poised at the point where east meets west in what is modern-day Turkey, with trade, and wonders, flowing into it from the Mediterranean and from Asia. But for all the comforting familiarities of the magnificent churches, the commerce, and the civilized values of art and law, those travellers would have found a world that was in many ways alien.

Constantinople was fading. After centuries as a seat of vast power, its finances were no longer on a sound footing and its army had deteriorated, relying heavily upon foreign mercenaries. The empire – essentially the eastern half of the old Roman empire – was beginning to crumble as enemies on every side began to nibble away at the territory under its control.

Those pressures were taking their toll internally. The court had become a nest of vipers, with any family that could lay even the flimsiest claim to the throne plotting to seize power. In the fifty years leading up to the English influx, Constantinople had seen twelve emperors. There were a great many claims.

When Hereward led his men into the city, Michael Doukas wore the crown. Only seventeen when he ascended to the throne on his father's death, Michael was more interested in books than political power. Into that vacuum stepped his mother and his uncle, John Doukas, who effectively governed as regents. John was the Caesar, at that time a title awarded to an influential relative of the emperor and one of the highest positions at the court. Cunning and cruel, with a long history of treachery, he also made a great many enemies.

One of those foes was Anna Dalassene, the matriarch of the Comnenoi, another family with a strong claim to the crown. Her brother-in-law, Isaac Comnenos, had been emperor. When he became gravely ill, Isaac wanted Anna's husband, John Comnenos, to succeed him. But despite Anna's lust for power, her husband refused, and Michael Doukas' father was chosen in his stead.

Anna Dalassene would never give up her desire to see her family rule the empire. That made her a dangerous rival in the eyes of John Doukas. He put her on trial for treason, and then had her banished to a monastery on the island of Prinkipos.

Soon after, however, the Caesar met his match. The emperor's adviser, the eunuch Nikephoritzes, eventually turned Michael against his uncle, and John Doukas was compelled to retire to his estates. But even at a distance, the Caesar's relationship with the emperor made him a force with which to be reckoned.

As the pressures upon the empire continued to grow, at court whispers of dissent mutated into a multitude of plots against the emperor. It was said that there was a knife in every shadow. But Emperor Michael had one thing in his favour, the ever-loyal Varangian Guard, his elite force of mainly English and Viking warriors who were perceived as the fiercest fighters in the world. Extremely well paid, celebrated, even adored by the people for their prowess, the Guard was the pinnacle of ambition for any half-decent warrior with an axe. But it was not easy to be accepted. Gold, and lots of it, was needed to buy a place in the ranks, and then the fighting men had to prove themselves. Still, the potential rewards were so great that many were prepared to try.

Constantinople was awash with simmering violence, intrigue and conspiracy, with dangerous enemies everywhere. As our story begins, Hereward and his spear-brothers must navigate a safe passage without knowing who can be trusted, who is friend, and who is foe . . .

James Wilde

# Prologue

*The Anatolian plain, east of Constantinople, 16 May 1073*

Deep in the hot night, death howled.

The man and the boy fled from it across a moonlit plain of jagged rocks and brown dust. Ahead of them, their shadows carved paths towards a twisted tree surrounded by clumps of scrubby vegetation. It was not enough. There was nowhere left to hide.

As he pulled himself over the stones with his one remaining hand, the man mewled like a babe. He could not rest, not even for a moment. Those full-throated shrieks demanded vengeance.

His face was ruined. A gaping hole whistled where once his nose had been. One eye was milky. His ears had been sliced off and his bottom lip was split in two. Some of his hair had been torn out or seared away, and what remained of his features was a mask of scar tissue.

His name was Ragener, once a sea wolf who brought terror to his victims on the waves, now little more than a frightened rabbit, less even than the wrecked man he had always considered himself to be. Ragener, a furnace of hatred, all of it burning for one man: Hereward of the English, the warrior who had taken his hand and thereby plunged him even deeper into hell.

On he staggered, glancing over his shoulder. The Turks swarmed in his wake, leaping like wolves at the hunt. There were six of them, dressed in felt *boerk* hats and belted *yalma* coats. He imagined he could see their single-headed axes glittering as they whirled above their heads.

Beside him, the boy seemed to care little. His face was like the moon above, pale and still, but his dark eyes were unnaturally large. Some would say Justin Verinus was no boy at all, but a ravening beast, and Ragener was inclined to agree.

'Why did you kill that girl?' the sea wolf spat. The words took odd shapes as they escaped from his misshapen mouth. 'There was no need. You have doomed us both.'

His thoughts flew back to the torn body lying among the rocks as the boy sat beside her, peering up at the stars as if nothing were amiss. Ragener had spent the previous hour creeping into the camp of the Turks to steal some flatbread to assuage their growling bellies. Those black-bearded warriors had been lost to their singing around their blazing campfire, swathed in the spicy aromas of roasting lamb. All had seemed well. He and the boy would eat a little and be on their meandering journey into the east before they were discovered. That had been his hope. But barely had he shaken the boy roughly for his stupidity when the querying shouts had rung out from the nearby village. Once the warriors had been roused to pursuit, Ragener knew that any hope that remained was thin.

Justin loped on without answering. Not a flicker of emotion crossed his face.

'To have come so far . . .' the sea wolf all but sobbed, 'all our suffering, and so close to our prize, for it all to be snatched away now.' He could almost taste the power that would have been his if the boy's father, Victor Verinus, had succeeded in his plot to murder the emperor and place Justin on the throne in Michael's stead. But now Victor was dead, slaughtered by his rivals the Nepotes, a family just as bloodthirsty, just as cunning, as the Verini. Ragener spat. All he had left was the life of an outlaw, fleeing from his many enemies in the court at Constantinople, with only this beast for companionship and the thin hope of finding the one ally on whom they could still count. For a moment, he thought about snapping the boy's neck to show his anger, but with only one hand he could not be sure he would come off best.

Clouds began to sweep in from the west on the dry wind. If only they could evade their enemies for a little longer, the bright eye of the moon might be obscured. But as he crested a low ridge, his foot clipped a rock. Over the top he spun, and rolled down the incline. He yelped as his bones cracked against stones, and then his head slammed against the hard ground and darkness engulfed him.

When next he looked up, he was lying on his back in the dust. Dark shapes loomed around him. Ragener choked off a cry of shock as he realized they were unmoving, yet still he felt his blood run cold. Though he was not a godly man, a muttered prayer crept from his lips.

Ten Turks hung from X-shaped timber crosses. All dead, a feast for the birds. Some had been flayed, others dismembered. *What demon-haunted land is this?* he thought. Whoever committed this atrocity did not fear those savage warriors, even though a multitude of them seethed across the east of the empire.

Ragener jerked his attention back to the ridge as one by one the Turks of the village war-band emerged. Their howls ebbed away and a silence fell across them that was somehow worse.

'It was not me,' he cried out, not knowing if they understood the English tongue. 'It was the boy!' He stabbed a finger towards where Justin crouched at the foot of one of the crosses. The lad was looking up at the sticky remains as if he had found a new game to play.

The sea wolf thrust himself back over the dusty ground, but when he looked up at the bearded warriors he realized that they had barely registered his presence. Their eyes had grown wide with fear as they gazed upon their tortured brothers, and they began to babble in their throaty tongue. If warning this was, it worked its hellish magic well, he thought.

The light dimmed. The clouds swallowed the edges of the moon.

As the Turks' chatter was plucked up by the rising wind, Ragener watched their attention fall back upon him. The warriors still desired their vengeance, but at least now they would not linger over it. He could see in their glinting eyes that it would be a quick death and they would be away before they were found by whoever had caused this slaughter. He tasted bitterness at the vile life he had lived, but one regret haunted him above all: that he had not slain the English dog Hereward who had lopped off his hand.

Trying to hide his fear in the face of his enemies, he bared his teeth. What came after death must surely be better than this miserable existence.

Behind him, Justin began to laugh, a thin, reedy sound, like a bird at twilight. Ragener felt a surge of rage. If he could have slit the boy's throat at that moment, he would have.

The wind began to moan. Whorls of dust licked up along the ridge. The Turks gripped their swords tighter, eyes flickering from the rotting corpses to their prey. Summoning their courage, Ragener thought. All around, shadows began to pool. Only a sliver of moon remained. The warriors became silhouettes against the lowering sky.

Raising his blade, the first Seljuk took a step down the slope.

Justin's high-pitched laughter spiralled up, drowning out Ragener's whimpers. The sea wolf blinked away tears. There was no justice in this world. He deserved so much more than this ignoble death.

The growing gloom snatched away all but the barest details. The Turk edged down one more step, his movements becoming more confident.

And then Ragener heard a whistling beneath the wind that

ended in a sticky thud. A shape flew through the air towards him. A moment later he found himself staring into dead eyes. The Seljuk's head lay in front of him, leaking blood into the dust.

A maelstrom of sound and fury swept along the ridge. Cries of alarm rang out. The warriors began to stumble back and forth in confusion, yelling as they hacked at the air with their swords. Ragener squinted, trying to pierce the dark, but he was as lost as those raving Turks.

Another whistle. Another wet thud. Ragener was reminded of his father preparing the lamb for the pot as the cold weather drew in. Raindrops swept on the wind, spattering the sea wolf's face. But then he smelled iron and knew it was not water.

The dying screams of the Turks became one voice, punctuated in the lulls by the boy's shrieking laughter. A body tumbled down the slope, flapping like a landed fish. Another head rolled among the crosses.

Terrified, the sea wolf jerked his head this way and that. The dark swallowed whatever prowled around him. *What devil is out there in the night?* he thought, his prayers rising in a wave. For surely this slaughter could be the work of no man. Too fast, too brutal, leaving not even a whisper of feet on dust to mark its passing.

When the last scream was cut short, and the final warrior crashed on to the stained ground, only the moan of the wind rolled out across the waste. Even Justin had grown silent.

Ragener's breath burned in his chest. Then, after what seemed an unbearable moment, a terrible silhouette loomed up on the ridge. The sea wolf whimpered, and waited for the end.

# Chapter One

The plume of dust hovered on the eastern horizon. Beneath a golden sky, the band of warriors lowered their spears and watched the cloud billow beyond the waist-high grass swaying in the hot breeze. Voices stilled. Faces darkened. Since dawn the high plain had been empty. But now, as the day turned towards dusk, every man there felt a grim sense of foreboding.

'What do you see, Guthrinc?' As Hereward of the English shielded his eyes his arm flexed, rippling the circular tattoos of a warrior. Though he had been born in the old English Kingdom of Mercia, he was a Dane by blood and his blond hair near glowed under that merciless sun. He had led the war-band for long years now, through the bitter, failed rebellion against the Norman cur William the Bastard who had stolen the English throne, and through the months of exile that had led them here, to these strange lands in the east.

Times had grown hard, and their enemies seemed to multiply by the day. His helm was dented, his mail-shirt torn here and there, each scratch telling a story of some hard-fought battle. His shield was splintered and needed a new lick of paint, but the golden hilt of his sword, Brainbiter, still gleamed as brightly as ever.

Guthrinc had the best eyes of all the spear-brothers. An

English oak who towered over the others, he had known Hereward longer than any man there. 'One rider,' he said. 'And riding hard.'

'Watch him. The Turks rarely venture this close to the city walls. But one day they will come in force, and then our new masters will regret paying so little heed to the enemy on their doorstep.' Hereward turned back to the rest of his men, irritated by the bitterness that had laced his words.

An angry voice rang out at the rear of the war-band. Hereward scanned his men: Hengist the Mad, Sighard, Hiroc the Three-fingered, Derman, Herrig the Rat and the rest; fifteen in all. Tempers had grown thin since they had been forced to take the coin of the Roman army to put food in their bellies. These were some of the bravest warriors he had known. In England, they had taken on the vastly superior Norman forces at the Isle of Ely. Only betrayal by the monks had brought about their defeat. But in Constantinople the Romans treated them like children who could not be trusted to raise a weapon, or, worse, like slaves. For day after day, week after week, they had roamed the deserted lands, watching for an attack that never came.

Pushing his way through the spear-brothers, the Mercian was not surprised to find Kraki at the heart of this disturbance. Wild of beard and hair, the Viking was a seasoned warrior, a former huscarl in the hall of Earl Tostig of Eoferwic, with a dark mood that rumbled away like a summer storm. Now the scar tissue on his face was crumpled in a scowl as he jabbed a finger towards Turold, a young warrior from Wessex who fancied himself a scop. His songs soothed the other spear-brothers at the end of a hard day, and every man listened, entranced, when he spun his riddles beside the fire.

'Save your brawling for the tavern,' Hereward commanded the Viking. 'These days you are snapping like a wounded bear.'

Kraki glared. 'This coward wants to throw down his spear and become a farmer.'

Turold held up his hands. ''Tis true. I have carried a spear with you ever since I wandered into the camp at Ely with nothing but the mud under my nails. I fought then because the Normans wanted to take everything we held dear. But there is not one here who would truly call me a fighting man.'

Hereward could not argue. Turold was always quick to smile and for the most part as gentle as a churchman.

'Some Roman girl has stolen his wits,' Kraki grumbled.

'Leave him be,' one of the others called. 'He has done no harm to you.'

Kraki rounded on them, his fists bunching. 'We are brothers! We stand together, we die together!'

Another warrior made a farting noise that only drove the Viking to even greater rage. Hereward stepped forward, placing one hand on Kraki's chest to hold him back. Beckoning, he walked to where Guthrinc was keeping watch. Still scowling, the Viking followed.

'You would pick a fight with Turold?' the Mercian said when only Guthrinc could overhear. 'No. Something else has been gnawing at you for too long now. What truly irks you?'

For a moment, Kraki chewed down on his anger. Then he swept an arm out towards the lonely countryside. 'What is there for us here? When we left England, you promised us gold and glory. But gold does not come any easier in Constantinople than anywhere else in this miserable world. We will not be able to buy ourselves a new beginning until we have earned it.'

'The coin will come. We have earned a little.'

'Little. Aye, that is a good word.' Kraki hawked up a mouthful of phlegm and spat at his feet. 'We are trusted only with work that would not tax a child. The Romans laugh at us, when they are not treating us like the dirt beneath their feet. And for what? Pay that barely stills my rumbling belly.' He hammered one fist against his chest. 'We are the warriors who risked all against the fiercest army in the west. Where are our rewards? We came here to join the Varangian Guard. Those bastards have more gold than they can ever spend, and more glory too.'

Hereward stared across the wide plateau to where the

mountains rose up in the distance, trying to find words. Kraki spoke true. For all their sacrifices, they deserved much more than this. Yet only gold, and a lot of it, would buy their way into the ranks of the emperor's elite guard. He felt the weight of his burden. Without a moment's doubt, his spear-brothers had followed him into a battle which had seemed unwinnable, and in defeat they had been forced to leave behind kin, friends, home. Where would he find the fortune required to repay them for such loyalty?

'If we stay here, the Romans will destroy us by degrees,' Kraki said, releasing the words he had kept tight inside him.

'And if we flee, we will be running for ever,' Hereward countered. 'Would you be known as the cowards who abandoned England, and then ran from every hardship?'

The Viking shook his head and looked away, wrestling with his doubts. He would not be easily placated, Hereward could see. This was not like Kraki at all. No battle had ever seemed too great for him to fight.

Guthrinc glanced over at his friend, a wry smile playing on his lips. 'Do I hear the whining of a babe in arms?' he murmured.

'You would be happy hunting fowl with your bow,' the Viking spat. 'Some of us want a just reward for the use of our strong right arm.'

'You are full of vinegar,' Guthrinc replied, chuckling. 'You would be sour even if the gold came up to the top of your beard.'

Kraki grunted. 'Chance would be a fine thing.'

'Wait.' Guthrinc's attention snapped towards the horizon. Narrowing his eyes at the dust cloud, he said, 'There is more than one rider. I count three . . .' He squinted. 'No, four . . . more. A war-band. It looks to me as though they are chasing the other one down.'

'Turks? Here?' Hereward furrowed his brow. At first the Seljuks had merely crept across the edges of the empire from the south and the east, but in recent years that trickle had become a deluge. Grown lazy on their wealth, the Romans had done little to fight for their land, as if this problem would somehow fade like the mist under the sun. Facing no resistance, the Turks had grown fearless. But surely any war-band would not venture this far west and risk waking the sleeping beast?

'Ready yourselves,' he called, turning back to his men. 'Lie low and wait for my command.'

As one, the spear-brothers fell silent, dropping down into the long grass so that it seemed they had never been there. Guthrinc kneeled to hide his huge frame. Peeling aside the green curtain, he watched the riders approach.

'If this is none of our business, we let them ride by,' Hereward breathed beside him.

At first the English could have been alone for a hundred miles with only the singing wind for company. But then the ground began to throb. The sound of hoofbeats rumbled across the grasslands. When Hereward peered over Guthrinc's shoulder, he glimpsed a dark smudge taking shape in the dust, gradually coalescing into a man hunched over the neck of his horse.

'A Roman,' Guthrinc murmured.

'How can you tell?'

'He carries a standard, the eagle with two heads. Tattered, it is.'

'He has been in a fight, then.' Hereward weighed this information, then craned his neck back and whistled a sharp blast through his teeth. The grass swished. Deep in their hiding places, his men would be stiffening as they raised their spears and shields.

If this was a Roman soldier being run down by enemies, Hereward knew they would have no choice but to act. He felt a tremor of passion run through him. It had been too long since his blood had been up, and he had grown afraid that the dullness of the days had taken the edge off him. Deep in his head, he heard a hungry whisper from the part of him that he had grown to hate, the devil that lusted for slaughter and filled him with a rage that made him blind to all reason.

As the riders left the barren landscape and plunged into the grass, the dust drifted away to reveal eight men hard on the heels of the fleeing Roman. To Hereward's eyes, they did not look like Turks – they wore hauberks and helms that gleamed in the setting sun.

Guthrinc cocked his head to one side. 'Can this be? Normans?'

'They are everywhere,' Kraki sniffed. 'They know how to make good coin with their strong right arm.'

When the leading rider neared, the Mercian could see that the warrior's face was twisted with terror. His leather armour was filthy with the dirt of the road, and his horse seemed exhausted. Spittle sprayed from its mouth as it veered through the grass. In contrast, the closest pursuer was bearing down upon them fast, sword raised to take the Roman's head.

Hereward tapped Guthrinc on the shoulder. The English oak knew the command without looking. Snatching his bow from his back, he nocked an arrow in one fluid movement, took aim, and loosed it. His shaft rammed into the forehead of the attacking warrior, flinging him off the back of his mount. When his horse reared up in shock, confusion erupted among the war-band. Milling in the long grass, the Normans searched this way and that for the enemies they now knew were hidden nearby.

Hereward felt the blood thunder into his head, and his devil cry out in anticipation, but he was no longer strong enough to resist it. With a roar, he burst into the open, axe in hand. At his heels, the rest of the English surged out, yelling. The Normans fought to keep their mounts under control, shouting warnings.

Guthrinc towered up, loosing another shaft in a blur, and then another. One arrow splintered harmlessly upon a shield, but the other smacked into the chest of one of the riders. Flailing, the man tried to wrench the arrow out, even as blood bubbled up over his fingers.

The Normans had the advantage of horseback, and they hacked down with their double-edged swords. But the courage of the English – some would say madness – had thrown the enemy into disarray. Spears herded their beasts into a frenzy and stabbed at thighs and arms. So many weapons bristled that the Norman shields were not enough.

As one rider tumbled back with a scream, Hereward thumped his axe down, splitting the man's face in two before he had even hit the ground. Kraki ripped his blade through the leg of another, and Sighard, Hiroc and Hengist unseated a third.

The surviving Normans were not stupid. Seeing they were outmatched, they rounded their horses and spat epithets as they thundered away. In response, the English shook their spears in the air and cheered. Hereward could see that even that short battle had been good for them. Grins sprang to lips and cheeks flushed with passion. Men whose spirits had been whittled away suddenly remembered who they were in the thick of a fight. He felt proud. Brave men, all of them. He would give them what they deserved, however much it cost him.

Sighard, the youngest of the English warriors, was beckoning frantically from where the Roman's exhausted horse roamed riderless. Under his shock of red hair, his pale face looked worried.

The Roman lay on his back in the long grass, shaking as if in the grip of a fever. He was barely more than a boy, his cheeks so hollow it seemed he had not eaten in days. Blood caked the corner of his mouth and a gash seeped on his forehead. Delirious, he jabbered as his eyes rolled white.

'What does he say?' Sighard asked.

Kraki peered into the lad's face. 'And why was he fleeing so hard?'

Hereward knelt beside the fallen man, noticing how his right fist was gripped tight. Gently prising open the fingers, he revealed the object the rider clutched as if his life depended on it: a gold ring with a large oval engraved with the sign of the two-headed eagle.

Sighard gaped. 'That is no warrior's ring. It can only belong to someone great.'

The Roman seemed to find peace now that he had delivered

his prize. For a moment his eyes swam, and then he looked clearly into Hereward's face. 'You must warn the emperor,' he croaked. 'We were not prepared. Now doom is coming for all of us.' And with that his eyes fluttered shut as exhaustion claimed him.

'What did he mean?' Sighard whispered, his eyes wide.

Hereward looked up and across the swaying grass into the west, where the red sun dipped towards the horizon. 'Make ready,' he said. 'We return to Constantinople this night.'

# Chapter Two

In Constantinople, even the night bowed its head to man. Outside the entrance to the hippodrome two vast stone bowls of oil blazed, and above them, along the whitewashed walls, torches sizzled. In the glare, sharp emotions burned too. Those who had not gained entry to the races haggled over bets, over winners and losers, jostling amid the stink of sweat and pitch. Desperation seethed in the ones who stood to lose more coin than they could afford. Greed, excitement, fury, all of it was at boiling point.

From within that grand stone building, the roar of the crowd boomed above the rumble of hooves as the horses thundered round the circuit. Riders yelled their encouragement, whips lashed flanks.

Hereward pushed his way through the throng, weary from the long journey back to the city. In his homeland, the villages would be quiet at this hour. Folk would be gathered with their kin around their hearth-fires, sharing tales of the day. Not here. They did things differently in this vast, greedy, hot, dangerous, scheming city. The Mercian looked round at the feverish men and women, cocking their heads as they tried to make sense of the din of the race. The lure of gold kept men from their beds, drove them out into the streets at first light. Gold was all that mattered to these Romans, and all that mattered to the desperate folk who streamed through the gates every day, fleeing from threat or hungry for a new dawn.

Sighard hurried up, his pale skin and red hair standing out among the swarthy Romans. 'The others are inside,' he said. 'They bid me wait for you.' His eyes were questioning.

'The Roman we found will live. The leech is tending to him at the Boukoleon palace.'

'The ring? His warning?'

'Whatever he knows is not for the likes of us,' the Mercian said, unable to hide his sardonic tone. 'He is saving it for the emperor's counsel.'

Sighard sighed. 'And a reward?'

Hereward shook his head, irritated. The guardsmen had shown him the door so fast he had barely had time to speak.

As the race ended, the cheers of the victorious surged up. Within moments, a knot of men swept out of the entrance. At their heart, Hereward glimpsed the emperor Michael, too bright-faced for a man who carried the burden of empire. He was young, an innocent. But as always the eunuch, Nikephoritzes, stood behind the emperor's left shoulder with eyes like brass. He was the true power, Hereward knew. Both men were swallowed up by ten warriors of the elite Varangian Guard, their hands never far from their long-hafted Dane-axes, their gaze continually searching the crowd for any sign of threat. They never smiled, rarely spoke.

Sighard followed the Mercian's stare. 'The emperor should thank his god that he has men like that at his back. He would have been torn from his throne and tossed to the wild dogs in the street by now, if not for them.'

'Aye,' Hereward agreed. 'This is a troubled city. Plots growing like weeds, the emperor loathed for his weakness. And beyond the walls, more enemies than any man can count.' He eyed the young Englishman. 'The emperor needs more men, men like us, to keep him safe. Soon he will see that.'

'I am sick of waiting for fortune to smile upon us.'

Hereward turned at the gruff voice. Kraki scowled at anyone who dared meet his eye. He and Guthrinc had emerged from the hippodrome with some of the other spear-brothers. The English oak was gnawing on hot lamb that he had bought from one of the street sellers, wiping the grease from his mouth with the back of his hand. 'I would be away, in the north,' Kraki continued. 'I miss the cold, and the rain, and the wind that cuts right through you. Weather like that keeps you hard. Here they are all too soft.'

Guthrinc frowned, seemingly sensing something else in his friend's words. Laying one of his big hands upon Kraki's shoulder, he said, 'You need some wine inside you.'

'I need mead.'

'Wine will drown your grumbles as well as anything. Come, we will find what passes for a tavern in these parts.' He gave the Viking a shove.

Once the warriors were shouldering their way through the crowd, Sighard leaned in and whispered, 'I worry for Kraki.'

'He has been walking under a cloud for too long. What troubles him?'

'Why, he misses Acha,' Sighard replied, surprised that the Mercian did not know.

Hereward nodded. Now he understood. His thoughts flew back to the first time he had seen Acha, in Earl Tostig's hall in Eoferwic on that cold, cold winter's night. Hair the colour of raven wings and skin like snow, she had used her beauty to bend many a man to her will there. But in the end she had given herself to the Viking. Though he hid it well, Hereward knew Kraki had been bereft when they had been forced to part. Acha had returned to her own folk, the Cymri, and the Viking had found himself here, in a strange world, where his worth was rarely appreciated. Little surprise that he yearned for England. 'Do not let him hear you say that,' the Mercian cautioned. 'He will cuff your ear so hard it will grow larger than your head.'

'When the blackness claimed me after the death of my brother,

Kraki dragged me back into the light. I would do the same for him.'

'He is a proud man. He does not take help easily.' Hereward felt concern for the gruff Viking, as he did for all his men. 'His spirits will recover once we have bought our way into the Varangian Guard.'

Sighard did not look convinced.

Curses echoed above the babbling voices and Hereward turned to see a bobbing head thrusting its way through the throng. A moment later, Alric shoved his way next to them. He was a monk who had found himself a companion of warriors and through it had seen as much blood and hardship as any of the other exiles. His face was flushed with anxiety. 'I was afrit you would be gone from here.'

'You are late,' the Mercian said. 'The others are already drowning themselves in wine.'

'There is talk of war—'

'There is always talk of war.' Sighard grinned. 'Have you not yet learned how these Romans are? They talk and talk and then fill their bellies with food and drink and sleep it off. When they are not plotting to murder some rival or other, that is.'

Alric shook his head. 'No, the Varangian Guard has been summoned to the palace. And the wise men, and the advisers. Never have I seen so many worried faces.'

'Calm yourself,' Hereward said, clapping a hand on his friend's shoulder. 'We are not dead yet.'

Sighard grabbed the monk's left arm and raised it high. A leather sheath capped the wrist where Alric's hand should be. 'Tell me, monk,' the young warrior teased, 'does God still hear when you pray with one hand? Or do you make as much sense to his ears as the thief who has had his tongue torn out?'

'God hears us all, even you when you have filled your skin with ale and make as much sense as a babe in arms.' Alric cocked one eyebrow in defiance. His skin had grown thick in the long years since Hereward had first met him, when they were both fleeing from death through that frozen forest in Northumbria.

Sighard spied Turold entertaining the crowd with one of his songs and wandered over, ready to be caught up in the skein of his friend's words. Alric beckoned Hereward to one side. From the leather pouch at his hip, he pulled a small object wrapped in a white silk cloth. 'A gift. For you.' Glancing around, he unfolded the cloth in the crook of his arm. On the silk lay a sliver of wood, capped with silver and attached to a leather thong. 'Do not judge,' the monk said with haste. 'There are some who say the power of God lies in that splinter. It is from a bowl St George himself once prayed over, which then made a blind woman see when she sipped from it, so it is said.'

The Mercian knew what value Alric's fellow monks would have placed upon such a relic. His friend must have gone to great lengths to secure it, perhaps even risking his own life. 'Why do you bring this to me?'

The monk searched for the right words. 'You have a devil inside you, one that drives you to slaughter like some beast, that puts at risk friend as well as foe when the rage eats your heart. We both know this is true.'

Hereward nodded. That devil had been with him for as long as he could remember. 'Aye. And with your prayers . . . your help . . . I have all but shackled it.'

'But I will not always be at your side, my friend. Now that you fight in the army beyond these walls, I cannot help keep it in check. You must do it yourself.' Alric pressed the relic into Hereward's hand. 'When you are on your own, when the night is dark, and you feel the devil's presence, take this in your fingers and ask for God's help, and he will give you the strength you need.'

Peering down at the fragment of wood, Hereward felt touched by his friend's concern. But as he murmured his thanks and slipped the thong round his neck, he felt a sudden movement at his side. Furtive fingers were closing about his purse. A blade flashed, cutting the strap.

'Hold!' he bellowed. 'Thief!' He lashed out, but his own fingers closed on thin air. He caught a glimpse of a young man darting away, his hair matted and his tunic filthy and threadbare. No doubt one of the rogues who preyed upon the rich men and women wandering through the streets.

Hereward barged a path through the stream of bodies. He would get no help from the fine folk of Constantinople, he knew that. They looked after their own business, and be damned to the rest.

The thief weaved through the throng like a rat. When he plunged into one of the narrow tracks that ran between the grand houses in the shade of the emperor's palace the darkness swallowed him up, but the Mercian's eyes were used to the fenland nights and he did not slow his pace. Rats fled from his feet. His nose wrinkled at the stink of middens. As the din of the crowd fell away, he fixed his attention on the pounding of feet ahead.

The track led into a maze of silent streets leading towards the Genoese quarter along the north wall, and Hereward began to close upon the fleeing youth. Finally, he found himself close enough to snarl a hand in the rogue's long hair and with a sharp yank brought him to the ground. His prey snarled and spat and thrashed. Hereward cuffed him once and pinned a hand across his throat. When his fingers flexed, the youth's furious resistance ceased.

'My coin,' the Mercian snarled. 'Now.'

Before the thief could respond, the night sang with the familiar clash of steel upon steel. An angry cry echoed. A curse. A threat. Hereward glimpsed rapid movement flashing in a street to his right: caught in a shaft of moonlight, a young man of some seventeen summers was surrounded by a gang of four cutthroats. The Mercian could see that the victim was of some standing. His tunic was well cut, and embroidered with gold or silver that glinted as he moved. Long black hair fell in ringlets around a serious face, dark eyes glimmering with sharp intelligence.

Short swords stabbed towards him. The victim whisked his own blade back and forth to hold them at bay, with some skill, Hereward could see. A robbery, no more. The young man had strayed too far from the crowds and now he would pay the price. And yet, as he watched, the Mercian saw that the rogues were hacking with concentrated fury. They seemed intent on ending the young man's days.

'Help me,' the victim called in the Roman tongue, breathless. 'I will make it worth your while.'

Seizing his moment, the cutpurse squirmed like an eel and broke free of the Mercian's grip. In an instant, he was up and running once again. Hereward knew that if he delayed for even a moment he would lose him.

In the next street, the rogues slashed with renewed vigour. The victim was outnumbered; not even his skill with a blade could save him. With a curse, Hereward spun away from the disappearing thief. He could not leave a brave man to be cut down.

Unsheathing Brainbiter, he barked, 'Leave him. Save your own necks.'

From somewhere nearby, another Roman voice said, 'Kill him too.'

The shadows were too deep for Hereward to see the source of that command, but now he knew one thing for certain. This was no mere robbery. It was murder.

Two of the rogues turned towards him. Their faces were hard, their eyes cold. These were not warriors, but men used to slitting throats in dirty alleys. They would fight like rats to the last.

Gripping his sword tight, Hereward braced himself. 'Come, then,' he snarled. 'You have picked the wrong man this night. My blade is thirsty for your blood.'

# Chapter Three

Moonlight glinted off steel. As Hereward stepped beside him, the young man hissed, 'Hesitate and you are lost. There is a high price on my head. These snakes will not let it go easily.'

Slow-witted they might be, but Hereward's two foes were cunning enough to strike as one. When they stabbed their blades towards his chest, he was ready, clashing their weapons aside with his own sword. Sparks glittered. Again they stabbed, one high, one low, growing more confident now they had the measure of him. Or so they thought.

The Mercian feinted left and lunged. His blade ripped into the stomach of the nearest rogue. As the man stumbled back with a shriek, his life-blood pumping between his fingers, the other rogue blanched. Hearing the cut-throat's dying cries, the one who had been the prey called out, 'First blood. Now we have a fight upon our hands.'

From the corner of his eye, Hereward glimpsed the youth slash and thrust with the poise of a seasoned warrior. No weakling there. A moment later one of his foes was falling back, trailing a ruby stream.

With a full-throated roar, Hereward's second enemy overcame his fear and threw himself at the Mercian in a frenzy of hacking and slashing. Within moments, the man lay twitching in a spreading pool. Gold or no, the final rogue had wits enough to see he was outnumbered and outclassed. Turning on his heels, he fled.

Hereward sheathed Brainbiter, pleased that he had managed to keep his devil in check. Perhaps Alric's relic did indeed work wonders.

His companion's face had been grim during the battle, but now a wry smile flickered on his lips. Prowling round the bodies, the young swordsman peered into the night in search of the one who had barked the order to end Hereward's life. His attention fell upon a pool of gloom on a narrow track between two houses. Levelling his sword, he called, 'Out, now, and answer for yourself.'

On the edge of Hereward's vision, movement flashed on the other side of the street. A sallow-faced man with hair streaked with silver separated from the shadows. Steel shimmered; a knife swept high.

Distracted by whatever he thought he had seen in the dark, the young man was oblivious of the enemy at his back. Snatching out his blade, Hereward lunged, impaling the silent assailant.

The young man whirled, cursing through clenched teeth when he saw the body tumbling to the ground. 'You have my thanks,' he said, clapping a hand on Hereward's shoulder. 'I let my guard down like a boy fighting his first battle.'

'These were not thieves.'

'No, they wanted me dead.'

Hereward eyed the younger man. He showed the confidence of someone twice his age. 'You owed them coin?'

The stranger grinned. 'I do not need to walk far to stumble across an enemy in Constantinople. There are many who do not like my name.' Crouching beside the fallen man, he turned the face up to the moonlight so he could study it. His smile drained away. 'Sabas Apion.'

'I should know of him?'

The young man pushed himself up. His thoughts could be

read in his expression as he weighed his discovery. 'Only if you spend your days at court. Sabas Apion is a powerful man, an ally of the eunuch Nikephoritzes. The emperor has leaned heavily on his counsel in recent times.'

'Why would such a man want you dead?' Hereward thought for a moment and added, 'Why would such a man be here, in the streets, wielding the blade himself? Powerful men do not dirty their own hands with killing. They pay others to spill blood while they are looking the other way.'

If he knew the answers to these questions, the younger man was not saying anything. He looked up and down the street and seemed to reach a decision. 'We must be away from here, and fast. The rogue who fled may be raising the alarm, and if we are found here, over the body of Sabas Apion, our heads will not stay on our shoulders much longer.'

'This cur attacked you—'

'That matters little. No one will believe our claims.' He gave a bitter smile. 'There are already many at court who are keen to judge me. And a man like Sabas Apion, a wise man, a friend of the emperor . . .' He shook his head. 'This will be enough to do for me, finally.'

'Perhaps that was the true reason for this attack.' Hereward sensed movement behind him and whirled, his sword flashing up. The younger man frowned, seeing nothing, but the Mercian knew better. 'Step out where I can see you.'

A figure separated from the shadows. Robes swirled, as black as a moonless sky, and a cloth of the same colour was wrapped around the head. The man's skin was dark, his eyes like coals, and his shaped beard, too, was the colour of pitch.

'Salih?' Hereward said. The other man gave a slight bow of greeting, but his mouth remained a grim slash in a face of granite. His hand rested on the curved silver dagger that hung at his hip.

Salih ibn Ziyad was as cold and unknowable as the ocean, a wise man who studied the movements of the stars, and the ways of animals, and the plants that could be used for healing. But his heart – that remained unknown even to those, like Hereward, who had travelled at his side. Yet the Mercian had seen enough to trust this earth-walker. Brave, he was, certainly, and fierce in battle. But it was the loyalty Salih had shown to his mistress, Meghigda, the queen of the desert tribe called the Imazighen, that Hereward would never forget. When Salih had encountered her as a girl he had helped her cope with the murder of her mother and father, and thereafter he had dedicated his days to guiding and shaping her into the great warrior-queen she had become in that harsh, hot land in Afrique. Her followers had believed her to be imbued with the powers of the gods, a trick that Salih had crafted to ensure the fealty of every Imazighen man and woman, and a part that Meghigda had played as if born to it.

But then Meghigda had been caught up in the great games of power played by the aristocratic families of Constantinople. The Nepotes and the Verini, between them, had brought her low. Maximos Nepos had professed love for the queen and then betrayed her for his own gain. That betrayal had seen her fall into the hands of the cruel Victor Verinus, where her life had finally been snuffed out.

In the end, it was for Maximos and the Nepotes that Salih reserved his deepest hatred, the Mercian knew. Maximos was the one who had lured Meghigda from her home, and from Salih's side. Maximos was the begetter of the ultimate misery. And so Salih slipped through the shadows of Constantinople, biding his time until he could gain his vengeance by using that knife on the throat of any of the Nepotes clan who rose before him. In his grief, he had become Death himself. He had no other purpose.

'Is it fate that our paths cross here, after so long apart?' Hereward asked.

'God guides us all, according to his plan. But this night . . .' Salih looked first into the face of the younger man, searching for the truth of him. Satisfied, he glanced down at the bodies. 'This city seethes with lies and deceit and plots. I walk a path among them, and they led me here.'

There was movement behind the wise man. A young girl of no more than eighteen summers hovered on the edge of the shadows. She was a ragged thing, so thin her cheeks were like the edge of his sword. Her eyes were dark-ringed, her red hair lank and greasy. Hereward frowned. Her name was Ariadne Verina, a girl who had been whipped like a cur by her own father, and, no doubt, had suffered even worse things at his hands. Bending women to submit to his monstrous desires was the inhuman hunger that had consumed Victor Verinus. But in the end it had proved the curse that had destroyed him. At the moment when all his plots seemed to be coming together, the women of the Nepotes, Juliana and Simonis, who had been victims of Victor's lusts, had risen up and unmanned him. How the Devil must have laughed at that ending!

Hereward narrowed his eyes at the girl. Did she feel any joy that her tormentor-father was now gone? And why, he wondered, was she now travelling with Salih ibn Ziyad?

Taking a step forward, Ariadne reached out a trembling hand. Her eyes rolled up to white, the muscles of her face growing taut so that her features subtly altered, and she shuddered before speaking. 'I am al-Kahina, slayer of devils.' Her voice was low and rasping, like a woman more than twice her age.

Hereward stiffened. Al-Kahina was the name that Meghigda had taken among her people. 'What is this?' he growled.

'I live on, as I will always live, for all time,' Ariadne continued in that voice that was not her own.

The Mercian glanced at Salih, but the wise man said nothing. Only the faintest smile danced at the corners of his lips. Hereward had seen that look before. Salih was playing with him. The wise man wanted him to believe that this wild girl was now the vessel that contained the spirit of Meghigda, a warrior-queen who would continue her fight for justice even beyond the gates of death. Perhaps that were so. Alric had told him how the power of God's spirit could fill a man, and how angels came down to earth to guide the needy. And yet Ariadne had faced agonies beyond measure at her father's hands, and Hereward had seen time and again on the battlefield how the madness of suffering could drive the wits to flights of wonder.

'What do you say?' he asked, playing along.

Ariadne pointed a wavering finger at him. 'You are in grave danger. Enemies rise up on every side who would see your doom.'

Hereward smiled. This was not news.

But then Salih nodded in agreement and cautioned, 'You must leave this place, now. The alarm will have been raised by the one who fled. The Varangian Guard will soon be here. There are some who would profit from seeing an English barbarian blamed for this night.'

'What do you know, Salih?'

'When I move through the city, unseen, I hear whispers; I divine the arc of plots that others can never see until too late. Constantinople is not a safe place for you, Hereward of the English.'

'You have my thanks, as always,' the Mercian said, bowing his head.

The words had barely left his lips when cries cracked the night. The thunder of running feet echoed closer. Hereward glanced in the direction of the tumult, and when he looked back, Salih and the girl were gone.

With a nod, the young swordsman darted along one of the tracks between the houses. Choosing another path at random, Hereward raced away just as the clamour reached the end of the street. He silently cursed his misfortune. The English had fought hard to gain a foothold in the city, with its strange rules and near-contempt for any who did not have gold to buy their place. He would not see it all destroyed for one good deed gone amiss.

The baked mud whisked by under his feet. The cries rose in pitch when the body of Sabas Apion was discovered, but the pounding of feet at his back did not seem to slow, and he could only guess his escape had been spotted. He ducked into another track where the gloom was so thick he could barely see a spear's length ahead of him and ran as fast as he could. At the far end, one of the broader streets glowed in the moonlight. With luck on his side, he would be able to lose his pursuers in the maze and find his way back to his spear-brothers before his face was known.

But as Hereward threw himself out of the path, he glimpsed rapid movement to his right. Something hard smashed into his face. Down he went, barbs of fire burning through his skull, and when he came round a moment later he could taste blood in his mouth. A figure hovered over him. A cloak of a colour turned grey by the night, but which he knew was blood-red. A leather breastplate, oiled and scented with sandalwood. A circular shield with a dragon sigil. And a familiar face framed by the steel helm, eyes incisive and filled with a cold humour. It was Ricbert, the right hand of the Varangian Guard commander, Wulfrun.

'Hereward of the English,' he said, weighting each word with a sardonic tone. 'Out dancing with the Devil again. This time there is a price to pay. The murder of Sabas Apion cannot be ignored. The emperor will demand your head on the morrow.'

# Chapter Four

The shadow swooped along the stone wall, in constant flight from the man who pursued it. Ragged breathing and rattling footsteps rushed in its wake. Along the line of sizzling torches in the monastery corridor Alric raced, his heart pounding to the beat of his leather soles. Muttering prayers, he tried to smother the pang of fear that God no longer listened to him, a guilty man. Would they never escape the doom that had pursued them for so long? Perhaps all of the English were cursed for taking up arms against a king, as some said.

He skidded to a halt, his feverish hands fumbling for the door to the church. He took a deep breath to compose himself in the Lord's presence and then pushed his way inside. Fat candles guttered in the draught. In the golden glow, Alric breathed deeply of the incense and felt a hint of peace.

An enormous shape crouched in front of the altar, surrounded by a halo of flickering candlelight. The eunuch Neophytos was at prayer. Alric gritted his teeth. The snakes of that hated, power-hungry clan, the Nepotes, were everywhere. Even here, in God's house. Neophytos was their spy in the Church, as Maximos Nepos now skulked through the emperor's court. Wherever power lay, there you would find one of the Nepotes sharpening a blade and plotting. Alric crossed himself. Sometimes he wondered if the entire bloodline was the Devil's own. The father, Kalamdios, had fought like a cornered dog during his family's long rivalry with the Verini, so the stories that circulated in the monastery told. His savagery had only been contained when his wounds trapped his mind in his frozen body. Now he was little more than a straw man with naught but a flicker of life in his eyes. Only the youngest, Leo, seemed to still have some good in him.

Alric steeled himself as he watched Neophytos at prayer. His fellow monk was no doubt trying to cleanse the stain upon his soul. If all had gone to plan, the eunuch's kin would now control the empire, and the emperor Michael would be cold in his tomb. Hereward had helped foil that plot, and Neophytos and the Nepotes had never forgiven the English for that. But whom else could he ask for aid?

Crossing himself, Alric strode towards God's table. On the edge of the circle of light, he hesitated, not wishing to interrupt those supplications, but time was short.

'Neophytos,' he murmured.

The eunuch jerked round as if the Devil were at his back. Guilt still haunted him. When he saw who had spoken, he scowled. 'What do you want?' he demanded in his sing-song voice. He levered his huge body to his feet. Beads of sweat glistened on his bald head and trickled down into the folds of flesh where his neck should have been.

'We have had our differences, you and I,' Alric began, choosing his words carefully. He hoped the eunuch would remember how the Nepotes had made Hereward and the English welcome when the travellers had first arrived in Constantinople. The rift that split them asunder only occurred when the Romans' true nature was revealed. 'But you are still a man of God. I cannot believe you would see an innocent man suffer.' He knew the Mercian would curse him for holding the naive beliefs of a child, but what choice did he have? 'Hereward faces execution before the sun sets. The Varangian Guard have accused him of murder . . . and a plot against the emperor.'

Alric expected a look of triumph, but Neophytos only fluttered his fingers as if wafting away smoke. His gaze flickered around the church. He was scared, the monk could see that now. But of what?

'You think this is of some concern to me?'

'I know there is no love lost between your kin and Hereward, but I implore you to call upon the Nepotes to help us. Simonis has the ear of the emperor. She could save my friend's life.' Realizing he was babbling, Alric tried to steady his tone. 'I would not expect you to do this out of kindness. We will find some way to repay you . . . gold . . .'

Neophytos snorted. 'You are mud-crawling rats, all of you. Soldiers and beggars. You barely have enough coin to keep your bellies full.' He smacked his lips. The talk seemed to have stirred his unquenchable hunger. Waving the intrusion away, he began to lurch towards the door.

'Wait,' Alric pleaded. 'We have no one else to turn to . . .'

'You should have thought of that before you made enemies of the Nepotes. In Constantinople, a man needs allies to survive, and thrive. And you have none. I will not mourn for your friend.'

'Tell me what you need—'

Neophytos whirled. The fear in his eyes burned clearly now. 'Will your prayers keep me safe? Will the spears of your brothers?'

'Safe from what?'

'Have you not heard the whispers? The prophecies of doom that sweep through this monastery like the cold northern winds? There is no hope here. Perhaps no hope for any of us. It may be a mercy that your friend loses his head this day and is spared from what is to come.'

Alric grabbed the eunuch's sweat-soaked tunic. 'What prophecies? Tell me.'

'Death is coming to Constantinople, death like we have never known before. Brother Joseph saw it in a dream. Our enemies will bear down upon the walls and sweep through the gates. No man, woman or child here will be spared.'

Alric knew of the rumours of the Turks massing to the east. Hereward and the others had talked at length about how Michael Doukas seemed blind to the threat that lurked on the edge of his empire.

'This very eve, the emperor sent out ten men to search for new relics. We must put our faith in old bones now,' Neophytos continued. 'Perhaps then God will look upon us fondly and spare us from the doom that is to come.' He threw off Alric's hand and lumbered to the door.

When Alric hurried out of the monastery, the low horizon was already glowing red. He felt his stomach knot. His friend had faced death before, many times, but this was different. The Varangian Guard always made good on their threats. Through silent streets he ran as the rising sun brought a glow to the grand stone halls, wishing they had never left England, wishing they had won their rebellion against King William, wishing . . . He made his way to the Kharisios Gate in the western wall and scrambled up the broad steps.

From the top of the wall, high above the stinking streets, he looked out across the sprawling city, so huge it took his breath away. Never in the days of his youth in Northumbria could he have imagined such a place existed. Nothing in England could compare. Some said hundreds of thousands of people lived there, ten times the number of even the greatest city in the west. His gaze swept across the sea of stone, the palaces, the churches, the statues, and in the distance the hippodrome and the dome of the Hagia Sophia. Few could deny it took the breath away. Yet it was a dream, nothing more. Beyond the grandeur lurked a pit of vipers. The Romans here had smiles on their faces and knives behind their backs. No one could be trusted. They called it the city of gold. To Alric, it was the city of death.

As he glanced along the wide wall, he glimpsed a solitary figure staring west, towards Normandy and England. He was not the only one who could not forget what they had left behind. The wind plucked lightly at the black ringlets framing Deda's face. The Norman knight was a man of wry humour, and gentle for such a seasoned warrior. A code of honour ruled his life. Perhaps that was why he had found so much in common with Hereward, though they should have been enemies. But now his expression was grim.

'No news?' Alric asked, anticipating the answer.

'No good news.' Deda brushed strands of hair from his face. 'I visited the house of the Nepotes as we agreed. They would not let me past the door. We will find no help for Hereward there.'

'How fare the others?'

'Kraki and Guthrinc hope to persuade Wulfrun of the Guard to show mercy.' He shook his head. 'The noble who was slain is too important. A head has to roll for his death, and better a man's who has no gold in his purse.'

Footsteps echoed on the steps. Alric turned to see Deda's wife Rowena emerge on to the top of the wall. She wore a white headdress to cover her brown hair, and her amber gown lit up in the dawn light. She had taken work with a rich merchant, assisting his wife in her duties. The pay was good, and she offered all she could to the pot to help the English buy their way into the Guard. But it was never enough.

As she neared, she shook her head, her face sad. Deda bowed his head in greeting. 'We all do what we can,' he said. 'There is no shame in trying.'

'I begged my mistress,' Rowena replied, 'but she would not risk her husband's standing by making a plea on behalf of . . .' She let her voice tail away.

'Hereward's name means nothing here,' Deda said in a quiet voice. 'He may be the greatest warrior England has ever seen, a man who almost brought a king's army to its knees, but here he is nothing more than troublemaker, rogue, and now murderer.'

'They say three other dead men were found in the street,' Rowena continued. 'Hereward would not have taken the man's life without good reason. He must have been attacked. There can be no other explanation.'

Alric bowed his head. 'Fate laughs at us. To have fought so

hard in England . . . to have defeated enemy after enemy . . . only to die here in Constantinople for little reason.' He caught himself. 'No. I will not give up hope. We will find a way.' He glanced at the sun floating on the horizon. There was little time left to redeem his vow.

# Chapter Five

Head down, the man in the red cloak swept along the ringing corridor. The flood of bodies parted around him as if he were a rock in a stream. Frightened nobles, robes flapping as they ran, afraid that the walls were about to come down. Bleary-eyed counsels roused from their sleep, or plucked from drunken stupors in the taverns. Others stinking of sweat and sex after the messenger boys had summoned them from the brothels. He saw slaves lumbering with amphorae of wine and arms filled with bread to sustain their masters in the long hours of anxious debate that were no doubt lying ahead. More boys racing with messages to those who had not yet heard the news. And leaders of the Church, faces like stone altars, ready to offer their prayers for victory or promises of salvation if all hell was about to break loose.

Wulfrun of the Varangian Guard had little time for any of them. If war was coming, it would be the men who raised the weapons who counted; his men, and the few axes-for-hire the Romans could scrape together from what remained of the army after that terrible defeat at the hands of the Turks in Manzikert, near two years gone now. Two years, and little had been done to rebuild the once-great Roman forces. No surprise, then, that the empire was falling into shadow.

If the word of the warrior the English had rescued could be believed, the Caesar had been captured. John Doukas, a man who was as untrustworthy as any other snake in this city. He had always wanted the power of the empire at his command, but he had never been brave enough, or clever enough, to grasp it. The emperor's advisers had tolerated his presence, preferring to keep him close where they could watch him, but now he had brought the entire empire to the edge of the abyss.

Torchlight glimmered off Wulfrun's vambraces as he thrust aside any man who dared venture into his path. The emperor's palace would normally have been still at that time of night, but now it throbbed with a din that would not have been out of place in the hippodrome. Perhaps these Romans were waking at last. They paid good coin for Englishmen like him to fight their battles, and he was grateful for that – his coffers had grown full since he had joined the emperor's elite fighting force. But soon they would have to take up weapons themselves if they wished to defend their city. Did they have the fire within them? Only time would tell.

When he came to the door to the feasting hall, he pushed aside his irritation. Adjusting his long-handled Dane-axe and the circular shield marked with his raven sigil, he swung the door open and stepped inside.

The wisest in the government clustered in groups, deep in quiet debate, low voices strained. In one corner, the emperor, Michael, was looking bewildered. His chief counsel, the eunuch Nikephoritzes, loomed over him like a stern grandfather with a mewling boy. With a forced smile, the eunuch ushered the emperor out and then glanced round and saw Wulfrun. As he strode across, he caught the arm of another man, short, with curly black hair shading to grey at the ears and blue eyes that moved quickly, taking everything in. Wulfrun thought he knew everyone who circled the court and the government, but he had not seen this one before, or thought he had not. The guardsman narrowed his eyes, trying to remember. How unthreatening that smiling face looked, how bland. Forgettable.

Another bloodless politician who would talk but do nothing.

Nikephoritzes steered the stranger over. 'You have met Falkon Cephalas? No?' he said by way of introduction. 'He will be taking the place of Sabas Apion.'

Wulfrun cared little for the constant rise and fall of those who sought power at the heart of government. Nothing ever seemed to change. 'The Caesar has been captured by Roussel de Bailleul? Is this true?'

'Forgive me,' Falkon interjected. 'I do not know this Roussel. He is a Norman?'

The eunuch's face darkened. 'He is a power in the east, one that has been growing by the day. One, I admit, to which we failed to give enough of our attention until it was too late.'

'An axe-for-hire, nothing more,' Wulfrun growled, 'except traitor.'

'By all accounts, he was one of the fiercest warriors in our army,' Nikephoritzes snapped, narrowing his eyes at the commander. 'An exile from his own people, and like so many he came to Constantinople seeking gold and glory. Our army has always relied upon strong arms from distant parts. They breed harder warriors in lands where the ice-wind blows.'

Falkon cocked his head, puzzled. 'We put our faith in them, but they betray us?'

'Roussel did,' Wulfrun said. 'He refused to bring his men into the battle at Manzikert when he knew he would soon be smelling his own blood on the wind. The Turks routed the empire's army, and set in place many of the miseries you see around you today.' He flashed a cold look at the eunuch. 'And still we paid Roussel good coin to raise his axe for the empire.'

Nikephoritzes showed an impassive face, refusing to be humbled. 'We do not dwell on the wrongs of the past,' he said in a cold voice.

Wulfrun felt his anger simmering, but he kept it pressed deep inside, as he always did when he wore the helm of the Varangian Guard. But he could not still his tongue. 'And despite his failings we sent Roussel into the east, to face the Turks, at the head of three thousand men on horseback.' He let the words hang for a moment. 'But he did not return.'

The eunuch's eyes glowed. Wulfrun held the older man's gaze, forcing him to respond. He had spent too long in silence, nursing his bitterness that these Romans would sup wine, and frolic, and dream of past glories rather than face up to the threats he had warned of at every turn. Perhaps he was tired this night.

'Roussel took his army and conquered land in Galatia, and there set up his own realm, with him as prince in his castle in Ancyra,' Nikephoritzes continued, each word like a pebble in his mouth. 'He follows the course of his Norman brothers to the west, in Sicily and Sardinia and Apulia.'

'We paid good gold to create our own enemy,' Wulfrun clarified. 'A realm with a great army, and riches, and a prince who sees what William the Bastard did in England and thinks he can do the same here. Who sees that slaughter buys a crown, and a mountain of gold, and power. And so we called the Caesar back from his estate where he idled away his days and sent him to challenge this Norman dog. And he was defeated. His army was routed, and he was captured. And now . . .' He looked to the eunuch. 'Do we pay a ransom? Do we wait for Roussel to burn this city to the ground? Do we—'

'We bring the Caesar back,' Nikephoritzes snapped, his voice cracking like a whip. The thrum of conversation stilled. 'No matter how many lives are lost in the doing.' The eunuch sucked in a deep breath to calm himself. 'These are dire times, Wulfrun. We must not fight among ourselves. And we must take care that we are not undermined from within while we face enemies without.'

Wulfrun gritted his teeth, keeping a blank face. How many times had he said those words to the ones who held the reins of power? How many times had he been ignored, rebuffed, quietly mocked?

'That skulking rat of yours . . . Ricbert? . . . knows all that transpires within the city walls,' Nikephoritzes continued. 'The moment he learns anything of import . . . anything that has more to it than the autumn mist . . . you must bring it to Falkon. Do you understand?'

The commander nodded.

'Good. See that you do.' The eunuch glided away to the nearest clutch of advisers and fell into deep conversation.

'I have heard nothing but good of your work, brave Wulfrun,' Falkon said, still smiling. His voice was oddly mellifluous.

'I serve the emperor to the best of my skills. And you, Falkon Cephalas, what part will you now play in these affairs?'

'You are a warrior. You know that great battles can change the course of empires. But sometimes small things can too. A wrong word here leads to anger there, turns to a desire for vengeance, becomes a lust for murder, ends in death. A life is lost, knowledge is lost, influence is lost, plans are changed, strategies fail. An empire falls. I have one small skill, Wulfrun of the Guard, and it is that I see the little things, and how they weave into the tapestry of the great things. Nikephoritzes saw that in me long ago, and though I was happy with my lot he chose to raise me to this great height so I can serve the emperor to the best of my skills too.' His warm smile softened his words.

Wulfrun nodded. 'You see the plans and the plots, the weft and the weave . . .'

'. . . both within the walls and abroad, and I advise those greater than me on what may or may not unfold.'

'May you find good fortune in your work, Falkon, for in Constantinople there is much advice but few ears to listen.'

Falkon nodded, his smile revealing nothing. 'I have made a vow to the emperor that I will let nothing escape my gaze.'

'That is a great vow indeed.'

'It is. But it is necessary. And the one who murdered Sabas Apion . . .'

'Hereward of the English.'

'He will be executed this day?'

Wulfrun hesitated, the doubts he had experienced earlier that night surfacing once again. 'There is no love lost between

Hereward and me.' He smiled inwardly at how bland those words sounded. Hereward had caused the death of his father. He could never forget that crime. 'He is a blood-crazed warrior, but all who know him say he is a changed man. His friend, the monk, says he keeps his devils locked deep within him these days. Hereward is the son of a thegn. To murder a man in the street like a rogue, that is the Hereward of old. But now . . .' As he gave words to his thoughts, he felt his doubts harden.

Falkon held out his hands. 'Still, he must die.'

'Even if he is innocent?'

'How you English stick together!' The Roman gave a silent laugh. 'He does not deny he killed Sabas Apion.'

'There were reasons—'

'Hereward killed him, of that there is no doubt. And he must be punished. His death will send a message to all in Constantinople that we will brook no challenges to the rule of law. No threats to the nobility. No plots against the emperor. For that message to be heard, Hereward must die.'

Wulfrun felt his racing thoughts begin to settle. There had been a quiet change in the city, but it was not a small one, and he wondered how much it would affect them all in days to come.

'Constantinople has suffered too long at the hands of those who seek to grip their fingers round the throat of power,' Falkon continued. 'No more. We shall not die from a knife at the back when there are so many blades levelled at our chest. I will watch, and I will listen. I will look deep into every face.' His smile faded for an instant and then sprang back with even greater force. 'No man is above suspicion.'

Though Falkon's expression said one thing, the commander thought he glimpsed a momentary hardness in those blue eyes. It seemed that Falkon meant his message for Wulfrun alone.

Once he had left the chamber, Wulfrun felt his unease begin to grow. Striding out of the gate, he made his way through the dark streets to the Boukoleon palace. Coming to a low stone building at the rear, he paused at the threshold and removed his helm. His heart, usually as steady in beat as a war-drum, began to flutter. His mouth felt dry, too, and he swallowed. These visits always turned him into a child again.

Steeling himself, he pushed open the door and stepped into the dark, smoky interior. His nostrils wrinkled at the vinegar reek of sickness. On a stool beside a low bed, the stub of a single candle guttered. As his eyes adjusted to the half-light, he forced himself to look at the figure lying under the woollen blanket. So wasted was it, there seemed to be nothing but folds. Bones, topped by a long white beard and hair.

Wulfrun grimaced and made a low noise in his throat. The figure on the bed stirred. That was good. Every time he visited, he feared the worst.

'I am sorry to trouble you at this late hour,' he murmured.

A hand rose from the bed, the fingers slowly beckoning.

Wulfrun pulled up a stool and sat beside the man who had guided him ever since he had arrived in Constantinople. Godred had once been the fiercest warrior the Varangian Guard had ever known. His axe had left its mark on battle after battle, and when he was made commander he was respected by all who followed him.

'I seek your guidance,' Wulfrun ventured.

A throaty chuckle escaped the old man's lips. 'You do not need to hear the ramblings of a dying old man.'

Wulfrun winced. Even now he could not bear to think that soon his mentor would be gone. 'You are still the commander of the Varangian Guard.'

'In name only. You have been commander for long seasons now, my eyes and ears out in the world, my voice. And in a month, or a week, or a day, you will be the true commander. Your wits will guide the Guard.'

'I am not worthy of that honour.' Wulfrun bowed his head.

'What troubles you?'

'Unrest grows by the day. The people are angry . . . hungry . . . weary . . . afrit.'

'You think they will rise up against the emperor?'

'If they do, the Varangian Guard will defend him to the last. No, my worries lie with Nikephoritzes.'

'That bitter old eunuch?' Godred broke into a coughing fit that seemed as if it would never end.

'Sometimes he thinks himself emperor, I am sure. And though he is wise, he is not as wise as he thinks. He will make the empire's troubles worse, if he lays a heavy hand upon the people.'

'You think he will do such a thing?'

Wulfrun thought of Falkon Cephalas and nodded.

Closing his eyes, Godred pondered. After long moments, Wulfrun feared he had fallen asleep, or worse, but then the old man let out a juddering sigh and said, 'This city wearies me. I think I will be ready for a long sleep in my tomb. There is more gold here than in our villages across the whale road in England, eh? Yet they plot and plot, and complain and fight among themselves like starving dogs.' He hawked up a mouthful of phlegm and spat it into a bowl beside the bed. 'There are times, now my candle is close to winking out, when I think, Take your axe to all of the bastards. The people know best. Let them decide what to do.' He groaned. 'But that is not the oath we took. You want my guidance, Wulfrun? Live life by the day. Suck every greasy mouthful of joy out of it. Worry not. What will be, will be. And you have proved yourself. I am proud of you. When doom comes calling, you will be ready.'

Wulfrun wanted to question the old man more, but this time he saw Godred's chest rise and fall with the measured rhythm of sleep. For long moments, he sat there, remembering all the things the old man had taught him, and all the wisdom he had imparted. When Godred finally went, this world, his world, would be a darker place.

Outside, the night was warm and the city was still. But the peace would not last. There were threats beyond the walls, and danger within, and now the cauldron was bubbling hard.

# Chapter Six

The sweet scent of the mullein flowers drifted in the air. And yet Wulfrun could only smell sweat and doubt and fear as he swept through the silent streets. Ahead, lamps glowed in the windows of the house of the Nepotes. Even now he barely recognized it. When he had first been entranced by Juliana Nepa, this place had seemed to be a home of misery. The family had suffered greatly at the hands of their rival Victor Verinus, their gold gone, Juliana's father, Kalamdios, locked in his body from a knife wound in the head, barely able to flutter an eyelid. And this once-grand hall a shabby relic, cracked and peeling and growing filthier by the day as the elements wore it down. But now that Victor was dead and the Nepotes had their fortune back, the house had been repainted. In the sun, it glowed white, like a beacon. The flagstones in front of the door had been scrubbed and cleared of weeds, the cracked and sagging roof tiles repaired. Inside, every chamber glimmered with gold.

And yet the Nepotes had still not found happiness.

On either side of the door, guards waited in the shadows, rough men with leathery faces that were maps of old fights. They nodded as he approached. He was well known there. A slave admitted him to the hall. Bathed in the golden light of a lamp, he stood for a moment, listening. From somewhere deep in the house drifted a soothing melody plucked on strings. A dim voice droned. And from the courtyard at the back came the clash of steel upon steel. He felt puzzled. He had expected to find the Nepotes in their beds.

Prowling to the far side of the hall, he peered out of the open door into the courtyard. Under the glare of torches, shadows danced on the central square beyond the trees. Two figures were sparring with swords. Maximos Nepos was teaching his younger brother, Leo, the finer skills of the blade. Maximos was wearing a fine emerald tunic. His long black hair gleamed, and his beard had been freshly clipped. Wulfrun did not like him. Too quick to grin, he had a sardonic look and eyes that suggested he was always quietly mocking. Leo, in comparison, was a strange lad, quiet and reflective, with dark eyes that seemed to look right through a man.

As they danced back and forth, Maximos made no attempt to hide the fact that he was toying with the boy. His grin was wide, his teasing insistent as he flicked at the lad's tunic with the tip of his weapon. Leo frowned, concentrating. Occasional clouds of anger crossed his features. With the back of his free hand, he wiped away the sweat that stung his eyes and attacked with even greater energy.

Maximos laughed. 'You try too hard!'

Simmering, Leo hacked wildly, but his brother parried with a lazy flick of his wrist. Before Leo could recover, Maximos grabbed the boy round the neck and spun him about, shaking the blade from his grasp. When it clattered on to the flagstones, Leo wrenched himself free and whirled, his eyes blazing. 'I am not a boy!'

Maximos only laughed louder, throwing his head back.

'When we thought you dead in Afrique, I was the one chosen to be emperor. Father chose me!' Leo hammered one hand on his chest.

Wulfrun could not allow himself to hear any more of this. The Nepotes had escaped death for treason by a hair's breadth after they had attempted to place Maximos upon the throne.

Only Hereward had been able to save the emperor Michael's life, and then only at the last. But he knew the family still yearned for the ultimate power, still plotted, still bided their time, and there was nothing he could do about it. The thought haunted him. How could he be true to the Varangian Guard oath, to protect the emperor above all, if he could not act as he ought in this? But his love for Maximos' sister Juliana had left him unmanned. The swell in his heart compelled him to turn a blind eye to the family's misdeeds because he could not bear to think of his love's being punished. Even though he knew Juliana was as murderous as the rest of her kin. Even though he knew her soul was scarred, aye, and her mind too. And yet he had sworn a second oath to Juliana to protect *her* at all costs. Wulfrun choked back a bitter laugh. As if Juliana needed any protection. In all Constantinople there had been no greater monster than Victor Verinus. A brutal, cruel beast whose blood ran as cold as the waters of the Rus. And yet Juliana and the Nepotes had lured him into their plots with their cunning, and then torn off his manhood and watched and laughed as his life drained away. Every man in the empire should fear the wrath of the Nepotes. And yet here he was. What a fool love had made him. What a whipped cur.

He stepped out into the courtyard, and called a greeting.

Maximos' eyes briefly flickered with suspicion, then he forced another grin. *Never trust a man who shows his teeth too much*, Wulfrun thought.

'Run along now. We will continue your lesson in the light of day.' Maximos ruffled his brother's hair. Leo threw the hand off and stormed away.

'Boys,' Maximos said to his guest, holding out one hand.

'You should be careful what words are uttered, Maximos Nepos. I am the emperor's eyes and ears here in Constantinople.'

Maximos grinned. 'You, Wulfrun? You are kin by any other name. And if you finally agree to marry my sister, you *will* be kin.'

Wulfrun winced. If another threat to the emperor emerged, where did he stand? Two oaths in opposition. No man should have to live with that terrible weight upon his shoulders. Yet it would only get worse until he had to choose.

'The hour is late,' Maximos said, sheathing his sword. 'What has drawn you from your slumber?'

'I have news, and a question. And I offer a warning, to use as you see fit.'

Maximos nodded, his grin fading. He ushered his guest back into the hall and ordered a slave to fetch wine.

'Sabas Apion has been murdered,' Wulfrun said. 'He was a good friend of the Nepotes, was he not?'

'Dead, you say?' Maximos showed no grief, but he could not hide the shadow that crossed his face.

Wulfrun sensed that the Nepotes were awake at that late hour because they had been expecting a visit from the murdered man. It was as he expected. Another plot. Another corpse. And, no doubt, another innocent man blamed. Here was one more thing he knew he should not examine too closely, unless he wished to choose between his duty and Juliana. He shivered. A part of him wondered if it was only love that kept him entranced. Whenever he was near Juliana his cock was afire. Every night he dreamed of her body, and every morning his bed was wet with his seed. Though he prayed in the church each day, he could not free himself of the spell of her flesh, of her scent, of the touch of her fingers upon the nape of his neck. Sometimes he wondered if that fire would finally consume him.

Waving away the goblet of wine that Maximos was proffering, Wulfrun said, 'The Nepotes know all who would attempt to wield power in Constantinople. Tell me of a man named Falkon Cephalas.'

Maximos frowned. 'I know of no such man. I will ask my mother, but . . . if he has one eye upon power, you are right, we would know him.'

Wulfrun felt troubled. How could someone rise so quickly without leaving a wake behind him? 'He has taken the place of Sabas Apion. And Nikephoritzes has charged him with uncovering all who might plot against the emperor.'

The other man laughed, waving his goblet in the air. 'And that is your warning? Why would such a thing trouble me?'

Wulfrun had no time for games. He had glimpsed the unguarded look in Maximos' eye and he knew the man would use the information to keep the Nepotes safe; more important, to keep Juliana alive. 'Is your sister awake?'

'Of course.' Maximos swilled back his wine. 'She would tug my hair until I howled if I let you leave without seeing her.'

Soon after the Roman had disappeared into the house, Wulfrun heard slight footsteps skipping nearer. Even now, even after everything, he felt his heart beat faster in anticipation.

A moment later Juliana appeared at the door, her blonde hair fairly glowing in the candlelight. Laughing with excitement, she hurried up to him. 'A surprise!' she exclaimed. 'But still so stern. One day I swear you will arrive at the door with a smile upon your face and I will not know you. Take off your helm so I can see the real Wulfrun.'

He could never deny her. Pulling off his helm, he held it in the crook of his arm. And she was right, as always; he felt the weight of his duties sliding off him.

And yet he must have shown his worries, for Juliana frowned with concern and stroked his cheek. 'How is Godred?' she murmured. 'He has been like a father to you. I know his sickness is a weight upon your shoulders.'

'He yet lives.'

Juliana seemed untroubled that his answer said nothing. Smiling brightly, she stepped back and took his hand. 'Soon you will command the Varangian Guard truly. You will wield the power.'

'The power is a burden,' he said, trying to keep the weariness out of his voice, 'and I have shouldered it for Godred for seasons now.'

'But still,' she replied, her eyes gleaming, 'you will be the commander. Come. My mother and father would see you.'

As he followed Juliana into the next chamber, Wulfrun pushed aside his greatest fear: once he was the emperor's chief defender, what would the Nepotes demand of him?

Her father, Kalamdios, sat on the wooden chair that had been his prison ever since Victor Verinus had thrust a blade through his skull and into his brain. His face was fixed in a permanent scowl, his fingers twitching at his side, though he could not lift his hands, nor walk, nor make any sound beyond an infant's mewling. A trail of saliva dribbled from the corner of his mouth, but his eyes rolled in greeting. Juliana's mother, Simonis, glided from the antechamber, holding out a goblet of wine for the guest. He thought how beautiful she looked, little older than her daughter, though silver now streaked her auburn hair. Wulfrun recalled how he had spied on Victor Verinus preying upon her body in a show of dominance over the whole Nepotes clan. He could understand why all of them had hated the man so. And yet, as he peered into Simonis' eyes, she seemed unaffected by all she had endured at her oppressor's hands. His gaze flickered towards Juliana. So beautiful, so young. She must have caught the eye of Victor the Stallion. He had thought he would have known if that bastard had laid hands upon her. But now, seeing her mother's untroubled demeanour, he was not so sure. Tortured by doubt and desire, he wrenched his gaze away and all but snatched the goblet from Simonis' hand.

Once he had swilled down a deep draught, he calmed enough to tell the Nepotes of the night's murder, and watched all their faces fall. He had been right – another plot in the making. 'Poor Sabas Apion,' Juliana said, righting herself. 'He was always kind to me.' She plucked at the sleeve of her dress, remembering something, and then said, 'I am worried, Wulfrun.'

'How so?'

'Once Victor Verinus was dead, we all thought our time of misery was over. But in the long weeks since then, it is as if death has been following us.' She looked up at him with limpid eyes. Her worry was real.

'What say you?'

Simonis rested one hand on her husband's shoulder. 'The men

we hire to keep us safe . . . many have been murdered. Yes, they are rogues and cut-throats and they spend their nights in the worst parts of the city. But soon we will not be able to find a single man who will take our coin to protect us.'

'You believe you have an enemy?'

Biting her lip, Juliana hesitated as if she were giving too much away. 'Maximos was followed one night by a dark-skinned man with a knife. He escaped with his life by a hair. A man he knows from the time he was a captive in Afrique.'

'Salih ibn Ziyad?'

Juliana nodded. Wulfrun frowned. Only once had he met this earth-walker from the hot lands to the south, but he had been left in no doubt that Salih was dangerous. He was a wise man who knew many things, yet he could take a life in an instant with that silver knife of his.

'And I . . . I too was followed,' Juliana continued. 'I ran through the market to escape—'

'You?' Wulfrun thundered, his hand falling to the haft of his axe.

'I saw the blade. And now this, with Sabas Apion . . . Wulfrun, I am scared.' She flung herself at him, burying her face in his shoulder.

Unused to such contact, he did not know what to do. After a moment he let his arms enfold her. 'I will keep you safe,' he murmured. Her breasts pressed hard against his chest and her hips ground into him, but she was young and innocent and she did not know what she was doing, he told himself. It was a prayer he had repeated many times. And pure she would stay until he had earned enough gold to gain the approval of Kalamdios and they could wed in honour. Then it would be he and he alone who would have her. Until that day Juliana would be beyond his reach, even though it would be torture to him.

Wulfrun pulled back before she felt him hardening. 'I vowed I would let no harm come to you,' he said, looking deep into her eyes, 'and I spoke truly. Whatever enemies you have are my enemies.'

'You are a good man, Wulfrun of England,' Simonis said with a smile. Her dark eyes glittered with triumph.

Before he could fathom the meaning of that look, a throat-rending cry echoed from the door. A death cry, such as Wulfrun had heard many times before. Urging Juliana back, he darted to the entrance hall. Swinging up his axe, he wrenched the door open.

Both guards lay sprawled on the flagstones, dead. Two figures waited on the other side of the street, their presence taunting whoever might discover the bodies. One was Salih ibn Ziyad, black bristles lining a grim slash of a mouth, eyes burning with a fierce intelligence.

The other was the young girl, Victor Verinus' daughter, Ariadne. As thin as a blade, her skin was dark from the dirt of the streets. Her stare had all the cold threat of a seasoned warrior. They held knives dripping with the blood of their victims.

'You will pay for this,' Wulfrun growled. But as he strode into the street, the murderers melted away into the shadows. Though he heard no running feet, he knew they were gone.

This was bad business. It was clear that Salih ibn Ziyad was hunting the Nepotes, though why he could not guess. But now Wulfrun would have to make good his oath: to defend the family who were in their own way as deadly as this new enemy, even though it could cost him his life.

# Chapter Seven

The rat gnawed on the knob of bread. Black eyes gleamed and needle claws raked the damp flagstone. From under hooded brow, Hereward watched the vermin in the shadows of the reeking cell. Humiliation heaped on humiliation. That was all he had endured since the English had sailed into Constantinople, and he had had enough. His anger simmered.

At his neck, his fingers closed around the sliver of wood imbued with God's power, and he felt the furnace in his heart die down. Alric had given him a great gift indeed. But if the Lord would offer him one more chance, he vowed there would come a time when he would choose to let that fire roar free, like a blaze in a tinder-dry forest, and then these Roman bastards would learn the meaning of regret. If he had to fight his way out of thc city, he would. He would not go meekly to his death.

And yet the hours of his life were creeping away from him. All night he had lain here, brooding upon a plan to escape, but in his heart he knew that it was vain hope. The Boukoleon palace was swarming with Varangian guardsmen, and it was only a short walk from this miserable cell to the yard where he would face the axe. Hereward stared into the gloom. Many times he had faced death, but never had he thought it would come like this.

Footsteps echoed along the corridor without, and a moment later the door groaned open. Thin dawn light fell across the filthy straw.

Stooping to step under the lintel, Wulfrun strode to the centre of the chamber. His face was like stone. He had waited for this day for a long, long time. To see the hated Hereward of the English, the man he blamed for his father's death, facing execution. How his heart must sing, the Mercian thought. He glowered at the commander, and felt surprised to see no hint of triumph there. The guardsman would not meet his gaze, and almost seemed troubled by what was to come.

'It was only ever a matter of time,' Wulfrun said, his voice like pebbles falling upon wood.

'You think I set out to murder that man?'

'I know Sabas Apion is dead. I know his blood was still wet upon your blade when you were captured. You may have enjoyed the emperor's favour for saving his life during the plot by the Verini, but even he will not forgive this crime, not the killing of a man held in such high regard at court.' He pushed back his cloak and let his hand fall upon the hilt of his short sword. 'Why did you kill him?'

'It seemed only fair payment for a man about to do murder.'

'Murder? Why would Sabas Apion care if a dog like you lived or died?'

'He cared not at all. But he had his heart set upon ending the days of another who was there. I was in the way, that was all.'

'Another, you say?' Wulfrun levelled his cold gaze at Hereward, weighing the truth.

The Mercian did not flinch. 'My tongue always speaks true.'

Wulfrun nodded slowly, seemingly accepting his captive's account. 'It matters little. This time your luck has run out.' He drew his sword and flicked the tip up.

So, the hour had come. Hereward pushed his back up the wall, steeling himself. 'You would see an innocent man go to his death?'

Snorting, the guardsman urged his captive out. 'Do not sully the word. You have not been innocent since you were a babe. If you are not guilty of this crime, there are more than enough others to suffice.'

Hereward eased out of the cell into a dank corridor, blinking at the sunlight breaking through a small window high up on one wall. There was little point in pressing Wulfrun further, he knew, however much reluctance he sensed in the guardsman. The judgement had been made.

Raising his chin, the Mercian strode along the corridor and up a narrow flight of steps. He was surprised by the images that rushed through his head unbidden. He thought of his wife, Turfrida, and the last time they had seen each other, on another bright dawn. And he thought of Alric and hoped the monk would bear his grief well. And then, as if from nowhere, a memory swept up of the son he had left behind in England. He could not understand his feelings – regret, hope that the lad would see better days than he ever had, worry.

In the yard, under a rosy sky, three guardsmen bore witness by the door into the palace. Hereward found his gaze drawn to the block, and the tall, broad-shouldered executioner who stood beside it.

'Dorlof is one of the Rus,' Wulfrun murmured at the Mercian's back. 'He is strong. He will take your head with one clean stroke.'

That was some comfort.

When he had crossed the yard, Hereward looked the unflinching Rus in the eye, then knelt. He felt a strange peace settle upon him. He had never feared death, and there had been times when he would have welcomed it. But one regret haunted him: he had failed his spear-brothers. What hope now for them?

Hereward heard Dorlof shift and the sound of knuckles cracking. He sensed the axe being swung up high.

He was ready.

'Hold!' A woman's voice cracked with authority.

Craning his neck, Hereward glimpsed a woman in a crimson

dress standing by the door to the palace. Tall and slender, her silver-streaked black hair was a mass of ringlets falling down her back. She was pointing imperiously at the executioner. 'Bring him to me.'

# Chapter Eight

'You have friends in high places,' Wulfrun growled.

Hereward's head was still swimming from the speed with which he had been snatched away from the jaws of death. The journey from the yard to this door on the first floor of the palace had passed in a blur. All he knew was that both the executioner and Wulfrun had not hesitated to obey the woman's command.

The guardsman swung the door open and steered him into a large chamber with a view over the gleaming blue-green sea. His saviour stood by the windows, sipping from a golden goblet. Hereward noted the languorous way she held her cup, the tilt of her chin, and decided that here was someone not used to being ignored. She narrowed her eyes as she sized him up.

'Hereward of the English,' Wulfrun said, bowing his head.

'You have my thanks,' the woman replied in a voice at once both lazy and weary. 'I can see why our emperor holds you in such high regard. You may leave us.'

Wulfrun frowned. 'He is a murderous cur,' he began. 'You would not be safe . . .'

'He will not harm me.' His saviour curled her lips into a seductive yet manipulative smile. 'I have learned much about Hereward of the English in these hours before dawn. He is a man of honour, I am told, not the cut-throat you threatened with execution.'

'I will not harm you. You have my word on that.' Why this woman had saved his neck, why she had taken the time to find out about him, Hereward could not begin to guess, but he was thankful none the less.

'I will remain without,' the guardsman said in his emotionless tone. He glanced at Hereward – a warning – and added, 'Should you need me, you have only to call.'

Once he had gone, the woman poured another goblet of wine and handed it to her guest. The Mercian took it, but he did not attempt to hide his suspicion. He had long since learned that in Constantinople nothing was given freely or without obligation.

'You know me?' she asked, that same smile playing on her lips as she watched him attempt to get the measure of her.

'I am rarely a guest at court.'

She laughed silently and began to circle him. 'My name is Anna Dalassene. I wielded power once, and could have wielded more. Once I had a husband, John Comnenos, the commander of the western armies. His brother Isaac sat upon the imperial throne. And when Isaac . . . sickly old Isaac . . . gave up his crown, my husband refused to press his claim to rule the empire. He saw no value in it.' A flicker of irritation crossed her face. Here was an old wound, still festering. 'And then my husband died. Now I only have my children.'

Hereward sipped his wine. It had a sweetness to it, far finer than the bitter swill they served in the tavern near the English hovel.

'This last night, you saved the life of my son.'

'The young swordsman, the one Sabas Apion tried to kill? That is why you saved my neck?'

'To give my thanks, yes.'

'If you can keep my head upon my shoulders, you still wield some power.'

'Some.' She fluttered fingers in the air, pretending to dismiss the words. 'In Constantinople, all men – and all women – need allies. Here, enemies lurk everywhere. There are few who can be trusted. But you rushed to Alexios' aid with no thought for your own safety. You fought for a stranger, because you saw one man threatened by four cut-throats, and knew there was no justice there.' Stepping closer, she peered deep into his eyes. Her stare was unflinching. Hereward thought he had never seen eyes filled with such confidence, such power, since he had stood before William the Bastard in Wincestre. 'A man of honour,' she added quietly, 'and they are rarer than hen's teeth in Constantinople.'

'Why did the man I killed want your son dead?'

'Many want Alexios dead. As many would see my blood spilled too. There is a war within Constantinople. A quiet one, but no less a war. You must know that.'

Hereward nodded. 'The emperor is not well liked. Some think the empire would fare better with a stronger man on the throne. Some covet the power that goes with the crown.'

'And there are those who believe I still covet the throne, for one of my sons.'

'Do you?'

'We have an emperor, a young one. I would not see him harmed.'

'A good answer, but not to the question I asked.'

Swigging back her wine, Anna set the goblet aside. Her eyes flashed. 'It matters not whether I see a path to the throne, merely that others think I desire it. For many a day, I could not set foot in Constantinople. The emperor's uncle, the Caesar, John Doukas, feared my claim to the throne. I have little love for him . . .' Anna caught herself. Hereward could see from her sour face that in truth they were bitter enemies. 'He branded me a traitor, saw me banished, to a monastery on Prinkipos. All to make sure I would be no threat to him. But power waxes and wanes, as we all know, and John Doukas no longer wields any at the court. Perhaps he no longer has aught to his name,' she added with an enigmatic smile. 'And so I am back.'

'But still you have enemies on every side.'

A cold smile. Anna poured herself more wine. 'I need a good man . . . a warrior . . . a trusted, honourable man who can watch over my son and keep him safe from the knives in the dark.'

'I am a soldier now. I aided your son in his hour of need, but I would not see out my days wiping the spittle from his chin.'

Anna's eyes narrowed. Hereward saw steel there. Here was a woman not accustomed to being questioned or denied. 'A soldier? The man who challenged a king? Who could have taken the crown of England for himself if he had not been betrayed? A lowly soldier?' Her words boiled with scorn. 'Wulfrun,' she called. 'Take him back to the cells.'

'Wait,' Hereward growled as the door ground open.

Anna waved the guardsman back out.

'So,' the Mercian said, holding out his arms to the chamber, 'this is no reward for an act of kindness. I must earn my life.'

Gliding across the room, Anna perched upon the stone of the window. A halo of sunlight glowed around her head. 'I need you, Hereward of the English. What you witnessed last night is only the beginning. My son's life hangs by a thread, and I would do anything . . . drive any bargain . . . to keep him alive. I can trust no one else in Constantinople. So, yes, if you would see another dawn, you must agree to my terms. It may yet cost you your life. But if you accept this offer, I will use what influence I have with the emperor to have your sentence lifted. The emperor will have his own terms, of course. He cannot ignore the murder of a man like Sabas Apion. But at least here is a chance for life. Do not turn your back upon it.'

Hereward stifled his simmering anger. He should have known that nothing in Constantinople came without a price. But as his thoughts raced, a flame flickered to life deep in his head. Smiling, he said, 'I will watch over your son, but let us haggle some more. I have a mind to strike a bigger deal by far.'

# CHAPTER NINE

The gulls wheeled across the face of the sun. Brassy light glinted off the swell below as the line of men stood in the sweltering heat at the front of the Boukoleon palace, their heads bowed. Ahead of them, a salty breeze stirred the banner on the sea wall. It offered little respite. The dull yells of the men working on the quayside to the east fell away, the shriek of the birds ebbed. A stillness descended on the waterfront.

Hereward eyed his spear-brothers as he stumbled out of the palace gate after more long hours locked in his cell. He felt a dull anger that his men had been rounded up. Sullen, the warriors peered out from under heavy brows, the looks of men seething at yet another unjustified indignation heaped upon them.

'You thought your freedom could be so easily bought?' Wulfrun whispered in his ear with barely concealed satisfaction.

The Varangian Guard flanked the captives, hands upon axes. Though they outnumbered the English two to one, they did not underestimate their prisoners. Hereward nodded. That was good. To one side, Alric, Deda and Rowena watched his approach. They could not hide the worry etched in their faces.

'You are no longer the lone beast running wild among the

fields of Barholme,' Wulfrun continued. 'Now every action you take affects others. Every word you speak in anger. Every drop of blood you spill.'

'These are good men. They do not deserve to be punished for my crimes.'

'Yet they will be. And in this way, perhaps, there is a chance to hold you to account. Your life and theirs are now entwined. Remember this the next time you would draw your sword.'

Hereward's gaze flickered to a small knot of nobles watching the scene, and to a short man with greying black hair standing a spear's length in front of the group, who appeared to command their respect. He showed a smile that did not seem to fit the moment as he looked out across the English warriors.

'You are dead men all, though your legs do not yet know it. It is for the emperor and the emperor alone to decide when you go to your graves,' he said in a lilting voice.

'Who is that?' Hereward asked.

Wulfrun grunted. 'His name is Falkon Cephalas. The strong right arm of Nikephoritzes. Look on him. He would not stand there if you had not murdered Sabas Apion. You may well live to regret raising this one to high station.'

In the group of nobles, Hereward glimpsed Anna Dalassene, her chin raised, with studied indifference. One other familiar face leapt out, Simonis Nepa, tall and slender and cold. She cast a gaze at Hereward that barely disguised its murderous intent. Her kin, the Nepotes, had offered a seeming hand of friendship when the English had first arrived in Constantinople, but all they had truly wanted was to use the spear-brothers in their plot to steal the throne. They had never forgiven Hereward for the part he had played in its failure.

'Stay strong, brothers,' Hereward said as Wulfrun steered him along the line towards the watching nobles. The Guard commander gave him a shove to silence him.

'Your life already hangs by a thread,' he hissed. 'A wise man would take care not to give any more offence.'

When they came to a halt, Falkon stepped forward, still

smiling. Hereward wrinkled his nose at the strong smell of flower-infused water that the women often used on their skin in the summer's heat. 'By rights, your blood should already be draining into the dust,' the Roman said with the faintest sibilance. 'Sabas Apion was a valuable servant. His counsel will be much missed by the emperor. And his kin are demanding justice. You have made many enemies.'

'Enemies I am not short of.' Hereward sensed Wulfrun flinch beside him.

'You saved the emperor's life. He will not forget it. But this crime is too great to be ignored.' Falkon glanced past Hereward's shoulder to the line of spear-brothers. 'The third one,' he said, counting heads with his index finger. 'Kill him.'

Stunned, Hereward whirled. Falkon had identified Turold. The Roman was clever: Turold wore his gentleness for all to see, in his easy smile, his open face. The death of such a man would undoubtedly be a blow to his brothers in battle.

Turold gaped in shock, not understanding what was happening. Grabbing his arms, the guardsmen hurled him to the ground. 'I have done no wrong,' the captive said, looking up in disbelief.

'Stay your hand!' Hereward demanded as a tumult of angry cries rang out from his men. Turning back to Falkon, he pleaded, 'He is no warrior. He has made plans to give up his spear . . . to marry a Roman girl . . .'

Falkon nodded to one of the guardsmen. Hereward jerked at the sound of steel upon flesh and bone. Anguished cries erupted from his men.

Hereward felt only cold horror. When he turned, he was gripped by the sight of Turold's head rolling to a gentle halt upon the flagstones. A growing pool of blood spread around the fallen body.

The spear-brothers threw themselves into a frenzy. In an instant, they were swallowed by the Varangian Guard, who rained blows down upon them.

'Hold!' Hereward yelled, fearing that more of his men would

be slaughtered. 'Harm no more.' Turning back to Falkon, he felt his anger boil and it was all he could do to contain it. 'Turold did not deserve to die,' he croaked. 'He had a gentle heart, quick to show kindness to all he met.'

The Roman held out both hands, his voice too light for the weight of the command he had just given. 'Someone had to pay for Sabas Apion's death. Now his kin will feel that justice has been done.'

Hereward swallowed, knowing that if his hands were free he would have choked the life from Nikephoritzes' counsel there and then, though it would cost him his life. He could hear the lamentations of his men, voices cracking with fury as they cried for vengeance.

'Still, it is not a fair balance,' Falkon continued, speaking as if to an old friend in the forum. 'One English cut-throat for a man like Sabas Apion. There yet may be other deaths among your men. You have been warned.'

'Is the hippodrome not enough for you Romans now?' Hereward spat. 'You must find your joy in tormenting good men who have done no wrong?'

Falkon levelled his implacable gaze on the Mercian. 'I have learned much about you this day, Hereward of the English. It would seem you are not merely a barbarian with a sharp blade, as I first thought. I have heard how you and your men fought against the Norman king who conquered your land, and how you came within a hair's breadth of defeating him. A great warrior, they say. A man who could be of some use to the empire in these difficult times.'

Hereward's eyes flickered towards Anna Dalassene, but she was looking dreamily out to sea, as if she were paying no heed to the confrontation.

'I have been moved to set aside your punishment. For now, at least,' Falkon continued. 'I have been told you have been axes-for-hire in the employ of our army. But now you will fight for your life, and that of your men. Succeed and you will live, as will your brothers, and I will consider the account of Sabas

Apion closed with the death we have witnessed this day. Fail us, and all of you will pay the price for the murder you committed.'

'Is that just?' Hereward snapped.

'It is what it is,' the Roman replied, holding out one hand, palm up. 'We do not allow a citizen, and a great one at that, to be slain with impunity. What say you?'

Hereward could barely hear the words for the thunder of blood in his head. Deep inside, he could feel his devil yearning to be set free. But there would be a time for revenge. For now, he had his men's lives to save. 'What do you demand of us?'

Falkon nodded slowly, a smile flickering on the edges of his lips. 'There may be wisdom in you yet.' He looked past Hereward to Wulfrun and called, 'Tell him what we demand of him in return for his life and the lives of his men.' Turning, the Roman walked back into the huddle of nobles and led them away. Hereward sneered. The man thought himself above giving orders to fighting dogs.

At the edge of the Boukoleon palace, Anna glanced back. She had kept her word. He was free. But had she also agreed with Falkon that one of his men should die to balance the account? Hereward knew he could not trust her, could not trust any of the Romans in this city of deceit.

'Know that I would not have seen one of your men killed.' Wulfrun had appeared beside him. The commander glanced at the headless body with a look of distaste.

'This will not be forgotten.'

Wulfrun nodded, understanding. 'Take the body away. And see it is treated well,' he barked to his men. 'I cannot put this right. But your man will get a good Christian burial, I will see to that.'

'Is this how things are done in Constantinople?'

'This is not England.' The commander spun Hereward round and slit his bonds. 'And there are some who say the days will get darker before the sun shines again.'

Hereward watched his men seething with passion. Faces turned towards him, demanding retribution for their fallen friend, their murdered friend, but he could only answer them with a look. 'I have already made one deal with the Devil,' he growled, 'in Wincestre, with William the Bastard, to save the lives of many. That cost us our home, our kin, our friends. Tell me what price is demanded this time.'

As he began to lead the Mercian back towards the Boukoleon palace, Wulfrun's face darkened. 'Constantinople is beset by enemies on all sides. Only the emperor and those close to him seem unaware of the axe that hangs over all our heads. One day the Turks will overrun this place, you heed my words, and then this city will be awash with blood. But now there is a new enemy in the east, one who is familiar to the emperor, and Nikephoritzes. A Norman. A seasoned warrior who styles himself upon William the Bastard.'

Hereward flinched. Even now the name made his stomach clench with disgust.

'Roussel de Bailleul sees himself as a conqueror, too. He has carved out a kingdom and built an army of Norman warriors and axes-for-hire. And now he has taken the Caesar himself, John Doukas, captive. Roussel may wish to ransom him for gold, to pay for his fighting men. But Nikephoritzes is afrit that there will be blood. That Roussel will take the Caesar's head. That he may even raise a challenge to the emperor's power.'

A shadow fell across Hereward as he passed through the great arch and into the palace courtyard. Puzzled, he looked around at activity everywhere, boys racing with messages, slaves hauling sacks of provisions. 'What unfolds?'

'War,' Wulfrun replied, his voice heavy. 'Bloodshed. Death. This is a bad business. You thought your days of killing Normans were done. But it seems that Anna Dalassene has convinced Nikephoritzes that you and only you know how the Normans fight, and the eunuch would put that knowledge to good use. You and your men will ride east, into the heart of this murdering bastard's kingdom, through his vast army, and rescue the Caesar. Or you will die trying.'

# Chapter Ten

The sky was on fire. Under the rising sun, the soaring dome of the Hagia Sophia glowed a dull red as a cool breeze licked over the rooftops. The greatest city on earth still slumbered. But in the yard of the Boukoleon palace, a line of warriors was on the move. At the head of his spear-brothers, Hereward paused and looked to the east. Soon it would be as hot as an oven. Waves of heat crushing down, dust clogging nostrils. England seemed but a distant memory at that moment.

The Mercian glanced back at his loyal war-band. They had tried to travel light. Their leathers and furs had been left upon their beds, but they were still weighted by their dented helms and hauberks, gleaming now that the rust had been scoured from them in sacks of sand. He caught the smell of paint from their shields, brightened for the coming campaign, as was the English way.

Nodding, Hereward felt proud of what he saw. Whatever was to come upon the hard road, they would face it together. But his men's knuckles were white where they gripped their spears and axes, their faces sullen and simmering with loathing. They wanted revenge for Turold's death perhaps more than they wanted the gold and the glory.

Stepping beside him, Kraki glowered through the mass of battle scars that glowed pink above his wild beard. 'When we leave the city behind, we should keep going. We have no friends here.'

'We have not run from a fight before.'

'This is not England,' the Viking said, words that seemed to have been voiced many a time in recent weeks by all of the men. 'What is there for us here?' His voice was strained, the emotion close beneath the surface. Hereward guessed he was still yearning for the woman he loved. But that was the dream of a child, though the Mercian would never say such a thing.

'We will carve out our place here or die trying,' he said simply.

Kraki snorted, not convinced.

Towering over his friend, Guthrinc narrowed his eyes at Hereward. 'I have seen that look before, when I dangled you over a bog for your crimes as a lad. You have a plan.'

The Mercian turned, giving nothing away.

The fruity stink of dung floated in the air. Horses stamped and snorted as boys scattered handfuls of hay. Low voices droned from the far side of the yard where around fifty warriors milled. More drifted out from the door to the palace refectory by the moment. Hereward studied the lines of the noses, the cheekbones, the dark eyes. The tunics were fine and ornate, brightly coloured in eggshell blue, and amber, and crimson, and embroidered with intricate designs, the clothes of wealthy men.

They were Romans to a man, Hereward knew. No foreigners here. That had been the order of Nikephoritzes. But for all the arrogance these strutting warriors showed, Hereward could see that they were only making a play at being soldiers. They were not seasoned. He glanced from face to face, but there were no scars. And they had yet to put on their armour. In heaps, the helms and mail-shirts shone in the sunlight, all of it pristine, never tested in battle. Hereward grunted. The Romans were soft. They had too much gold, too many comforts, and nothing that they held dear enough to fight for with their lives. Even the emperor knew this. That was why he filled his Varangian Guard with English and Vikings who knew how to fight to the death, the fiercest warriors in the world.

Kraki snorted. 'We are to ride with them? Should we tuck them in at night too?'

'Nikephoritzes dreams of past glories,' Hereward replied. 'He knows his army is little more than a tattered shroud over a rotting body. The empire's enemies laugh at the forces the Romans can command.' He shrugged. 'Since the battle of Manzikert, his best fighters – axes-for-hire from the north, all of them – have drifted away, or sided with those who seek to unseat the emperor. And all the empire is left with—'

'Is the mud beneath our feet,' Kraki grunted.

Guthrinc shielded his eyes as he watched the Romans. They were laughing, clapping each other on the shoulders. 'You would not think it by looking at them. They swagger as if they were the heroes of this godforsaken place.' He frowned. 'War is serious business.'

Hereward glanced back at his spear-brothers. They looked a shabby band by comparison, wild-bearded, scarred, their tunics torn and mended time and again, their helms dented. Those who did not know them would have thought them rogues and cut-throats. Their eyes flickered with contempt, their faces like stone, as they studied the ones they were meant to fight alongside.

'Nikephoritzes is no fool,' he continued. 'Though the emperor seems blind to every part of his business, his counsel knows the empire is crumbling. The Romans cannot afford to squat here in the city with no army of any worth to defend them. He would build it up to be a powerful force.'

'With these?' Kraki spat, sweeping one hand out towards the milling recruits.

'They call them the Athanatoi, the ones who are without death.'

Kraki sniggered. 'We will see if they still hold that name after the first battle.'

'In days long gone, the empire had a great army, one to be feared,' Hereward went on. 'And among the *tagmata* was a war-band called by this name. These Immortals swooped down upon the Rus like a bolt from the heavens and left only a sea of blood in their wake. They were knights on horseback, sheathed as much in gold as iron, nobles all of them.'

'Ah, magic!' Guthrinc said, raising one finger in the air. 'Nikephoritzes thinks that if he gives these ones the same name he will summon up the spirits of those warriors.'

Hereward smiled. 'Aye, you may well be right. But he is clever too. These are also all Roman nobles, because Nikephoritzes believes they are the only ones to be trusted to be loyal to the emperor. And if they find glory in these coming days, the word will go out and their fellows will join the army once more. And all in Constantinople will give praise to these wondrous warriors with the spirits of old. And to Nikephoritzes too,' he added in a sardonic tone.

Guthrinc cracked his knuckles. 'A trial, then.'

'Aye, by fire.' Kraki spat into the dust. 'And when they all die on the end of Norman blades, I suppose we will be blamed.'

'You have taken many blows to that thick skull of yours, but they have not dashed out your wits,' Hereward replied with a nod. 'I would wager that is another reason why they are sending a band of barbarians to war alongside their fine sons.'

'Who told you all this?' Guthrinc asked with a pointed note of suspicion. 'That woman?' When Hereward did not reply, the tall man added, 'And I wonder what else she told you that you are keeping in your tunic. I have never known Hereward of Mercia to ride into battle without a plan, and a good one at that.'

'All in good time.' Hereward spied a familiar face in the crowd of soldiers. Alexios Comnenos strode among the men readying for battle as if he were not part of them. None spoke to him. He did not smile, nor did he nod in greeting. He passed among them like a ghost, heading towards the horses. Hereward understood the Romans' contempt. Alexios was younger than all of them, yet his renown in battle surpassed every one. And they knew, as Hereward knew, that Alexios' mother was a force in their city. She would not rest until Alexios had achieved a level of success that she deemed worthy. A boy hero with a powerful mother who always thrust her son to the front. Hereward grinned. No surprise that these warriors only had cold looks to mask their jealousy.

Yet the Mercian liked what he saw. There was a strength in this young man's face that was not visible in the others. Here was someone who *had* seen battle, aye, and hardship too.

When he caught Hereward's eye, he grinned and walked over. Clapping a hand on the Mercian's shoulder, he said, 'I did not have the time to give you the thanks you deserved for saving my life.'

Kraki eyed the new arrival with suspicion. 'Is this the lamb we are supposed to wrap in blankets and keep safe from all harm?' The Viking looked Alexios up and down. 'I see why your mother thinks you are still a babe in arms.'

The Roman grimaced. 'Why speak you of my mother?'

Kraki leaned into the young man's face and bared his teeth. 'She begged us to form a shield wall around you because she thinks you a poor little rabbit who cannot stand up for himself.'

Alexios' cheeks flushed, as much with anger as embarrassment, Hereward thought. 'Pay no heed to Kraki. It is his way to push you until you push him back.'

'Is what he says true?' Alexios demanded, rounding on the Mercian.

'No. And yes. Your mother does not doubt that you are a fine warrior. But it is the knife at the back in the dark of the night that she fears.'

'Ready yourself for a few more knives at the back when those good Romans see the filthy English are on your side,' Guthrinc said with a rumbling laugh.

'I need no one to watch my back,' Alexios snarled.

Leaning in, Hereward whispered, 'You have enemies who

may well call themselves friends. And in that kind of battle, all men need allies.'

Alexios hesitated, then nodded. 'It would be an honour to ride with you.' His gaze flickered to Kraki. 'You, not so much.'

The other English drew in to study the man they had been told about. Hereward felt pleased that Alexios did not recoil at their fierce expressions and ragged appearance. 'You will know all their names soon enough. They will defend you with their lives, of that you can be sure.'

'My mother must be paying you well,' the Roman said.

'She bought my life,' Hereward replied, 'and after that . . .' He paused, thinking. 'She gave me words that are worth more than gold. Or at least as much.' He smiled when he saw Alexios' baffled expression, and Guthrinc's and Kraki's too.

The sound of iron clattering on wood rang out across the yard and the babble of voices stilled. A man with a hooked nose was banging his sword upon his shield. The commander, no doubt, ready to give the orders.

As Hereward led the English towards their comrades in arms, Alexios jabbed a finger into Kraki's face. 'You,' he said, 'need a bath. You reek of vinegar.' He strode ahead to the sound of Guthrinc's chuckles.

When the war-band gathered on the edge of the group, Hereward could see the Romans eyeing the new arrivals with barely concealed contempt. The commander allowed himself a brief, and obvious, smile when he looked across at them, then turned his attention back to his men. 'Welcome our new brothers,' he said. 'They know how the Normans fight, so I am told, and we might find some use for them once we are in the thick of battle.'

Laughter rippled through the assembled Romans. Hereward saw Sighard's cheeks colour. Kraki clenched the haft of his axe until his knuckles turned white. But every one of Hereward's men showed a cold face, undeterred by the mockery. They all knew that the proof would come once they were knee-deep in blood and shit, and the screams of the dying would drown out any laughter.

The speaker turned back to the English and held Hereward's eyes. 'My name is Tiberius Gabras,' he said. 'I command the Athanatoi, and while you ride with us I command you too. If I say you ride into the enemy's arrows, you ride. Do you hear me?'

'We fought in your army. We know what an order is,' Kraki said, glaring.

With a smirk, Tiberius looked around his men. 'They fought in our army,' he repeated to much laughter. 'And can you ride?'

'If we ride badly, it is because your army's commanders taught us,' Hereward boomed. Some of his men did ride badly, he could not deny that. Only a few had spent much time on horseback while they were in England. But he had forced them to persevere in their learning, for among the fighters of Constantinople it was a skill that was much valued. A few had taken to it well, Sighard for one. But he would not want to risk sending them into battle on chargers. They fought their best with their feet on the ground, behind a solid shield wall.

Tiberius held his gaze for a moment, sizing him up. Hereward flashed a grin so the commander would know that here was a man who would not be easily cowed. The Roman's face darkened and he looked away.

'The slaves will find you horses,' he said. 'Ships are ready to take us across the Bosphorus, and then we ride east . . . to glory. We will fall upon the Normans like a storm of steel, and they will know once and for all the might of the empire. The Caesar will be in our hands before their blood has drained into the dust.'

The Immortals cheered, raising their blades high so they glinted in the light of the rising sun. They were too confident, Hereward thought. And that was the first step on the road to the boneyard.

But as Tiberius moved among the throng, revelling in the

pride, Hereward was looking elsewhere. Three faces leapt out at him, all of them like stone, the only ones still turned towards the English. He took in the dark, intense stares, ones he knew well across the field of battle, and then caught Alexios' arm. Whispering, he asked the men's identities.

'The squat one with the staring eyes is Isaac Balsamon,' Alexios murmured. 'The one who licks his lips like a snake is Lysas Petzeas. And the one with the almond eyes who watches without blinking, that is Zeno Oresme.'

Hereward nodded. 'The boar, the snake and the wolf. I will remember them.'

'I see no threat there,' Alexios replied with a shrug. 'I have supped wine with them all. They were among the first to step forward when Nikephoritzes asked for men to join the Athanatoi.'

The Mercian flashed one last glance at the three Romans. He could not be sure if they meant harm, were simply curious, or were angry that these interlopers were encroaching on a pure Roman *tagmata*. But he would be watching them closely from now on.

'Come,' he said, turning to his men. 'Let us choose our mounts. We shall show these Romans how fortunate they are to have the English fighting alongside them.'

But as the spear-brothers strode towards the horses, Guthrinc caught his leader's arm and pointed to the door to the palace. A straggler had emerged, a new recruit, grinning as if he were the lord of all he surveyed. It was Maximos Nepos.

# Chapter Eleven

Jewels of light glittered on the swell. The ship ploughed a furrow through the wide river, the creaking hull flexing against the current as the oarsmen droned their song. Amid the stink of horse dung wafting from the beasts in the pen, Hereward leaned on the ship's side and contemplated the line of vessels transporting the Immortals and their horses to the eastern shore. It was not the greatest army he had ever seen, but Nikephoritzes had assembled enough warriors to make Roussel de Bailleul think twice about keeping the Caesar captive.

'Word has reached the emperor from the scouts sent out to the east. The Norman has been paying good gold for more axes-for-hire.' Alexios balanced on the rolling deck, the breeze stirring his dark hair.

'Save us from little men with big plans,' Kraki growled. 'He is holding out for more gold for his coffers. He will send the Caesar back once he thinks he is rich enough.'

'We shall see,' Hereward replied. 'He has his own land now, and he is the king of it. A man will not give up that power lightly. And the emperor will not let him keep it. A threat in the east is not what he needs now as his empire crumbles around him.'

'What do you say, Little General? Have you a plan to win this coming fight?' Maximos stepped over the oarsmen's benches and wandered to the aft deck. His teeth were white in his broad grin and his dark eyes sparkled.

Alexios' cheeks flushed, but he did not rise to the bait.

Maximos clapped an arm round the younger Roman's shoulders, refusing to relent. 'Did you know his mother sent him out to prove himself in battle when he was barely big enough to hold a sword? And the general sent him home the same day because he did not want babes in his army?'

Pushing up his chin, Alexios stepped aside from the other man's grasp. He would not let this mockery wound him; Hereward admired him for it. 'I have proved myself in battle a hundred times since then,' he said in a calm voice.

'Aye, what stories they tell about you now, eh? You have polished up your name like a fine gold plate.' Maximos' easy grin grew harder, his gaze colder. 'The bravest warrior in all Constantinople, they say, and yet still barely more than a boy. A wit as sharp as a blade. Skills upon the field of battle that dwarf those of seasoned fighting men. Why, soon you will command your own warriors. And then . . . the army itself? And then . . . the empire?'

'I am a loyal—'

Maximos snorted. 'You? You have no say in these matters. Your mother rules you, and her ambition is as hot as a furnace.'

Alexios flinched, his hand twitching towards the hilt of his sword.

'You do not like to hear of your mother?' Maximos pressed, feigning innocence.

'It seems all you Romans know your duty to your kin,' Hereward interjected.

For a moment, Maximos looked out across the waves. The words had stung, as the Mercian had known they would. Maximos had danced to the tune of his own mother and father for too long. He had murdered his best friend, the man he loved, and then betrayed the woman who loved him, Meghigda, all in pursuit of the Nepotes' lust for the crown. Plots within plots. Maximos' life had known little else.

The young man found his grin soon enough. 'I mean nothing by it,' he said, clapping Alexios on the arm. 'We will be brothers in this battle, and we will sing songs about it in the taverns when we return.'

Alexios held the other man's eyes for a moment and then walked away.

'He is a rival,' Hereward said.

Maximos shrugged. 'You will find men grasping for the throne on every street in Constantinople. The emperor is weak. Power ebbs away. The people starve. Enemies march towards our walls by the day. Sooner or later the crown will slip into new hands. Every man and woman in the city knows that.'

'And you would rather it were you,' Hereward said.

'I have no trust left in my heart for you,' Kraki snarled, glaring at the Roman. 'I have never known such a lust for power. It hollows a man out.' He strode away, following Alexios towards the pen where the horses snorted.

'My sins are great, I know that,' Maximos said to Hereward, looking back to watch the glowing dome of the Hagia Sophia as it retreated behind them. 'And you well know that I have been haunted by all that has been demanded of me by my kin. I am sick of the plots.'

'Then turn your back upon them.'

Maximos laughed without humour. 'Were it only so simple. And if only I were stronger.'

Hereward studied the Roman. His troubles had carved hollows under his eyes. There could be no doubt that he hated the road his kin were forcing him to walk, but still he could not be trusted, Hereward felt sure. For these nobles, plots and power were a way of life. It was all they thought of, aye, and likely all they dreamed of every night.

'You will understand, then, if I watch my own back while you are around,' the Mercian said.

His eyes fixed on the city, Maximos nodded. 'No man would

blame you.' Pausing, he glanced around to make sure he would not be overheard. 'Take care in the days to come. I am the least of your worries. I have heard whispers . . . it has been made plain to some who ride with the Athanatoi that it would be good if the English did not return from this journey into the east.'

'Made plain by whom?'

'I can say no more. Watch your backs, that's all.' With a nod, Maximos walked away.

Hereward could not tell if the Roman was trying to buy trust, and if so whether with lie or truth. But that the English had powerful enemies in Constantinople there could be no doubt. His knuckles whitening, he gripped the rail and peered into the swell. He was sick of smiles that hid murder, and lies, and deceit and plots. But if death waited for them in the east, they would give a good account of themselves.

Once they had landed, the English made their way to the Roman's camp where, privately, Hereward passed on Maximos' warning. He was pleased to see his men meet it with defiance. As dusk fell, the spear-brothers wandered among the tents, ignoring the mocking stares. A gloom had descended upon them after the murder of Turold. The Mercian glimpsed an anger there too, one directed at the Romans, and at the world. They needed a victory, soon.

The Immortals sat around their campfires deep into the night, singing songs of battle and women and feasting. They laughed and drank as if the war had already been fought and won. Hereward watched them, frowning. If he was commander here, the mood would be different. War needed to be respected, as did Death. If not, a price would be paid, there was no doubt of that.

He slept fitfully, haunted by dreams of his dead wife Turfrida, and, once again, the son he had left behind in England. Before the morn of his execution, he had not thought of that lad in many a season. He prayed the boy would have a good life.

When dawn came, the Athanatoi broke camp. Hereward

gathered his spear-brothers and soon they were trailing away from Constantinople at the heart of the army. Ahead lay an unknown land, and threats on every side. Ahead lay victory or defeat, death or glory.

# Chapter Twelve

The wind had fallen and the smothering heat crushed down upon the ridge. Only the music of chirruping insects sang out. Lying on his belly in the long grass, Hereward felt thankful for the shade of the trees hanging over him. How he yearned to slake his thirst from the waterskin on his horse, but that was far behind him, where most of the war-band waited.

Peering down the slope, he watched a trail of blue smoke rise up from the rough huts of logs and turf. The dwellings reminded him of those deep in the fens, each one carved from the land by poor folk who made do with only the flimsiest shelter from the elements.

Beside him, Kraki swept aside the grass and thrust his scowling face forward. 'Why is it always us crawling like worms? Those Roman bastards will never sully their fine tunics.'

'Let them laugh at us filthy with dust; I would rather see the dangers ahead with my own eyes.' He did not trust the raw Romans one bit, not their skills, nor their battle-senses, and certainly not their sense of brotherhood. All warriors who raised an axe knew that you watched out for every man who trod the bone road with you. But he suspected these Immortals would send the English to hell if it would save their own necks.

It had been four days now since they had left Constantinople. Hereward recalled the Romans' curses as the English showed little skill on horseback, keeping the pace slow. As they moved east the land had turned wilder, the golden crops giving way to woods and grassland, rock and dust. The bustling villages grew sparser, and further apart, and eventually the army reached one that was abandoned. Doors hung open, the shacks empty of all possessions, the livestock gone. In that part of the empire, the fear was so strong Hereward could almost smell it. The Turks smelled it too, and so they inched westwards day by day, taking whatever they found.

Squinting in the bright sunlight, he watched a dark shape flicker across the grassy slope beyond the shacks. It could have been the shadow of a bird, but he knew it was Herrig the Rat creeping closer to the huts than any other man would dare.

'We are wasting our time here,' Kraki rumbled. 'These Turks are no threat. They are *farmers*.' He spat the word. 'We will question them about the Norman dogs, find out all we need to know about numbers, and be on our way.'

Before he could voice his agreement, Hereward heard the sound of running feet at his back. Maximos Nepos crashed into the grass beside him, grinning as if he had just bedded the most beautiful woman in Constantinople. The Mercian wondered if that grin was the last thing Maximos' best friend had seen before the Roman plunged a knife into his side.

Maximos must have glimpsed Hereward's unguarded expression for he furrowed his brow in a rueful look. 'You do not trust me. I understand that. How could I not? But I will not forget that you set me free in Afrique, perhaps saved my life, and I will earn that trust back.'

'I hear a dog farting,' Kraki muttered from somewhere in the long grass.

Undeterred, Maximos grinned once more. 'My brothers grow restless. They wish to question these dogs.'

As if from nowhere, Herrig the Rat rose up from the long grass. All three men started. Through his gap-toothed grin,

Herrig said, 'Only women and children are here. The men are away at their work.'

Hereward studied the village. His gut still advised caution, but he had no time to give voice to his doubts. Maximos jumped to his feet and exclaimed, 'Then let us be at it. A glorious battle awaits, and we have no time to tarry here.' He pushed his fingers into his mouth and let out a piercing whistle.

The thunder of hooves boomed through the still air. Cresting the ridge along the narrow track leading to the village, the Immortals swept down on the cluster of huts. As one, the doors crashed open and women and children flooded out across the baked mud, eyes wide with fear.

When the Romans had surrounded the entire village, Tiberius Gabras urged his mount forward. The Turks cowered back, babbling in their strange tongue as they plucked at the cloth of their plain dresses.

'Our leader likes to show he is a strong warrior,' Kraki sneered, as Hereward led the war-band down the slope. 'Frightening women and children.'

Looking down his hawkish nose at the women, Tiberius boomed a question in the Roman tongue. When the women only gaped, the commander snapped round to his men and barked an order. Sullenly, Lysas the Snake slipped down from his horse and began to converse haltingly with one of them in her own tongue. She replied in a hesitating, reedy voice, her gaze never straying far from the knight's blade.

While Lysas relayed the information to Tiberius, Guthrinc leaned in and whispered, 'What are they saying?'

'Our Norman foe is known to these Turks,' Hereward replied. 'He has paid them off with much gold so he can build his kingdom in the north. But since he has captured a powerful man . . . the Caesar . . . he sends out scouts and war-bands to smite down any who would try to free him.' As he spoke, he watched Roman heads rise and eyes search the hills and woods, their bravado fading.

'If this Norman dog is anything like William the Bastard, he will carve these Romans like hot meat, and us with it,' Hiroc hissed. He was a dour man, always scowling at some imagined misery or other, but few could doubt his words.

Sighard stuck out his chin in defiance. 'Did they think Roussel would let us ride up to the borders of his kingdom without any challenge? What manner of warriors do we follow?'

English heads turned towards Hereward, questioning, hoping, as always, that he could save them from the fate they now all saw darkening the horizon. But the Mercian found his attention caught by Alexios, who sat upright on his steed with a grim expression. Even he sensed the failings of the men around him, and the threat that came with it.

Shouts rang out from the shadows among the trees further along the ridge. Hereward whirled to see Turkish men spewing from the wood. Their heads were covered with felt *boerks*, the bowls intricately embroidered with the brims turned up to protect their eyes from the sun. Woollen *yalmas* were pulled tightly across their chests and fastened with loops under the arms, and straight-legged trousers were held up by belts from which hung bow-cases and quivers. Some whirled their swords over their heads; others brandished sticks and rocks. Though they roared ferociously, the Mercian could see there were not enough of them to challenge a large, armed war-band.

He raised a hand to hold his men back. The Turks' faces were contorted with fear for their women and children. Any man would have felt the same to see his village surrounded by such a force. This was a show of defiance, an honourable outcry to warn the Romans away from their kin, nothing more.

But as the Mercian glanced back at the Immortals, he felt his chest tighten. Scowling, Tiberius seemed to see something different. As the Turks hovered on the treeline, shaking their sticks and yelling their throats raw, the commander barked, 'Kill them. Kill them all. We will not have them warning the Norman scouts.'

Though Hereward yelled to stop this cruel order, his voice was drowned by the rumble of hooves as the Athanatoi hurled their mounts up the slope. Through the din, Tiberius roared, 'The women and children too.'

The English stared in slack-jawed dismay as the remainder of the Roman force rounded on the cowering villagers. Swords and axes hacked down. Screams rang out and innocent blood drained into brown earth. Hereward could barely comprehend what he saw. In England, the Normans had committed such atrocities, but never his own allies.

Alexios forced his horse back, watching in horror. Though there were years between them, when he glanced back and locked eyes with the Mercian, Hereward felt a common bond.

'What do we do?' Guthrinc's voice was breaking. He held out his hands as if he wanted to cover his eyes to blot out the terrible sight.

But Hereward could see that Tiberius would not be satisfied until all the Turks had been slaughtered, and his men were only too happy to oblige. Their fear for their own lives outweighed any disgust at their personal actions.

'This is madness,' Sighard gasped, his eyes rimmed with tears. 'Madness.'

Finally the screams ebbed. The sword arms stilled. Some of the Immortals cheered, though others looked around, bewildered now that the blood-lust had left them. Only the English stood with their heads bowed.

As he glanced up the slope to the treeline, Hereward glimpsed some of the Turks fleeing into the woods. Tiberius would send his men in pursuit, but the chance of their being caught was slim. They knew the paths, the hiding places. They could go where no horse could follow. By this course of action, Tiberius had almost certainly brought about what he had hoped to prevent. The tormented Turks would want to exact their revenge, either by their own hands or by the Norman war-bands'.

Fools, he thought. You have damned us all.

# Chapter Thirteen

The candles guttered in the sudden breeze. Shadows swooped across the stone wall behind God's table. On aching knees before the altar, Alric glanced round, still murmuring his prayer that Hereward and the English would return safely.

'Who goes?' he called into the dark.

The monastery of St George had been still for some time. The hours while Constantinople slept had always been Alric's favourite time for reflection. He could imagine himself back at the cathedral in Ely, when life had seemed simpler, for all its threat. Only Neophytos, the eunuch, had been moving around the church, replacing the spent candles, and for all his vast bulk he made barely a whisper.

'Is this the one? Alric of the English?' The voice floated out of the gloom.

'It is.'

Footsteps clattered on the flagstones as a group of six men swept into the circle of light round the altar. Alric recognized Wulfrun, his crimson cloak swirling around him; the others were unfamiliar. Four looked to be rogues from the street, with scarred faces and broken noses. The fifth was a slight man, with greying black hair and piercing blue eyes.

'I am Falkon Cephalas,' he said in a soft voice. 'Keeping order in this troubled city is my burden. And it pains me to find that those troubles extend even here, under God's watchful eye.'

Alric clambered to his feet, puzzled. From the corner of his eye, he glimpsed the outline of Neophytos cloaked by the shadows. The eunuch was taking care not to give away his presence. 'I do not understand—'

'Plots,' Falkon interjected, 'against the emperor himself.'

Alric furrowed his brow. 'I am a servant of God, nothing more. I have no interest in earthly power.'

'And yet you travel with the English warriors who would have killed a king and stolen his crown, no doubt for Hereward alone.'

'William the Bastard stole the crown first,' the monk protested.

Falkon held out his hands, showing how little he cared. 'Who would have killed a king,' he repeated in a quiet voice.

Alric pushed up his chin in defiance. 'There is no man in Constantinople who would accuse me of any plot against the emperor.'

'That may be so. And yet my eyes and ears upon the streets tell me that this monastery houses men who would see the emperor dead.'

The monk forced his gaze to fix upon the intruders so he did not draw their attention to Neophytos.

'Since the murder of Sabas Apion, I have learned much about Hereward and the English and their rebellion against the crown.' Flames flickered in those cold blue eyes. 'None of it good.'

'They wish only peace—'

Falkon held up his hand to silence the monk. 'Your words mean nothing.'

'I do not lie.'

'All men lie, monk. Even the servants of God.' He flicked his raised hand towards the door. The four rogues turned on their heels and swept away. 'Too many enemies of the emperor now circle the crown, every one of them brazen. They think they are untouchable because of their position, or because, so far, they have been seen to do no wrong. They are mistaken.'

'You would seize them before they commit any crime?'

Falkon only smiled, a tight, humourless expression.

A scuffling echoed in the corridor that led to the church, punctuated by loud cries. When the four rogues surged back into the circle of light, they were dragging another man among them. Alric gaped. It was the monk Amyntas, a devout man even by the standards of the monastery. His nose was caked with blood and his left eye swollen shut.

'Leave him,' Alric protested, stepping forward to free the captive. 'He has done no wrong.'

'Stay back, English,' Falkon cautioned, 'lest you be seen as an ally of this traitorous dog.' When he wagged a finger, the rogues stepped back so he could stand face to face with Amyntas. 'Do you deny that you have worked with others in matters of treason?'

'Yes, I deny it,' the bewildered monk cried. His teeth were stained with blood.

Undeterred, Falkon continued, 'And that you spent evenings at a house in the Pisan quarter, where my spies tell me enemies of the emperor plot his downfall.'

Amyntas hesitated for only a moment, but it was enough. Falkon's smile broadened. Sensing what was to come, the monk threw himself back along the nave. At Falkon's nod, the four rogues whisked out their short swords and fell upon him. Alric cried out in horror. The blades hacked down time and again, as if the men were slaughtering a pig. Amyntas' blood flooded into the seams between the flagstones and flowed towards the altar.

'What have you done?' Alric cried, clutching at his head with his single hand. 'Here in God's house.'

'Let this be a lesson to you, and to your English friends, and to any who would harm our emperor,' Falkon said, turning his back on the ruined body. 'No longer will we stand by and watch the seeds of dissent sprout and flourish. Justice will be swift, and harsh.'

Alric flashed a look of dismay at Wulfrun. The silent

guardsman only stared into the dark of the church. Yet a tremor at the corner of his mouth spoke volumes.

'You moved too slowly, Wulfrun,' Falkon said as if he could read the minds of those present. 'These days I wonder if I can trust even the Varangian Guard. You have failed to stop these treasonous plots spreading like weeds across Constantinople.'

'The emperor still wears the crown,' the guardsman replied, his voice wintry.

'Still. Perhaps it is best if I find my own men to serve my wishes, what say you?'

Wulfrun turned his eyes back to the dark. 'Whatever pleases you.'

Falkon's piercing gaze darted back to Alric. 'As if I did not have worries enough about you and your English friends, I am told that you also brought with you the adviser to the Imazighen, Salih ibn Ziyad, a man whose hands are drenched with blood.'

Alric gritted his teeth, saying nothing. He felt sickened by this man who killed at a whim, who had no respect for the rule of law. If Falkon Cephalas were not stopped, there would be hell to pay for all of them.

'Do you know where he is?' the Roman pressed.

'I do not.'

Falkon shrugged. 'For now, I will take your word. But know that my men will hunt him down like a dog. He is a threat, and his days will be ended.'

Turning on his heel, the Roman strolled back along the nave. A trail of bloody footprints followed him after he crossed the pool around Amyntas' remains. Wulfrun and the rogues followed.

Once they had gone, a scuffling echoed from the dark on the far side of the church. Neophytos was hurrying out. Though Alric felt disgust at the murder of Amyntas, the speed of the eunuch's exit stung his curiosity. Creeping out, he followed Neophytos through the deserted corridors until the Roman stepped into the night at the front of the monastery. A small figure waited by the wall.

Squinting out of the doorway, Alric recognized Leo Nepos, Neophytos' cousin. The boy listened intently as the eunuch hissed some message at him, an urgent one by the sound of it, and responded in a voice made loud by anger. 'Maximos has abandoned us when we need him most. I am the one. I.' He beat his chest for emphasis.

Resting both hands on the boy's shoulders to calm him, the monk leaned in to whisper. Though he strained to hear more, Alric knew he was too far away. Easing along the front of the monastery, he flitted to the shadows close to where the two Nepotes spoke, but he was too late. Neophytos was already hurrying back to the monastery as Leo jumped the low wall into the street.

Alric looked from one to the other, weighing his options. If any in Constantinople should be worried by the threat of Falkon Cephalas, it was the Nepotes. Perhaps he could learn something here that would help his friends upon their return. Reaching his decision, he clambered over the wall and followed the boy.

At that hour, the streets near the monastery were deserted. An owl hooted from one of the trees in the garden of a large house. The breeze carried the fragrance of the white, night-blooming flowers that the Romans seemed to love so much. After a while, Leo's insistent pace slowed. His shoulders sagged, his head bowed; his anger appeared to be draining away. In that moment, Alric thought the lad looked as if he had a great weight pressing upon him.

An urgent whisper rustled out from somewhere near by. An unguarded foot scraped on the ground. Leo stopped and looked round. Only silence followed. With a shrug, the boy continued on his way. Alric felt his heart beat faster. Did the lad not realize someone else was keeping pace with him in the shadows?

As the monk glanced this way and that, a shape swept out of a side street. Black, it was, darker than the night itself. Alric gasped when he saw a flash of silver: a knife arcing down towards the oblivious boy's neck.

His heart leapt into his mouth – he could not even manage a

cry of alarm. But before the blade drank blood another figure dashed forth, smaller this time, and paler. A girl. Grabbing Leo, she dragged him out of harm's way.

'He is just a boy,' the girl cried, 'and unlike my own brother, this one has a good heart.'

Shaking himself out of his stupor, Alric recognized Ariadne Verina, the waif who had known more miseries in her short life than most grown men ever experienced. Then the would-be assailant could only be the one who had befriended her, Salih ibn Ziyad, the man who hated the Nepotes more than any other in that city – enough, it seemed, to slay a boy.

The girl thrust herself between the black-robed man and Leo, reaching up her arms to bare her own chest to the blade. 'Do not harm him,' she pleaded. Alric heard a tenderness in those words that went beyond mere concern. And when she glanced back and locked eyes with the lad, he could see the affection that lay between them. 'He deserves your mercy, Salih. We are of a piece, he and I. Both of us overlooked, ignored by our kin, treated like the mud beneath their feet. Both deserving of so much more. That is our bond.'

Salih snarled, refusing to sheathe his knife. But Ariadne would not back down either. Whirling, she thrust Leo away. 'Run,' she urged. 'Run like the wind. I will hold him off.'

The boy darted away into the night.

When Salih moved in pursuit, Ariadne grabbed his arm. Alric watched a curious change come over her face, a hardening as if of age, and when she spoke her voice was deeper. 'I am al-Kahina. The spirit of Dihya burns in my breast. I am one with the sand and the sun and the rocks. You have told me this a thousand times. We too have a bond that can never be broken. You must trust me.'

Alric edged closer, puzzled by what he was seeing. The girl sounded just like Meghigda, the queen of the Imazighen, who was now in heaven. Was this why Ariadne now followed Salih like a novice monk behind the abbot? Because she believed she could grow to be as strong and powerful as Meghigda and needed the wise man's guidance? Or had her suffering made her as moonstruck as Hengist?

Finally, Salih slipped his cruel blade back into the leather scabbard hanging from his waistband. Turning his burning eyes upon Alric, he showed his white teeth. 'This is none of your business, monk.'

'You want vengeance for the murder of your mistress Meghigda,' Alric said. 'But while you hunt, you yourself are being hunted.'

Salih narrowed his eyes. 'Of what do you speak?'

'There is a cruel power in this city. It has smelled the blood of Hereward and the English, and mine too. And now it has turned its gaze upon you.' A shadow crossed Salih's face. It seemed to Alric that the other man knew something of these matters. 'It will not rest until all our days have been ended, I can see that now.' The monk held out his hands, pleading. 'If you value your life, or this girl's, you must heed me. Join with us again. Our only hope is to stand together.'

# CHAPTER FOURTEEN

The moon turned the dry land to silver. Under its glare, dark shapes crawled like rats, belly down in the dust and the yellow grass. Not a sound did they make beneath the whisper of the warm wind. Far behind them, down the slope, on the plain where an approaching enemy could be seen long before they arrived, the ruddy embers of a fire glowed.

Those slow-moving vermin clawed their way up to the ridge and pulled themselves into the dense, spiky trees. Enveloped in the sweet aroma of oily resin, they rose up, becoming men, taking slow steps as they eased into the deep shadows.

At the treeline, Hereward glanced back to where the Athanatoi slept, no doubt dreaming of victorious slaughter. His nose twitched with distaste. The Romans had left one of their younger warriors to keep watch by the fire, but his eyes had soon drooped. It had been easy for the English to creep away once the snores began.

Crunching across fallen twigs, Hereward strode into the heart of the circle where the spear-brothers squatted in silence. Here they could give voice to their doubts without risk of being overheard. Since the destruction of the village, the Mercian had sensed the growing dissatisfaction.

Slowly he looked from face to face. It still hurt him to see how few remained from the full ship that had left England all those seasons ago. Some peered up at him, yearning for answers that would solve the troubles that had descended upon them. Some stared at the ground, lost to their thoughts. Kraki was the worst. His scarred face was rigid, his gaze seeing only the dark between the moonlit trees.

'I know your hearts feel the winter chill,' Hereward began, his low voice rolling out through the woods. 'You struggle and strive and wonder when you will achieve the rewards that have been promised you.'

'These days we have worse thoughts than that,' Guthrinc said. His tone was wry, but his words struck too hard with the men there.

Hiroc scratched his greasy scalp with the three fingers remaining on his left hand. 'We do not ride with warriors. These are spoiled children. Drunks. Swaggering oafs who think they are riding out to hunt deer. They will be the death of us, mark my words.'

'Aye.' The word floated through the branches. Mad Hengist was dancing among the trees. 'Enemies fight harder . . . demand blood . . . when they are angry at the way their kin are treated. We know that, we all. In England, we knew that.' Sane words from a crazed tongue.

'In England we were heroes. We fought for honour . . . for justice.' Sighard plucked at the leaf-mould between his knees. He was the one who looked to Hereward most for answers. 'But since we came to Constantinople we have been treated as less than dogs. And now there are many who want us dead, any man can see that.' He paused, letting his words rustle away. 'Is it not time to give up on our dreams of gold and glory? To move away, to a new land, new fights? At least then we will keep our heads on our shoulders.'

'Run?' Hereward said in a quiet voice. This sentiment was reaching his ears too often these days. 'Is that what the warriors of Ely would have done?'

Kraki raised his head, his eyes glowing under his heavy

brow. 'A good warrior knows when it is time to retreat,' he growled. 'A clever man does not wait until his legs have been hacked out from under him, until his spine has been shattered, his hands cut off, his eyes gouged out, before he says *Enough*.'

Hereward looked beneath the Viking's glowering expression and saw the blackness gnawing away inside him. Kraki was the strongest one there, with a spirit of iron and leather, yet he was the one who had been cut the most by their failure. Finally his long-stifled anger simmered, and then boiled over. The Viking hauled himself to his feet, his fists bunching.

'Speak your mind,' Hereward said. 'That is why we are here. To give voice to our grievances so they do not eat away at us from within. Brother can say anything to brother.'

'Aye, speak I shall,' Kraki said, jabbing a stubby finger at his leader. 'For these things need to be said, and I am the only one who dares utter them.'

Hereward looked around at the war-band and saw moonlit eyes flicker away. Could it be true? Had he been blind to the true extent of his men's feelings? If that were so, he was not fit to be leader.

'You are full of promises,' Kraki said. 'The sun will shine. Gold will fill our purses. We will find a heaven upon earth. One more dawn. One more day's march. One more battle. One more night with a growling belly. How long should we listen to these empty words before we say enough?'

'This is not an army. I am not a king. I do not ask you to follow me—'

'No, it is worse than that.' Kraki stepped forward, his voice rumbling with passion. 'We put our trust in you. We saw your sacrifices in Ely. You never led us wrong. There are some who thought you more than a man. The hero with the magic sword, who could kill giants with his bare hands.' He choked down his emotion. 'But you are only a man after all. And all men have failings.'

'What say you? That it is time for a new leader? You?' Hereward demanded.

Kraki shook his head slowly. Before he could speak, Guthrinc clambered to his feet and rested a hand on the Viking's shoulder to silence him. 'We could never ask for a better leader. No one doubts you, Hereward. But there are times when the fighting must end.'

The Mercian looked around the spear-brothers again. 'Is this what you all say?'

Mutterings rustled out, but none would commit himself.

'You, Herrig?'

The Rat snickered and rattled his necklace of bones. 'Find me more Norman fingers and I am happy.'

Someone groaned.

'All your promises of gold and glory,' Kraki continued, calmer now, 'each day they sound more and more like dreams made of mist. Our choices fall away. Our chances fade. And in the morn when I wake, I now see only our days ending, and soon, for all of us.'

'And you have a better plan?'

'Any plan is a better plan!' Kraki raged. Guthrinc squeezed his shoulder once more.

Hereward hesitated, reading the other man's mind. He remembered what hurt lay behind the Viking's anger, something that Kraki would not admit even to himself. 'You would return to England?'

'Aye. William the Bastard will have forgotten me . . . forgotten all of us. My axe will earn me good coin. And if I get the chance, I will take the king's head for good measure.'

*And you will seek out Acha, the only woman who ever meant more to you than gold and ale,* Hereward thought.

Some of the others murmured their approval.

'It does not have to be England,' Hiroc said in a quiet voice, 'if you think our lives are still in danger at home. We could go north, east . . . We could follow the whale road until it falls off the end of the world. Anywhere would be better than this place, where they see us as lower than farmers.'

'And run and run and run, still chasing the gold, the glory?' Hereward said, holding out one hand.

'At least every man we meet would not want us dead.'

The Mercian laughed. 'That sounds more like a dream than anything that ever left my lips. Since we first came together in Ely, wherever we turned we have found someone wanting us dead.' He began to pace around the circle, listening to the crunch of his feet in the stillness. 'I know you all better than your kin,' he continued. 'We are brothers, born from blood. I see before me men who have cleaved heads with axes. Who have ripped open bellies and hacked off arms. We deal in death. And to the Romans of Constantinople we are little more than barbarians. They send us out to fight and kill their enemies so they do not have to sully their pale hands.' He paused, drinking in the stares of the rapt men. 'But I see here men who would rather end their own days than kill women and children. Who would turn away rather than slay an innocent man. I see men who fight not for greed or power, but with honour in their hearts. There are easy roads to reach our just rewards, but men like us will never walk them. We take only the right road, however hard it is. The road of honour.'

Kraki dropped back down to his haunches, still glowering, but listening.

'All is not yet lost—'

'You say,' the Viking growled.

'Have you ever known me to throw myself to the winds of fate? To wait for God to deliver to us what we need?'

Sighard's eyes brightened. 'A plan? Is that what you have?'

'I always have a plan.' Hereward gave a wolfish grin. 'On the hard road, we must always wait for our day. But now it is here.' His thoughts flew back to that hot chamber in the Boukoleon palace where he had bargained with Anna Dalassene to keep his head upon his shoulders. He recalled his mind racing as he stared into her cold eyes, wondering if there was more he could gain than his miserable life. So many sins weighting his soul, so many failures. It seemed scant reward for his bargaining. But if he could find some way to aid his brothers in their misery, to pay them back, finally, for all their sacrifices during the war in England, then that would be a prize worth fighting for.

'Are you ready to risk everything?' His low voice rumbled among the trees. 'At stake, all our lives. Our reward: the gold we need to buy our way into the Varangian Guard and all the riches that will follow.'

'That, or keep walking the hard road until we are driven down to our knees?' Guthrinc said with one eyebrow raised thoughtfully. 'And wait for the Roman bastards to kill us while our backs are turned? Aye. I will take that wager. Better a good death than to be butchered like a stag for the feast.'

'Where is this gold?' Kraki snorted, unable to hide his suspicion. 'Hanging from the trees so we can pluck it as we pass?'

Crouching, Hereward lowered his voice to a whisper. Every man leaned forward to catch his words. 'When Roussel de Bailleul captured John Doukas, he also took ten coffers of gold plate and goblets and jewelled relic boxes, stolen from the Church when the Caesar was driven out of Constantinople. Unlike John Doukas, the Norman leader is a God-fearing man, like all his folk. He would not dare use that gold for his own gain for fear of damnation.' The Mercian looked around the faces of his men, watching their eyes brighten as they grasped his meaning.

'Those coffers are there for the taking,' Sighard exclaimed.

'While the Immortals do their best to save the Caesar . . . when they no doubt plan to sacrifice us to earn their victory . . . we will be making away with all the riches we ever needed.' Hereward let the words settle on them. He glanced at Kraki. The Viking would do anything to return to England, he knew that. But as a babble of excited whispers rustled out, the Mercian knew that every man there was ready for this fight. Kraki would not betray his brothers. The Viking gave a reluctant nod.

Hereward felt his heart swell. He had planned to keep this secret close to his heart until they were near their prey, in case he decided the risks were too great to take. But his brothers had decided for themselves. If they were to die, it would be as warriors, fighting for the chance of a better life.

Their hopes renewed, the men buzzed with excitement as they began to make their way back to the camp. Hereward urged them to stay silent, for fear they would wake the Romans. But as he led them quietly out of the wood, a figure hailed him. It was Maximos.

'I have been looking for you everywhere,' the Roman said with a broad grin. 'I was sure the Turks had stolen you from the camp and slit your throats.'

'We are well, as you can see,' Hereward replied. 'It is our way to tell stories of our home so we do not forget the ones we have left behind. Here we could speak freely.'

Maximos nodded. 'Home pulls at the heart . . . unless you have kin like my own. I would have given anything never to have returned to the schemes of my family. But return I did, and now I must live with it.'

Turning, he led the way down the slope back towards the camp. Hereward watched him, understanding the emotion that lay behind the Roman's words, but still not able to trust him. How much had Maximos heard, he wondered? Were they now at even greater risk?

# Chapter Fifteen

Shafts of light dappled the forest floor. Under the thick canopy, the air was dry and hot, and fat flies droned lazily. Dim at first, a rumble ruptured the peace. The sound of thunder rolled nearer until a rider hurtled among the twisted trees. His flushed face was contorted with fear and his sky-blue tunic clung to his body, dark with sweat. With fierce exhortations he urged his foaming mount on. The track had long since been lost, as had his axe and shield. He had been too confident, expecting no resistance in these empty lands where only farmers toiled.

Hereward watched the Norman scout slow his pace. The dark-haired man was filled with desperation as he tried to negotiate tangled roots that could bring his horse down. Ducking under hanging branches, he glanced this way and that. His eyes widened. He could see no way out.

Away in the shadowy woods behind him, more hooves pounded. The cries of the hunting Athanatoi rang out, as eager as boys at play.

Sliding back down into the hollow, the Mercian breathed deep of the rich aroma of leaf-mould, then gave a curt nod to Kraki, Sighard and Guthrinc. The Immortals had done their part. Now it was down to the English.

Looking up at the sunlight shimmering through the swaying

branches, he listened to the snorts of their prey's horse as it drew closer to their hiding place. Three days had passed since their night-time conclave, when he had revealed his scheme. Three days drenched in sweat and burned by the hot eastern sun. The Romans had lost some of their bravado as they rode into Galatia and the green plains gave way to brooding mountains in the distance, grey against the blue sky. Bands of Turks roamed everywhere, their mouths red slashes in black bristles. In their strange bowl hats and long coats, they herded sheep or goats as they moved from farm to village, where they held their markets. The Romans could not look them in the face, no doubt uneasy lest word had spread of the slaughter. But these were not fighting men, anyone could see that. And when the shrill voices of these strange folk were softened by gifts of food, Tiberius Gabras' cold face softened a little. But all the men there knew the greater threat lay ahead.

The beat of hooves drew nearer. Now Hereward could hear the rasp of the rider's breath, and his curses. Raising one finger, he cautioned his men to wait.

At least Tiberius had shown some wit as a leader. They had heard whispers of Roussel's fortress at Amaseia, and the warriors the Norman had garrisoned there, but hard facts were few and far between. Why had he left his palace at Ancyra where the rest of his army waited? And so the Romans had bided their time, knowing a leader such as Roussel would send out scouts to ensure his new kingdom was safe from attack. One lone rider was easy to capture.

Shrieking birds took wing above the green canopy as the whoops of the Athanatoi soared. The scout's horse whinnied in response, its hooves thumping on the forest floor very close to the hollow.

Hereward let his hand fall.

The four warriors bounded from their hiding place with a roar. The horse reared up, its rider howling in shock. Thrown, he slammed into the forest floor. The English were upon him before he could shake off his daze.

Snarling one hand in the scout's tunic, the Mercian yanked him up. 'Lie still and your head will remain on your shoulders,' he hissed. The other three warriors crowded around, fierce faces saying more than any raised weapon.

Swallowing, the scout nodded his understanding, and Hereward let him fall back to the ground.

Once the Immortals' horses had trotted up, the riders leapt from their saddles, clapping each other on the shoulders and laughing as if they had ridden down a deer. There were twenty of them, enough to put the fear of God in the scout, not so many that they would struggle to pass through the dense forest. Lysas the Snake wandered up, slaking his thirst from his hide. He splashed some water on the captive's face and laughed.

'You English have your uses after all,' he said, showing his teeth.

'Aye.' Kraki could not bring himself even to look at the other man. 'We show you what seasoned warriors can do, if only you could learn which end of an axe to use.'

Lysas laughed without humour. 'Bring the Norman to Tiberius. He will tell us all about Roussel before the sun has set, if he knows what is good for him.'

'We do not answer to you,' Sighard snapped, flushed.

'Do as you will, then,' the Snake replied with a shrug. 'You will answer to Tiberius.'

As the Roman stepped back towards his raucous comrades, Kraki growled, 'One day I will take my axe to the lot of them.' The Viking lowered himself to balance on his haunches, staring at the ground. He seemed even more sour than Hereward had feared.

As the Mercian weighed the other man's spirit, he realized Guthrinc was standing apart, looking deep into the forest. He had eyes like a hawk, missing nothing.

'What do you see?'

For a long moment, Guthrinc continued to stare, his face emotionless. 'A boar, perhaps, if they have such things here,' he said eventually. 'Leaves trembled. Something is there. If I could hear myself think over the din the Romans are making, I might know more.'

The Athanatoi's laughter boomed out. Hereward cursed silently at their lack of experience. No good warrior would rest for even a moment away from his hearth-fire. Stepping beside his friend, he searched the green world. Nothing moved. But he knew better than to doubt Guthrinc. 'Drag the Norman to the Immortals,' he commanded Sighard. 'Let him be their burden.'

Once the younger man had hauled the trembling scout to the Romans, Hereward turned back to the tangle of trees caught in the patchwork of sunlight and shadow. Kraki was moving across the foot of the hollow, easing from cover to cover to get a better look.

'We are not alone,' Guthrinc said.

The words had barely left his lips when shadows separated from the trees across the forest, scores of them. Hereward stiffened. At first he thought they were ghosts, so silent were they. But an army had waited there, hidden in plain sight, their footsteps making not a whisper. Turks, he could see now. Their faces were like stone, their eyes coals. As one, they plucked arrows from the quivers at their belts and raised their bows.

Hereward roared, an animal bellow torn from the depths. His men knew the meaning of that guttural sound, recognized it from every battlefield where they had fought shoulder to shoulder. Throwing himself on to his belly on the ridge of the hollow, he glimpsed Guthrinc and Sighard doing the same. His nostrils filled with the choking scent of peat as arrows whined over his head, hundreds of them it seemed. The screams of the shafts were punctuated by dead thuds as they thumped into trunks, and then by real screams torn from the throats of the Romans. The horses whinnied, hooves pounding. When he looked up, he saw five of the Immortals staggering around, arrows bursting from torsos and faces. Blood soaked into the sweat of their tunics.

Before he could move, rough hands grabbed him and spun him on to his back. Enveloped in the reek of strange spices,

Hereward looked up into a grimacing mouth slashed through black bristles and eyes brimming with hatred. Cursing in his throaty tongue, the Turk swung up his sword.

As the blade whipped down, the Mercian rolled to one side. Kicking out at his foe's legs, he heard the knee crack. A howl rang out. The weapon thudded into the forest floor a hand's breadth from his head. Before the Turk could recover, Hereward hurled himself up. The top of his head smashed into the other man's jaw. As his stunned enemy spun away into the hollow, he clawed his way to his feet and ran.

Figures flitted all around. The marauders crashed through the undergrowth, pausing every now and then to loose a shaft. Hereward felt an arrow whisk by his head. Another rammed into the ground at his feet. The Turks were trying to herd their prey, like boar to the slaughter. Weaving among the trees, the Mercian realized they had only moments to escape before the enemy had them surrounded.

His feet flew over the forest floor. Ahead, he glimpsed Guthrinc and Sighard already on horseback, both of them beckoning wildly to him. But the Athanatoi were in chaos. Scrambling and cursing in their panic, they fought to get back upon their mounts. Fear had washed away their raucous mood. All of them knew they were outnumbered, and far from reinforcements.

Bow-strings cracked. Hereward dropped to his haunches, sheltering behind his shield. Four arrows punched through the wood. And then he was running again, reaching the huddle of rearing horses. Grimly determined, Lysas had the scout at his back. The wide-eyed Norman had seemingly decided his captors were the least of his worries.

As Hereward dragged himself on to his steed, he saw the advancing Turks swarming all around. More surged out of the depths of the forest by the moment.

'Kraki?' he yelled to Guthrinc, who was fighting to keep his bucking horse under control. But his friend could only shake his head.

Hereward searched the confusion of Romans. The Viking was not among them. He felt desperation grip him.

As the Athanatoi fought their horses under control and began to ride away, Hereward scanned the forest. Beyond the milling Turks, he glimpsed the flash of an axe. Kraki was hacking wildly at a ring of five enemies. Though Hereward knew the Viking would never give up, he could see there were too many foes on every side. It was only a matter of time.

Kraki lashed out, even as his enemies swallowed him. A Turkish sword rose, and then plunged down.

Arrows flashed by. The Mercian raised his shield, recoiling as a shaft glanced off the rim. When he lowered it again, his spear-brother was nowhere to be seen.

Blood thundered through his head. He would not, could not, accept that the Viking had been lost. Snarling, he tried to force his horse to turn.

'Leave him,' Lysas shouted at his side. 'He was dead the moment he fell behind.'

But Hereward could not accept that. He would ride back, find the man who had once been his enemy but now, grudgingly, had become a man he could trust with his life. He would find him even if a hundred Turks barred his way.

But then Lysas stabbed the tip of his sword into the flank of Hereward's mount. The horse bolted. The Mercian felt the branches tear at his face as they hurtled between the trees. The whine of arrows fell behind. Though he felt as if a spear had been thrust through his heart, Hereward knew he had no choice but to accept the truth.

Kraki was dead.

# Chapter Sixteen

A shower of sparks swirled up towards the glittering stars Around the campfire, a knot of warriors sat brooding, English and Roman alike. On every side, tents stretched out across the dusty plain, the cloth cracking in the night breeze. The wind moaned, the burning logs crackled and spat. On the evidence of nights past, there should have been singing, laughter, the jubilant voices of men who believed the world bent before them. But tonight all voices had been stilled, all heads bowed.

Except one. In the distance, a bestial howl soared into the night, a terrible sound that seemed to have been wrenched from the abyss. Guthrinc was mourning his dead friend.

Hereward stood at the entrance to the largest tent, arms folded. His heart was heavier than it had been for many a day, perhaps since he had stood on the quay at Yernemuth and said farewell for ever to the land of his birth. Brooding would do no good, he knew that. But his moods gripped like a storm, and were just as uncontrollable. Inside his head he could hear the whispers of his devil, demanding vengeance, berating him for leading his men from one disaster to another. Though he clutched the sliver of relic that Alric had given him, that voice would not be stilled. He felt his blood pulse in his temples. The shadows clotted his mind, and he knew there would soon be a reckoning.

From the depths of the tent came the dull slaps of fists upon skin. In one corner, Tiberius glowered, his face ruddy from the dancing light of a torch, watching three of his men circle the kneeling scout. The Norman's wrists were bound behind his back, his face bloody and swollen, his lips split. He mewled, pleading for mercy.

Tiberius was not a man who had mercy in his soul. The attack by the Turks had put the fear of God in him. Hereward knew the Romans were worried about the approaching battle with Roussel de Bailleul, but now they realized they were surrounded on every side by a multitude of enemies. If the Turks attacked in force, the Immortals would be wiped out in the blink of an eye. And they had brought this down upon their own heads, though no one would give voice to this harsh truth. But they could not ride back to Constantinople like whipped curs, Hereward knew. The emperor would never forgive them. They would be scorned by all; no doubt lose their standing, their gold, their land. All they could hope now was to strike against the Normans as fast and hard as they could, capture the Caesar and ride back like the wind.

Hereward gritted his teeth. This foray went from bad to worse. Hope was now thin on the ground.

'How many men does your master have at Amaseia?' Tiberius barked.

'Three . . . three thousand,' the scout murmured.

Tiberius threw back his head and laughed. 'An army that great? Do you expect me to believe these lies?'

'It is no lie,' the scout said, his voice rising, then breaking.

A shadow crossed the Roman commander's face. 'No. I cannot accept that.'

''Tis true. Three thousand men. Seasoned Norman warriors, the fiercest fighters in the east. And axes-for-hire, bought with the gold Roussel has flowing from his coffers.' The scout tried to hold up his head with defiance, but a shudder of pain ran through him. Hereward could see that the Norman was not lying, and he knew Tiberius must see it too.

The Roman commander turned away so his men would not see his expression. Hereward guessed what was passing through the man's mind. Three thousand men. More than five times the numbers of the Athanatoi, and more skilled too. The Romans were riding to a slaughter.

Tiberius glanced towards him and for a moment their eyes locked. The Mercian sensed a moment of understanding between them; if they were in hell, they were there together. Turning from the tent, he walked back to the campfire. His spear-brothers looked up from the dancing flames. Hereward glimpsed Alexios among the number. The Roman seemed to spend more time with the English than with his own countrymen. The other members of the Athanatoi always fell silent when he was around, as if he could not be trusted. The Mercian guessed that it was more because they feared the power, and the vengeance, of his mother, Anna Dalassene.

'We should have mead,' Hiroc said gloomily, 'and raise our cups to Kraki. He will not be easily forgotten.'

'When I stumbled over my spear while we sparred in Ely he tossed me into Dedman's bog, and held me under until I thought I would drown,' Sighard murmured, his chin resting on the heel of his hand. 'I hated him for that. But I learned my lesson.'

Hiroc cracked his knuckles. 'I can say this: he could be a miserable bastard with a temper like an angry bull, but he would not want to see us here, squatting like old men dreaming of days long gone.'

Hengist the Mad was roaming through the shadows beyond the circle. Snarling his fingers in his long, greasy hair, he bounded up to the fire, threw his head back and bayed like a moonstruck wolf. Answering Guthrinc's grieving howl, the cry rolled out across the tents. Hereward felt his neck hairs prickle erect.

'You are right. Kraki would have cursed any man here who let the heart-fire dim at his loss,' he said once the mournful sound had ebbed away. 'When we first met in Eoferwic, he would have gutted me for daring to open my mouth. He did not make friends easily. He was boastful and his temper was like a forge. But on the field of battle, no warrior would have wanted a better man at his side. Kraki would have given his life for any of us. That is how we will remember him.' He paced up to the fire and dropped a hand on Hengist's shoulder. At the touch, the smaller man calmed. 'But hear me now,' the Mercian continued. 'We have no mead to swill back, but when the time comes we will sing his name loud on the field of battle. We will honour him as he would have wanted, by seeing his enemies fall before us. We will spill oceans of blood. Kraki will hear us, in heaven or Valhalla, or wherever he walks now, and he will be pleased.'

The spear-brothers nodded, defiance driving the sadness from their features.

After a moment, one of the men at the back of the circle stood up. When the flames lit his features, Hereward saw it was Derman, the Silent Warrior, whom the others called the Ghost. He was tall and slim, black hair framing a face that oft seemed drained of blood. So stealthy was he, it was said that he could walk through an enemy army and not be seen. Rarely did he speak, but now it seemed he could not contain his thoughts. 'First Turold and now Kraki,' he said, his whispery voice almost lost beneath the crackle of the campfire. 'Neither would now be dead if these Romans had acted with honour. They betray us by turns. I say they are our true enemy.'

'You are dogs, all of you.' Heads wrenched round as a figure stepped from the shadows among the tents. Hereward recognized the squat form of Isaac Balsamon, the Boar. Contempt glimmered in his staring eyes. 'You should thank God that you have been allowed to ride alongside us. The Viking, he was little more than a beast, not fit to be among civilized men. He was a drunk. He reeked of sweat and vinegar. He would shit in the street if we let him.'

Hereward saw his men bristle. Fists bunched. Hands snapped to the hafts of axes and spears. 'Stay,' he commanded. The spear-brothers obeyed, but they remained rigid. The Boar only laughed.

But then Alexios stood up, his face flushed by the heat of the fire, or so Hereward thought. 'Still your tongue,' the youth spat. 'Speak no ill of the dead, and not one who has shown only courage on the field of battle.'

Isaac eyed the other man, hesitating to speak. After a moment, he growled, 'Why would you defend him?'

'All who have been baptized in blood on the field of battle are brothers.'

'And there is your error.' Grinning, Maximos stepped beside the Boar and slapped an arm across his shoulders. 'My good friend Isaac is still a virgin. No blood has yet been spilled. And he would not know a field of battle from a field of barley. What say you, Isaac?' Maximos' grip on the other man's shoulders grew tighter, too tight for a display of friendship, and he shook him like a dog with a stick. The Boar grimaced and tried to wrench himself away. With his free hand, Maximos reached over to ruffle the other man's hair, a playful gesture that reeked of mockery. He gripped the Boar's scalp, shook his head roughly and then thrust hard. Isaac tumbled on to his back.

While the English laughed and jeered, Maximos held out both hands and grinned, playing to the crowd. The Boar jumped to his feet, but Maximos was bigger, stronger, and a warrior who was never afraid of a fight. Thinking better of a confrontation, Isaac brushed himself down and walked away with as much nonchalance as he could muster. But when he glanced back, Hereward saw the glint of murder in his eyes. Humiliation had made a bitter enemy.

Maximos walked over to stand beside Alexios, flashing his broad grin at the spear-brothers as he passed. He was telling them he was one of them, Hereward knew. But was this more of his cunning? Hereward studied Maximos' face, remembering when they had travelled across Afrique together and he had thought the Roman could have been a brother. They had seemed so alike, men of honour in a grim world. But then the scales had fallen from his eyes. The Mercian frowned. Maximos defied easy measure.

'We must take care.' Tiberius had come up quietly behind him. When Hereward turned, he saw that the commander's face was drawn, his mood flat. What he had discovered from the scout lay heavily upon him. 'Lines are being drawn,' the Roman continued. 'We must not fight among ourselves. It will be our undoing. We have had our differences, Roman and English, but we need every good warrior to trust the man beside him if we are to survive the battle ahead.'

'Easy words,' Hereward replied. 'These divisions run deep.' *And you have only made them deeper*, he thought, but there was no gain in giving voice to those words. 'My brothers will do what is demanded of them, do not doubt it. Look to your own. If weakness lies anywhere, it is there.'

Turning, he walked away into the night before his simmering anger got the better of him. Kraki's death had been a blow too far. It threatened to release the man he once had been, the wanton killer. And if that happened all would truly be lost.

# Chapter Seventeen

The rat scurried down the centre of the street, a knob of bread clutched between its needle teeth. The hot morning reeked of sweat and fish sauce as the rodent weaved among the jumble of wooden stalls laden with amphorae of olive oil, game birds and fruit. But the crowds that throbbed past the bellowing merchants were oblivious of the life speeding by their feet.

From the shade beneath the colonnade, Deda watched the creature pass by. Rats scrambled everywhere in that city; he sometimes wondered if there were more there than men. They were not starved, of that he could be sure.

The stalls tumbled out into the thoroughfare from the entrances to the shops that lined the way. Scraps of food fell everywhere. The rats danced with delight. With a lopsided smile of bafflement, Deda remembered the times his stomach had growled with hunger when he had trudged with Hereward and the rebels through the snowbound forest in England. And now, here, in the suffocating heat of the east with an abundance of victuals on all sides, still it growled. But he would not complain. He had suffered worse in his life than an empty belly.

With glistening brows, men and women bustled past the knight without even the slightest acknowledgement. Perhaps they saw in him nothing more than a filthy beggar. Perhaps they recognized the bearing of a swordsman, but did not care.

Shrugging, Deda looked past them for his wife. Rowena was buying some of the flatbread the Romans liked, and some olives, if what little coin they could spare would go that far. He nodded. Life, after all, was good.

A hand fell on his arm. A voice rustled at his side, the words laced with ironic humour. 'Do not look round. Keep your fingers from your sword.'

'If you have plans to rob me, you could have not made a worse choice.'

'We do not trust Normans here. Sometimes we pay them to fight for us, but we do not really like them.' A snicker. 'And I am English, so I have even less reason to trust you than these Romans.' The speaker edged forward until Deda could see it was the Varangian guardsman, Ricbert, the small, sly, thin-faced warrior who was Wulfrun's eyes and ears in the streets of Constantinople. 'And yet now I find myself the guardian of your miserable life. God makes strange plans for us poor mortals.'

Deda raised one eyebrow. 'I have never seen much need for a guardian before. Nor have all the men who have died on the end of my blade.'

'Perhaps it is time to think anew,' the guardsman said, pointing along the street.

Men with helms and shields and axes were pushing their way through the throng around the stalls. Cold eyes searched faces and peered into shadows. Soldiers, by the look of it, Deda thought, but not of any kind he recognized. Every man wore a brown tunic, and a brown cloak too.

'We call them Shit-dogs,' Ricbert said, lowering his voice as he stepped back out of sight, 'and they have come for you.'

'I have done no wrong,' the knight said, frowning.

'Falkon Cephalas believes you, your wife, some of the other English here, to be a threat. He has heard rumours that you scheme against the emperor, and, as we have found, Falkon Cephalas will do anything within his power to crush even the whisper of a plot. Even build his own army of bastards, rogues and cut-throats because he no longer has faith in the Varangian Guard.' Ricbert gripped the knight's arm. 'Your life is no longer safe. You must come with me, now, or you will be taken.'

'My wife—'

'There is no time.'

Deda wrenched his arm free and pushed his way into the crowd. He kept his head down, his eyes flickering under his brow. Ahead, he glimpsed Rowena emerging from one of the merchants' residences with a loaf wrapped in a white cloth hugged against her chest as if it were made of gold. He thought how weary she looked. But then she saw him and her face lit up with a smile.

Nearby, the soldiers filtered among the stalls. Axes twitched in their hands.

When Rowena opened her mouth to hail him, Deda pressed a finger to his lips. Her smile fell away as she read his dark expression. Words were rarely necessary; they were like one mind. Her white headdress covering her brown hair, she lowered her head and walked towards him. Once she had reached him, he slipped a hand under her arm to urge her back to Ricbert.

Behind him, Deda heard a harsh voice crack through the drone of conversation and the barks of the merchants trying to sell their wares. He did not look round. Gripping Rowena's arm tighter, he forced her on, feeling proud that she showed no fear, and asked no questions. She trusted him implicitly, as she had through every peril they had encountered on the long road from England.

One of the soldiers snarled an order to stop. When they did not obey, a tumult of angry cries rang out and Deda heard the crash of an overturned stall. In the confusion, he barged through the men and women who had stopped to puzzle over this display. But when he reached the shadows beneath the colonnade where he had been standing he could not see Ricbert anywhere.

'We cannot tarry,' Rowena breathed under the furious sounds of pursuit.

Deda felt his chest tighten. The crowd was too dense, their routes for escape too few. A whistle rang out, and when he jerked round he saw Ricbert standing in a side street, barely more than a rat-run, with the towering buildings on either side throwing it into deep shadow. He pulled his wife into the alley.

'You have scant regard for your life,' Ricbert spat when they reached him, 'and for mine too.' He glanced past Deda's shoulder towards the milling crowd at the end of the alley. 'I must not be seen here.'

With rough hands, he thrust the other two through an archway into a cool courtyard fragrant with the scent of herbs. Darting past them, he beckoned without looking back and raced ahead, leading them on a meandering path through the ringing chambers of a deserted house, into another courtyard, another alley, past a stinking midden, through a shady garden and into a third alley. There he paused briefly before ushering them through a door into a house that reeked of sweat and sour wine. When the door slammed shut, Deda heard moans of passion coming from all corners. A brothel.

Rowena crumpled her face. 'These poor souls.'

'The girls are well rewarded,' the guardsman muttered as he strode on.

'You would not say that if you endured the same!' Rowena's voice cracked. Ricbert only snickered.

Deda rested a comforting hand on his wife's shoulder, remembering her suffering at the hands of the Normans in England. No words would ever suffice. She bit her lip, and with the back of her hand she brushed away a stray tear.

Once out of the brothel they walked quickly, keeping away from the marketplaces. Finally they arrived at a grand house in the east of the city, not far from the emperor's palace. Ricbert ushered them inside, first glancing up and down the street to make sure they had not been observed.

Within, Deda breathed in perfumed air. Gold plate gleamed, jewel-encrusted caskets shimmered. There was wealth here, and lots of it.

In a chamber at the rear, Alric sat hunched on a bench, fretting as he plucked at his tunic. When he saw them he leapt to his feet, beaming.

'You are safe,' he exclaimed. Deda saw that the monk still reached out with his missing hand. Sensing his error, Alric switched to the other hand to give his friend's arm a squeeze.

'I would have thought there was no one in Constantinople who cared if we lived or died,' Deda mused, looking around.

'You have friends here.' Deda turned to see a tall, slender woman. Her chin jutted in the manner of someone used to commanding those who stood before her and, though she smiled, her eyes were dark and unknowable. 'My name is Anna Dalassene,' she said. 'You are now under the protection of the Comnenoi.'

Ricbert, who must have slipped out of the chamber to fetch the woman, eased back in with Wulfrun. The commander of the Guard glowered from beneath his helm. There was still no love lost between him and any friend of Hereward, Deda noted.

'I have never known such a gathering,' the knight said with a wry smile. 'The Varangian Guard, a noblewoman, a monk, and two wanderers without a land to call their own.'

'War makes for strange allies,' Wulfrun growled.

Rowena frowned. 'War?'

The commander hesitated, then removed his helm and tucked it under his arm. 'We must await the return of the Athanatoi before we know if there will be war in the east. But there is a war brewing here at home, of that there can be no doubt. Falkon Cephalas has taken to his work with the drive of a virgin boy given free run at a brothel. He has brought in his own men, some soldiers, axes-for-hire, cut-throats, Romans all. Men he can trust.'

'Because he cannot trust the oath-sworn guardians of the emperor,' Ricbert interjected in a sour voice.

'We are all under suspicion,' Anna said. She poured herself a goblet of ruby wine and touched it to the edges of her smiling lips as she surveyed her guests above the rim. Weighing them, judging them. Rowena raised her chin, refusing to submit to such scrutiny.

'Falkon sees plotters everywhere,' Wulfrun continued, adding with a shrug, 'and oft-times he is right. But this cure may well be worse than the sickness that has afflicted Constantinople for too long. Men and women are dragged from their beds to face his questions in the blood-rooms beneath the Boukoleon palace. Eyes have been put out. Hands and feet lost. Aye, and lives lost too. It is said they have set aside a new quarter in the cemetery at Petrion for Falkon's victims.'

'Falkon Cephalas believes the only way forward for Constantinople lies with pure Roman blood, but even Romans can be dangerous,' Anna murmured.

Ricbert wrinkled his nose in disgust. 'Never have there been men more loyal to the emperor than the Varangian Guard. We have all sworn an oath to defend the crown with our lives, if necessary, but that dog thinks we are all liars or traitors.' His knuckles grew white on the haft of his Dane-axe. 'But he has the protection of Nikephoritzes, and through him the emperor himself. So we must skulk like rats, staying beyond the reach of his cold eyes.'

'For now,' Anna added in a cool voice. 'We wait silently in the shadows, unnoticed by Falkon Cephalas, and we watch. The hour will come when we act.'

Deda sensed a presence at his back. Even as he was turning, he saw Wulfrun grimace and swing up his axe.

'You dare come here?' the guardsman snarled.

Wreathed in black, Salih ibn Ziyad stood in the doorway to the next chamber, one hand resting on the hilt of the silver knife at his waist. Beside him, the girl Ariadne watched the other occupants with uneasy, darting eyes, her gaze somehow older than her years.

As Wulfrun moved, Anna snapped up a hand and commanded, 'Stay. He is my guest.' The snap in her voice brooked no dissent, and the warrior held back.

'He is a murdering dog,' he said.

'Every man here has killed,' Salih said. 'There are wars and there are wars.'

Alric stepped between them and faced Wulfrun. 'If you have a complaint here, it is with me. I pleaded with Salih to join us. All enemies of Falkon Cephalas are our allies.'

'He cannot be trusted.'

'I have no argument with you,' the wise man said, his unblinking stare fixed upon the guardsman.

*No*, Deda thought. *But you would slay the woman Wulfrun loves in an instant, for she is one of the Nepotes.*

'Sometimes our friends look like our enemies,' Anna said, 'and our enemies, friends. Judge a man by his heart and that alone.'

Deda watched Wulfrun's struggle play out on his face. Finally he lowered his axe, but his burning eyes never left Salih ibn Ziyad.

Rowena stepped forward to break the simmering tension between the two men. She bowed her head to her host. 'You have brought us beneath your roof, and for that you have our thanks,' she said.

Anna sipped on her wine, her stare unblinking, unnerving. 'You have Hereward to thank for your safety. He agreed to protect my son's life from the blades of plotters. In return he asked that I make sure his friends were safe from harm here in Constantinople. He knew this city was a pit of vipers, that death comes when least expected, but even he could not have foreseen the threat posed by Falkon Cephalas.'

She set her goblet down with more force than Deda suspected she intended. It rang out like a hammer in the stillness of the house.

'I have endured much in my life.' She eyed each one there in turn. 'I know your stories. You have all stared defeat in the face. You have been driven to your knees. But no more. Now we will fight back against those who would crush us, and we will earn what is rightfully ours.'

Her eyes glittered as the echo of her words died away. And in that moment, Deda felt that if anyone could save them all from the jaws of Falkon Cephalas, it was this woman.

# Chapter Eighteen

Under the cruel sun, two men trudged along the dusty track through the mountains. White cloths swathed their heads and their robes were sullied with the dirt of the road as if they had travelled from distant lands. Hereward and Tiberius kept their eyes down, their faces in shadow. They were all but invisible to the farmers who tramped past with donkeys laden with full baskets.

When the track crested a ridge, they looked down into a narrow, steep-sided valley. Apple orchards covered the lower slopes, the fruit heavy on the branches. Green and slow under a cloud-streaked blue sky, the Yesilirmak river carved through the cleft towards the northern sea. Skiffs were moored at a wooden quay, the sailors and fishermen sitting lazily in the sun. Two more ships drifted at their moorings, low in the water from the weight of the merchandise stowed on board. Perhaps supplies for the Norman army, Hereward mused. A force so great meant many bellies needed to be filled.

On the flat valley floor, bounded by the soaring walls of the purple mountains, the ancient city of Amaseia squatted behind its walls. Under a jumble of orange-tiled roofs, the halls were wooden, like the ones Hereward remembered from England, but here the walls were painted white to reflect the heat of the eastern sun. Above the city, tombs had been carved into the cliff-face. On the far side of the walls lay another city, this one of tents and makeshift huts spreading out to the trees and the very edge of the water. Cocking his head, the Mercian listened to the sound of hammers and the cries of workmen. New homes were still being built. The army was growing. And yet . . .

'That is not three thousand men. The scout lied to us,' Tiberius murmured.

Hereward could not disagree. They might still have a chance.

Tiberius trudged on, his eyes flickering around uneasily. 'I should not be here,' he growled.

'A leader should not be afraid of seeing the field of battle for himself,' Hereward replied as they walked slowly down the track. 'Victory could lie in the way the sun falls, or the weariness in your enemy's face. No scout could tell you all you need to know.'

Five days before, the moon had set and the night had grown dark before Hereward had persuaded the Athanatoi commander that they should scout the enemy fortress for themselves. But this had been a Tiberius humbled by the weight of what lay ahead. At first light, the Immortals had broken camp and ridden east before turning towards the row of brooding mountains in the north. Hereward had sensed the changed mood in the warriors. No whoops, no laughter. Eyes turned down, faces graven. Word had spread about the size of the army they were riding to confront. What had seemed like a procession towards glory and riches had become a fight for survival.

Tiberius had sent scout after scout ahead so he could steer a path through the vast, empty spaces not yet filled by the streams of Turks drifting from the east. One thing remained in his favour: that these fierce, dark-skinned people lived in small tribes and were not yet part of one great, conquering force. But that would change soon, Hereward thought, once they recognized how much land and gold could be gained if they worked together. Any warrior could see that.

The woods and green plains criss-crossed with gushing, cool streams had eventually given way to dustier land scarred by outcrops of brown rock. When they reached the foothills of the mountains, the Romans had breathed sighs of relief. Here they could hide themselves from the eyes of roaming war-bands. In the shadowy, forested crook of two hills they had set up camp, and feasted that night on deer and wild boar. The next day, Hereward had walked out of the camp with Tiberius beside him, and for three days they had followed the narrow tracks across the wild mountain country. He knew that Tiberius had been praying that the captured scout had been lying, that Roussel only had a rag-tag band of axes-for-hire who were growing fat and lazy on their spoils. Now, as he looked upon that unassailable fortress, he could no longer deny the truth.

'What hope is there?' the commander breathed. 'If we rode into this valley, we would be slaughtered.'

Hereward narrowed his eyes, watching the warriors wander through the camp. 'There are other ways. Offer Roussel gold. Buy back the Caesar. The Norman likes to live like a prince. Perhaps he has grown sick of war now he has his comforts.'

Tiberius chewed on a nail, pondering. 'Aye. That may well be our only way,' he replied after a moment. 'At least we could live to tell the tale.' He thought on, and his face sagged. 'But the emperor will not tolerate this land within the boundaries of the empire. He wants the Caesar saved, true, though more to keep face among his people than out of any love for John Doukas. But he . . . or Nikephoritzes . . . wants this rival dead more. As long as Roussel sits upon his throne here, it shows how weak the emperor truly is.'

'If you return to Constantinople with the Caesar, you can claim victory. You have learned your enemy's weaknesses. And you can ride back with an army that dwarfs this Norman force and crush Roussel. How can the emperor not fail to reward you?'

Tiberius grinned.

'Or,' the Mercian continued, his voice steady, 'you can take the Caesar, now, without offering gold, and claim an even greater reward for your courage.'

Tiberius frowned, eyeing the English warrior as if he had gone mad. 'Do we fly in on the wings of angels?'

Hereward eased himself out from behind the rock where he had been hiding.

'Wait. You will be seen,' Tiberius exclaimed, reaching out to grab the Mercian's arm.

'We are just two poor travellers. So close to the northern sea, they must see many strangers here. We are no threat. Let us find out where this Norman's weaknesses lie.' Without looking back to see if Tiberius was following him, Hereward bowed his head and wandered on down the track.

As he neared Amaseia, his nose wrinkled at the reek of the middens mingling with the smoke from the home-fires and the aromas of unusual spices. The walls were crumbling stone, as old as the earth itself, it seemed. They had not been well maintained. Mildew mottled the front, and yellow grass and weak saplings sprouted from cracks. This was not a place that had had to defend itself in living memory. Calls and song rolled out from the other side of the ramparts. Some tongues he recognized – Norman and Roman – but some were strange to his ears.

Sweating in the sun, men cursed as they heaved bales up the steep path to the gates from the ships at the quay. Boys tossed handfuls of hay to horses in pens on terraces below the city walls. From the corner of his eye, he glimpsed others winding their way along the tracks, merchants and farmers mostly, bringing in their wares on shaking carts or strapped in bundles on their backs. He had been right – two more earth-walkers would not draw attention.

When he sensed Tiberius picking up his step to arrive at his side, he did not look up. 'You seem at ease,' the Roman murmured. 'Are you not afraid that you will be found out?'

Hereward smiled to himself, remembering the times he had walked under the noses of Norman soldiers across England as he scouted. The part of him that had welcomed his devil into his soul enjoyed the thrill. 'Men have too many cares to pay heed to strangers, unless you give them good cause. Show no fear and all will be well.'

The gates hung open. They were cracked and weather-beaten, and he mused how a strong man could probably push them down. Laughing and shrieking, children splashed in a pool from a spring in the shade of the walls. He stepped in behind two merchants with bales resting on their shoulders as they passed through the gates. Tiberius kept close behind him.

Amaseia bustled in the sun. With no other towns nearby, it was the centre of commerce for the surrounding countryside. The street running along the inside of the walls was a makeshift market, with merchants booming as they tried to outdo each other in selling their cloth and beasts and jewellery and swords. Dogs yapped, fighting with each other over bones tossed out by the butcher.

Hereward looked into the faces of those he passed and saw no worry there, only smiles and cheery greetings. Tunics and dresses were made of good cloth. Heads were raised, backs were straight. Amaseia thrived, it seemed, and its citizens felt secure. Clearly Roussel de Bailleul treated his new subjects well; at least in that respect he did not cast himself in the image of William the Bastard.

Pushing into the flow, Hereward meandered along the streets. Warriors strode everywhere, some with their heads shorn at the back in the Norman way. They walked with their chins raised, as if all the world were theirs. Hereward felt a pang of anger. Sometimes he believed the raw pain of what these bastards had done to England would never go away. There were plenty of axes-for-hire, too: wild-bearded Vikings, still swathed in mail and leather despite the heat, pale-skinned Vlachs and long-haired Franks. He sensed Tiberius stiffen beside him. These men made most of the smooth-skinned Athanatoi look like children. The few seasoned warriors among the ranks of the Immortals would never be enough.

Beyond the wide streets, near the walls, there was a labyrinth of steep, narrow ways among the timber-framed houses. In the shade, the air was cooler.

'Have we not seen enough?' Tiberius snapped. 'I would be away before we are found out.'

'A man who would carve his own land out of the empire would demand a palace, I wager,' Hereward replied. 'That is where we will find the Caesar.'

Tiberius looked askance, studying his companion. 'I have heard the stories of your battle in England. A great warrior who all but brought down the might of the Norman army. A giant-killer. The owner of a magic sword.' He laughed coldly. 'You English are a strange breed. You brag as if there are no greater folk on earth – no greater warriors, no greater artists or merchants. And then you are drunk and crying for all that you have lost and the women you have bedded and the green fields of home. But you have fire in your heart, I will give you that,' he added in a grudging tone.

Hereward raised his hand to silence the Roman. Ahead, the winding way opened on to a courtyard, beyond which was an old stone building with grand columns along the front like many of the great Roman halls he had seen in Constantinople. But parts were falling into ruin, the stone crumbling, the roof sagging. Here there were guards, Normans all by the look of them. They lazed in the sun or squatted in the shade, helmets and mail heaped to one side. But if the palace was attacked, they would be ready in an instant.

As he watched, a tall, strong man strode out of the hall with a knot of older men following close behind. When his voice boomed across the courtyard, the guards leapt to their feet and feigned alertness. This could only be Roussel de Bailleul.

Grinning broadly, the nobleman swung his arms wide as his powerful voice echoed round the courtyard. This was a man who appeared afraid of nothing, who, Hereward thought, seemed to relish the life he had. He laughed easily, a rare thing in these grim Norman warriors. His brown hair was long and swept back from his forehead, his skin tanned from his time in this land, and he wore a fine purple tunic embroidered with silver leaves that shimmered in the sun. There was a swagger to his step as he walked out into the courtyard and looked across his domain. He nodded to himself, pleased.

'All is ready?' he demanded in the Norman tongue.

One of his advisers stepped forward, an old warrior by the look of him, still powerfully built but with a growing paunch, silver hair, and a lined face that puckered into a scar along his cheek. 'We await the final supplies,' he said.

'Good.' Roussel clapped his hands. 'Then we will eat our fill the next few nights before all we have is the grumbling of our bellies.'

Hereward frowned, unable to understand what the Normans were discussing. Their mood seemed high. But then a surprisingly familiar voice rose up from the back of the group and the Mercian was jolted alert. He squinted, trying to see through the wall of bodies. Why there should be anyone there that he knew, he could not guess.

But as he waited for the speaker to reveal himself in the crowd, Tiberius gripped his arm and hissed, 'Someone comes.'

Hereward glanced over his shoulder. Three figures were walking through the shadows of the winding street towards the palace.

'Come,' Tiberius insisted, his voice low but urgent. 'We must not be caught here spying on Roussel.'

Nodding, the Mercian turned back. He kept his head down, his face turned towards Tiberius as if they were in intense conversation. As they walked back down the street, Hereward glanced quickly at the three figures passing them. At the front was a boy. The Mercian glimpsed an emotionless face, pale like the moon. He felt almost as if the boy were not there at all, a ghost. His feet made not a whisper on the baked mud, and he seemed to leave no sense of his passing.

But Hereward felt the hairs on the back of his neck prickle erect when the second figure went by. He could not see the man's face, but he was tall and broad-shouldered, his stride powerful. The Mercian's chest tightened at the odd sensation that he had walked past a blazing forge.

The third figure was smaller, and now Hereward stiffened at the sense of something familiar: the shambling gait, perhaps, the unpleasant vinegar odour.

Once the trio had passed, Hereward flashed a glance back. With a jolt, he saw that the third figure was looking back at him too. Now there could be no doubt. Instantly, he took in the ruined face, the wheezing holes where his nose had been, the milky eye, the missing ears, the raw scalp where the hair had been torn out or burned away. This was Ragener, the Hawk, who hated Hereward perhaps more than any other in this world. The Mercian recalled hacking off the sea wolf's left hand, then tossing him into the sea to die. But Ragener clung on to life like a cornered wolf, and every time it seemed his end was near he found some way to survive.

Hereward jerked his head back, hoping the ruined man had not recognized him. 'Quick,' he whispered. 'We must get away from here.'

'Hold!' The command was shouted from the edge of the courtyard. It was Ragener, the word distorted by his ragged lips.

The Mercian did not look back. Urging Tiberius on, he turned in to a narrow alley and broke into a sprint. Cursing under his breath, the Roman followed close behind.

The crack of running feet echoed behind them.

Hereward darted down another street, and then another, trying to lose the sea wolf in the maze as he made his way towards the gate. Finally he could not hear any sound of pursuit, but he knew that would not be the end of it. Ragener had not seen his face, he was nearly sure of it, but on some level the ruined man must have sensed an implacable foe, as Hereward had sensed the Hawk.

'We must be away as fast as we can,' he insisted. 'The alarm will be raised. And while Roussel's men will not know what stranger they are looking for, the gate will be closed while they search, and they will now be on their guard.'

Emerging on to the bustling street along the walls, they slipped into the throng. Loud voices echoed behind them, and warriors thrust their way through the crowd, axes gripped. The Norman army had been lazy in the sun only moments ago. Now the beast had stirred.

Avoiding the flashing glares as he pushed through the bodies, Hereward pressed on towards the gate. Eyes darting, Tiberius caught his arm and hissed in his ear, 'They are coming from both sides. We will be pinned between them in no time.'

The Mercian glanced towards the gate. Three guards had gathered, listening intently to a stern-faced commander. Only moments remained before the only way out of the city was barred.

'Stay close to me, and utter not a word,' Hereward growled to the Roman.

A two-wheeled cart was trundling by, piled high with what looked like bales of silk. Stepping beside it, Hereward dropped down so the cart would hide him from the eyes of the guard. He crept forward, matching the slow turn of the wheels. He sensed Tiberius slip in behind him.

When the little procession neared the gate, the Mercian glanced back and nodded to his companion. Before the Roman could register any understanding, Hereward pressed his shoulder against the side of the cart and braced himself. Somehow Tiberius read his intention.

Together, the two men heaved. The cart lifted up on one wheel, hovered for a second, then crashed on its side, spilling its wares across the mud. The merchant who had been leading the cart roared his anger, torn between calming his skittish horse and watching that no one stole his possessions. Men and women milled around, their curiosity caught by the disturbance. And then the guards too were hurrying over.

Hereward flicked one hand towards the now unguarded gate. With Tiberius close behind, he darted away from the cart and slipped into the surging crowd. Within a moment they were through the gate and hurrying along the track back through the mountains. Only then did Hereward allow himself to breathe easily.

He was troubled by the presence of Ragener. It seemed like fate speaking to him, perhaps warning him. The last he had heard the ruined man had been hiding in Constantinople, but when his patron Victor Verinus was murdered he had disappeared from sight. The sea wolf was savage and cunning and there was no vile act he would not consider to gain advantage for himself. If he was here in Amaseia, with Roussel, then no good could come of it.

# Chapter Nineteen

An arc of blue sky filled the warrior's vision. On the fringes he could glimpse the jagged peaks of brown mountains and daggers of light as the sun slipped towards the horizon. The dip and splash of oars echoed rhythmically on all sides, and the creak of timbers as the hull flexed against the river currents. His nostrils wrinkled at the spicy sweat of the Turks as they rowed in the heat. Every now and then they would break into song in their strange throaty tongue.

But he lived, he yet lived. That in itself was a miracle.

Kraki was lying on his back, his hands bound behind him – his punishment after he had attempted to claw out the throat of one of his captors. His ankles too were strapped together with a leather thong – his reward for kicking one of the Seljuk warriors in the balls. And he tasted a filthy rag stuffed deep into his mouth to stop his stream of curses and abuse.

But he still lived.

Lances of pain stabbed his ribs. Blood was crusted around his left eye and his right had closed up. His lips were split. He grinned to himself. He had had worse.

The Turks' song started up again, a lilting refrain that matched the rhythm of the oars. As he drifted with the music, his thoughts flew back to the battle in the forest. If he had been quicker, he would not have been separated from Hereward and the others. He was a poor excuse for a warrior these days. Too many nights yearning for Acha, the only woman to tame his wild heart, that was what had taken the edge off his battle skills. If his father had been there, the old man would have clubbed him round the head with the haft of his axe and told him he was a mewling child.

The Turks had surrounded him in an instant. Three had fallen under his blade. But then the flat of a blade had clattered against the back of his head and that was all he remembered of the fight. The gods had little time for the affairs of men, but that day they must have been watching over him. If the sword had been turned even the slightest degree it would have taken off the top of his skull, and he would have been swilling mead with his ancestors in the ringing halls of Valhalla.

When he had woken beside a campfire under the night sky, his first sight had been of a Turk holding a sword above his bared neck. The others had been laughing and dancing around him, tearing at chunks of lamb from their victory feast. For long moments they had barked questions at him, but he could not understand a word. The warrior had waved the sword, threatening to bring it down time and again. But the Viking had not shown any fear, and that seemed to have angered them further.

Once the blows had stopped raining down upon him, he had spied another captive on the other side of the campfire, one of the Romans. He was young and frightened. These were probably the first enemies he had ever looked in the face.

Kraki closed his eyes. The painful memory was easier in the dark of his head. He recalled yelling words of encouragement to the lad. But when the Turks had realized what he was doing, their swordsman had swung up his blade and taken the Roman's head to show they meant business. Even now he could feel the burning as his rage surged through him like wildfire. He had thrown himself at his captors, and not for the last time. He felt proud that he had drawn blood and broken bones before they had beaten him into unconsciousness again.

'Are you dead yet?'

The Viking opened his eyes at the oddly inflected words. At first the sun's glare blinded him. Then a head hove into view. Suleiman ibn Qutalmish was the only Turk Kraki had ever heard speak English. His teeth were white among the black bristles of his beard, his grin was wide, and his eyes sparkled with humour. His broad shoulders and the way he balanced on the balls of his feet as he moved showed he was a warrior, used to wielding a sword. Even if the other Turks had not bowed their heads in deference whenever he neared, Kraki would have known he was a leader from his fine clothes. Gold thread glimmered in the swirls of embroidery on his purple coat, and his bowl cap was studded with rubies. When the Viking's captors had taken him on horseback across the plain to a vast tent city and thrown him on to the ground in front of this man, Kraki had thought his head would soon be resting beside the poor Roman lad's. But Suleiman had been wise. He knew death was only the right course when it served a purpose, and some men were worth more alive.

The Turk crouched beside him, prodding Kraki's leathers with a finger. 'No, dead men do not scowl so,' he grinned.

'Set me free,' the Viking growled. 'I will show you that the fire still burns in my chest.'

Suleiman threw back his head and laughed. 'You Northmen. You are bags of wrath, as bad-tempered as a wolf with a thorn in its paw. Life is good, Viking. Open your eyes and you will see it.'

Kraki snorted and looked away. He would not give this enemy any satisfaction.

'You slaughtered my people, Viking,' the Turk said, his grin falling away.

'I had no part in that.'

'A man is judged by the ones who stand at his side.'

'The Romans are like frightened children. They lashed out.'

Suleiman peered at the mountains. 'They will lose this land

because they do not know how to fight for it,' he mused, almost to himself. 'I know how to fight, Viking. My father Qutalmish craved the throne of the Seljuks and he fought his cousin Alp Arsan for the right to sit upon it. He did not fight hard enough. And when he fell, I was made to flee with my three brothers into the mountains. We lived with the Qguzes, the tribes who did not bow their heads to Alp Arsan, but we did not forget our father's desire, and we plotted and we waited. And Alp Arsan did not forget. He sent war-band after war-band to hunt us down. My brothers are all dead now. But I still live. And now Alp Arsan is dead too, and the tribes fall in step behind me, one by one.' He smiled. 'Your god smiled upon you when you were brought to me, Viking. Others might have taken your head without a second thought. But I see the currents of this great river of life, and I know where to steer to get where I want. There are many different ways to fight. The Romans would do well to learn that lesson.'

Suleiman stood up, stretching. Kraki eyed him. He had seen worse leaders. The Turk was not cruel, like William the Bastard, nor was he weak like the Roman emperor. But still he could not understand why his captor had not killed him.

The ship plunged through cool shadow, the spray dousing him. After a moment, he drifted with the rhythm of the oars and found himself back in England, in a glade with Acha. She was caressing his brow and telling him all would be well. More than gold, more than glory, he yearned for her. It made him feel weak, like a babe crying for his mother. He should be stronger than that, strong like his father, who had trudged across frozen wastes after his wife had died, carrying her body to the hill where they burned it and offered up her soul to the gods. His father did not yearn. He fought hard, all his life, and put meat in the pot for his son, and instructed him in the ways of the world. Kraki never saw him shed a tear, or complain about his lot. He was a good man, who did his best for his kin. Sometimes, though, Kraki thought he remembered his mother's face, though it was as if she were looking at him through the autumn mist.

The ship jolted and he jerked awake. As the oars dragged up the side and clattered on the boards, the Turks stood up, stretching their weary muscles. They had arrived at their destination.

Kraki pushed aside a glimmer of apprehension. His end-days were near, he knew that, and he would face them like a man. Rough hands dragged him to his feet. Swaying on the bobbing deck as two men tied the mooring rope to a post on the quay-side, he looked out across a town of white-painted wooden houses at the foot of soaring cliffs.

'Amaseia welcomes you,' Suleiman said at his side. 'And soon, Roussel de Bailleul will too.'

The Turk was clever, Kraki acknowledged. He knew the Athanatoi had been riding to confront the Norman warlord. Now Suleiman would trade his captive for favour or gold, and Kraki would face days of torture while Rome's enemy tried to extract all that he could of the emperor's plans to defeat him. Kraki owed the Romans nothing. They had heaped misery upon misery upon him since he had washed up in Constantinople. But he would never speak, however much of him they sliced off. No man of honour would betray his spear-brothers, no matter the degree of suffering.

One of the Turks sawed through the bonds at his ankles. Two men gripped his arms and all but carried him over the side and on to the quay. Grunting, he thought of tearing at one of his guards' throats with his teeth. Better to die now than suffer days of agony. But the Turks seemed to sense his thoughts, for they stepped back, one of them pressing the tip of a sword into his back.

As he strode up the uneven path to the gate, he glanced back and saw Suleiman walking just behind him. The leader had his hands behind his back, a smile ghosting on his lips as he surveyed the merchants and their wares. Never had a man seemed more at ease. Here was a leader who feared nothing, Kraki thought.

His captors prodded him through the gate on to a busy street. The Norman guards paid them no heed, as if these new arrivals were old friends. Kraki pushed his chin up, baring his teeth at anyone who dared look at him. Suleiman laughed, amused by this display.

'You are not like the Romans, I will give you that,' he called. 'I see now why they need you to fight their battles.'

Wincing from the dull throb of his bruises, Kraki trudged along a winding street to a courtyard in front of what he took to be the warlord's palace. Two of Suleiman's men had hurried ahead to announce their leader's arrival, and the Turkish band was beckoned inside by a fierce-looking warrior with a mass of red hair and one empty socket.

Looking around, Kraki saw that the palace lacked the opulence the Romans enjoyed. Though it seemed to have been raised up by the same hands that built Constantinople, with its columns and large windows that flooded the chambers with light, the stone was cracked and blistered, the floor crumbling. A pool of dark water gleamed where the roof had leaked. But no gold plate shone like the sun; no ornate tapestries hung on the walls. There were no comforts at all. This was a warrior's home, not a king's.

Within moments, three men marched in. One was the red-haired man with the missing eye, his hand never straying far from his axe. Kraki smelled a seasoned war-leader, perhaps the commander of the Norman warriors. The one at the front could be none other than Roussel de Bailleul. His clothes were finer, silver leaves emblazoned on a tunic of purple, the colour of emperors. But it was the way he moved, with the confidence of a man used to victory, that betrayed his station. Tanned, tall and strong, his chin was raised and he sported the grin of a man who did not need to hide his thoughts for fear of attack.

But Kraki stiffened when his gaze fell upon the third man, someone he had thought he would never see again. Drogo Vavasour was tall and muscular, with a swaggering gait, but his eyes still skittered with an uneasy movement that carried a light Kraki had only seen before in Hengist's gaze. The Viking's thoughts flew back to the sweltering heat of northern Afrique and the glaring sun of Sabta, where this Norman bastard had lured the spear-brothers into what he believed was a trap. Fired by his hatred of Hereward, who had killed his brother during the English rebellion, Drogo had been too confident on that day. His men had been slaughtered and Drogo himself had fled to save his miserable neck. It was only fitting that he had found his way here, to Amaseia. These Norman dogs always ran in packs. And in this part of the world, Roussel's reputation was rising fast.

From under his heavy brow, Kraki studied Drogo. The warrior was unlikely to recognize him; the fighting had been too fierce. For now Kraki was safe from threat, he knew. But Vavasour was wild, unpredictable, and dangerous. His hatred of Hereward made Roussel's army an even greater threat when they encountered the English.

Suleiman and Roussel embraced, laughing as they clapped each other on the back like old friends. Talking quietly in each other's ears, nodding and grinning, they renewed bonds with memories of shared times. Then they both looked to Kraki.

'I bring you a gift,' the Turk said with a sweep of his arm.

Roussel feigned turning up his nose. 'It is not much of a gift, brother. Is it a bear? A wounded wolf?' Roussel began to circle the Viking, a smile dancing on his lips as he enjoyed his game. 'A bedraggled wretch, perhaps? What have you caught yourself, Suleiman ibn Qutalmish?'

Kraki pushed down his defiance. Even now, when hope seemed so thin, he could not find it within himself to take any course that would cause his doom. Fighting to the last, that was in his blood. It was there in all his father had taught him in the cold wastes as they ran from the packs of enemies who hunted them. He could never forget that life-lesson. And now he had to live to warn Hereward of Drogo Vavasour's presence here. He gritted his teeth. The warrior's way was never easy. He would endure.

'Gold mined from the earth seems no more than rock, brother.

But once it has been polished, it gleams,' the Turk replied. 'This bedraggled wretch has a fire in him. But he also has knowledge of an attack set to strike at you, by the Romans. A war-band has picked its way east. At first they wailed like a child demanding attention . . .' Suleiman shook his head, unimpressed. 'These are not warriors like your own good men, brother, ones who know how to carry themselves into battle. But they learned fear on the road, and now they creep through valleys and forests, drawing towards Amaseia.'

'Is this true?' Roussel demanded, stepping in front of his captive. Kraki watched the warlord's eyes. They were calm, perhaps even amused.

'Aye. A storm of steel is about to break over you,' Kraki told him. 'Be afraid.'

The Norman laughed. 'The Romans have grown fat and lazy through their long rule. They have known victory and wealth for so many years, they think it their God-given right. But men have to fight, always, for the things they value. Let us see, then, who fights the hardest.'

The Viking spat on the floor. 'Cut these bonds. Then I will show you all I know about your days yet to come.'

'You will speak. In time.' Turning away, Roussel raised one hand and snapped his fingers. The warrior with the missing eye held out a leather pouch. Kraki heard the clink of coin.

Suleiman grinned. 'You are too kind, brother,' he said, taking the pouch.

Kraki showed a cold face, hoping it would hide his thoughts. The Normans seemed distracted, as if they had larger game to hunt than the Athanatoi. And the longer Roussel waited to get answers, the more chance there would be to escape.

'Take him away, Drogo,' the warlord said with a dismissive flap of his hand. But as Vavasour unsheathed his sword to prod the captive out of the chamber, the sound of approaching feet echoed.

Three figures emerged from the shadowy depths of the palace. At the front was a moon-faced lad with dead, unblinking eyes.

But Kraki found his gaze drawn to the man who towered over him. He was big, bigger than Guthrinc, with shoulders broad enough to carry a mule. His tanned skin was like leather, but he was not young, for all the power that was revealed in even the slightest movement. Deep lines were carved into his face, and his hair was the colour of steel, sweeping from his brow and falling down the back of his neck. Yet he had lost none of his potency, Kraki could see. Here was a warrior who would give a good account of himself on any field of battle.

'How much longer must we wait?' he demanded, the voice of a man used to being obeyed.

'All goes to plan, Karas Verinus—'

But a snarl of anger from Suleiman cut off Roussel's words. The Turkish leader whisked out his sword, all humour draining from his face. His men swept up their own weapons. 'You side with this devil?' he barked.

Roussel held out his arms. 'There is no need for argument here—'

'No need?' Suleiman spat. He narrowed his eyes. 'This Roman dog slaughters my people. Men, women, children. He straps their remains to crosses to warn off others, as if they were crows on a gibbet.'

Karas did not flinch from the accusation. 'My land is my own,' he said, his voice low and rumbling. 'I am not like the other Romans you meet, who roll over and bare their throats when you Turks sweep in and steal every patch of earth you cross. Come in your tens, your hundreds, your thousands – the soil will run red with your blood and still you will not gain what is mine.'

Kraki frowned. He knew the name of the Verini from his time in Constantinople. Their head, Victor, had had his cock torn off and his body dumped in the street, a feast for the wild dogs and the rats. Was this warrior then kin?

'Stay your arm, brother,' Roussel insisted. This time Kraki heard an edge to his voice. 'This is talk for another day.'

Suleiman finally drew his hard gaze away from the man he

loathed. Nodding to the warlord, he sheathed his sword. 'Another day.' But as he strode towards the door without any other pretence at pleasantries, he flashed one murderous backward glance at Karas.

Kraki almost grinned. Already they were fighting among themselves. These cracks would only get deeper.

But he felt his confidence ebb away when he glanced back at the new arrivals and saw that the third one was the ruined man Ragener the sea wolf. Kraki lowered his head. He doubted he would be recognized – the dog had been pleading for his life the first time they encountered each other, and hiding from the thick of battle the second time. But he knew he could not take any risks. Though he was a coward, Ragener was also vicious, with a heart filled with hate. He had carved away the flesh of Alric while the monk was his captive, a barbarous act that had cost the churchman his hand. If he could, Kraki knew he would take Ragener's head and tie it to his belt by the hair for that crime.

The sea wolf lumbered forward, his gait rolling as if he were still aboard ship. He waved a finger at Kraki, words tumbling out of his misshapen mouth. 'Do I know you?' he mumbled, leaning in so that the Viking could smell his vinegar breath.

Kraki grunted. 'I have seen you in my nightmares.'

Ragener scowled. 'This is your captive?' He prowled around like a hungry rat.

Kraki averted his eyes, regretting his inability to hold his tongue. His father had always said it would be the death of him.

Roussel was distracted. Karas was looming over him, talking in a low voice. His fierce unblinking eyes glowed. The warlord waved a hand as he tried to dismiss whatever was troubling the Roman.

'I will watch over him,' Ragener breathed, like steam escaping from a bubbling pot. With the exclamation, he lunged forward until his eyes were a hand's breadth away from Kraki's. In that moment, the Viking could see that the ruined man knew him.

He hungered for revenge, against Hereward, against fate for the iniquities that had been heaped upon him, and he would take it out of his captive one chunk of flesh at a time.

# Chapter Twenty

The setting sun ignited a line of fire along the jagged rim of the black mountains. And across Amaseia too, flames flickered into life. Torches blazed in the fora and the main street and folk chatted lazily under their light, stretching their exhausted muscles. From the river came the creak of timbers and the calls of the men on the quayside as they moored the last of the ships.

As Hereward watched the peaceful end to another hard day, he felt oddly adrift. Faces floated through his mind. Memories of similarly peaceful days long gone, in England, when the dying sun set the fenland waters alight and the birds shrieked their final calls over the wide, empty land. Turfrida was there, whispering words of comfort, his wife whom he still missed as if she had only just been lost. Aye, and Kraki too, drunk on mead and roaring with laughter. He missed his quiet conversations with Alric, the only true friend he had found in his life. And he thought again of his son, the boy he had never even named. Three summers had passed since the babe had been left with the monks at Crowland Abbey. How tall would he be now? Was he even still alive? Hereward slipped his fingers around the sliver of wood at his neck. He had abandoned the boy for good reason, or so he thought. The Mercian dipped his head. He had always feared becoming a man like his own father, who used his fists on those around him. His son deserved better than that.

Hereward jerked from his reveries. A dark shadow was flitting through the scrubby trees and thorny bushes, up the slope from the town to the cleft in the rocks where the knot of warriors waited.

'He has returned,' he murmured. Sighard and Three Fingers nodded. But the Romans did not have the Mercians' keen eyes, forged in the long, dark fenland nights. Maximos and Alexios leaned forward, squinting. Zeno Oresme, the Wolf, did not stir, his almond eyes calm as he sat on a rock, his sword already in his hand. He was a cold man, murderous by all accounts, but like the other Romans he could identify the Caesar. And as a veteran of the brutal battle at Manzikert, he had more experience in a fight than most of the others.

The warriors strained to hear, but only the whisper of the wind rolled up the hillside. But then, as if from nowhere, Herrig the Rat appeared at their backs. The men all jumped.

'God's wounds. He is like a ghost,' Maximos breathed, irritated with himself.

Herrig was frowning, puzzled, Hereward saw.

'What did you find?'

The Rat clambered on to a rock and peered down towards the tent city where Roussel's forces camped beyond the walls of Amaseia. 'Half of his army are nowhere to be seen. Long gone, from the cold ashes of their fires. Of those left . . .' He pursed his lips. 'The horses have been fed and watered, and the carts have been loaded with bales and hides. They smelled of bread and olives. And the Norman bastards are cleaning their hauberks with sand and sharpening their swords with whetstones.'

'Could they know?' Maximos asked.

'If they are preparing their carts, they are readying for a journey,' Alexios said. 'Perhaps Roussel has bigger plans than we thought.'

'I fought beside him at Manzikert.' Zeno's lisping voice floated from their backs. 'He is not a man of small dreams. I wager he would see this land he has here grow and prosper. With the Normans and the Turks carving chunks out of it daily, soon there will be no empire fit for that name,' he added with a note of bitterness.

'If Roussel's men are ready, we may have lost what little chance we had to surprise them,' Sighard breathed. 'Should we turn back?'

'To what end?' Hereward said. 'We will still be a flea biting a bear's back. This plan is all we have. We must see it through and hope we are still alive to greet the dawn. Put fire in your hearts, brothers. After all, we have only half an army here now to trouble us.'

'Aye,' Maximos added, 'and we will still surprise them. This plan will work. I feel it in my heart.'

Their resolve strengthened, the warriors watched the city fires, waiting.

Once the sun had disappeared behind the mountains, the night came down hard. A crescent moon glowed, providing just enough light for their business. The steep-sided valley grew still.

After long moments, a full-throated scream of terror echoed from upriver. It rose and fell, rose and fell, seeming as if it would never end. Even though the warriors had expected it, they stiffened, chilled to the bone. The sound was filled with so many agonies, they could imagine the gates of hell had been opened.

A loud roaring erupted, not quite drowning out the dreadful cry. Away in the dark an inferno appeared, heading towards the city. The men stared, gripped by the sight of that unholy light.

'It begins,' Hereward said. 'Raise your weapons.'

# Chapter Twenty-One

The fire swept towards Amaseia. Shards of orange light glimmered off the black water. Along the river banks the glow marched, until a blazing ship emerged from the night. Aft, the conflagration roared up from a pile of bales almost to the top of the mast, smoke billowing around it like grey sails. The scream was tearing from the throat of a man bound in the prow: a Norman scout, gripped by terror as the flames licked towards him.

All was going to plan.

'Wait,' Sighard said, pointing. 'That is not what we agreed.'

Hereward squinted into the dancing glare. Now he could see a second man, strapped to the mast, another scout no doubt. His head rolled on the deck by his feet. The Mercian grimaced. 'That is not Guthrinc and Hengist's work. Tiberius has left his own mark upon this.'

Across Amaseia, torches flared into life and a terrible clamour rang to the heavens. Folks rushed from their homes. The alarm sprang from throat to throat.

The Mercian flicked his hand towards the city. Cloaked in darkness, the men crept out from the rocks and crawled down the slope. As they neared the walls, Hereward's nose wrinkled at the acrid reek of the burning ship. A torrent of bodies flooded through the streets and out of the tent city, down to the water's edge. So great was the din, the English could have been bellowing to each other and not been heard. Hereward grinned. This was how he had seen the night unfolding in his mind's eye.

When they were close enough to the quay to hear any exchange, they slipped into a copse of scraggly trees and waited. Shadows swooped across the harbour. The light that chased them illuminated the faces of the gaping men trying to make sense of this disaster.

Watermen armed with long poles braced themselves along the quayside to fend off the drifting ship so it did not ignite any of the vessels moored nearby. But Hereward could see it was already listing. Soon the hull would split and it would sink in a hissing cloud of steam.

A handful of brave souls threw grapnels into the prow, then leapt into the water and hauled themselves up on to the deck to wrench the Norman scout free of his bonds. Together they dived back into the churning river.

Surrounded by warriors, the dripping scout crouched on the quay, catching his breath. Hereward cocked his head, listening, as questions were barked. The response was picked up by one man and yelled to another, and then another, a chain unfurling all the way to the city gate.

*The Immortals are coming. The greatest warriors in all Constantinople.*

Grinning, Hereward and his men exchanged a triumphant look. Now they only had to wait and pray the Normans would react as they hoped.

Loud voices surged deep into the city as news of the impending attack spread. For a while, the English and the Romans waited in the copse while the panic unfolded around them, and then Hereward stiffened. The response had been decided and the order given. Pulling on hauberks and helmets, warriors flooded out of the gate and into the turmoil of the tent city, where men were racing along the tracks between the shelters, stirring their drunken brothers. Axes were gripped, swords unsheathed. In the pens, nervous horses stamped and whinnied. Riders found their mounts and galloped out of the valley towards the plain.

Hereward felt no pride that his plan was progressing as anticipated. Any seasoned war-leader would have known that the plain was the best place for a force to gather to defend the city.

Sighard clawed his way forward and watched with him, his breath tight in his chest. 'How many will they send?' he breathed.

Too few and their chance of escape from Amaseia would be slim, Hereward knew. They could not ghost in and out of the palace and leave no trace of their passing. At some point an alarm would be raised.

Maximos loomed over the younger warrior as the first force rode out en masse. 'And still they ready themselves?' he whispered. 'Is Roussel leaving the city undefended?'

'He knows not how many ride with the Immortals,' Alexios replied. 'He can take no chances.'

Unable to believe their luck, the warriors watched as the Norman forces swept away from Amaseia. Soon the tent city was deserted.

'Let us not tarry,' Hereward hissed. 'There will still be swords and axes waiting for us. We cannot know how many warriors Roussel has kept to guard his prize.'

Creeping out of the trees, the war-band eased into the throng bustling along the dusty track running between the river and the gate. All around, frightened faces glowed in the firelight. Their new masters had kept these people safe from the incursions of the Turks and let them go about their business in peace. Now they were wondering if it was all coming to an end.

Maximos recognized the source of their anxiety. 'We are the enemy here,' he murmured. His voice hardened. 'The emperor's weakness has left these poor souls to seek solace in the arms of an invader.'

The crowd was swelling. Hereward pushed through the

churning bodies at the gate, hoping the confusion would be cover enough. The remaining Normans were distracted, their attention focused on the threat they feared was rushing towards them from the open plain, not on a handful of men wandering into the city in full view.

Once they'd fought their way across the wide street by the walls, Hereward plunged into the narrow alleys winding between the houses. They were dark, deserted. The din ebbed away. Soon only the whisper of running feet followed him.

When they reached the end of the alley opening on to the wide courtyard, the Mercian raised his hand. His men pressed into the shadows by the wall at his back. Torches glimmered in the depths of the palace. Only two guards were visible. Huddling together as they whispered intensely, they flashed glances towards the orange glow rising above the rooftops from the river.

Grinning, Maximos cracked his knuckles. Alexios nodded in reply. Feigning worried faces, the two Romans darted out from the alley. The guards whirled, hands flying to their swords.

'At the gate!' Maximos glanced over his shoulder in seeming panic. 'You are needed. Now!'

The guards gaped, unsure, and that was their undoing. As soon as the two Romans were close enough, blades flashed. Maximos rammed a knife into one of the guards' guts, wrenching upwards, then planted his free hand on the man's mouth and forced him to the flagstones. Smaller and lither, Alexios danced behind the other guard before he could unsheathe his sword. Another short blade ripped across the Norman's throat and he collapsed, clutching at a spray of crimson.

A moment later, the war-band was racing across the empty courtyard to the palace. Easing through the door, Hereward looked around the deserted hall. Torches flickered along the walls. At first, all seemed silent. Then, cocking his head, he heard a faint laugh and the thrum of distant voices.

Responding to a snap of the Mercian's hand, the warriors ghosted across the hall in the direction of the sound and paused outside a chamber beneath the stone steps leading to the first floor. Hereward pressed his ear against the age-cracked door. Three men were conversing in the harsh Norman tongue, their voices edged with laughter. From the sound of it, they were supping and swilling back wine.

At a glance, his men raised their weapons. Thundering one foot against the door, the Mercian crashed into the room. The guards were hunched on benches. Wooden bowls of spicy stew and cups of wine flew as they jerked round in shock. But they were too slow to react, their weapons abandoned in one corner.

Hereward rammed Brainbiter into the chest of the nearest man. Before the Mercian had even withdrawn his sword, Sighard had fallen upon another. The third man threw himself across the chamber, clutching for his blade. Maximos cuffed him with the hilt of his sword and he crashed against one of the benches. Hereward was on him in an instant, snarling his fist in the man's tunic.

Yanking the Norman up, the Mercian glared into his eyes and hissed, 'The Caesar. Where is he held?'

The guard stuttered for only a moment before the answer gushed out of him. Once the Norman had been laid low by the flat of a blade, the war-band darted back to the hall. For a moment they paused, listening. When they were sure they had not been heard, they bounded up the stairs. Though each was fast, Herrig the Rat was fastest of all, snickering to himself as he took the steps three at a time.

Hereward had expected the Caesar to be bound in the dank dark beneath the palace. But the chambers on the first floor where the guard said the noble was confined were as sumptuous as any king's hall. Through one door, gold plate, jewelled caskets and gem-studded books gleamed; the riches of the Church that had been taken from John Doukas. Richly embroidered tapestries, marble statues and bolts of Syrian silk filled every space. Yet there was no order to these riches. Looted, all of them, and cast aside by a warlord who now had what he valued even more – his own empire.

'Make haste,' Hereward hissed to Sighard and Hiroc. He jabbed a finger towards a box of dark wood carved with angels.

The two men nodded. Soon the box was stuffed with gold.

Alexios and Maximos loomed in the doorway. 'Is this the hour to rob?' the younger man said, incredulous. 'The Caesar is all that matters.'

'I would not begrudge a man some coin for his pouch,' Maximos added, pursing his lips in thought, 'but that coffer will slow you . . . us . . . down. And it is not so much of a fortune that it is worth risking our lives.'

'For us English, it will suffice,' the Mercian replied. 'And if you find us falling behind, keep going. But my men are strong. We will outrun you, even with a chest of gold.'

A shadow appeared behind the two Romans. Zeno the Wolf stabbed his sword towards the Mercian. 'Are you mad? Talking like wives at the market in the enemy camp? Come, now. Or I will take the Caesar myself.'

Soon they were creeping towards the chamber where the guard had said John Doukas was being held. Outside, Sighard and Hiroc set down the coffer and crouched beside it while Hereward rested his fingertips against the wood of the door. At the least, he had expected heavy iron bolts, but there were none. It seemed Roussel was treating his captive with the respect his station deserved.

The Mercian shoved and the door swung open.

A man in an emerald tunic sat on a bench, looking out of the window to where the orange glow lit the night sky. At first Hereward thought the guard had lied and this was some monk, for the man's hair was tonsured to show his devotion to God. But his back was straight and his chin raised with the arrogance that the Mercian had seen in all Roman nobles. He turned slowly, no doubt expecting his captors. When he saw who stood in the room, he stood up, frowning.

'Is this he?' Hereward asked.

'It is,' Maximos said with a hint of mockery. 'Once a general, once the most powerful man in the court, and now king . . . of his vast lands in Thrace and Bithynia, and nothing more. But he has gold aplenty, I will give him that.'

'Who are you?' John Doukas demanded. His voice was strong and low. His pale eyes gleamed beneath dark brows.

'It is I, Alexios Comnenos.' The younger Roman stepped forward, holding out one hand. 'You know me.'

'Aye, your mother hates me and would see me dead. Is it not enough that I was sent to risk all in battle with the Normans, only to see my most trusted men betray me and flee?' He curled his lip, implying that he had been meant to be defeated, the Mercian guessed. 'Does your mother hate me so much that she has now sent her favoured offspring into this den of enemies to kill me?'

'We have come to save you. You are to be returned to Constantinople under our guard,' Alexios protested.

For a long moment, the Caesar looked from one face to another, a smile creeping across his thin lips. Then, with quick steps, he backed to the window, and threw back his head. 'We are attacked,' he yelled so loudly it must have torn his throat. 'Save me! Save the Caesar!'

# Chapter Twenty-Two

Deep in the palace, a lone voice responded. The cry was taken up by another, and then another. Soon the stone walls were ringing.

Hereward gripped the hilt of his sword. When his eyes locked with the Caesar's, he could see a cold calculation. There was more here than a fear of Anna Dalassene's retribution. A chill smile flickered across John Doukas' lips.

'Seize him,' Alexios demanded. 'He will see sense once we are away from this place.'

'No.' Hereward raised his sword to prevent any warrior from coming forward. 'The Caesar will resist us every step of the way. Our enemies will be upon us before we can even drag him outside.'

Alexios began to protest. The Mercian could sense the disappointment in all the men. There would not be another chance to free the captive. They would wear their failure like a brand when they returned to Constantinople. But at least they would still have their lives.

Maximos understood. 'Come,' he urged, pushing the younger Roman towards the door. He flashed a cold glance back at the Caesar, one that promised an accounting. And then they were out in the corridor, where Sighard and Three Fingers waited with the chest held between them.

'Bring it,' Hereward commanded.

'Now *you* will be the death of us,' Maximos said, as he ran at the side of the Mercian warrior.

'At least there will be some reward for risking our necks.'

'Aye, for you.'

Herrig the Rat waited at the top of the steps, beckoning. The sound of running feet and alarmed voices echoed through the palace.

Hereward bounded down the steps into the hall. Glancing back at Sighard and Three Fingers struggling with the weight of the chest, he could see they would soon be snapped up in the jaws of their enemies. Yet he would be damned if all this had been for naught. He would not go back to Constantinople and see his men treated like dogs again.

Whirling, his gaze fell upon the shadows swirling across the stone wall. He grinned. Snatching up a pitch-soaked torch, he held the spitting brand to tapestry after tapestry. Flames roared up. Choking smoke billowed.

Maximos wrenched open the door and with a furious swing of his arm urged the others out just as three Norman warriors stumbled into the hall. Their axes hovered, their fear-filled eyes darting towards the inferno. Hereward set his jaw. They had dropped their guard, just as he had hoped.

With a lunge, he rammed his blade into the chest of the nearest man. At the death-cry, the attention of the two others snapped back to the fugitives. Hereward danced forward. Brainbiter swept up, deflecting a swinging axe. Sparks flared in the thick smoke.

In the corner of his eye, he glimpsed another figure beside him. It was Maximos. The Roman was strong, but light on his feet too. Stabbing with his short sword, he drove the third Norman back. With a fluid move to one side, he hacked across his foe's forearm. The warrior's axe tumbled from his grasp and he went down on one knee, howling in agony. Maximos placed one foot on the man's chest and thrust him back into the flames. Screams tore through the hall as his tunic caught fire.

Hacking high, then low, Hereward pushed his own opponent back towards the blaze. Once the heat swelled at his back, the Norman lowered his axe and leapt to escape his fate. The Mercian seized his opening and slashed his blade across the warrior's face. Before the man had fallen to the blood-slick flagstones, Hereward had spun on his heel and was darting through the open door with Maximos at his side.

Cries rang out behind them. More Normans were flooding into the hall. He heard alarm, fear that the fire would engulf the palace, and anger too, that what they had no doubt considered a fine redoubt had been attacked with seeming impunity while their backs were turned.

When Hereward flashed a look over his shoulder, his eyes locked with another, familiar, pair. Bathed in a ruddy glow from the hellish inferno, Drogo Vavasour was rigid, gripped by the sight of the last man he had expected to find there, and the most hated. In an instant, he was swallowed up by a crowd of men shipping hides filled with water to extinguish the blaze. Hereward ran on.

'You have bought us some time, but not enough,' Maximos said as they raced across the courtyard. 'If I had John Doukas here, I would have tossed him into the flames too. He might as well have killed us himself.'

'We are not dead yet,' the Mercian grunted. But in a city filled with enemies, surrounded by rugged countryside that would slow their escape, he knew they would need God and fortune on their side if they were to live to see the dawn.

Herrig loomed out of the shadows of an alley on the other side of the courtyard, a ghostly figure beckoning. When Hereward and Maximos plunged into the narrow space, they found Sighard and Three Fingers leaning breathlessly against the wall. Zeno waited beside them. 'Stay close at my heels,' the Rat breathed, dropping low like his namesake. Darting down the alley, he scrambled through a narrow gap between two halls. Close behind him, the warriors squeezed through the space and followed the scurrying figure along winding tracks as black as pitch. Sighard's and Three Fingers' breath rasped as they heaved the laden chest between them.

When they reached the wide street running along the walls, they waited in the shadows for their moment. Now that the burning ship had sunk beneath the waves, the crowd had started to thin. It would not be so easy to lose themselves in confusion, Hereward could see.

Zeno pushed his way past Hereward to peer into the dark beyond the walls. 'Do we go to the river? Steal a ship?'

'Our enemies will be upon us before we cast off into the current,' Alexios said. 'No, our only hope is to take horses and ride to the plains. Any who watch will mistake us for stragglers joining Roussel's army. Once we have joined with the Athanatoi we will find safety in numbers.'

Maximos grinned, but his eyes remained cold. 'We should heed the Little General.' Even now he made no attempt to hide his mockery.

Alexios bristled.

Stepping between the rivals, Hereward growled so that the others could not hear, 'Put aside your differences or I will leave you behind.' He turned his gaze on Alexios, adding, 'Whatever vow I made to your mother.' Without waiting for a response, he jabbed a finger at Sighard and Hiroc and jerked it towards the gate. Both men nodded. Steeling themselves, they kept their faces low as they edged out of the alley. Hereward nodded, satisfied. Carrying the coffer between them, they looked like two merchants taking their wares down to their ship. No threat at all.

As the English warriors reached the gate Zeno walked out of the alley, then Alexios and Maximos. Hereward looked round for Herrig. When he glanced back, he glimpsed the Rat already on the other side of the wall, out of sight of the guards.

When he could afford to wait no longer, Hereward lowered his head and dropped in close behind a local man walking towards the gate, almost as if they were together. He could see the guards pacing around, their hands tight on their sword hilts.

Steeling himself, he let his own fingers close on Brainbiter. If they had to fight their way past the whole city, they would.

Under dancing torchlight far along the street, bodies were churning, heads turning. Roussel's palace guards were racing to close the gate.

Sighard and Three Fingers were already in the shadow of the stone arch over the gate. Near them, the guards cocked their heads, straining to make out the meaning of the distant cries.

Hereward picked up his step, ready to break into a run. But as he half drew his sword, he glimpsed the gate guards pushing through the small crowd towards the uproar.

The confusion had acted in their favour.

The two English warriors slipped through the unguarded gate, followed by Zeno, Maximos and Alexios. When Hereward caught up with them, they were darting through the dark away from the track, towards the pen where Roussel's army kept their horses. Behind him, he heard the sound of the gate grinding shut.

Maximos flashed him a grin.

'We are not out of hot water yet,' the Mercian cautioned.

When they reached the pen, he could not help but breathe a sigh of relief. The remaining horses stamped and whinnied as the strange men approached, but their unease would not be heard above the din coming from beyond the walls.

'We failed.' Alexios sagged against the fence. 'How will we hold our heads high now, when we return home?'

Hereward eyed the coffer and grinned to himself. The English had not failed. He cared little whether they took the Caesar back with them or not. This was all he had wanted out of this foray – enough gold to buy their way into the Varangian Guard.

But then the grinding of the gate echoed again, and the furious voices began to tumble out of the city.

'They will be on our tail soon enough,' Maximos said, looking towards the glow of torchlight. 'Let us hope we can outride them on strange mounts.'

'Then let us make it hard for them,' Hereward said. He glanced down at the chest, knowing its weight would slow his men down. 'I will take our spoils and ride south, making the trail clear so it will draw them away. The rest of you, ride for our brothers as fast as the wind.'

'Alone?' Sighard protested. 'Who will watch for attack in the night? How will you hunt for food when there are Norman dogs running you down?'

'You will not ride alone.' To Hereward's surprise, Maximos stepped forward.

'Aye,' Alexios insisted, 'and I will be at your side too.'

'And I,' Zeno said. Turning to the three English warriors, he said, 'This is for the best. We know this land. We can find the tracks that will take us away from the Normans. You, ride hard for your brothers, and tell Tiberius to wait for us at the Sakarya forge.'

Sighard hesitated, but Three Fingers gave him a rough shove, knowing there was no time to argue. With Herrig, they mounted their steeds and urged them out of the pen. Soon they were galloping towards the track that led to the plain.

When Hereward had climbed on to his chosen horse, Maximos heaved up the coffer and set it in front of him. 'We will find a way to strap it to the beast once we are away from here,' he said. 'Let us hope you get a chance to spend it.'

Walking away from the pen, Zeno struck his flint and wafted the sparks towards the dry brush at his feet. Soon flames were leaping. 'Fresh meat for the wolves,' he said. 'They will follow us now.'

'Come, then,' Hereward said, digging his heels into his horse's flanks. 'We have woken the Devil. Let us make certain he does not drag us down to hell.'

# Chapter Twenty-Three

A sliver of amber light danced. All around it, a dark as deep and lonely as a moonless night pressed down. Here, in this dank pit reeking of urine and shit, the rats scurried without cease, their claws clicking on the cold stone.

Kraki had been in worse places. From somewhere in the palace above him muffled sounds floated – running feet, cries – and he could smell smoke. A fire had been discovered, he guessed. Perhaps he would simply roast to death, instead of the slow ending he imagined.

Watching the torchlight flicker under the door, he pressed his back against the slick wall. Few would find it comforting, but he did. His memory swept across the plains and the fields and the great, wide whale road to the cold land of his birth. He remembered the reassuring feel of sturdy rock at his back as he sheltered in a cleft in the mountains against the knife-wind. His father was there, telling him tales of bloody battles, and Odin's will. He felt surprising regret for those lost days, and he realized how much he missed the old wolf, with his face carved raw by the gales, and his wild grey beard, and the pink scar of honour that ran from temple to chin.

But then his father's face faded and Acha's rose from the mist, raven-black hair and skin like snow, her eyes stern, accusing.

Yes, 'twas true, he thought bitterly – she had made a farmer of him. He yearned for days long gone, for the comfort of the home-fire, for his woman. The fire in his belly was dying, he thought with a pang of fear. There was no place for his axe here. If he survived this pit of misery he should fly back west, across the plains and the fields and the whale road, to England, to Acha. He had no value here any longer.

When he heard the shuffling steps approaching his cell, he gritted his teeth. He knew who was visiting him long before the door swung open and flooded the tiny chamber with torchlight. Blinking in the glare, his eyes gradually revealed the silhouette of Ragener looming over him.

The ruined man eased the door half shut with his foot and squatted in front of his captive. His split lips turned his grin into grimace.

'You are brave when I am trussed up like a deer for the slaughter,' Kraki growled. 'Cut my bonds and we will talk like men.' He strained at the rope round his wrists at his back, though he had tried to break it a hundred times.

'I am no jolt-head, Viking,' the sea wolf said with a throaty laugh. 'A man with one hand is no match for a great warrior like you. But over time I will even the score a little.'

Kraki sensed the other man's hunger, like a dog waiting for the scraps on his master's plate. 'That knife of yours will even the score for you, that is what you are saying. As it did with the monk.' In his mind's eye, he saw Alric's blood-drained face floating on the edge of death as the black rot ate its way from his ravaged hand.

'Aye,' Ragener replied, his voice edged with pride. 'I took his fingers, one by one. God gave him the strength to take his suffering, I grant.'

'He is stronger than you.'

The Hawk flinched at the bald statement. 'It was a small price to pay,' he snapped. 'Your leader, the bastard Hereward, took my hand.' He raised his stump and shook it in Kraki's face.

'And he took the monk's hand, but that was an act of mercy,

to save his friend's life from the black rot.' The Viking's voice was low, steady, betraying no fear. 'Hereward will never forgive you, you know that? He will pursue you to the ends of the earth to make you pay for what you did to his friend. He will take your other hand, your feet, your eyes, and then, when you can bear no more, he will take your head.'

Ragener's one good eye glowed like fire. His mouth gaped like a codfish, and for a moment the Viking thought his enemy was going to wail like a child. Knives did not make men. The forge of the heart did that.

As if the sea wolf could read his thoughts, Ragener pulled out his short-bladed knife and waved it under his captive's nose. 'Let us wait no longer. I will start with your tongue. Then I will not have to listen to any more of your whining.'

The ruined man lunged, pressing the tip of the blade against the Viking's throat as he forced him back against the stone with his stump. He was stronger than he looked, with the strength of someone filled with a rage against the world. Kraki felt the hot needle-burn of the knife against his skin. He would be dead in an instant if he resisted.

'Let us see how much you love life.' Ragener's whisper was laced with wicked glee. 'Put your tongue out. Let me slice it off and you will live to see another day. Resist and I will carve away your lips to get at it, then I will chop your throat like a piece of venison.'

Kraki held the sea wolf's gaze. He knew this man was capable of anything. There was no honour in him.

The noise in his throat rustled out, barely audible. The sea wolf frowned, unable to tell if this was assent. 'Speak up!' he yelled. 'Are you so afraid of me?'

This time Kraki moved his lips, but no sound came out.

Ragener smiled in triumph. 'Now you know what it is like to live with fear,' he hissed. Leaning in, so he could revel in Kraki's croaked plea, he let the knife fall away.

Kraki's teeth clamped on the sea wolf's cheek. The blade clattered to the floor as Ragener clawed the air, howling. But he could not pull free. The Viking felt blood bubble in his mouth, tasted iron, but still he held on. When he finally wrenched his head back, a chunk of cheek came with him. He spat it across the cell, a feast for the rats.

Ragener reeled as the agony stole his wits for a moment. Seizing his chance, Kraki rammed his head into the ruined face. The sea wolf spun back. But the Viking did not stop there. Shuffling on his knees until he loomed over his victim, he hammered his forehead into Ragener's face time and again until the flesh was pulped.

When he sat back, blood streamed down his scarred features. 'I have a thick head, half-man. You know that now,' he murmured. Falling back, he fumbled around until his fingers closed on the sea wolf's knife. His best chance now, he knew, was to use the confusion upstairs to his advantage. Pushing himself up the wall, he lumbered to the door and nudged it open with his nose. He nodded, pleased. The din from the main hall had grown even louder.

Gritting his teeth as he twisted the knife to saw at his bonds, he stepped out into the long corridor that ran the length of the palace and stalked towards the steps leading to the halls. Chambers led off on either side. Stores for wine and food, he thought, wrinkling his nose.

Then he winced, and all but cursed aloud. The blade had sliced into his wrist and blood was trickling over his fingers, but he could not stop, not now that he had been given one slim chance to escape. He felt a touch of elation, and unease too. All hinged on the next few moments.

But as he reached the foot of the steps, he juddered to a halt. Perched on a step halfway up the flight was the strange moon-faced boy, no doubt waiting for the sea wolf. Kraki tried to find words that would reassure, but he had never been good with children. For a moment, the lad stared at him, unblinking, and then he put his head back and made a keening sound, like the gulls on a grey winter's day.

'Quiet, damn you,' the Viking snarled.

Too late. Thunderous footsteps raced at his back as if a bull were bearing down on him. Half turning, he glimpsed a mountain of muscle and bone racing towards him. It was the Roman, Karas Verinus.

'You are the key to winning the throne, and by God you will not escape me,' he snarled. His huge fist slammed down like a hammer upon an anvil, and Kraki knew no more.

# Chapter Twenty-Four

'I will bring you back his head!'

The words throbbed in the void, almost lost beneath the pounding of blood. Kraki blinked once, twice. As the darkness ebbed away, he realized he was lying on cold stone amid the reek of charred wood. Pearly curls of smoke wafted through the air. He glimpsed arches and tapestries and knew he was in the main hall of the palace. At his back, a drone of low voices and the grinding of objects being dragged across the floor told him the fire had been extinguished. A blast of cool night air from the open door washed over him.

But he found his attention drawn to the man who had spoken with such passion. Drogo Vavasour was like a madman. His hands clutching at the air, he ranged around Roussel de Bailleul. His cheeks were flushed, his eyes staring at horizons far beyond that chamber. 'Ten men, that is all I need,' he spewed, spittle flying.

Roussel, though, was calm. Arms folded, he watched the prowling warrior, a fixed smile on his lips. His demeanour suggested that he thought the other man was less than sane, Kraki thought. 'Take them, and do not return until he is dead,' he said, placating.

'I will follow Hereward of the English to the ends of the earth, if that is what it takes.'

'Hereward?' Kraki jerked up, his head ringing.

'Your friend was here this night,' Drogo spat, 'trying to steal the Caesar from under our noses. He failed, and we ran him out of here like a rat.'

Kraki gritted his teeth. To have come so close! If Hereward had known he was captive here, he would now be riding back to the Athanatoi, his life his own once more.

Drogo strode forward and made to vent his frustration upon the captive with a kick to the gut.

'Leave him,' Roussel commanded. 'He has his uses, yes?'

From behind Kraki, the towering bulk of Karas Verinus stepped forward. 'He has his uses,' he said, looking down at the man he had battered into unconsciousness.

Roussel turned to Drogo and said, 'Our plans have of necessity been brought forward a day or two at most, but we are ready. We will ride tonight and join our army on the plain. Once you have sated your blood-lust, find us. You know where.'

Vavasour nodded. Animated, he snapped his fingers at the one-eyed warrior Kraki had seen earlier, and a few others. They trailed after him out into the night. Kraki felt his heart sink. If any man could track down Hereward, it would be Drogo Vavasour. His hatred for the Mercian made him a relentless enemy.

A tonsured man in an emerald tunic wandered over, a goblet of wine held loosely in his hand. He raised his cup in a toast.

Roussel nodded. 'You did well to raise the alarm, John Doukas. If my men had not been half asleep, our enemies would be dead now.' He shrugged. 'It matters little. They are fleas upon a dog.'

Pushing himself up, Kraki studied the Caesar. Something was amiss here. The warlord had said *our enemies*, and John Doukas seemed not to be a captive at all.

As if he could sense the Viking's thoughts, Roussel smiled. Crouching so he could look his prisoner in the eye, he said with a confident smile, 'The Romans sent you out here to die, Viking. Do you trust your new masters?'

'I trust no one.'

'Wise words.' He nodded. 'You will be well treated, do not fear.'

'I am not afrit of any Norman. I killed enough of you bastards in England.'

'I have heard the stories of Hereward of the English and his rebels. Brave men all. Still, we share blood, you and I.'

'You are not my kin.'

Roussel laughed silently. 'You have not heard the tales of days long gone, then. Vikings from the cold north found a new home in Normandy. We are fierce folk, both. We should not be enemies.'

Kraki glowered. 'Any man who learns his ways from William the Bastard will always be my foe.'

'Is that what they tell you?' Roussel chuckled. 'I am no William the Bastard, Viking. I would not slaughter babes in arms and old men, as he did in the English north. I believe in honour above all. But I like the gold he has in his coffers, and the land that spreads out before him, I admit.' Standing, he looked around the hall. 'There is much to be said for being king.'

Kraki shrugged. He had no quarrel with this man. In other times, he may well have liked him. They were brothers of the field of battle. But the Viking stared past the warlord to where Karas was lurking in the shadows. The Roman was a different matter. He reeked of threat, as did his dog Ragener, aye, and the moon-faced boy too. It was only fitting that they travelled together. Why they had come to the warlord, he did not know, but he sensed that here there were plots within plots.

Leaning down, Roussel caught Kraki under the arm and hauled him to his feet. 'You will soon get some food in your belly, and wine too. I would wager you would not say no to that?' He laughed, slapping the Viking on the back. 'But first we must put some miles behind us.'

With a gentle shove, he urged Kraki towards the door. Accompanied by a knot of warriors, they crossed the town and passed through the gates. In the east, a pink sliver edged across the horizon. Kraki came to a halt, looking around in surprise. The tent city of the warlord's army was empty. Silence hung over the once bustling town. Nearby, horses had been readied and carts were laden with provisions.

'You need all your men to hunt down Hereward? Or to crush the Athanatoi?' the Viking asked.

Roussel grinned. 'Aye, crush them we will.' He looked to the lightening sky. 'They may well be already lying in their own blood. They will have found a surprise waiting for them. But that is not all, Viking.' Leaping on to the back of his mount with the skill of a seasoned horseman, Roussel waved a hand to command his men to throw Kraki into the back of one of the carts. 'My army will not be returning this day. No, today we leave Amaseia behind.'

# Chapter Twenty-Five

It was the hour of dawn. Around the dome of the Hagia Sophia, a halo was forming. The rooftops were limned with gold, and the whitewashed halls were starting to emerge from the night like ghosts. But in Constantinople's lonely streets the shadows still swelled. As the first birdsong trilled, a faint beat echoed. Footsteps clattered nearer. Two children raced from the dark, faces flushed, wide eyes darting as they searched for a place to hide.

'We were too confident,' Leo Nepos gasped. He glanced over his shoulder as he ran. The men at their backs were drawing closer.

'If you would live a life without risk, be a farmer.' Ariadne Verina narrowed her eyes. They were close now. There was still a chance they could escape by the skin of their teeth. But then she too looked back. Shapes moved in the dark, four, perhaps five of them. Her voice deepened, her face growing harder. 'Do not be afraid. Should they catch us, we will gut them like deer. This is the vow of al-Kahina.'

Clasping her companion's wrist, she yanked him to the right, down a filthy alley where the light had still not licked. Her head spun with thoughts, memories of the woman she would be, she believed herself to be: Meghigda, warrior-queen of the desert tribes, a woman who would never show fear, never be beaten like a cur, never die. *The spirit of Dihya burns in my breast*, she repeated silently in her head; a prayer, a spell.

For a moment, she stumbled over shards of shattered amphorae and discarded sacks until she found the pile of rotting fish guts, tossed out by one of the merchants, where she had come across it the other day. Leo gagged at the foul stink. Pressing a finger to her lips, she thrust the lad down on the other side of the heap and crushed in close to him. The blush of his skin warmed her cheek and she felt her heart trip faster.

Ariadne's breath burned in her chest as the crack of footsteps rattled past the end of the alley. She counted the passing bodies, then pushed her head up just as the final pursuer ran by. She glimpsed a sword, glinting in the first light.

'Are we safe?' Leo breathed.

Ariadne glanced at the lad fondly. He was weaker than she. He could never survive the hardships she had endured. Yet she understood his yearning to be something more: to gain respect, and, perhaps, power. Without respect he was nothing, and no one could bear to be that way. When her father died, she had been left with no value in this cruel city. But she had found some worth through Salih ibn Ziyad, and some purpose too. And she had found her power in Meghigda. 'For now,' she said. 'But they will be searching for us. We will wait here until the merchants arrive, and then lose ourselves in the crowd.' She fumbled for his hand and gave it a squeeze. After a moment, he responded.

Ariadne thought back to earlier that night: her desire to escape the confines of the house of Anna Dalassene had made her too reckless. Once she had found Leo she had persuaded him to join her in spying on Falkon Cephalas, the architect of all her misery. After following Nikephoritzes and his closest advisers from the Boukoleon palace, they had eventually found themselves at the back of a filthy tavern not far from the Petrion Gate on the north side of the city. More of his men had gathered there, spies it seemed, far away from prying eyes. Talk had been unguarded, and Ariadne and Leo had heard too much. When they had been discovered by a drunken rogue stumbling out into the night to drain his bladder, Falkon could not let them escape with what they now knew. His dogs had been loosed, a host of bloodthirsty warriors, hunting them through the streets with a relentlessness that told Ariadne she would never be able to rest easy again.

'Why did I follow you?' Leo moaned, hugging his arms around his knees.

'To find the truth. Falkon Cephalas will come for your own kin soon. You must know that. He seizes any that he feels threatens the emperor, never mind if they are noble. It is said that he has a chamber deep beneath the Boukoleon palace where he tortures them until they plead for death. The cries that rise from that place would chill the blood, they say.'

'Who say?'

'People.'

Leo turned up his nose. 'He would not dare come for the Nepotes.'

Salih ibn Ziyad would lash her with his tongue if he knew that she was in the company of one of the hated Nepotes. If only he could see that Leo was still an innocent. The boy could not be blamed in any way for the death of Meghigda, queen of the Imazighen and the woman Salih had loved above all others. No, that stain was upon the soul of Maximos Nepos alone. But her teacher believed that vengeance should follow blood. In his eyes, all of the Nepotes must pay.

For a moment, Leo's brow furrowed, and he shook his head, puzzled. 'Why do you help me? Your kin have been rivals of the Nepotes since before we were both born.'

'I have no kin,' Ariadne snapped. Catching herself, she forced her voice to soften. 'My father cared only for his sons. He treated me worse than a dog, forcing me to crawl beneath the table waiting for scraps from his meal, locking me in the dark for days at a time, beating me till I bled . . . beating me, and worse . . .' She choked on the words, the memories burning her mind. 'I am glad the Nepotes murdered him.' She spat into the pile of fish guts. 'But the Verini live on. My uncle, Karas, is worse by far than even my father. He too is ruled by his lust for power, a hunger that will make men do aught to gain what they want.'

'But you are not like the rest of your kin,' Leo murmured. 'I see kindness in you. You pleaded for my life. You have even tried to help the Nepotes this night.'

'We do not have to be ruled by our blood, or by days long gone,' Ariadne said, passion igniting in her voice. 'I can see that clearly now.' Her thoughts flew back to when she crept through the catacombs and discovered the cell where her father had imprisoned Meghigda. 'My eyes were opened by a woman . . . a wanderer from Afrique, a queen, a warrior—'

'A warrior?' Leo's brow furrowed. 'A woman?'

'Yes! She was filled with fire and fury, and filled with hope too. She led her people in battle, and cared for them as a mother, and taught them that they should never bow their heads to any man. They called her al-Kahina, slayer of devils.' Her voice hardened, her eyes flashed. 'And now that she is dead, I am al-Kahina, and all that she believed lives on in me. You must trust me.' She closed her eyes, feeling herself become the woman who had showed her a light in this miserable life. 'We will survive this night.' She heard her voice echo as if from the depths of a well, the voice of another. It was as if she were standing in the dark at the back of her head, observing herself. 'Falkon's men are dogs who smell blood, and like dogs they can be easily deceived. We will let the shadows of the city cloak us. We will move through it like ghosts. And if they dare confront us, they will know our wrath.' She felt the blood pulse in her temple. Fire swept through her, the fire of al-Kahina.

Leo let these words settle on him, giving no sign that he believed them. 'And what of this strange man who follows you everywhere?'

Ariadne opened her eyes. For a moment, the fire dampened. 'Salih ibn Ziyad is a great man, a wise man, and he has a heart bigger than a lion. He teaches me everything that he taught al-Kahina, so I can grow to be like her—'

'A good story, little mouse. But now you are dead.' The shadow loomed over them both and Ariadne jerked in shock. One of Falkon's rogues leered down at them. He must have chanced upon them while searching the alley.

The short-bladed knife leapt into her fingers and she rammed it upwards without a moment's thought, under the chin of the rogue and into his throat. Twisting the weapon as Salih had taught her, she ripped it to one side. Hot blood gushed down on her. As the man staggered back, gurgling, Ariadne fell upon him like a wolf. He tumbled back on to the heap of fish guts, and she crashed down on him, plunging the knife over and over again into his chest, lost to the frenzy, seeing only her father's face.

When the fury finally ebbed, she swayed back. Trembling, she wiped the back of her hand across her mouth. Leo was gaping at her, in horror or dismay, she could not tell. But there was no longer time to talk. In the growing light, two silhouettes lurched into the end of the alley and a cry of alarm rang out.

'Come,' she said, wrenching Leo to his feet. 'There is a place near here where we can hide. But we must be quick.'

Through the shadows they weaved, with the shouts of pursuit echoing at their backs. Ariadne gritted her teeth. For years, she had been like a rat fleeing the light, unnoticed by all. She knew Constantinople better than anyone: the alleys, the drains, the empty houses, the filthy holes where no one ventured, the secret places. Clambering over a midden, she dragged Leo to a door in a mildew-streaked wall. Inside it was dark and reeked of piss and sweat.

'Where are we?' the boy whispered.

'The place where my father stored the wares he looted from those who fell before him.' She fumbled by the door until she found a candle and a flint. Once the flame leapt up, Leo gasped. Across the mud floor, a multitude of children lay under blankets of rags. Most of them were girls. Some still slumbered, but others stirred, pushing themselves up to stare with sleepy eyes. The pale faces were streaked with dirt, the cheeks hollow from hunger. Ariadne felt her heart ache. It was the same every time she ventured here.

'They have no homes, no kin,' she said, swallowing. 'They had been beaten, raped, left to die, but I brought them here, gave them shelter, and what food I could steal. Now they have some hope, thin though it may be. And together they will help each other survive.'

'Al-Kahina,' one of the girls near the front murmured, her eyes welling with tears of gratitude. She lowered her head in respect.

A figure loomed at Ariadne's shoulder and she whirled, the knife flying to her fingers once more. Only at the last did she catch herself. It was Rowena, her features shifting from worry to annoyance.

'I knew I would find you here,' she snapped.

'How?' Ariadne exclaimed, incredulous. This place had been her secret and hers alone.

'I have followed you here time and again. You think only Salih watches over you?'

The girl felt shocked that anyone would care enough to be her guardian. 'You should not be here. It is too dangerous.'

Rowena laughed bitterly. 'Once I was like you. Filled with so much anger at the hardships the world had thrown at me. I cared so little for my own life, I risked it all for vengeance.' In the candlelight, her eyes gleamed and Ariadne thought how haunted they looked. She had never seen this side of the woman in the time they had spent together in the house of Anna Dalassene. Rowena had always seemed distant, even cold. 'The price I paid was high,' the woman continued. 'I would not see you suffer so. You are just a girl. Do not throw away what joy awaits you.'

'I will come and go as I please,' Ariadne said, her voice growing flinty.

Rowena hardened. 'You do not realize the danger—'

'Nor do you,' the girl snapped. 'Falkon Cephalas has more spies abroad than we all feared. And tonight we learned how far he plans to go. Those he accuses will be executed, swiftly, their bodies hanged in the public places. And thus his message will be made clear to everyone in this city.'

'The emperor will never allow it.'

'He will look the other way as long as Falkon ends the plots that have besieged the throne for so long. He is coming for all of us now, anyone who has spoken out, anyone he decides is a traitor. If I were just a girl, we would never have been forewarned—'

The door thundered open. The candle guttered and went out. There was enough thin light outside to see that three of Falkon's men had forced their way in. Once the rogues saw that they had found what they were looking for, they drew their swords. Ariadne stiffened. She could see from their faces that no one would be allowed to leave this place alive.

'Why did you come here, Rowena?' Gripping her knife, Ariadne readied herself to fight to the last. 'You will die now, and all because of me—'

'No one dies here unless I command it.' The voice rang out of the dark.

Ariadne felt her heart swell, even as the first rogue fell with blood gushing from his neck. The second cut-throat wrenched around, flailing, but the assailant was invisible in the shadows, his blade too swift. In an instant, all the soldiers lay dead in their own life-blood.

Salih ibn Ziyad stepped into the shaft of wan light breaking through the doorway. Ariadne watched his glittering eyes fall upon Leo and feared what was to come. But then he looked at Rowena as if he had seen nothing at all. 'Rest easy. No harm will come to this girl while I yet live.'

Ariadne felt a rush of warmth. Her teacher, her friend, always there, always protecting her. She had been in darkness so long, but now she was blessed.

'There is more to you than meets the eye, Salih ibn Ziyad,' Rowena replied, relief edging her words.

'For too long we have been lambs,' Salih said, looking from one face to the other. 'We thought if we hid away, the wolf would never find us. But now we know he will never relent until he hunts us down. It is time to put aside our differences and find our own teeth.'

# Chapter Twenty-Six

Across the plain where a wall of dust marched, thunder rolled. But this was a storm of horses and steel. The ground throbbed as Roussel de Bailleul's army raced towards where the lines of Athanatoi waited. Their silvery armour glowed like embers in the ruddy light. Reflected barbs glinted off their helmets, but not from their weapons. Swords were sheathed, lances resting in their hoods.

The hot wind was rising. The air reeked of fire and iron. The world trembled.

On his horse, Guthrinc shielded his eyes against the glare of the dawn and watched the force loom out of the misty distance. So many of them, he thought, but still not the numbers of which they had been warned. Tiberius had been right. If the Immortals wished to take a stand, they might yet carve out a victory, though it would be a bloody one, with many losses.

But that was not the plan.

Beside him, Mad Hengist began to laugh as if he had seen the most wondrous sight. ''Pon the wings of angels we will be carried away,' he gasped, and laughed some more.

Beyond him, Tiberius leaned along the neck of his horse and watched the cloud of dust eat its way across the plain. Now the time had come, the unease that had knotted his features had ebbed away. He was calm, ready.

'You English are good warriors. You have earned your place at the front of this line,' he said to Guthrinc. 'I know you think most of my men are too raw for battle. Many have not yet been hardened by seeing a friend cut down, or feeling a sharp blade rip through their flesh. And you would be right. But they will learn.' He glanced over at the English, no doubt seeing the nicks in their hauberks, the dents in their helmets, their greasy fur and tortured leather, the scars of too many bloody campaigns. And then he looked along the lines of his own men in their pristine armour, nary a scratch to be seen. 'No, they are not yet good fighters,' he continued, 'but they are good horsemen. Can you say the same? For that is the skill you will need if you wish to see the sun set.'

'We will give a good account of ourselves.' Guthrinc forced a smile, but if he dared admit it to himself, he had his doubts. He had seen seven summers when he rode his first horse, but it had been a lumbering old beast, useful for pulling his father's cart to market and little else. Only the wealthiest had been able to afford a horse in his village, but if truth be told there had been little use for them in the sodden fens. Oxen pulled ploughs. Legs were better for clambering past the watercourses and skirting the sucking bogs. No, his spear-brothers had only been forced to learn to ride when they had clawed their way into the Roman army, and it had been as if they were careering down a steep hill towards a lake of swords. 'You will be watching our hooves disappearing over the horizon,' he said with a confident nod.

Mocking laughter rumbled out. Isaac Balsamon, the Boar, jabbed a finger towards the English. 'I would make a wager if I thought there would be someone left to pay the dues.'

'Make the wager.' Derman the Ghost's voice was barely a whisper, almost lost beneath the pounding of approaching hooves. His face impassive, he sat upright upon his horse, his coal-dark eyes fixed on the wall of dust. 'I will return to pick the coin from your pouch once the birds have picked the flesh from your bones.'

'Silence,' Tiberius commanded. 'In camp you may be rivals. Here on the field of battle you are brothers.'

Chastened, the Boar looked away. Derman nodded his agreement.

Roussel de Bailleul's army thundered closer still.

Tiberius stiffened. The moment had almost come. 'They will have seen the sun upon our armour. They know that we are outnumbered. The battle-lust is upon them. Their blood will be up, the fires in their bellies burning hot. Reason has fled and they will not think to slow, or stop.' Drawing himself up, he raised his right hand and boomed, 'Upon my order.'

Along the shimmering lines, heads turned towards him.

For a moment, Tiberius waited, until he was sure the distance between the two armies was just right. His arm snapped down and he bellowed, 'Ride!'

Guthrinc felt as if the world around him heaved into life with one great shrug. The air boomed with the sound of a multitude of hooves pounding as one, the clank of armour and the roar of full-throated battle-cries. He lurched forward. His eyes stung as grime billowed up. The din filled his head, driving all thought away. Ahead, the line of dust swept closer, and now he could see the dark shapes at the heart of it.

An age seemed to pass as the Immortals thundered towards near-certain doom. But then the riders on the right flank began to turn in a great, slow arc. Along the lines, the turn flowed in perfect timing. The Roman army began to change direction. Guthrinc waited, his knees gripping the powerful beast beneath him. He glimpsed Derman begin his turn, and then Hengist, and then he urged his steed to join the martial dance.

The Immortals turned, and turned. A vast cloud of dust swallowed them. Choking on the grit, Guthrinc screwed his watering eyes shut tight. His head spun from the deafening pounding, and the sensation of being swept along by a mighty river swelled by spring floodwater.

His thoughts whirled back to the long conversations around the campfire. 'They will think us afrit. They will want to ride on, and on, desperate to bring down the cowards and put them to the sword. But we will be fresh, our mounts rested, and they will already have had a long ride from Amaseia. And so we will lure them on, far away from their fortress. Draw them out into the vast plain, to the edge of the forests, until their mounts are so weary it will take them an age to return to their home.'

*And in that time, Hereward will lead his war-band away from Roussel's palace, with the Caesar in one hand and a chest filled with gold in the other.*

Guthrinc grinned. If God was smiling on them, they would snatch victory from what had seemed like certain defeat.

Opening his eyes, he blinked away the sweat. Now there was only the riding, as far and fast as they could manage.

Though his muscles ached from gripping on for dear life, he snatched a glance to one side. His spear-brothers all seemed to be commanding their steeds well. No man had fallen behind. The dust trailed behind them, and now there was only the clear plain ahead, sweltering under an arc of blue, and the black line of the forests in the distance.

And yet, as he stared ahead, he felt unease creep over him. On the edge of his vision, beyond the left flank, he sensed movement. Another long line of dust was starting to swell. Telling himself it was nothing, he fought to keep his attention on the ground sweeping beneath his horse's hooves. But he felt his gaze drawn back as if he had a hook in his skin.

The dust cloud was sweeping towards them. Beside him, he glimpsed Tiberius' head jerking round. The commander had noticed it too. As Guthrinc watched the Roman's face drain of blood, he knew what they were seeing. The scout had not lied. Roussel de Bailleul's army was as large as they had feared, but it had been divided into two forces, for some reason he could not divine. And now they were caught between the pincers.

Tiberius roared his command until his throat was raw,

but under the drumming of the hooves the words barely reached even Guthrinc's ears. The Immortals rode on, oblivious.

By the time the ranks of Athanatoi had realized what was happening, it was too late, Guthrinc could see. The riders on the left flank tried to steer their mounts away from the approaching army, but they were too slow. Even if they had succeeded, they had lost the advantage.

With hope of escape draining away, Tiberius wrenched out his sword and stabbed it aloft. Guthrinc saw the act repeated along the lines. A battle-cry rang out, filled with defiance. There was no choice but to fight, they all knew that. And they all knew that death was close. But these were not cowards as he had feared. They would look their fate in the eye and go down fighting.

Guthrinc turned to the English on his left and bellowed, 'Brothers! Fight as you never have before!'

His call jumped from lips to lips. Eyes filled with sparks. Axes leapt to hands.

The only hope, if hope it was, was to cut a swathe through the approaching army before the warriors at their backs fell upon them like wolves. As Tiberius leaned low, thrashing his horse on to even greater speed, Guthrinc could see this was the plan in the commander's mind.

Soon the Normans and Roussel's axes-for-hire were visible in the swirling dust, row upon row of some of the fiercest fighting men in this part of the world. But Guthrinc silently vowed not to be disheartened. He had stared into the faces of William the Bastard's men while Ely burned around him – he, a simple farmer – and he had lived to tell the tale. Bowing his head, he urged his horse to keep pace with Tiberius.

When the two sides came together, it was like the waves of two great oceans crashing against each other. The air boomed. Hooves pounded like hammers on an anvil and the whinnies of rearing, terrified horses rose like screams. Steel smashed against steel. Sparks flew. Shields splintered. Throat-tearing cries ripped out.

Guthrinc felt his senses reel from the tumult. The ordered lines collapsed in an instant and chaos swirled on every side. There was no sky, only clouds of dust, hacking swords and bristling lances. No ground, only a turbulent sea of horses and men.

The world closed in. Guthrinc glimpsed only flashes as the battle heaved around him. His mouth a rictus, Tiberius stabbed his sword into the face of a shaven-headed Norman. Hengist slashed around him with his axe, his lips pulled back from his teeth in a bestial snarl, no doubt seeing the Normans who had slaughtered his kin back in England and driven him mad.

Guthrinc felt a bolt of pain in his thigh as a charger slammed into his mount sideways on and his leg was pinned. Wrenching round, he looked straight into the face of a warrior driven half mad by his battle-lust. Mouth wide open, he was laughing as he thrust his sword. Somehow Guthrinc swivelled and the edge of the blade sliced across his upper arm instead of plunging into his heart.

Pain seared into his shoulder, but it was enough to drive the confusion from his head. He would have preferred to be using a bow – that was his weapon, mastered by hunting wildfowl in the rain-soaked fens – but he was a big man, stronger than anyone he knew, and when he used his axe it counted.

His arm came down in a blur. The blade smashed through the Norman's skull and down deeper still, almost to the centre of his chest. Guthrinc wrenched it out, spraying grey matter and blood.

Gentle Guthrinc, they had called him back in his village, and he hated what these wars had made of him. But as he looked round, he saw that his savagery had served his purpose. The Normans urged their horses towards easier victims, giving him a wide berth.

As a space opened up around him, his breath caught in his throat. The Immortals were being slaughtered like oxen for the king's feast. Before his eyes they fell one by one, their clumsy sword skills no match for Norman warriors who had lived for battle since they were children.

The ground had become a bloody marsh, miring the horses in the bog. Eyes wide with terror, they frothed at the mouth as they tried to drag themselves free. Roman bodies, or what remained of them, lay crushed face down into the mud.

One steed galloped by in front of him, its headless rider lolling upon its back. It ranged back and forth, directionless. In that terrible sight was the sum total of the fate of the Athanatoi.

Craning his neck back, Guthrinc peered through the churning mass of bodies. The other half of Roussel's army was bearing down upon them. Once they arrived no man stood a chance of surviving this massacre. Hengist saw it too, and in that moment all madness fled his face. The bleak sanity that settled upon him was somehow even worse.

Guthrinc felt clarity descend as the mad din of battle ebbed away. In the silence in his head, he turned this way and that until he caught sight of Tiberius. The Roman commander's pristine armour was now clotted with gore.

Urging his horse forward, Guthrinc clutched for Tiberius' arm. Spittle flew from the Roman's mouth as he whirled, his axe swinging up. But the battle-madness cleared enough for him to recognize his ally.

'If we fight on, we die,' Guthrinc bellowed above the clamour. 'Give the order to flee.'

'My men will not obey me,' Tiberius said, his face streaked red. Tears of desperation flecked his eyes. 'I will doom them if we go.'

'They are already doomed.'

Tiberius looked around and saw the truth. Despair crumpled his features. But for all his faults he was a good leader, Guthrinc saw, one who was prepared to shoulder the guilt for the sacrifice that was to come. 'Ride!' he roared. 'Ride! Follow my lead!'

His command sped through the ranks closest to him. Digging his heels into his mount's flanks, Tiberius rode hard through a narrow space. His sword whipped right and left to force a wider way. Raising his arm, Guthrinc snapped it forward, and as one the English swept into the Roman's wake.

Like a knife, the remnants of the Immortals carved through the milling mass of Roussel's force. With each spear-length that passed beneath the horses' hooves, more of the Athanatoi followed.

Guthrinc hacked at any Norman who dared come close. But their enemies had easier prey, and they turned their attention to picking off any of the Romans who were floundering.

For a moment, a wall of warriors blocked the way ahead, making the path seem impenetrable. Guthrinc felt a pang of anguish that their last gasp had died on their lips.

But Tiberius drove on with the Immortals close behind him, and the barrier parted. The last resistance flowed away and then all that remained of Constantinople's hope flooded out into the wide, open plain. Guthrinc sensed the palpable relief of the blood-spattered men riding beside him, but the feeling was tempered by despair. At their backs, the screams of the dying rang up to the heavens. Guthrinc felt sick to the pit of his stomach when he thought of the true meaning of the Athanatoi name: the ones who are without death. That battlefield had now become the graveyard of their arrogance.

The Immortals rode on. No one looked back.

# Chapter Twenty-Seven

The carrion birds swirled in a black cloud. Their shadows roiled over a red field, baking under the cruel sun. In the centre a ragged banner of a double-headed eagle fluttered, the blood-spattered standard of the Immortals. Among a jumble of torn bodies, its pole listed, wavering. It had been rammed into the corpse of the warrior who had no doubt carried it, the victors' mockery of the promise it held. Reeking of iron and rot, the wind lashed across that desolate plain to the four men who stood on the high ground, taking in the haunting scene of loss.

'Why did they not flee?' Alexios breathed. 'There was no need to stand and fight.' The young warrior's drawn face was too pale. Anyone who looked at him would think he had aged ten years or more in the time since he had left Constantinople.

Hereward narrowed his eyes, knowing there was no hope of recognizing any of his friends who might be lying among the fallen, searching none the less. He would not give in to despair. His spear-brothers had survived many a desperate battle in bygone days. 'All that matters now is that the Athanatoi are not coming back for us,' he said. 'We are on our own.'

Maximos watched the birds feast. 'We can as easily make our way back to Constantinople on our own.'

'But not the way we came. Roussel's army may well be

hunting survivors. We would not want to ride straight into the middle of them.'

'South, then, and cut to the west along the road from Iconic. But the Turks have driven deep into that part of the empire. Their war-bands roam wherever they choose, looting from any village they come across.'

Hereward strode back to where they had tied their horses. The beasts needed watering and resting; they had been ridden hard from Amaseia. He rested one hand on the coffer strapped to his mount's rear with the rope they had taken from one of the villages on the way. If his men had survived, all this would have been worthwhile.

'Maximos speaks true.' Alexios stepped past him and stroked the flank of his own horse. Though his wit was still as sharp as a knife – no man in the Athanatoi was sharper, Hereward thought – the young man's humour had been dulled in recent days. His worries seemed to be weighing heavily on him. 'The emperor is too weak, too distracted by his own selfish needs,' he continued. 'Every day that passes while he is on the throne is another betrayal of all Romans.'

'And you think you could do better?'

'It is not something I desire.'

Hereward laughed without humour. 'I cannot walk a street in Constantinople without stumbling over someone or other who thinks he deserves the crown.' He glanced towards Maximos. The Roman was watching them both like a hawk while Zeno continued to scan the battlefield. 'There is no love lost between you and Maximos.'

Alexios shrugged. 'He thinks highly of himself, and less so of me. But I do not know him. I know his kin. How they fell on hard times when the Verini gained the upper hand in the rivalry that had consumed them for years. I am told that since Victor Verinus' death, the Nepotes are once more rising up.' He looked up to the clear blue sky where the ravens still swooped, shrieking. 'I think Maximos now sees me as a rival, perhaps everyone. There are some who want, and some who want too much.'

'Hold.' Zeno's voice rang out. When Hereward whirled, he saw the Roman pointing back along the trail edging the plain. The two men raced to his side. 'We are not alone.'

A dust cloud billowed and the sound of drumming floated through the hot air. Men on horseback were approaching, around ten, Hereward guessed from the sound, and they were riding hard. Squinting, the Mercian watched their dark shapes emerge in the hazy distance. Warriors, there was no doubt of it.

'Roussel de Bailleul must want us dead badly if he has sent a war-band on our tail,' Maximos mused as the four men turned back to their weary mounts. 'And all for a few burned tapestries.'

Hereward frowned. 'There is more to it than that, I am sure.' He remembered the hate in Drogo's face when their eyes locked at the palace. If any man would track them down across the long miles, it was Drogo, he was sure of it.

'Roussel wants his gold back,' Zeno said. 'Toss it aside, here, where they will find it, and they will leave us alone.'

'Never,' Hereward insisted. He would not sacrifice his spear-brothers' hopes, not after all they had endured.

Eyes blazing, Zeno gripped his arm. 'Are you mad? You would throw us all to the wolves over a little gold?'

Hereward hurled off the other man's arm. 'Ride on, if you must. I will not hold you back.'

'We will not abandon a brother,' Alexios said, adding in a hesitant voice, 'but our horses are weary and the weight of the gold will slow us . . .'

Hereward leapt on to his mount's back, his eyes flickering towards the nearing dust-cloud. 'They have a scout, a good one. Someone who can track four men across the land with ease. All we have to do is hide our trail.'

'Easier said than done,' Zeno snapped. He clambered on to his own horse, simmering at being rebuffed.

'Then it is decided,' Maximos said with a laugh. 'God knows, I love gold as much as any man, and if I had the chance to take a little joy from all this misery I would seize it with both hands.' Narrowing his eyes, he looked towards the south. 'Our horses are drained. We cannot outride these Normans. But we can use our wits. The land ahead is wild. Thick, untamed forests. Rivers and streams where we can ride along the bed and hide our tracks. Not even the greatest scout on earth can follow us through there.'

Zeno spat. 'And there are also Turkish war-bands roaming everywhere. Once they smell gold, we will have packs of wolves bearing down on us from all sides.' He looked around the three faces and saw there was no deterring them. With a curse, he urged his horse down the slope from the ridge towards the forest that reached out as far as the eye could see.

Maximos grinned as if this were the greatest adventure he could imagine. He followed Zeno, riding as hard as he could. While Alexios set off, Hereward glanced back towards their pursuers. He could feel his devil starting to whisper deep in his head. He would not abandon the gold for which he had fought so hard; he would not be defeated again. God help any man who tried to stand in his way.

# Chapter Twenty-Eight

The bodies shifted in the breeze blowing through the lonely forum. The ropes at their necks groaned with each swing; the wood of the gibbet creaked. Four men there were, two nobles and two merchants, and a woman. The sixth was little more than a child. The crows had already feasted, and soon, as the grey light of dawn gave way to rose and blue, they would feast some more.

Wulfrun eyed that final, tiny frame and felt a pang of cold deep in his heart. Could a boy truly have been any threat to an emperor? But Falkon Cephalas cared little for such details. He knew that any men or women who passed through the forum would see their own faces on those rotting remains. And they would hold their tongues when they felt like complaining about the one who ruled them, and they would not let their growling bellies drive them to fight over the price of grain in the market. These six were only the latest. Bodies hung everywhere in the city, ripe fruit reeking of decay. And there would be more, many more, in the days to come, Wulfrun had no doubt.

Constantinople had not known such peace in his lifetime. No whispers of plots reached his ears. No grumbles about uprisings.

But at what cost.

At that hour, the forum was deserted. Through the eyelets of his helm, he searched the side streets and the doorways for any sign of Falkon's dogs. Those cut-throats pretending to be soldiers were everywhere these days. Nothing seemed to pass their notice.

Once he was sure he was not being observed, he whistled, long and low. After a moment, he spotted movement in one of the streets leading on to the forum. A hooded figure stood in the half-light, beckoning to him with a slender hand.

Wulfrun strode over. As he neared, he felt his heart lift when he glimpsed Juliana's pale face in the depths of the hood. Anger twisted his features for a moment, and he felt a hot rush of hatred for Falkon Cephalas. Too many days had passed since he had last seen the woman he loved, but he could not risk being seen entering the house of the Nepotes.

'Is it true?' she hissed once they had stepped deep into the shadows where no one would notice them.

Wulfrun felt shocked at how the brightness seemed to have drained from her. Her face was filled with sadness. Removing his helmet, he softened his face and his voice. 'Take your mother and father and Leo and leave your house the moment you return.'

'Then Falkon Cephalas suspects the Nepotes.' Juliana's eyes widened in fear as the future unfolded before her. 'Who would have pointed the finger of blame at us?' Her face hardened and she bared her teeth. 'Who would have dared?'

'Folk lie to save their own necks.'

Juliana blinked away hot tears. 'There is no fairness in this. Our plan unfolds. All is within our grasp—' She caught herself when she realized whom she was with. They would continue with their dance – he pretending he did not know of the Nepotes' treachery, she pretending he thought only good of them. The lies had become so great he could barely shoulder them. But he loved her, and he lusted after her, and that stew of fierce emotions had swallowed any sense he might have had.

'Hurry now,' he urged. 'Leave the city with only what you

can easily carry. Falkon will have no reason to pursue you once you are away from Constantinople, and I will send word when it is safe for you to return.'

Juliana's eyes flashed. 'If the chance presents itself, kill him,' she snarled.

Wulfrun all but recoiled. He had never seen such savagery in her before. 'Go,' he said.

Putting on a smile for his sake, Juliana leaned in to kiss him upon the cheek. But as her lips brushed his skin, he felt her stiffen. 'Oh,' she breathed.

Ten of Falkon's brown-cloaked men were racing across the forum, swords drawn. Wulfrun knew then that this could only have been a trap. Falkon must have planted the seeds to ensnare not only the Nepotes, but also an enemy at the heart of the emperor's court. Wulfrun of the Varangian Guard. Wulfrun the traitor.

'Run,' he yelled. 'I will hold them off.'

'There are too many,' Juliana cried as she edged away. 'You cannot defeat them. Come with me.' She reached out to grab his hand, but he turned his back on her.

The commander sized up the force sweeping towards him, with the rising sun glinting off their helms and the bosses of their shields. Juliana was right: there were too many and they were too fast for both of them to escape. He was strong, but Juliana would have no chance. He knew what he must do.

He looked just once in her eyes, peeling back the layers of deception in search of the honest love that he had always hoped was there. It was a child's wish, he knew, but he had lied to himself too much to back away from the truth this time. Silently, she begged for him to go with her. But he only spun back to his foes and slipped his helm on. He heard her footsteps race off.

Wulfrun felt cold blood chase his feelings away. This was what he needed to be now – a savage warrior of the Varangian Guard, who cut down all enemies in his path, a man who would give up his own life for the oath he had sworn.

When the first soldiers reached him, he glimpsed the fear in their eyes and felt good. The long-handled Dane-axe felt like an old friend in his hands. In a full arc, he swung the weapon. The impact jolted up his arms. But the blade was sharp, and it sliced through meat and bone as if through water.

The first head lolled forward on a strip of skin and sinew.

For a moment, his opponents hesitated. These were not true soldiers, forged in the heat of war. Their battlefields were night-cloaked streets, filthy alleys and desolate cemeteries, their choice of attack a quick stab with a short-bladed knife or a rip across a bared throat.

Wulfrun hooked another, ripping out the man's side in a gush of blood.

He whirled his blade with all the skill he had learned over the years, but his thoughts were flying with Juliana, racing to safety and the promise of days yet to come. He prayed he would see her again, but knew in his heart he would not.

His enemies began to order themselves better as they remembered they had the advantage of numbers. From every side they came at him, swords thrusting. Wulfrun felt barbs of pain and heard his own blood spattering. Two more fell before they wrestled his axe from his grip. And then the blows were raining down upon him and the silver sky spun overhead.

There had never been any hope that he could defeat them all. But he had bought Juliana's life, and that was enough.

Rough hands dragged him into the forum. Through his daze, he found himself looking into the smug face of Falkon Cephalas. The Roman was pleased that he had caught the fish he really wanted. 'Wulfrun of the English,' he said, 'you have betrayed not only your oath, but yourself. Like a virgin boy, you have sacrificed everything you had earned for the love of a whore who cared less about you than the earth beneath her feet.' Smiling, he swung his arm out to the bodies swaying on the gibbet. 'Now, feast your eyes upon your new home.'

# Chapter Twenty-Nine

*Windsor, England, 15 September 1073*

The double-edged sword trembled over the bared neck. In a tunic filthy with mildew smudges from the sprawling forest, the kneeling man mewled. Beside him, the carcass of a deer leaked blood, an arrow still protruding from its neck. A breeze swept through the treetops to the grassland at the foot of the hill, plucking up the bitter tang of the hunter's fear-sweat as his terror-filled eyes rolled up to the Norman nobles gathered in a circle around him. Though he tried to plead for his miserable life, his throat had closed and only splutters and gulps came out.

The warrior holding the sword looked towards the man who held this wretch's life in his palm. For now, King William gave no sign of his thoughts. He was a mountain of a man in his emerald tunic embroidered with gold leaves, broad of shoulder and heavy with muscle. The monarch showed power in every sinew, not just in the crown he had stolen. And that was how he kept his grip upon the throne – by exhibiting strength on a daily basis. He knew how folk saw him, nobles and commoners alike: as the Bastard he had been dubbed since his earliest days. He couldn't have cared less.

King William eyed the pathetic thief. His tunic was little more than rags, his arms were like straws, his cheekbones sharp beneath the skin. Starving, no doubt. Even so, the ceorl should have known better than to hunt the king's deer, and so close to the grand new castle soaring up on the bailey nearby. The thief could not claim ignorance. This had been a royal hunting ground for the old English monarchs since the days of the Romans, or so he had been told.

'What say you, my lord?' William de Warenne was a fighting man, lean, with a good length of bone. But these days the noble had a weak stomach for bloodshed. He would need to stiffen his resolve if he was to govern England. After so many years of struggle, the Bastard hated leaving this rain-soaked isle in the hands of another, but Normandy was beset by trouble on all sides and his leadership was required.

The king raised his eyes to an overcast sky the colour of steel, pretending to seek guidance from God himself. 'I am inclined towards mercy,' he murmured.

William de Warenne nodded, relieved. 'England is yours. The rebels have been cowed, angry voices stilled. Few complain, now, about aught but the hardships that burdened them before your grace arrived upon these shores. Now that peace has arrived, finally, the English look to you as a stern father who has dealt punishment and now offers the hand of kindness.'

The king choked down his contempt. William de Warenne always thought flattery was required. If he truly knew his liege, he would realize that obedience was the only thing that was necessary.

'You must feel that fortune has deserted you,' the Bastard said to the cowering man. 'To stumble across the king himself as you go about your crime, when I have been absent from this place for so long.' He clenched inwardly. Behind those words hid a deluge of misery. The invasion of Scotland and the crushing of Malcolm after that monarch had dared to try to conquer the north of England. Before the blood had even dried, his presence had been needed in Normandy to counter the invasion of Maine by the repulsive Fulk le Rechin, the Count of Anjou. He had hoped his swift campaign to seize le Mans would have been the end of it. But no. The new Count of Flanders was flexing his muscles, and Philip of France was determined to do all in his power to contain the Norman might.

Sometimes he wondered if this was his curse. To fight and fight but never reach satisfaction. As soon as one threat was destroyed, another rose up.

Pressing his hands together, he feigned a prayer. But from under his half-closed lids, he studied the faces of the nobles around him. They were Norman lords who had been well paid for their support in seized English land, and three visitors from the court of Bleddyn ap Cynfyn, King of Gwynedd, who had come in a show of respect when they had heard he was back on English soil. They still feared him, he could see that, even though silver had started to streak his hair and some of his girth had turned to fat. That was good.

The king jerked from his reflection at a loud hail. Looking back, he saw Richard fitz Gilbert striding down from the sturdy timber walls of the castle he had been constructing, on and off, these last three summers. A brother to the king in all but blood, the Norman noble was a tall man, strong where William de Warenne had grown weak. The king nodded. He had made the right decision. Richard would be a perfect counter-balance to William de Warenne as joint Chief Justiciar in the coming months.

The nobleman was not alone. Another man was stumbling to keep up on the steep, muddy slope from the castle's gate. From his tunic, he looked like a monk. He was squat, his spine twisted, his dark hair lank against his head.

When he had bowed to the king, Richard's eyes sparkled with mockery as he held out a hand towards the trembling monk. 'This is Centwine, a faithful servant of the Lord who spends his days in service at Crowland Abbey, to the east,' he said with ironic respect.

The king stifled his smile. 'I have heard of this abbey. The monks there are said to be the most devout in the land.'

''Tis true, my lord,' Centwine said, bowing his head almost to his waist. 'And we are faithful servants of our king. We offer prayers for you every day at Matins.'

'This *faithful servant* has journeyed alone from the east with a tale to tell,' Richard continued. 'One of some value, I would wager.'

The monarch heard the edge in the other man's voice. The business had grown serious. 'Speak,' he commanded.

'I . . . I come with news of Hereward of the English, who led the war against you from his fortress in Ely,' the monk stuttered, his eyes fixed firmly on the sodden grass.

William snorted with scorn. 'Hereward is long gone from these shores. By now, he is probably dead.' He felt surprised at how even the mention of the English dog's name still roused him to anger. Of all the men he had faced across the field of battle, Hereward was the only one who had come close to defeating him.

'Not . . . not Hereward as such, my lord,' Centwine burbled, 'but his son.'

The king stiffened. 'Hereward has a son?'

'My lord, when his wife Turfrida was slain, the child was placed in the care of the monks of Crowland Abbey. They were charged with nurturing him and guiding him as he grew to be a man.' The monk looked up, resolve hardening his face and his voice. 'Some of my brothers are still loyal to Hereward, and they treat this boy as if . . .' He all but choked on his words. 'As if he were sent by God himself. This is blasphemy!'

'Hereward's son has seen but three summers. For now, he is unknown beyond the abbey walls. But when he grows, the story of his birth will spread, as these stories are apt to do.' Richard locked eyes with the king, his look adding all that his words had not said. He was a wise man. He knew the threat this boy posed. The English were like children. They dreamed of heroes who would rise up and save them in their hour of need. Whatever William de Warenne said, the king knew that they still resented the fact that their land had been taken from them. They resented the Norman rule. They resented him. The boy would be a rallying point for those who secretly harboured desires to challenge their conqueror. Perhaps, in time, he would grow to lead a new rebellion, one that all the people could stand behind.

The king smiled, resting one hand upon the monk's head. 'You have served me well, good Centwine. This news has captured my interest. Your abbey will receive the full weight of the king's gratitude. Your brothers will know a time of plenty.' As the monk fawned and scraped, the monarch wiped his hand on his tunic and looked to Richard. 'An abbey is no place to raise a boy. Find him.'

Fitz Gilbert nodded. He knew his king's mind well enough. The boy would not see a fourth summer.

The king turned back to the circle of nobles, his gaze falling upon the forgotten thief, and then the warrior who still held his sword above the man's neck. William the Bastard waved a dismissive hand. 'Take his head.'

# Chapter Thirty

Flames flickered in the vast gulf of night. Like the spirit-lights that the doomed see wandering along the ghost-paths on All Hallows' Eve, the points of illumination floated through the gloom, winking out then reappearing as they passed behind trees. No sound floated through the vast forest, no hoot of owl nor rustle of leaf. Under the dense canopy the air was still, and oven-hot.

Hereward lay flat on his belly, his fingers dug deep into the leaf-mould as if he were gripping on to the world for dear life. Sweat slicked his brow and soaked through his tunic. He blinked away the stinging droplets, watching that trail of torches for any sign that they were changing direction. If they moved towards where Hereward and the others lay hidden in the undergrowth, there would be no more running. The Turkish war-band would have picked up their trail and would fall upon them in no time.

Behind his eyes, his devil called to him, cajoling, mocking, urging. He imagined creeping behind those prowling Turks, ghosting from the dark to trace his knife across a throat, then disappearing back into the shadows before his victim had even gurgled his last. Whittling them down, one by one. But he knew it was a futile dream.

The Turks swarmed over these parts like ants, moving closer to Constantinople by the day. When this war-band was destroyed there would be another to take its place, and another, and another, and if they found their brothers slaughtered it would only drive them to wilder excesses. Then there truly would be no escape.

The torchlight bobbed along like summer fireflies for a little longer before juddering to a halt. Hereward's fingers closed around Brainbiter. For an interminable moment, his breath burned in his chest. Just as he had convinced himself that the Turks had decided to rush their hiding place, the flames jerked to life once more and continued on their way.

Sighing, he rested his cheek on the dirt. Exhaustion tugged at his limbs. It seemed an age since he had slept. In the dark, his thoughts swept back across the long miles and the four days since they had left the ridge with Drogo Vavasour close on their trail. Through the grasslands they had ridden and deep into the forest, where the way was harder. Their pace naturally slowed in that trackless, gloomy world, but they knew it would slow their pursuers too. Soon they had found the babbling stream they had been searching for, and led their mounts along it till they found the river that carved through the forest's heart, as Maximos had promised.

Splashing through the cool shallows, they had reached a bend where the river widened and became slow-moving enough to cross. Waist deep, they had waded to the other side, and continued along the shallows before finding another spot where they could cross back.

As they had trudged on, heading south, they had laughed together, sure now that no scout could ever follow them. But that night Zeno had woken them from their sleep. On his watch he had heard the distant whinny of a horse. Creeping along the water's edge, he had come across the Normans, closer than they could ever have imagined. The warriors had no choice but to flee through the dark, risking the chance that one of their horses would break a leg on the uneven ground.

Over the next three days, they had covered their tracks with branches and leaves, had plunged again and again into the cold water, all to no effect. Drogo and his men were relentless, undeterred by any obstacle. They seemed never to rest. Zeno had started to wonder if they had some talisman that guided them – he could think of no other explanation. But Hereward knew it was only Vavasour's hatred pushing him beyond the limits of any ordinary man.

Weary, with their bellies growling, they had managed to catch a little fish along the way, which they had gnawed on, raw and slimy. And then they had been seen by the Turks.

Hereward ground his teeth. This journey had become more cursed by the day. They had been forced to flee faster, and further off their course, to save their necks as the Turkish war-band also pursued them, hungry for whatever wares they might be carrying. Only when night fell could they seize one slim chance to hide.

Craning his neck up, Hereward peered among the trees and saw the last of the torches fading away. Relief flooded him. At last God had smiled on them. It was a thin hope, but he would seize it with both hands. Dragging himself to his feet, he edged past the wall of blackthorn to where the other three men hid with the horses.

'Gone?' Maximos whispered.

Hereward nodded.

Closing his eyes, Alexios pushed back his head in a silent prayer of relief.

'Soon our luck will run out,' Zeno said, scowling. 'We do not need enemies. We are killing ourselves by degrees.' His long-repressed anger rising, he jabbed a finger at Hereward. 'He is killing us.'

'Hold,' Alexios said, laying a hand on the other man's arm. 'There can be no gain from fighting among ourselves.'

Shaking the younger man off, the Wolf stepped towards the Mercian. 'We have one slim chance to survive. Leave the gold for the Normans—'

'It will not deter them.'

'You think—'

'I know. Drogo Vavasour wants my head. Nothing less will satisfy him.'

Zeno bared his teeth. 'That can be arranged.'

'Hold,' Maximos cautioned, his eyes narrowing.

'I will not die because this one wants to be rich.'

Hereward flinched. The voice of his devil grew louder. Despite himself, he found his hand reaching towards the hilt of Brainbiter.

Zeno's gaze snapped towards the movement. 'Come, then. Let us have it.' He levelled his own blade at Hereward's chest.

'Enough,' Maximos commanded. He and Alexios thrust themselves between the two men. For a moment, the Wolf's blade wavered before he sheathed it. Half turning away, he flashed a murderous look at the Mercian. 'The gold must go.'

Together, Maximos and Alexios glanced back at the English warrior. Hereward could see in their eyes that they both felt the same. They were trusting that good sense would soon return to him. Neither of them understood why he risked all to take that gold back to Constantinople.

'The gold stays,' he growled, walking away. He answered to no man.

In brooding silence, they led their horses through the sweltering forest. Sometimes they would glance back and see their enemies bearing down on them, but it was only a trick of the light. Sometimes they heard the whinny of a horse, and a whistled call and response. It was impossible to tell if the sounds were a day's ride or only moments away.

There was no rest, no easing of worry. They snatched sleep when they could, usually sagging on the backs of their mounts as they trundled along animal tracks between the trees. They hungered and sweated, pausing only to scoop handfuls of water from the streams they crossed.

'Why will they not give up?' Alexios muttered at regular intervals, as if he were murmuring an incantation.

Finally, two days after they evaded the Turkish war-band, they saw the sun again. Emerging from the treeline, they looked out across rolling grassland, studded with copses and rocky escarpments.

Looking up to the sky, Maximos closed his eyes and enjoyed the warmth on his face. 'We have come far south,' he said. 'We should start to head towards the west.'

Zeno spat a mouthful of phlegm. 'You think we will survive this open land?'

'Enough talk,' Hereward growled. 'Ride.' He urged his horse on, but he could feel it protesting beneath him. Sometimes it nearly stumbled. Every step seemed an effort. He felt sorry for the beast, but there was little he could do to help it.

Down a gentle incline they rode, the grass swaying like green waves. Glittering dragonflies whisked by. Hereward wiped the sweat from his brow. The sun was high, the heat suffocating. No breeze stirred the leaves in the copses that dotted the landscape. Looking back, the Mercian saw the lines they had made through the grass, stabbing like a sword towards them. He felt his unease grind up. 'Faster,' he urged. 'Faster.'

Grim-faced, the Romans dug their heels into their horses' flanks. The steady thrum of hooves became a drumming on the earth that matched the pulse of blood in Hereward's head. His neck prickled as a sense of dread descended upon him.

Barely had the dark mood settled when a cloud of shrieking birds swelled up from the edge of the forest. Wrenching round, Hereward saw four riders burst from the treeline and hurtle down the incline. Drogo had sent his men on different tracks to run the prey ragged, and then trap them between two groups. The others would be along soon enough.

The Romans saw their pursuers at the same time. As one, they urged their horses on to greater excesses. The world blurred.

Hereward leaned across the neck of his mount, feeling the wind tear at his hair. The Normans' beasts would be weary too. Everything now depended on outriding them, until they could find another location where they could attempt to lose their pursuers, or some high ground where they could take a stand if that was all that was left to them.

Slowly, the Romans began to pull ahead of him. Hereward dug his heels in, pressing his mount on, but its mouth foamed and its eyes were wide and white.

*Cut the coffer free*, he told himself. Yet even then he could not betray his spear-brothers.

He saw Alexios glance back, worried, and then fate snatched all choice away from him. His horse crashed down as if its legs had been hacked from under it. Hereward spun through the air and landed hard on the earth. When he pushed himself up through the swaying grass, he saw that his mount lay dead, its heart having finally given out as the last of its strength ebbed away.

Hereward could feel the hungry stares of Drogo's men upon him. Sensing blood, they thrashed their steeds towards him and thunder filled the air.

# Chapter Thirty-One

'Run to me!' Ahead, Alexios had brought his skittish horse up sharp and turned it round. Beckoning wildly, he yelled, 'I will carry you.'

In the moment that Hereward took to glance from the young Roman to the Normans bearing down on him, he reached a decision. His enemies' armour flashed in the blazing sun. Their double-edged swords glowed in their hands. And yet his devil called to him, deep in his head, the voice growing louder by the moment, matching the pulse of his blood in his temple.

Under the neck of his sweat-stained tunic, his fingers closed around the relic that Alric had given him that night in Constantinople. He felt God's power throb beneath their tips. From the moment they had met, his friend had fought hard for his salvation, had suffered and sacrificed, and he himself had struggled through years of fighting what lay inside him. Now Hereward knew he was damned, come what may, and only the beast that controlled him could save him.

With a yank, he tore the leather thong that held the relic over his head and tossed it away. He never saw it land in the long grass. His hand was already leaping to the hilt of Brainbiter.

'Go,' he yelled to Alexios. 'Leave me. This is my fight.'

He could feel the young Roman's incredulity. What kind of

madman turned his back upon rescue and looked death in the face?

The Normans were only three spear-lengths away now. Bounding to his fallen horse, the Mercian gripped his sword in his hand and stared down the enemies racing towards him. Already tasting victory, mouths flickered into smiles. Blades swung high. They could hack him to pieces or smash his bones beneath the trampling hooves of their steeds.

But from the moment he had been taught how to ride into battle, Hereward had studied these beasts. He knew they always leapt the obstacles in their path. When his foes were a spear-length away he dropped to the ground, tucked tightly behind the carcass of his mount. When the riders sailed overhead, he jabbed his blade up and ripped through the belly of the steed that passed above him.

Hot blood showered him. Blinded by the flood, he only heard the cries of the riders and the thunderous sound of the dying horse crashing into another. Both of them slammed to the ground.

Blinking away the gore, Hereward was up in an instant. As the world closed in, only the booming of his heart reverberated through his head. He was dimly aware of two riders bringing their mounts round, but his gaze fell upon the two men he had brought down. One squirmed on the ground, wrenching at his right leg, which was crushed beneath his dead steed. The other horse heaved itself up and began to canter away. Its rider staggered to his feet, dazed.

As the man's senses returned to him, he glanced around and saw Hereward stalking towards him, stained from head to toe in blood. This fierce vision of hell gripped him. Gaping, he reached for his empty sheath. When he saw the fallen blade lying in a circle of flattened grass, he hurled himself towards it. Too late. Hereward was upon him.

The booming in his head had grown louder still. The Mercian thrust Brainbiter into the warrior's side, and as the man went down he whisked his sword up and took the head. Without slowing, he plunged his blade into the chest of the trapped man.

The other two riders were circling. Now they had seen what had happened to their brothers, they were not about to take any risks. Through the haze, Hereward watched them make their calculations. Two of them, one of him. They had the advantage of horseback. Yet even so they were hesitant.

The Mercian grinned. 'Come,' he roared. 'Your days are ending.'

As the pounding of hooves rose up, their heads jerked round. Hereward followed their gaze. Alexios was riding hard towards them, his sword drawn. Maximos and Zeno followed behind him. Maximos was laughing, pleased that here was a problem his blade could solve.

Digging in their heels, the two Normans drove their horses back the way they had come. This was not a fight they could win.

Hereward sheathed Brainbiter and strode towards his fallen horse.

'Come,' Alexios insisted, knowing full well what the Mercian planned. 'Drogo Vavasour will be along soon enough with the rest of his men. We must be away.'

Ignoring him, Hereward pulled the coffer free from its strap. With a grunt, he heaved it on to his shoulder. When he turned back to the others, the young Roman was staring at him incredulously.

'You have already killed one horse,' Zeno snarled, scowling. 'Will you not rest until we are all at the mercy of our enemies?'

'Leave the gold,' Alexios said. 'You must see we will not live if we are weighted down.'

'Ride on,' Hereward said. 'I will walk.' He began to stride through the long grass, one arm crooked around the chest. His actions were as mad as the other men believed, but he would risk anything for his spear-brothers.

Maximos threw back his head and laughed even louder. 'You

and Hengist are of a kind,' he roared. 'Both moonstruck. Here, I will take the gold. You ride with the Little General.'

'Have you lost your wits too?' Zeno spat. 'When your horses both die under you, I will not look back.'

'You are a sour man, Wolf,' Maximos said. 'Our days are dark enough as it is, and the chance of us seeing another dawn over Constantinople is thin. Find a little joy in your heart.'

Snorting with contempt, Zeno urged his horse away.

Once Maximos had strapped the coffer to his mount, and Hereward had climbed behind Alexios, they rode after him towards the west.

'Maximos finds light where there is none,' Alexios said, his mood grim. 'That is his way. But Zeno speaks true. We cannot outride Drogo so burdened. You must see reason.'

'I will walk back to Constantinople alone, if need be. But the gold stays with me.'

Alexios cursed. 'This truly is madness. What man places gold above his own life? Do you hear me? If you try to take this gold back, you will die.'

'I am not afrit of death.'

Realizing there was no point in talking further, Alexios leaned forward in brooding silence. With two men upon its back, the horse could barely canter. Maximos' mount, too, struggled under its burden. Soon, Zeno was little more than a smudge in the hazy distance.

When the wind fell, they paused on a ridge above the grassland and looked back. Once again Hereward could hear the sound of hooves rumbling across the heat-seared landscape. He had hoped they would have been able to put more miles between them before Drogo picked up their trail. Glancing ahead, he saw the high land was wilder, with scrubby brush and jagged chunks of rock poking from the earth.

'Cappadocia,' Maximos said, surveying the landscape.

Cocking his head, Hereward thought he could hear water. A river.

'Set me down,' he said.

'I will not see you die,' Alexios replied.

'And I will not see you end your days. I have chosen this path for myself. It is not your burden.' Slipping to the ground, he took the chest from Maximos and set it back on his shoulder. 'I can pick a way through this land where horses will find it hard to follow,' he said. 'If you find the river, you may have another chance to hide your tracks.'

Maximos looked down at him, his dark eyes glinting. No humour softened his face. 'You have not eaten. You have not slept. This sun is a harsh mistress. She will suck the rest of the life from you before night falls.'

'Go,' Hereward said. He looked across the sun-drenched wastes, but in his mind's eye he only saw the English fenlands, sodden after the rains, and his spear-brothers marching away from their kin to follow him into battle. 'Go,' he murmured, lost to his memories. 'I must walk this road.'

Alexios was frowning as he scrutinized the Mercian. He sensed that this was about more than gold. But no more words would change things. Without another glance at his two companions, Hereward trudged down the slope and into the wild country.

When he glanced back, he saw the two riders silhouetted against the silver sky, still watching him. But then the wall of thorny brush closed behind him and he plunged down among huge outcroppings of rock into an empty land of stones and dust.

Nothing moved. The wind had dropped and the sun was fat and high. Suffocating waves of heat seemed to rise up from the rock to envelop him. Squinting into the shimmering middle distance, the Mercian eyed an arduous route among the sharp brown rocks. He would find it slow going, he knew, and dangerous to negotiate, but not even the best horseman would find it easy to follow him.

His shadow marched ahead of him, growing shorter as each mile fell under his feet. Blood seeped from his torn palms and knees where he had clambered over the jagged rocks. Soon his hide was as dry as his throat. He had hoped to find the river, or one of the many streams that must feed it, but he had come across nothing to replenish his supply.

As the ground began to rise up again, he sheltered in the shadow of a boulder that was as big as a hall. Shielding his eyes against the glare, he glanced back over the waste. At first he could see only the strange formations and the black brush. But then he thought he made out dark figures picking a path towards him. He blinked, unsure. It could have been Drogo and his men, but he could no longer trust his own eyes. He felt near-delirious from the heat and the thirst and the exhaustion.

As he carried on, the coffer crushed down upon his shoulder, seemingly growing heavier by the moment. Yet he would not, could not, set it aside.

And the sun beat down.

Once his shadow moved behind him, he thought he saw figures emerging from the rocks on every side. His father, Asketil, was there, grey-haired and hunched in old age, but his hands still sticky with the blood of his wife, Hereward's mother. In the corner of his eye he glimpsed his brother Redwald, walking beside him, whispering how he had cut off the head of Turfrida, Hereward's wife.

And others, shades of days long gone, haunted memories of suffering and death and harbingers of miseries yet to come. However much he ran, he could never escape what had been. Like his devil, Death walked with him always.

'I will not abandon the gold!' he yelled, shaking his fist at the shadows. And on he trudged.

Twilight fell, but the heat barely seemed to ease. His exhausted limbs trembled, demanding rest. But he knew that if he lay down he would sleep too long, too deep, and then Drogo Vavasour would be upon him and the chest would be snatched from his grasp.

And then night came down hard, and though he squinted into the gloom he seemed to be wading through a black sea. Feeling his way, he edged up rising ground along what seemed to be a soaring cliff face. Once, twice, he crashed down to his knees, his legs scarcely able to carry his weight. After a moment's respite, he forced himself up and took another shaking step.

When he looked up at the few stars sprinkled overhead, he realized he could no longer remember where he was.

A moment later, he had crested yet another ridge. He could feel the ground falling away under his feet. The hard rock had given way to small stones that seemed to shift like water. Leaning back, he tried to dig his heels in to slow his progress, but the pebbles rushed away from him, and he felt himself dragged along with them.

Down he flew, and down, going faster and faster, until he was spinning head over heels. The coffer flew from his shoulder. In the scream of cascading stones, he heard it crash and splinter and he thought, *No! I cannot fail you!*

And then his head slammed against rock and he knew no more.

# Chapter Thirty-Two

This time his mother's face floated in front of him. She was holding out her hands, imploring him, but though she mouthed passionate words he could not hear them. In the deep dark, Hereward realized that when his mother was speaking was the only time he didn't hear the dim whispers of his devil.

He struck out from the depths, rising upward through the black waves. When he felt a gentle swaying, he thought he was being tossed around on the surface of that great dark ocean. But his fingers brushed across soft warmth and he heard a steady beat. Hooves. He breathed in the musk of the horse that carried him, thrown across its rear.

Hereward opened his eyes. Rocky ground was moving beneath him. The light was thin. Had dawn already come?

In the rush of his returning wits, he realized Drogo Vavasour must have captured him. Steeling himself, he felt the life slowly returning to his limbs. When finally he was ready, he hurled himself backwards. Crashing on to the rough ground, he rolled and launched himself into the deepening gloom.

Laughter rang out, accompanied by a familiar voice. 'A madman, I tell you!'

Whirling, Hereward saw the horse that had carried him belonged to Maximos. Alexios rode behind, his expression sullen.

Zeno was some way ahead, glancing back with contempt.

'We could not let you kill yourself,' the young Roman said.

'We found you with your skull all but bashed in,' Maximos added, leaning down, 'your lips as dry as the desert. A little water poured down your throat saved your life. You may thank me later.'

Hereward looked around. The landscape was still rocky, but he could see the dark outline of trees in the thin light. 'Where are we?'

'You slept for a day,' Maximos said. 'We feared you might never wake.'

Alexios slipped down from his horse. 'Your plan had some value. In the wild lands we lost Drogo Vavasour for a while—'

'But not long enough,' Zeno snapped. 'His men are now closer than ever. These two dogs have damned us all by trying to save your miserable life. They should have let you end your own days, as you seemed to want.'

Hereward listened. The throb of hooves echoed dimly through the dusk.

'Come,' Alexios urged, grabbing Hereward's arm. He glanced back along the track as if he could pierce the gathering dark. 'We cannot tarry—'

'Where is the gold?'

Hereward watched the shadow cross the young Roman's face. But then Alexios raised his chin in defiance. 'The gold was killing you as surely as any axe. It had stolen your wits and it would have taken your life. I threw the chest away.'

Hereward heard no more. Blood thundered into his head. Thrusting Alexios to one side, he took three steps back along the road. 'We must recover it.'

'That was a day gone,' Maximos said. 'It will be in Drogo's hands by now.'

Wrenching out his sword, Hereward spun round and thrust the blade towards Alexios. Jabbing the blade against the younger man's throat, he fought with all his will to stop himself taking Alexios' head there and then.

'Do you know what you have done? With that gold, my brothers could have bought their way into the Varangian Guard. They are good, brave men. They sacrificed all to fight against the Norman bastard in England . . . their kin, their homes, their friends, aye, their wits too. That battle drove Hengist mad.' Spittle flew from his lips. Alexios had fallen to the ground – the Roman might be dead for all he knew. Instead the faces of his spear-brothers floated in front of his eyes, those still suffering and those long dead. 'I am their protector. I promised them victory, and when I could not give them that, I promised them a new dawn, gold and glory. But here in Constantinople, you Romans have treated them worse than dogs. They have been beaten down, lied to, spat upon. They are heroes, all of them, and now you have damned them to a life of suffering that they have never deserved.'

A pang of pain stabbed into his heart as sharp as any sword. He had failed them again. He was no better than Asketil, his father.

Drawing back Brainbiter, his hand shook as he prepared to strike.

'Yes, kill him.' Maximos' droll voice cut through the haze that filled his head. 'Slay the Little General and all your worries will be over.'

The sword wavered.

'Your men will thank you for this great act of vengeance.'

Blinking, Hereward felt his vision clear. He looked round at Maximos. Making no effort to restrain him, the Roman sat on his horse, feigning a concerned expression. The Mercian felt a rush of revulsion. Stepping back, he wiped one shaking hand across his mouth and sheathed his sword. He had lost everything, and in his weakness he had almost killed an innocent man. This was the Hereward of old, one ruled by his passions. What he would not have given to have Alric there, his friend, to guide him, to tell him what he needed to do to be a good man. But this was the path he had chosen.

'We will talk of this further,' Alexios said, clambering to his feet. 'But not here, or we will be talking when an axe cuts through us. Agreed?'

Hereward nodded.

'Ride with me,' Alexios said, climbing on to his horse without a backward glance.

As they set off into the night, the beat of hooves at their back had grown louder. Hereward knew – as they all knew – that they had reached the end of their journey. Now it was only a matter of finding a place to make a stand.

As they crested a ridge, the well-used road broadened. Peering ahead, Hereward could just make out shapes darker than the night. Houses, by the look of it. The Mercian felt a glimmer of hope in his heart. If they could find Romans who would stand with them, they could drive Drogo and his war-band away, perhaps even inflict a defeat upon them.

But as he looked around, he saw that no light burned in any window, and when he breathed in he could smell no wisps of smoke in the air.

Soon after, they entered a moderately sized town. Stone halls lined the road, as ancient as every residence Hereward had seen in that part of the world. But the place was still. There was no chatter, no women singing to their babies, no drunken men laughing; the only sound was the wind whistling among the buildings.

'Where is everyone?' Alexios murmured, unsettled.

The four men leapt down and threw open doors. The halls were deserted, the home-fires cold. Hereward could see no signs of battle, but every house was stripped clean of anything of value. When he plunged into barns, he found no grain, no olives, no wine. There were no dogs, no horses, no cattle, pigs or other livestock. It was a town of ghosts.

'What happened here?' Alexios whispered.

A crash echoed behind them. When they ran back to their horses, they found Alexios' steed lying on its side, eyes rolling, breathing shallow.

'No more riding for you,' Maximos said. His eyes darted

back along the road. The rumble of hooves had reached the high ground now.

Zeno leapt back on to his horse. 'We must go for help,' he said to Maximos. 'Find the people of this place and bring them back here.' The horse stamped skittishly, sensing his anxiety.

Maximos looked to the west, where the last rays of the dying sun glimmered on the edge of a deserted landscape. 'You will find no aid.'

Zeno flashed him a look. Hereward could see that the Wolf knew Maximos was right. His words were only designed to offer an excuse. He was saving his own neck.

Maximos slapped the last horse on the rear, and it cantered away. 'I am sick of riding. And sick of running from battle. We will make our stand among these empty houses, fight to the last.' He nodded to Hereward. 'As we did in Sabta.'

Hereward nodded in return. Perhaps he had misjudged Maximos.

Zeno's mocking laughter rolled out. 'You coddle yourself with dreams, like children. Drogo is a bloodied war-leader. Do you think he will let you pick his men off one by one? He will set the town alight, or starve you out, or ride you down like deer. If you stay here, you die.'

'When you reach the first tavern, set aside a cup of wine for me,' Maximos said. 'Ride fast now.'

With a snort, Zeno urged his mount away.

The last of the light died.

As the sound of the Wolf's horse ebbed, the booming of the approaching war-band carved through the stillness of the town. Hereward drew his sword, his eyes searching the narrow tracks between the houses.

'They may ride by,' Alexios suggested, unsheathing his own sword.

'Aye, and it may rain gold,' Maximos replied, looking around. He kept his voice bright, but Hereward knew he too believed the end was near. With a firm nod, the Roman reached a decision. Resting one hand on the Mercian's shoulder, he pointed to where the cluster of houses rose up on an area of higher ground. 'Let them come to us. We can—' His words died on his lips. Hooves beat the ground behind them.

The three warriors whirled, only to see Zeno riding back to them at speed.

'Follow me,' he barked, breathless. 'I have found . . .' His voice tailed away. It seemed he did not know what he had found. And yet Hereward could sense his excitement. He turned his horse round, and the three of them raced after him. Behind them, the Mercian could hear the cries of Drogo's men as they entered the town. They scented blood.

On the edge of town, a narrow track wound down a steep incline, littered with boulders and scrubby brush. Hereward, Alexios and Maximos skidded down the path in Zeno's wake. Thorns tore at their skin. One wrong step would send them spinning into oblivion. But they had nothing to lose.

At the top of the incline, in the town, they could hear the shouts of their pursuers as they began to search. The path would not stay hidden from them for long. At the bottom, Zeno waited for them before riding along the side of a sheer rock face.

Alexios caught Hereward's arm and pointed. 'Do my eyes deceive me?'

Away in the dark a thin line of light glowed in an arc.

The Mercian frowned, unsure of what he was seeing.

Maximos pushed ahead. 'Listen,' he hissed. 'I hear voices.'

And now Hereward could too, dim, rustling, as if emerging from the depths of a deep well.

The three warriors prowled towards the light. When they reached the glimmer, they found that Zeno had dismounted and was pressing his cheek against the rock, listening. As Hereward's vision adjusted, he saw that the illumination was leaking out of the gap around a large boulder.

Alexios shook his head. 'What is this place?' he whispered.

# Chapter Thirty-Three

The torch guttered in the night breeze blowing through the open tent flap. Shadows danced across the billowing cloth as the two Turks knelt, heads bowed. Their muttered prayers were almost lost beneath the cracking of the guy ropes. In the ruddy glare, fear-sweat gleamed on their bare backs. Their wrists were bound, and their ankles too. They knew what was coming. There was no escape for them.

In the far corner of the tent, Kraki watched. His own wrists were lashed with rope, as they had been much of the time since they had left Amaseia. The guards let him flex his muscles a few times a day, but all there had heard what he had done to Ragener and they knew how dangerous he could be. No chances would be taken.

There was no escape for him.

A moon shadow swept across the entrance, and Karas Verinus strode in with his brother's son, Justin, at his heels. The Turks began to whimper. It seemed that they knew this towering oak of a man, or knew his reputation. His pale eyes flickered with a cold fire as he glanced over. This display was for his benefit, Kraki knew, but whether warning or threat he was not sure.

The two captives had made the mistake of wandering too close to the camp as they spied on the Normans, trying to discover for their masters why this army strayed so far from its fortress. Roussel and his men had cared little. They were good friends with the Turks, both groups happy to carve up the empire to their own advantage while the emperor hid away in Constantinople.

But Karas Verinus had been driven into a rage by the bravado of the dark-skinned scouts. He had ridden out into the wilderness alone, with only his sword for his defence. Within an hour, he had returned with the two spies stumbling and falling and howling, tied to his horse.

The Turks started to babble in their strange tongue, no doubt pleading for their lives. Kraki grunted. They should hold their tongues and face death like warriors. A man like this Roman would never be moved to mercy. Kraki had seen enough of him to know that. On the journey from Amaseia, Karas had treated the Normans who travelled with him with disdain. He always held his chin high, like a king surrounded by slaves, never joining in the laughter, never talking. Even Roussel de Bailleul tolerated his behaviour. The warlord showed no man fear, but Kraki had seen him eye Karas as if he were a mad dog.

'Pay heed,' the Roman called across the tent, as if he could read the Viking's mind. 'Feast your eyes on how a hero of the empire treats his enemies.'

From his tunic, he pulled out a long-bladed knife of the kind that hunters used for gutting deer. Pointing one finger at the nearest captive, he held out the weapon on the palm of his other hand. The boy took it.

Kraki watched the lad, trying to read in his face what he intended to do next. But those features were like a still lake at midnight. Justin stared at the Turk, unblinking.

When the attack finally came, Kraki jerked in shock. The lad had been unmoving one moment, a blur of hacking the next. A frenzy settled on him. Though most of his face remained as calm as ever, his lips pulled back from his teeth and his empty eyes widened, luxuriating in every instant of that butchery.

The screams of both Turks ripped out, spiralling up into a

chorus that reached to the heavens. Kraki imagined every warrior in that camp cowering, refusing to investigate, all of them afraid to consider what could draw such a sound from a man's throat.

The blood sprayed. A fine red mist settled around the victim and his killer. On Justin's face, speckles merged into streaks that became one crimson mask.

Now Kraki understood the boy's true nature. Perhaps there was something in all the Verini, in the blood itself, that set them apart from normal folk.

Karas watched as if revelling in a student's fine work. Then he rested a hand on Justin's shoulder and the lad fell still in an instant. What had once been a man lay unmoving at his feet.

Though he was sickened to the pit of his stomach, Kraki refused to look away. That was what Karas wanted.

The other Turk continued to wail. Stepping behind him, Karas hooked a hand in the captive's bonds and lifted him as if he weighed no more than a babe. With a flick of his wrist, he swung the screaming man so he could grasp his legs and then he smashed him down across his knee. The Turk's spine shattered with the sound of a breaking branch. Karas tossed the remains aside without a glance.

'This . . . this is how the Verini treat their enemies,' he said, fixing his eyes upon Kraki. 'These rats swarm across our land and the emperor does nothing. He is too weak. But when they came to steal what was rightfully mine, I showed them how a Roman defends what is his. And if I have to, I will kill every last one of them I can find.'

'If a man does not have honour, he has nothing,' Kraki said, unmoved. 'And I see no honour here.' If Karas was going to break his bones one by one, he would not plead. He would go to the great halls of Valhalla dreaming of Acha, and he would be happy.

'Honour?' Sneering, Karas strode across the tent. 'Let me tell you of honour. Victory upon victory I achieved for the empire in battle. The bodies of my enemies lay before me to the horizon like the rocks of the earth. The emperor sits secure upon his throne because of the blood I have spilled, a sea of it. But I was not lauded for my troubles. No, I was called butcher. I was despised by the pale-skinned cattle of Constantinople.' He fluttered a hand in the air. 'Perhaps feared. It is good to be feared. But they would not have me among them. They wanted the safety that my butchery brought them, but they did not want to see me, or think upon the things I had done. And so I was sent far away from the city, to live out my days on a patch of miserable land in the east.' He shook his head. 'No more.'

Kraki craned his neck up at the general towering over him. He sensed the resentment radiating off the Roman. If the emperor only knew what he had unleashed. 'So you ride back to Constantinople for vengeance. What will you do – slaughter every man, woman and child in the city?'

Reaching one hand behind him to indicate the red-faced, dripping boy-devil, Karas said, 'Once my plans have reached fruition, this will be our new emperor, as my brother intended, and I will stand behind him, guiding him. The empire will be great again. And I will be praised upon high, by all.'

The Viking looked from Karas to Justin in disbelief. These Romans were all drunk on power, or mad, or both. What man in his right mind would see a monster like that boy wearing the crown? Once again he yearned for the simple days of England. There, every man knew the reason for the battles he fought. There, it all made sense.

The night breeze gusted and the torch roared. In the shower of sparks, Kraki glimpsed a figure standing just outside the entrance to the tent. It was Roussel de Bailleul. He was watching the boy standing over the torn and broken bodies.

'What need do you have of me?' the Viking asked.

Karas dropped to his haunches so he could scrutinize his captive. 'Ragener the Hawk has told me of my brother's death in Constantinople.' The Roman turned up his nose. 'Victor was a weak man. I had only pity for him. His hungers were . . . distasteful. He thought himself far better than he was, but in truth he was a failure as a general, as a warrior, as a man. Yet for all that, he was my own blood. He deserves vengeance.' The Roman leaned down so that his cold grey eyes bored into Kraki. 'And the Hawk told me what part you and the other English played in my brother's death.'

'We did nothing.'

'You stood with the Nepotes. You are tainted by their reek. And so it is only right that you carry a message – that Karas Verinus is coming for them, and that the Verini will be restored to power.'

'I will not speak for you.'

'Speak? No.' Karas grinned. 'The Nepotes demand more than weak words. When we arrive in Constantinople, your days are done. I will cut out your heart and ram it down your throat. Then I will tear out your guts and fill that space with vipers. Once you are stitched back up, I will deliver you to those bastards in time for the serpents to eat their way out of you.' He sniffed dismissively. 'A message, nothing more. But they will know that I am back, and I am coming to take their heads, one by one.'

# Chapter Thirty-Four

Shards of gold stabbed out from the rock face. As the boulder ground away from the cliff, the dark fled from the flickering light. A rush of warm air scented with spices blasted out, accompanied by the music of a plucked instrument, and singing, and the lively chatter of excited voices. The shadows of the four warriors rushed away from them as they were swallowed by a circle of illumination. Each man was gripped by the revelation of this mysterious hidden world.

Yells of triumph shattered the spell. Hereward wrenched around, looking up the narrow track leading to the abandoned town. He could not yet see any sign of Drogo Vavasour's warband, but from the tone of the cries there could be no doubt that they had discovered the way their prey had gone. That was no surprise. The Romans had been hammering upon the boulder for long moments, pleading and cajoling with whomsoever was in the cave behind it to admit the new arrivals to the hiding place.

For a while, there had been no response. The voices within had stilled, the sounds of life retreating into the recesses. Hereward had watched the desperation settle on his fellow warriors. They all realized this was their only chance of surviving to see another day. But finally Alexios had convinced those in hiding that he and his allies were good citizens of the Roman empire and not marauding Turks. A gruff response had rumbled out: they would be admitted, but swords and axes waited to greet them. One hint of threat, one lie, and they would be put to death there and then.

The boulder ground out further. Now Hereward could see the Romans straining to push it, eight of them, all broad and strong. Torchlight flooded into the night.

'Make haste,' Zeno called, his voice breaking as he craned his neck round to search for their pursuers. Terror carved deep lines in his features. The sound of running feet and bellowed threats was drawing nearer.

When the gap was wide enough, the four warriors thrust their way inside. In his desperation, Zeno tripped and fell to the ground, bringing Alexios down on top of him.

Straining, the eight men heaved on ropes attached to iron bars struck into the stone of the boulder. The weighty obstacle juddered back into place, and not a moment too soon. Steel clattered against the other side. Furious threats rang out.

Zeno scrabbled away from the entrance, his eyes wide. But Hereward only sheathed his sword and looked around their hiding place. It was clear Drogo Vavasour and his men would never be able to smash their way in. They were safe, for now.

With faces like iron, the eight men now gripped their axes, barring the way into the caves.

'Where is this place?' the Mercian demanded.

A man in a pale-blue tunic pushed his way through the defenders, so old his face resembled a melted candle. 'You are welcome in Malakopea,' he said, looking Hereward up and down, 'if you come in peace, and abide by our rules.'

Grinning, Maximos boomed, 'Grandfather, we are your servants. You have saved our miserable necks from a Norman war-band, and for that we will always be grateful.'

'Normans, you say?' the old man replied, curious. 'Not Turks?' Cocking his head, he listened to the words echoing through the stone door and then nodded to the guards. When they moved apart, Hereward marvelled at what he saw waiting beyond.

Carved out of the very stone was a tunnel wide enough for three men to walk abreast. It seemed to run deep into the earth. On either side, chambers had been hollowed out, each one flickering with candlelight. Laughing children raced around as if they were outside their homes far above. Men and women, young and old, emerged from the rooms to puzzle over the new arrivals, or gathered along the tunnel to chatter. Amid the din of a community at rest, Hereward thought he could hear the bleating of goats and, far away, the lowing of cattle.

'Whatever you have witnessed in your life,' the old man said with a note of pride, 'you have seen nothing like Malakopea, our city beneath the city.'

Alexios wandered into the tunnel, gaping as he looked around. 'You live down here, like rats in the earth?'

'We live like kings,' the old man corrected him, grinning. 'Well fed from our stores. Good water from deep wells. Cool air from the shafts that run up to the world above—'

A young boy ran up and grabbed the old man's leg, half hiding behind him. 'Clovos. Clovos. Are these our enemies?' he said, peeping out.

Clovos ruffled the lad's hair. 'No, Damian. These are Romans, like you, and an Englishman, if I am not mistaken. They are not the Turks who drove us from our homes.'

'This is sanctuary, then,' Maximos suggested.

'When it is safe, we live in Malakopea-above. We farm the land, and trade with our neighbours. We live as all Romans do. But when we face an enemy, we hide here until the threat has passed. Why, we could live here for an age, if need be. Come.' He beckoned and the four warriors followed him into the depths of the fortress.

As he walked, Hereward scraped his fingers along the surface of the wall. The rock was soft, but still he could not imagine the work involved in creating this place. Glancing up at the encrusted soot from the torches, he said, 'These caves are old.'

Clovos shrugged. 'Malakopea-below has always been here. Some say it was built before the Flood.'

Along the tunnel they wandered, and into branching tunnels going deeper and deeper beneath the earth. Hereward felt stunned by what he saw. Never had he seen the like in England.

Stone steps led down to new levels, and down and down. Eighteen in all, Clovos said, large enough to house twenty thousand inhabitants. Hereward saw large chambers for kin, and smaller ones too, stables reeking of animal dung, olive presses and wine cellars, stores where merchants made and sold their wares, rooms filled with weapons, a chamber lined with stone containers and smelling of herbs and spices where the leech healed the sick, tombs for those he failed, and even a chapel where the devoted knelt in prayer before God's table. Everything that was above ground was here below too.

'This is like a rabbit's warren,' Maximos breathed, amazed. 'It is safer than any fortress.'

'Good,' Zeno grumbled. 'I will sleep soundly for the first time in days.'

Hearing the word sleep, Hereward realized what little strength remained in his limbs. His belly growled, and he was filthy from the road.

Clovos was one of the city elders. After three weeks sheltering from the marauding Turks who had raided the city and killed many, he seemed pleased to see new faces. He found them empty chambers where they could sleep, and bread, cheese and olives, and fresh water.

Hereward fell into a deep sleep the moment he laid down his head. No dreams assailed him, and for that he was thankful.

For the next three days, the four warriors ate their fill and slept like the dead. The Mercian could feel his strength returning by the hour, and with it a desire to push aside his bitterness at the loss of the gold, and his despair at what it meant for his brothers. There was little to be gained in dwelling on failure – that was a lesson he had learned when he first became a warrior. Battles ebbed and flowed. Friends died. Loved ones were murdered. Defeat swept in at the moment of seeming victory. And yet the hard road went on, and it was the warrior's task to walk it, through rain, and bog, aye, and fire too. But at some point there would be sun, and God's rewards; he believed that with all his heart.

He only had to find the way.

Alexios spent much of his time with the monks who taught the children in their large study chamber. From the shadows in the doorway, Hereward watched him tell of great battles, and horsemanship, and read the lessons from God's book. When the Roman was alone with the youngest, it seemed that the responsibilities of war slipped from him. He laughed more, and he charmed the girls and wrestled with the boys. Hereward could see an innocence there that reminded him of Alric.

Later, Hereward prowled the long tunnels, exploring the marvels of that hidden place. The underground city throbbed with life everywhere he turned. Standing beneath the narrow shafts that rose up through the rock to the surface, he closed his eyes and let the cool wind blow down on to his face. He found a central air shaft that was wider than three men standing with their arms outstretched. Could there be a wonder greater than this anywhere in the world?

But as he went deeper, and deeper still, more chambers became unoccupied. The lowest two levels were deserted. Only the sound of his whispering footsteps rustled through them. When he took a torch and began to creep into the darkness, he felt an unsettling atmosphere that made the hairs on the back of his neck prickle. He peered down into the deep wells and dropped in a pebble. He held his breath, listening, but the splash, when it finally came, was almost too faint to hear. What kind of men could have cut those pits that seemed to go down to the very depths of hell itself?

In one chamber, the dancing light of his torch pulled faces from the dark. Daubed on the walls, they seemed very old indeed. The ochres and blacks had faded, so that they looked like ghosts emerging from the stone. As he peered closer, he decided those features did not resemble any man he knew. They looked like devils. He was not superstitious, but he felt unsettled, as if he had uncovered something that was not meant for him to see.

When he walked away, he thought he could feel those eyes on his back.

As he moved through the last of the dark towards the brightly lit stone steps leading up to the inhabited levels, a figure stepped out of the shadows. Hereward snatched out his sword, and thrust the torch in front of him. A pale face flared in the dark: it was Zeno. The Roman had been following him. 'You were close to losing the weight upon your shoulders,' Hereward spat. 'Why are you lurking here?'

Glancing over his shoulder to make sure they could not be overheard, Zeno said, 'You cannot trust Maximos Nepos.'

'Why do you say so?'

'You cannot trust him,' the other man breathed. 'He is not what he seems to be.' Before Hereward could question him further, he had hurried up the steps and away.

Turning the warning over in his mind, the Mercian climbed up through the warren of Malakopea-below until the city folk started to buzz around him. A puzzle that had troubled him since he had left Constantinople now seemed clearer.

Searching through the tunnels and chambers, he found a gloomy tavern that smelled of vinegar. In the half-light, old men squatted on stools, sipping wine from cups. Hereward heard the Roman's laughter before he saw him. Maximos was leaning against the tavernkeeper's table, arms folded, flirting with two women, whores by the look of them. When he saw the Mercian, he whispered something in one of their ears that brought a peal of giggles, and then he wandered over.

'That is a face that needs some wine inside it,' he said.

'I am not here to drink with you.'

Maximos studied the Mercian's eyes, noted the hand upon the sword hilt, and nodded. 'Bad business, then.' He led the way to two stools in a dark corner at the rear of the tavern.

'You were prepared to fight alongside me in Malakopea-above, and likely die beside me too,' Hereward said, sitting, 'and for that you have my thanks.'

'And yet?'

'I know why you chose to ride with the Athanatoi.' He allowed the words to sink in, but the Roman's face gave nothing away. 'It was not because you were prepared to sacrifice yourself for the emperor, not even for all the riches he could shower upon you. Everything you have done in your life . . . all the death you have dealt . . . has been to one end: to advance the cause of your kin, the Nepotes.'

Now Maximos winced and looked away.

'No, you have ridden to war for one reason only,' Hereward continued. 'To find a way to murder Alexios Comnenos without blame falling upon you or your kin.'

Maximos took a deep breath, his shoulders sagging. 'There you have me.'

'Alexios is a rival, with a better claim to the throne than anything the Nepotes could ever show. Your kin failed once in their plot to seize the empire. You will not risk another failure. Does it eat away at them? At your mother, and your sister, and your father? The Nepotes think it is their destiny, and yet they are as far away from their goal as ever.'

Maximos wagged a finger to summon a cup of wine from the tavernkeeper.

'That is why Anna Dalassene tasked me with watching over her son,' Hereward continued. 'It puzzled me. He is as sharp as a blade, a fine warrior with good command of his sword, and like all good warriors he never lets his guard down. But now I see that his mother feared treachery. A knife in the back. A throat slit while sleeping. She sent me to protect him from you.'

Maximos sucked on his lip in thought for a moment. 'If that were so, why did she not warn you that I was the enemy? That would have made your work easier, would it not?'

Hereward had no answer. 'Do you deny your kin sent those cut-throats to murder Alexios in the street on the night I was taken by the Varangian Guard?'

Taking his cup of wine, Maximos let it hover on his lips for a while as he weighed his response. 'No. And yet I could have taken his life time and again on the ride from Constantinople. I did not.' The Roman swilled back his wine. When he had wiped his mouth, he bowed his head, his shoulders sagging. Hereward watched the bravado fall away from him. He thought how the man who emerged looked hollowed out by life.

'I am a vile canker, Mercian,' Maximos said in a low voice. 'I know my worth. I murdered a friend I had had since childhood, a man I loved more than any other, for the sake of my kin. And I betrayed a woman who loved me, Meghigda, and she died because of it. These two things haunt my nights, and my days. There is only so much misery a man can inflict before it starts to eat away at his soul. I have had my fill.'

'You would deny your kin? Their desire for power?'

'I would.' His eyes flashed with passion.

'Can a man walk away from his blood?'

'You did.'

Hereward flinched. The Roman was right. His father, Asketil, had been a stain upon God's earth, and his brother too. He had found the strength to tear himself away, to walk his own road, however lonely that might be.

'I will not do my kin's bidding any longer. I will be my own man,' Maximos vowed, 'even if that means I have no kin.'

'You think they will let you walk away? You are key to all their plots.'

Maximos gripped his cup so tightly Hereward thought it might shatter. 'I will make amends.'

The Mercian peered into the other man's face. For all his protestations, he still could not wholly trust him. The Nepotes were masters of deception, and Maximos had shown time and again that he was skilled in twisting words to his own ends.

'I know I must earn your trust. Time will show you I am a changed man.'

As Maximos held up his cup for more wine, cries of alarm rang through the tunnel outside the tavern. Armed men rushed past the doorway.

'Come,' Hereward said, jumping to his feet. 'I smell Normans.'

The throb of anxious voices swelled. Hereward and Maximos raced past worried mothers pressing their children into their skirts and uneasy men with twitching hands. Word of some troubling discovery was rushing back through the tunnels, though no one seemed to know exactly what.

As the two warriors reached the entrance hall, they spied guards jostling for space, their faces drawn. Their worried eyes darted towards Clovos as the old man pushed his way into their midst.

'Stand aside,' he croaked, his voice hardening. 'Stand aside.'

As Hereward and Maximos edged in behind the elder, Alexios and Zeno ran up behind.

'What is amiss?' Zeno asked. 'Are we under attack?'

For the first time, Hereward saw that a slit had been cut in the rock wall beside the entrance, invisible in the dark when they arrived. Clovos peered through it. When he turned back, his face was drained of blood.

'Open it,' he commanded. 'Now.'

The eight strong guards pressed their shoulders against the boulder and heaved. The grinding of the rock reverberated. In rushed a blast of warm night air scented with vegetation. As Clovos pushed his way through to the threshold, the Mercian stepped behind him. It was dark outside. All sense of night and day disappeared in that underground world.

'What do you see?' Hereward asked.

The old man raised a trembling arm and pointed to the edge of the half-circle of light. 'Our scout,' Clovos said in a creaking voice.

On a flat rock, stained and dripping, stared a human head.

# Chapter Thirty-Five

'You have until dawn to deliver your four guests into our hands or worse will follow.' The voice cracked through the night.

As Hereward watched, Drogo Vavasour emerged from the dark on the edge of the semicircle of light. His hands were dark with blood – he had performed that foul deed himself. His face brooked no dissent. The ghostly outlines of his men appeared at his back, their weapons raised and ready.

The guards of Malakopea stepped forward, spears bristling. They were ready to defend their city to the last. But the Mercian knew Drogo would not attack such an overwhelming force. He did not need to.

Once one of the defenders had reclaimed the head of the scout, Clovos ordered the boulder to be dragged back into place. Hereward felt the stares of all the men there turn towards him and the Romans. They were being weighed, measured, the coming days mapped out.

'We have other scouts outside this place,' the elder said, the implication heavy in his voice.

'If you force us to leave, you are sending us to our deaths,' Hereward replied. 'Our blood will be on your hands.'

'And if another of our scouts is murdered, his blood will be on your hands.' Clovos' stare was cold, all sign of hospitality gone.

'You cannot deliver us into the hands of our enemies,' Alexios insisted. 'Not in the name of God.'

The old man hesitated. 'This requires some reflection,' he said, frowning. 'I must seek guidance.' He pushed away through the throng, disappearing into the network of tunnels. The four warriors looked at each other, feeling the simmering suspicion on their backs.

'Come,' Hereward murmured, 'we must find somewhere away from these watchful eyes.'

Down into the depths they hurried until they found one of the deserted chambers. With a single guttering candle for light, they huddled in a corner where they could not be overheard.

'This is not good,' Maximos whispered. 'We are trapped like rats here. Enemies without, and if Clovos turns against us a city filled with enemies within.'

'There is a secret tunnel to escape this place if needs must,' Alexios said, looking around the anxious faces. 'One of the churchmen told me. It winds up to a hidden doorway in Malakopea-above. If we can find it—'

'Have your wits gone?' Zeno spat. 'No one will tell us where it is. It is hidden for a reason. And Clovos will not risk our escaping if we are to buy the safety of their scouts.'

'Then we sit here and wait for our fate to be decided by others?' Alexios leaned forward so that the candlelight pooled shadows in his eyes. 'That is not my way.'

'Nor mine,' Maximos agreed.

Hereward peered into the dark. 'Damn this place. Who can tell the hour? How long do we have till dawn?' He sensed the tension rising in the other men. They all knew time was fast running out. 'We search for the escape tunnel,' he said. 'We have no other choice. Pray we find it.'

'We will cover more ground if we go our separate ways,' Zeno said, standing.

From under his brow, Hereward eyed Maximos. If the Roman

was to murder Alexios, this would be as good a time as any. A knife across the throat, the corpse hidden, then a rapid escape with no time to look back. 'Let us make haste,' the Mercian said. 'We will meet at the tavern through the night to tell what we have found. May God go with us.'

As the Romans returned to the thronging parts of the city, Hereward hung back, watching which way each went. Alexios disappeared into the mass with Zeno behind him, but Maximos struck off in a different direction, and Hereward followed in his wake. He kept his head down so he would not be seen, but after some time he began to think his quarry had no intention of attacking the Little General. He seemed too engrossed in his task, too aware of the gravity of the threat facing them all. Hereward was about to fall back and begin to search on his own account when he saw a youth of about twelve summers stagger out of a tunnel, his face like a winter field. Pressing his back against the stone, the lad looked this way and that as if he expected to be beset by enemies at any moment.

'What ails you?' Hereward growled, not wishing to alert Maximos to his presence, but the Roman's hearing was good and he turned round, surprised.

'M-murder,' the lad croaked.

Maximos hurried over. 'Does the boy know something?' he asked.

Hereward crouched so he could look the youth in the eye. 'Murder, you say? Show me.'

The boy led them back through the maze of tunnels to a chamber away from the main throng. At the entrance, he pointed inside with a wavering hand. What looked like a bundle of rags in a growing dark pool lay in one corner. Nodding to Maximos to stay with the lad, Hereward darted in and lifted the head. It was Clovos.

Now the Mercian began to see a shape to these events. Glancing over his shoulder, he called to the boy, 'Tell no one of this, do you hear? Whoever murdered this man will come for you if you speak out. Leave this business to us.'

Terrified, the boy nodded furiously. A moment later he was racing away.

'The lad will hold his tongue for a little while, but not long enough,' Hereward murmured to Maximos. He lifted the head once more so the other man could see the identity of the victim.

Squatting, Maximos leaned in to examine the remains. The throat had been slashed, but that was not what interested the Roman the most. He traced his finger along the edge of other cuts on Clovos' face. 'Tortured,' he said. 'This was no robbery, no murder in a fit of anger.'

Hereward bowed his head, seeing only one solution. 'Tortured to reveal where the escape tunnel is hidden. Alexios would not be capable of this.' He held the other man's gaze for a moment, but he could see immediately that they had an understanding.

'If this murder is uncovered, we will all be blamed. Our time will be done,' Maximos breathed.

'Agreed. Then the body must not be found until we are away from here.'

They searched the chamber for a large cloth in which to wrap the remains, and then Maximos kept watch while Hereward carried the corpse to a deserted store. Maximos was simmering. 'Zeno has risked everything,' he murmured as they raced back to the tavern.

But neither Zeno nor Alexios waited there. 'Clovos must have known where to find the escape tunnel,' the Roman hissed. 'Why is Zeno not here to tell us?'

Hereward felt the hairs on his neck prickle. 'Zeno does not wish us to join him on the way out of Malakopea-below,' he said quietly. 'Come. We must find him, quickly.'

Once the way had been pointed by someone who had seen Zeno only a short time before, Hereward and Maximos leapt down the stone steps to the lower levels. When they neared their destination, Hereward pressed his finger to his lips.

From somewhere nearby, Alexios' voice floated back. 'I see nothing here. We should tell the others . . .'

The Mercian did not wait for the response. Following the echo of the words, he snatched out his sword and looked into the chamber from which it had come. Alexios stood with his back to him, tracing his fingers over the stone wall.

From the corner of his eye, Hereward glimpsed rapid movement. Zeno was lunging to cut Alexios down.

Maximos barged into the chamber. With one fluid movement, he thrust his own blade into Zeno's belly. Howling, Zeno crashed on to his back, clutching at his wound with both hands. The other men there could see he would never live after such a blow.

Zeno looked down at the blood bubbling through his fingers and laughed coldly. He could see it too. The Roman did not plead, though, or wail like a child. He took his fate like a warrior.

But as Maximos knelt beside the dying man, Hereward was surprised to see the look of contempt upon Zeno's face. 'Your kin said you would fail them,' he sneered, a bubble of blood floating on his lips. 'They sent me to do what they knew you could never do. Your own sister called you coward.' His eyes gleamed with a faraway look and he murmured 'Juliana . . .' with the tenderness of a man who had lost his heart.

'My sister never loved you,' Maximos snapped, his face icy. 'She is the greatest whore in Constantinople. But the reward she seeks is power, not gold.'

The words struck home as sharply as his blade. Zeno's eyes widened as the warrior suddenly feared that he had sacrificed his life for nothing but his own weakness.

Standing, Maximos turned his back on his victim, not even offering Zeno the respect of watching him die. When he heard the rattle of the last breath, he spat on the floor and said only, 'It is done.'

And yet in Maximos' drawn features Hereward could see the pain of Zeno's taunt, and fear too. If the Nepotes had lost faith, they would turn their backs on him. The Mercian clapped a hand of comfort on the other man's shoulder.

'You saved my life,' Alexios said, humbled.

Maximos shrugged. 'It may not be enough.'

'Our time is nearly done,' Hereward said. 'And Zeno took the secret of the escape tunnel with him into the Grim Lands.'

The words had barely left his lips when cries of alarm began to ring through the city. Maximos grinned without humour. 'And that is the sound of our last hope fading away.'

# Chapter Thirty-Six

The keening cry carved through even the boulder that closed off Malakopea-below. The throat-rending sound carried with it agonies untold for most of the silent, ashen-faced men gathered in the entrance hall. But Hereward had heard its like before. He had brought that very shriek from a man's throat.

'They are flaying him alive,' he said.

The heads of the guards jerked towards him. He had given voice to the fears they had tried to push aside when they had first heard that terrible noise.

'You must save him!' A black-haired woman thrust her tear-streaked face through the men who had gathered by the entrance. Whirling from one to another, she held out her hands, desperate. 'Save my husband.'

'Where is Clovos?' someone asked. 'He will know what to do.'

Hereward glanced at Maximos and Alexios. Having followed the cries of alarm, they had found the guards talking about another scout who had fallen into the hands of the Norman war-band. Drogo Vavasour had clearly decided he could not wait until dawn. He wanted his prey tossed out to him now, so his wolves could fall upon them.

When the woman caught sight of the three strangers, she

reached out an accusing finger. 'You brought this hell to our door,' she snarled. 'Why should my husband suffer, for you?' She turned back to the guards. 'Send them out so Kostas will be freed.'

In the absence of Clovos to keep the peace, the guards began to shift uncomfortably. Hereward watched hands waver over swords and axes. Eyes darted. Choices were weighed.

'Let us be away from here,' Maximos breathed in his ear. 'This business will only get worse.'

Before the guards could reach a decision, the three men hurried back into the tunnels, hoping to lose themselves. But they could hear the voices growing louder behind them. Debate was turning to anger. As they thrust their way through the crowds, the shouts rang out. 'Seize them.' 'Take them to Clovos.'

'I am sure Clovos will have little to say on this matter,' Maximos murmured.

Alexios glanced over his shoulder. Heads were bobbing. Bodies pressed their way. 'Where do we hide?' he whispered.

'There is nothing to gain by hiding,' Hereward replied. 'These tunnels do not go on for ever. They will find us soon enough.'

'Then what?'

Ahead of them, more cries leapt from mouth to mouth. The Mercian heard a familiar name. Each time it was repeated it was louder still. 'They have found Clovos' remains.' He cursed. He had hoped they would have more time to find a way out.

'These are not choices I like,' Maximos said. 'Lose my head in here for a murder I did not commit, or be thrown out into the hands of a dog like Drogo Vavasour. Death or death?'

'This is not over yet,' Hereward said. His mind was racing.

'You have a plan?' Alexios asked. Maximos cocked an eyebrow.

'I saw something when I came through this place . . .' Hereward choked off his words when he saw guards surging towards him. Men began to clutch for his arms, hoping to restrain him. 'Follow me,' he snarled. Throwing off the hands, he barged his way through the throng.

With every chamber they passed, it seemed another man or two leapt out to answer the guards' call. Soon Hereward found himself battling through a sea of bodies. Hands snarled in his tunic. Women clawed at his bare skin.

Finally he found a space to snatch out Brainbiter. 'Away,' he yelled, whisking the blade in an arc. Maximos and Alexios drew their own weapons, watching every side.

The folk of Malakopea fell back, glowering at the enemy revealed in their midst. Hereward did not wait for them to recapture their bravery. Crashing through the line of bodies in front of him, he found a branching tunnel where they could run. A din of fury immediately swelled at their backs. It sounded as though the entire city was now hunting them.

Knowing the crowd would probably rend them limb from limb for Clovos' murder, they raced through tunnel after tunnel. Hurling their bodies down flights of steps they progressed deeper into the bowels of Malakopea, and after a while the roar of the crowd began to fall away. A brief respite, nothing more. As they stumbled on to the lowest level, Hereward slumped against a wall to catch his breath.

'Thank God,' Maximos gasped. 'I thought you had decided to take us straight down to hell.'

'Why have you brought us here?' Alexios hurried back to the foot of the steps to listen for sounds of pursuit. 'We will be trapped like rats.'

'We were trapped like rats the moment we stepped into this place.' Hereward grasped a torch from the wall and led the way into the dark ahead. 'We have time here,' he said, his voice echoing off the slick walls. 'These depths are empty.'

'Time for what?' Alexios asked.

Hereward came to a halt beneath the vast central air shaft that rose up through the darkness to, he hoped, the ground above. 'Time to climb.'

Alexios gaped. 'Are you mad?'

Maximos laughed. 'Aye, he is mad. He thinks we have the wings of angels.'

Stepping forward, Hereward pushed the torch towards the wall of the shaft. As the shadows flew away, the flickering light revealed footholds cut into the stone reaching up into the dark. 'Made by the men who carved this out of the very earth.'

Maximos craned his neck back so he could peer up, even though the top of the shaft was lost to him. 'Mad,' he said with a nod. 'You believe we can climb that, all the way up to Malakopea-above?' Forming his hand into a claw, he stared at his fingers. 'Clinging on with only our nails and toes?'

'I believe we have no other way of saving our necks.'

The din swelled once more as the crowd began to make its way down to the lowest levels.

'Those holes may stop there,' Alexios said, pointing just beyond the circle of light. 'Or halfway up. You cannot know—' He caught himself, listening to the growing sounds of pursuit. 'You speak truly. We have no choice,' he said, his shoulders sagging. 'Better to die fighting to the last than giving ourselves up to our enemies.'

'I will go first.' Handing the torch to Alexios, Hereward sunk his fingers into the lowest handholds, then scrabbled his feet up the tunnel wall to haul himself into the shaft. As his eyes adjusted to the gloom, he felt the next holes and began to climb.

Below him, he could hear Maximos and Alexios bickering before the elder Roman clambered up next. The light winked out as Alexios tossed the torch away, and then Hereward found himself swimming in a sea of darkness. His fingers and his toes would have to be his eyes.

Hand over hand, he pulled himself up.

Heights did not trouble him. When he was a child in Barholme, he had climbed to the top of the tallest oaks, where the winds whisked the branches so savagely that it felt as if any moment he would be torn free. But this was different. In the deep dark, the void sucked at him. He imagined the shaft going down beneath his feet, and down, and if he fell he would fall for ever.

From below, he heard voices rumble as the crowd searched

along the tunnel. He knew they would not see the climbers even if they looked up, but he still felt relief when no voices were raised in alarm.

Hand over hand. Feet feeling for each hole. Maximos and Alexios were like ghosts behind him, but he did not dare call out for fear of startling them into losing their grip.

After a little while, his fingers began to ache. Bolts of pain lanced up his arms from the strain of clinging on for dear life. Every now and then he paused for breath, tried to rest, but the agony in his limbs never eased. If he allowed himself to, he would have wondered if he had the strength to reach the summit.

But his devil would not let him. Whispers rustled through his head. Blood throbbed behind his eyes. That slow-burning rage put fire in his belly and drove him on. Perhaps the devil was not the enemy he had always imagined. While it dragged him down to hell by degrees, it also helped him to survive another day.

His breath rasped. No light shone above, no sign of any end to this torment. Even though he knew his eyes were open, he felt as if they were screwed tight shut and he was swimming inside his own head. How easy it would be to let go, fall back, float.

Cursing, he shook his head to rid himself of the spell. This weakness would be the end of him, if he let it.

*Climb*, he urged himself. *Climb.*

After a while, his whole body began to shake. An icy numbness spread through his fingers until he could barely feel them. Afraid that he was about to lose his grip, he drove all his attention into his hands. And in that instant, his left foot failed to find the next hole. His toe scrabbled against the wall, and as he flailed he felt his hand begin to drag away from the stone.

His heart throbbed into his mouth. The world whirled. His head flopped back.

Just at the moment when he was sure he was falling, his foot slotted into place. Somehow he managed to hold tight.

For a moment, he pressed his forehead against the dank stone, trying to steady himself. If the others had called out to him, he would not have heard for the thunder of his blood.

How he found the strength to go on, he did not know. One hand over the other. Refusing to allow himself to think any further than the next hole.

But then he felt his hand alight on a flat surface, one that seemed to have no end. As he pushed his arm forward, he realized that it was a ledge. With a surge of relief, he dragged himself up and over the edge. Joy swelled in his heart. Beyond the ledge, he found a recess where the builders of the shaft could rest. Never would he have thought such a simple thing could bring him so much comfort.

For a moment, he rested there, gathering himself. When the rasp of Maximos' breath rose up through the shaft, he knew he could tarry no longer. Yet where there was one hollow, he hoped there might be others.

'Have courage,' he hissed into the dark. 'There is a place to rest just above your heads.'

Exclamations of desperate joy rushed back to him.

Gingerly he hung his legs over the edge and shuffled along the ledge. Once he passed the edge of the recess, he pressed his back against the stone for fear he would pitch forward in his disorientation. Barely an arm's length further along his resting place, he found another hollow, and beyond that, another. Falling into it, he closed his eyes and sucked in a deep, juddering breath.

When he heard Maximos wheezing as he pulled himself up, he called, 'There is a cave near you. Rest in it, then follow me along the ledge. There is another. Leave that one free for Alexios.'

Once they were all safe, they talked in low murmurs, afraid their voices would carry down to Malakopea-below. None of them wished to survive this ordeal only to climb out into a forest of spears. Within no time, the chatter ebbed. Exhaustion claimed them.

Settling against the back of his cave, Hereward stretched out his aching limbs and peered into the swimming dark. How strange it was to be suspended there halfway between heaven and hell, between life and death. In his weariness, his thoughts drifted like the tide, and he found the blackness became another world, one in which memories and thoughts and dreams played out, merged, became one.

Red lines danced before his eyes, drifting into the shape of the devils he had seen scrawled on the walls of the chamber at the lowest level. He blinked once, twice, but they would not leave him alone. They sensed that he was one of them, he knew.

As they faded, he saw his son, no longer a babe in arms but running through the dripping fenlands, his face always turned away. He ached to see the lad more than he had ever dreamed.

A wave crashed over him, one of the great waves that had almost drowned him off Flanders, and he was swept away into the gulf. Turfrida, his dead wife, was smiling as if she was filled with the joy that had consumed her in life. She told him he was a good man and he felt tears burn his eyes.

Sleep came.

When his eyes flickered open again, he realized the black had become grey. Crawling out of the hollow, he craned his neck up. A circle of blue sky glowed above. The light of this new day reached its fingers down the walls of the shaft, illuminating the ladder of handholds and another resting place. No more would he be lost in darkness. Now he could see the challenge ahead of him, he knew he could beat it.

When Maximos and Alexios emerged from sleep, they hailed each other in cheery whispers. The daylight had worked its spell on them too.

Soon after that they began their climb again. This time Alexios led the way. The handholds were easier to see, and they scaled the wall at twice the speed of the previous night. As the circle of sky grew larger, that prize drew them on, putting fire in their bellies at a time when they should by rights have been flagging.

And then Hereward was hauling himself over the lip of the shaft into the heat of the day. After the chill dark of the long climb, the glare of the sun blinded him. He rolled on to his back, one arm thrown across his face, relishing the feeling of freedom.

'That is the easy task done.' Maximos' voice floated over from nearby, laced with dark humour. 'Now we face mile upon mile on foot and a good chance we will starve to death, not to mention roaming bands of murderous Turks who would like nothing more than to lop off our heads.'

'Then let us waste no more time,' Hereward replied. 'I have had my fill of running, and a bellyful of bowing my head to those who see me as little more than a dog. Now I am ready to fight for what is rightly mine.'

# Chapter Thirty-Seven

The hot coals glowed like a furnace. The circle of ruddy light cast by the brazier boiled, but it barely reached into the suffocating darkness that choked the chamber far beneath the Boukoleon palace. In this miserable corner of Constantinople, one that few even knew existed, the air was hotter than hell and the reek of blood was stronger than in any butcher's yard.

Wulfrun lay strapped to rough boards leaning against one glistening stone wall. He had been savagely beaten time and again. Blood caked the corner of his mouth and his skin was mottled with bruises. Lances of pain stabbed into every joint. Somehow he forced open his swollen right eye just a slit so he could see the man who stood before him.

Falkon Cephalas wrinkled his nose at the stink. He was a man used to giving orders, but rarely seeing their consequences. Today he was wearing an emerald-green tunic embroidered with gold thread, the finest piece of cloth ever to be seen in that foul place. In contrast, Wulfrun was bare-chested, and his filthy breeches were soaked in blood.

'We have gone easy on you, Wulfrun of the English, because of your service to the emperor,' Falkon said, folding his hands behind his back. 'But you know that cannot continue, surely? When I give the command, Kobol of the Blades will draw agonies from you. Every secret you have kept locked away will be torn from your throat. Save yourself the suffering. Speak now.'

'I know nothing.' His words sounded like stones dropped upon ice.

The Roman paced closer so he could peer into his captive's face. 'I ask little. Tell me where the Nepotes are in hiding and your misery will be over.'

'I know nothing.'

Falkon sighed and stepped back. 'She is a whore, Juliana Nepa, you know that? Your true love. Sabas Apion enjoyed her flesh on many an occasion. She led him by the cock into treason, and then to his death. But that was how she wielded her power, by spreading her thighs and twisting the wits of any man fool enough to be beguiled by her. You have no need to protect her.'

Wulfrun closed his eye. There was nothing here that surprised him. He had simply chosen to ignore it.

'My patience wears thin.' For the first time Wulfrun heard a note of frustration in the other man's voice. 'For every traitor I hang, another two appear. There seems no end to this work.' He strode away into the dark, his leather soles clacking on the flagstones. 'But I cannot rest. Soon, God willing, the Athanatoi will return with the Caesar, and if they are not already dead, those English bastards will be swinging on a gibbet too.'

'What wrong have they committed?' Wulfrun's croak was almost lost beneath the hissing of the brazier.

'Have you heard how the travellers speak of them in the taverns? Tales of heroes, and magic swords, and warriors who almost brought a king to his knees. Stories that spread. And if men would bring down a king, why, how easily would they be persuaded to unseat an emperor? For a little gold, the adulation of women.' The low voice roamed through the dark. 'No, better to send a message to all within this great, shining city that even men who would be kingslayers can have their flames snuffed out as easily as beggars. The moment they return, Wulfrun, they will be gone.'

Wulfrun felt sickened. He had nothing but hatred for Hereward, but still the Mercian had not earned such a fate. Falkon Cephalas would, it seemed, only be pleased when Constantinople was a city of the dead.

'When I was a boy, in Barholme, in the east of England, my father gave me a spear and a task. I would go into our barn and stay there until I had slain every rat that ate our food for the coming cold season. The first night I slaughtered a pile that came up to my knees. I slept well, thinking the work was done. But the next morning there were more rats, more seemingly than there had been to begin with. I set about killing them too. By the end of the second night, with the bodies heaped higher than my head, I was weary and hungry and filled with despair that I had failed.' He licked his lips, but there seemed no moisture left in his body. 'But my father carried me back to our hall upon his shoulders, and he fed me and thanked me. He had taught me a lesson that day – for he was a good man, with a big heart, and he wanted his son to thrive in the world.' Wulfrun felt a wave of fondness wash over him, and sadness that his father was no longer alive. 'Where there is plenty, there are always rats,' he continued, his voice cracking. 'No amount of slaughter will drive them away, for it is the need that draws them in. The hunger for what is there. A wise man does not waste his time in the killing.'

The Roman laughed, without humour. 'This is the father Hereward murdered, yes?'

'Who are you, Falkon Cephalas? What made the cruel man I see before me?'

'I am nobody. I have no import. No purpose save to serve. I am not haunted by days long gone. I have not been shaped, twisted, compelled, made wise, made cruel.' The Roman stepped back into the light. A wry smile ghosted his lips. 'I have no stories to tell you of when I was a boy. I think nothing of what was. I could scarcely remember it, even if I tried. My life has been uneventful. Only here, only now, matters. I do what needs to be done, and then I sleep. I do the same the next day, and think not of the day that has gone.' He held out both hands as if this was a great revelation. Wulfrun thought that perhaps it was.

'You will never be the true commander of the Varangian Guard,' Falkon continued. 'Your days of glory are behind you. You will be shamed across all Constantinople. And soon your life, too, will be done. Make your peace with God, for an ending is coming.'

# Chapter Thirty-Eight

Smoke as black as Hades billowed overhead. Tongues of flame licked up from the piles of rubble that had once been a thriving town. Ragged corpses sprawled across the streets as if they had been torn from their feet by a mighty gale, and in truth they had: the storm of Roussel de Bailleul's army. From the moment of the first charge, it was clear to any witness that these defenders had not stood a chance.

In his hauberk and his leathers and his furs, the warlord stood on the plinth of a statue which now lay shattered in the mud behind him. Turning slowly, he looked out across his handiwork, past the death and the destruction, to the crowds of wailing women and children. His face showed no joy in this victory. It was necessary, no more.

Kraki glowered at the warriors who picked over the bodies and the contents of the houses for any booty they could steal away. Yet for all his contempt, he had to admit to a grudging respect for the savage skill and strength of this army. The Normans lived for battle, and every man fought like two.

As the shrieking ravens swooped down to feast on the dead, the Viking looked out across the carnage and frowned. He could not divine Roussel's mind. Why had he attacked this town and wrought such complete destruction? There was little gain in it for him. He had as much gold as he needed in his palace at Amaseia, and no doubt more still in Ancyra. An assault such as this could only bring the wrath of the emperor down upon him.

The one-eyed Norman, Roussel's second-in-command, and another warrior with wild grey hair dragged a Roman out of the ruins. Sporting a swollen eye and a gash on his forehead, the dazed captive did not yet seem aware of his good fortune. As far as Kraki could see, he was the sole survivor of the force that had tried to defend the town.

The two warriors flung their prisoner on to the ground at Roussel's feet.

'Kneel before me,' the warlord commanded.

Scrabbling to his knees, the Roman craned his neck up at his captor.

'I have shown you mercy for one reason and one reason alone – so you can carry my message to Constantinople, and to the emperor himself. Will you do so?'

The Roman nodded.

'That is good. Watch well. Listen. Pay heed, for on this great day the course of the empire will be changed for ever. And you, lowly warrior, have been chosen to proclaim it to the world.' Raising his right arm, Roussel beckoned towards the ranks of his army. After a moment, the mob parted and a man pushed himself forward. It was the Caesar, John Doukas. Unlike the filthy, blood-spattered warriors around him, he was dressed in a clean mauve tunic embroidered with fine gold thread. Kraki grunted. He looked as if he had prepared himself in his finery for a morning in church. With his chin high and his gaze fixed upon the horizon, the Caesar walked to the plinth with a measured step.

When he came to a halt, Roussel boomed, 'The fate of this great Roman empire has been thrown to the wind by the betrayals and the failings of the emperor, Michael. He has proved himself too weak to wear the crown. No longer can this be tolerated. No more will his subjects suffer, starve, or die at the hands of the empire's enemies. Today, all good men must cry *Enough*.' The warlord peered down at the Roman aristocrat. 'John Doukas, brother of the emperor Constantine, no man has a greater claim to the throne. Will you accept this call to lead the people back into the light?'

'I will,' the Caesar said in a loud, clear voice.

'Then I proclaim you emperor. Once the pretender Michael Doukas has been removed, you will take your rightful place upon the throne, and all will be well again.'

A cheer rang out through the army. The warriors thrust their swords and axes into the air and stamped their feet. But as Kraki scanned the ranks, he saw only knowing grins and sly looks.

The Viking nodded, sneering. Now he understood why the Caesar had seemed more like a guest than a captive when he wandered through the halls of the Amaseia palace. John Doukas' loyalty had been bought, or he had reasoned that Michael's days were done, and better to be on Roussel's side than facing him across a field of battle.

Kraki glanced around the devastated town. All was now clear. This was a message, to the emperor and his advisers, that Roussel was a force to be reckoned with. They could no longer treat him with contempt.

'Tonight there will be a feast the like of which has never been seen before,' Roussel boomed to his men. 'And tomorrow . . . tomorrow we ride on Constantinople.'

Frowning, Kraki ignored the raucous whoops of the men and watched the warlord walk towards him. Could it be true? Was the Norman leader so brave . . . or so arrogant . . . as to take on the might of the greatest city on earth?

'You think me mad?' Roussel said, his smile wry.

'I think you have weighed your actions well,' the Viking grunted. 'You knew the emperor and that snake of a eunuch Nikephoritzes would never let you rest. The kingdom you have carved out for yourself in Galatia would always be a threat to their rule.'

'You have some wisdom, for a scar-faced old dog.' Roussel grinned, enjoying himself. 'Once they sent the Caesar to bring me low, I knew they would never relent. Attack after attack would follow.' He shrugged. 'If they had left me alone, I would have been happy to enjoy my land and my gold.'

Kraki snorted. He did not believe that for a moment. Adventuring was in the Norman's blood. 'And now you have seized the upper hand.'

Roussel raised his face to the sun, basking. 'John Doukas is an ambitious man, filled with resentment at the way he was treated by those who surrounded the emperor. Nikephoritzes, in the main. That eunuch is a threat to himself.'

'With your own dog upon the throne, you can keep your lands, your riches, *and* act as general to the new emperor.'

Roussel's smile faded as he looked towards his milling warriors. Karas Verinus, Ragener and Justin pushed their way out of the crowd. The Roman clutched a large basket to his chest. When he saw the Viking he gave a sly smile and started towards him, but the sea wolf hung back. His yellow teeth were now visible through the hole where Kraki had torn away part of his cheek. He would not make the mistake of coming too close again.

Kraki spat a mouthful of phlegm. He was no fool, this Norman. If John Doukas was to fall, the warlord had already allied himself with the brutal general and that mad, blood-slaked boy who would be the next to steal the crown. 'Karas will accompany that Roman survivor into the city to deliver your message to the emperor, filled with shock and despair, and to vouch for all that is said,' the Viking went on. 'And then, as you lay siege, he will be a power on the inside, twisting things to your . . . and his . . . advantage.'

'He is a hero of the empire, for all his faults,' Roussel said, watching the general stride over, Justin at his side. 'He will have the ear of the emperor's circle. If he says he fears our power, so will they.'

'At last we no longer have to hide behind pretence,' Karas said when he arrived. 'Soon Constantinople will fall.'

'In time, all traitors fall too, to the axe,' Kraki growled.

'And you are above such games,' the general sneered. 'A man of honour.'

Justin leaned forward to peer into the Viking's face. His eyes were glassy, unblinking. Kraki felt the odd sensation that there was nothing behind them. He understood war, but he did not understand this.

'Do you see the sands of his life running away?' Karas said to the boy. 'Do you see the flesh falling from the skull?'

The boy continued to stare.

Kraki broke that gaze and looked to the general. 'If you put this thing upon the throne, you will damn yourself.'

Karas smiled. Pushing the basket beneath the Viking's nose, he whipped off the lid. A mass of snakes roiled in the dark depths. 'Your new companions. After the feast this even, I will come for you. You have my word on that.'

Placing one hand upon Justin's head, the general steered him away, back towards the camp. Roussel watched them go, his expression wintry.

'I judge a man by his friends,' Kraki said.

'This is war, Viking. You have seen enough blood to know that if we only found allies in friends we would die alone on the battlefield.' Without looking back, Roussel strode away.

# Chapter Thirty-Nine

Silvery moonlight carved a path through the deep shadow of the tent. In the triangle of open flaps, stars glittered in the sable sky. Drifting in on the breeze, the sweet scent of roasting lamb mingled with the tang of woodsmoke. From far across the camp, where the great fire roared, jubilant voices rang out, and raucous laughter, and song. The feast had been in full flow for long hours now, since the fat red sun had turned the landscape ruddy. Soon it would be done.

In the corner of the tent, Kraki salivated. His belly was empty and had been for more than a day. There was no need to waste good food on a man who was not long for this world. But he had years since made his peace with death. He had always dreamed it would come on the battlefield, with his blood thundering in his head, and his good right arm laying waste to his foes. An ending that would earn him a place at the high table in Valhalla. But here he was, trussed up like a deer waiting to be butchered for the pot. Aye, justice, there was little of it in this world.

One dream remained: that his spear-brothers had survived and would bring vengeance down upon the heads of Karas Verinus and all who walked with him.

The voices echoing from the campfire dimmed. The silences

in between the songs grew longer. He found himself straining to listen for the sound of a foot on the baked mud of the track. For the whisper of his death approaching.

A shadow fell across the moonlit path and he jerked. He had heard nothing.

His moment had come.

'Do not tarry there,' he growled, struggling into a seated position. 'Look into my eyes, if you dare.'

'You are so tired of life you would rush to the end?' A silhouette loomed in the entrance to the tent. So certain had he been that it was Karas Verinus approaching that Kraki found himself struggling to recognize the man who stood there. But then the figure shifted and the pale light lit the features of Roussel de Bailleul.

Kraki snorted. 'You have come to watch my gutting? Is there not enough song and wine at the feast?'

The warlord raised his right hand to show the goblet he was holding. A toast. He sipped it, his gaze never leaving the glowering captive.

'Karas will be here soon enough. He eats his meat and watches the fire,' the warlord murmured, adding, 'while he sharpens his knife on a whetstone.'

'You know that Roman bastard will turn on you the moment he sees an advantage.'

Ignoring his words, the warlord began to circle the prisoner. 'You could join my army. I can always use good fighting men. Even Karas Verinus would not dare attack you then.'

'You would have me standing at your back in a battle?' Kraki laughed without humour.

'You would not attack me if you agreed to fight under my banner.'

'You speak without any doubt.'

'Aye. I have no doubt.' Roussel squatted in front of the Viking, levelling his unwavering gaze. 'Men of honour know each other.' He raised his index finger to his left eye. 'We see it, here. We know it with a look, as one wolf recognizes another, as a brother knows a brother. And we know men without honour too. They are our true enemies, not the ones we face across the field of battle. They are the ones who steal life away, grain by grain.'

This was true; Kraki had learned as much from his father. 'I would kill an honourable man, if it meant I lived to see a new dawn.'

'Aye. But you would not gut him and fill him with vipers.' Standing, Roussel wandered into the shadows at the rear of the tent. His voice floated back, thoughtful. 'Some of my men fought with William at the battle of Ely. They told me of the courage of the English they faced. Stories of Hereward and his war-band, few in number, near-starving. To come so close to victory, to smell it on the wind, and then be betrayed . . . that must feel like a spear to the heart.'

'It is war.'

'True.' Sipping at his goblet, Roussel wandered back in front of the captive. 'Instead of freeing your land from my countrymen, it was you who were sent into exile. A harsh judgement, but you kept your heads upon your shoulders. To fight another day. But a defeat like that wounds in ways the eye cannot see. I know. Tell me . . . if all had changed, where would you be now?'

Kraki peered into the dark, and saw across fields and forests and the wide whale road to a rain-lashed bog. And standing under the willows he saw Acha, hair like raven-wings, skin as pale as snow. He felt peace. There would be no more running, no more fighting. 'England,' he muttered.

'We are all haunted by days long gone. What was, what if, what might be again.' Roussel drained his wine and tossed his goblet away. Striding to the entrance, he glanced out into the night and then returned. His voice lowered. 'Days long gone. Times that shaped us. The land on which we walked, the people we knew. And in days of hardship we long to be back there, to feel the gentle touch and loving embrace. To hear laughter we barely remember. There is an oak tree on the edge of my village, where my father liked to sit. There he would tell me tales of when our folk came to Normandy in their dragon-ships, filled with fire and fury. Stories of great battles, of warriors who made the earth shake. There are days when I would hear those tales again. When I would sit with my father in the sun and learn from his wisdom.'

In the moonlight, Kraki glimpsed the flash of silver. Roussel was holding his knife. The Viking felt his heart leap. Now he knew why the warlord was there, what all these strange words meant. An honourable death. Freedom from the suffering that Karas Verinus promised. Raising his head, Kraki sucked in a breath of cool air. He was ready.

'But it is all like the mist,' Roussel was saying. He weighed the knife in his hand, watching the way the light reflected off the blade. 'The oak has been cut down for firewood. My father . . . I will never sit beside him again in this life. This is the trap of days long gone. They still shape us, even though they lie beyond the horizon, and we cannot find those places again. All we have is here, now. We must hold on to that, brother. We must make it bend to our will, live lives of joy if we can. My father's words still stay with me. They will never go, and that must be enough.' The warlord's fingers closed tight around the deer-horn hilt. 'What is gone is done. There is no going back to find another path through the forest. Only forward. Only forward. That is where our true salvation lies.'

Before Kraki knew what was happening, Roussel stepped behind him, grabbed the bonds at his wrists and hauled him to his feet. Closing his eyes, Kraki bared his throat, waiting for the blade to free his life-blood.

Instead, he felt the warlord sawing at the ropes. When they snapped free, Roussel shoved him forward. 'Run,' he said.

Kraki staggered a few steps, then glanced back. His thoughts tilted.

Roussel slipped his knife into his tunic and turned away. 'Run,' he said again.

As he grasped what had been done, the Viking felt a wave of

gratitude. His judgement of this man had not been amiss. Rubbing his wrists, he lurched out into the night, scarcely able to believe that he had been given a second chance to live his life. But his legs were weak and unused to walking far, and after so long without food in his belly he had little strength for a fight.

Run, the warlord had said, and run he would.

Beyond the camp, the flames of the great fire spun a swirl of glittering sparks up towards the stars. Bursts of song still rolled out, but the jubilation he had heard earlier had all but ebbed away. Soon the feast would be over and the drunken warriors would be staggering back to their tents to sleep off their stupor.

Picking a path among the guy ropes, the Viking crept away. Barely had he gone more than a few steps when he felt his neck prickle. Looking back, he saw a mountainous figure silhouetted against the glare of the fire. With flames flickering around the outline, the shape was moving away from the feast. Here was Karas Verinus, now ready for his butchery, he was sure of it.

Kraki ducked down, hoping the night had been dark enough to cloak him. At first nothing reached his ears, no roar commanding him to stop, no thunder of feet. But at the last tent he thought he heard something, a sigh perhaps, a whisper of footsteps. When he glanced back he glimpsed a flitting shadow in the moonlight, far away. A trick of the light, he told himself, nothing more.

Beyond the camp, the flatland seemed to stretch almost to the horizon, where a dark smudge of trees lay. It was a patchwork of dusty soil, clumps of tough yellow grass swaying in the breeze and ridges of brown rock like the fins of great fish breaking through the surface of the whale road. He could see few places to hide. Yet if he could reach the forest before dawn he could find some roots and berries to assuage his growling belly, and then he would be ready for anything.

Cursing his weakened legs, he broke into a loping run. His chest was soon burning from exertion. What a ghost of himself he had become. Trussed up for too long, beaten and abused, and deprived of sound sleep. When he reached the nearest slab of rock he paused to catch his breath. Looking back towards the camp, he stiffened.

A figure was moving across the wide expanse with a steady gait, relentless, remorseless, hunting. As Kraki watched, he realized this was not Karas. His pursuer was smaller, and slight of frame. It was the boy, it could be no other, the mad, blood-crazed boy who was not a boy. The Viking cursed again. A boy! But he was too weakened to face even that savage. He was a sheep being pursued by a wolf.

Blinking the stinging sweat from his eyes, he weaved among the rocky outcroppings, hoping the lad would lose sight of him. But every time he reached another open stretch, he saw Justin closing upon his heels.

The forest seemed to draw no nearer. He imagined the boy with his knife, leaping around him. A cut here, a cut there, his blood draining away into the dust, until finally he would collapse. And then that moon-faced bastard would fall upon him.

Kraki roared his anger. All the battles he had fought, all the enemies he had defeated, and his days would be ended by a mere boy.

And then he felt his feet fly out from under him. Sweat-blinded, he had not seen the hollow. Down the slope he flew, turning in the air. With a crash that drove the breath from his lungs, he slammed into the earth, rolled and came to a halt looking up at the edge.

The boy reared up there. His blade glinted in the moonlight.

Raising his huge hands, Kraki snarled, 'These are waiting to choke the life out of you. Feed them!'

Justin showed no fear, no emotion of any kind. Then, even as he swung up his blade, other shapes seemed to rise up from the very land around him.

The boy paused, looked around.

Kraki shook the surprise from his head. For the second time that night, he had been dumbfounded by a sudden appearance. They were Turks, he saw, each one armed with a sword.

'God smiles upon you, my friend,' a familiar voice boomed. Suleiman was standing on the other side of the hollow, grinning. 'But I would not have thought you to flee from a mere stripling.'

'Wait!' the Viking urged as the warriors closed in on Justin. 'Take care—'

The boy lashed out with his knife. Blood gushed from the throat of the nearest warrior. The man's hands clutched for the wound, his wide eyes showing his disbelief that such a thing could have happened.

Roaring as one, the Turks whirled their swords, but they were too late. The beast was already gone, sprinting away into the night.

His face now grim, Suleiman helped Kraki to his feet. 'Karas Verinus has been the bane of all Seljuks, slaughtering us like cattle whenever we dared walk on the land he claimed. It seems his foul blood has tainted the boy too.' The commander looked towards the ruddy glow over the camp, his dark eyes glinting beneath heavy lids. 'There will be a reckoning, make no mistake.'

'What brings you and your men here?'

'Since Roussel de Bailleul's army rode out of Amaseia and Ancyra we have been watching from afar. We would know his mind.' His grin flickered back, his eyes sparkling once more. 'There may be some gain for us here. What say you?'

Kraki grunted. 'Spoils aplenty, I would wager.'

'Good, good.' Suleiman clapped an arm across the Viking's shoulder and added cheerily, 'And what for you now, my friend? You have your freedom again. Do you return to Constantinople and be a running dog for the Romans? Or let God's wind carry you to a new life?'

Kraki looked to the west. He thought of England and Acha. He thought of the peace he could find once the ache in his chest had been assuaged. And he remembered Roussel de Bailleul's wise words. Here was the crossroads. The choice was his.

# Chapter Forty

Shafts of sunlight punched through the forest canopy. Shadows flashed around them as shrieking birds took wing from the branches. Three men weaved among the trees, their breath rasping as they leapt gnarled roots. Their grim gaze was fixed on the green world ahead. At their backs, dark shapes swept through the half-light. The ground throbbed with the beat of hooves.

Sweat-slick in the baking heat of midday, Hereward grimaced. Would there never be any respite? Would the running never end?

Maximos skidded down a bank and snarled his ankle in a loop of bramble. With a curse, he crashed on to the soft leaf-mould, only to roll and come back to his feet without missing a step.

'It is Drogo Vavasour, I tell you. He has found our trail,' Alexios gasped as he ducked a low-hanging branch.

'Save your breath,' Hereward snapped. They could not keep this pace up for much longer. Their legs burned from weariness and they were near-starved.

Since they had left Malakopea-above, striking out west, only morsels had passed their lips. They had trapped wildfowl when they could, but the meat was never enough to fill their bellies.

They had torn out edible roots and gnawed them, and they had begged at the only dwelling they had passed, a small farm where the wife looked terrified when they appeared at her door. A knob of bread had been the reward for their pleadings. That had been a mistake. He felt sure the woman had set these dogs on their trail. Drogo and his war-band or Turks, it mattered little. They would still end up dead.

A whistle rang out. Their pursuers had them in their sights.

Hereward's eyes darted, but he could see only the seemingly endless forest. Nowhere that offered them any advantage.

A figure bobbed up from the wall of blackthorn ahead of him. Maximos cried out in surprise. The Mercian's hand flashed to his sword. Before he could draw it, a voice called out, 'Hold. It is I.'

Hereward skidded to a halt. He could scarcely believe his eyes. Maximos and Alexios slowed, then stopped to gape at the nut-brown, gap-toothed face grinning at them.

Herrig the Rat bounded out from his hiding place and snickered. 'I have seen a wounded boar cover its tracks better than you.'

Behind them, the sounds of pursuit ebbed away. Hereward turned to the line of horsemen. Familiar faces grinned down at him.

'Did you think we would abandon you? We roamed across these godforsaken lands for days until we found your trail,' Guthrinc called, his face ruddy from the exertion.

The Mercian looked along the ranks, taking in Hengist, Sighard, Hiroc the Three-fingered and the rest, with a few Athanatoi taking up the rear. He was more than delighted to see they had all survived.

Slipping down from his mount, Guthrinc strode over and with a hearty laugh swept Hereward up in a bear-hug. 'You might be a great war-leader these days, but I could still hang you upside down from the branches as I did when you were a lad.'

'You put the fear of God in us. Is this how you greet friends – by running them down like rabbits?'

'How many yet live?' Alexios demanded. 'We saw the field of battle . . . the standard . . .'

Guthrinc's face darkened. 'Perhaps one in every ten made it away with their lives.' He glanced at Hereward. 'The Romans have been humbled by this defeat, brother. It is a harsh way to learn any lesson, but in time some good may come from it.'

Hereward drew himself up. 'The gold is gone.' He expected to see dismay cloud the faces of the English, but only shrugs met his admission.

'There is always more gold,' Sighard said, unperturbed. 'We have our heads upon our shoulders and our good fighting arms. That is enough for us to give thanks.'

The Mercian felt chastened. Never give up, that was the lesson they had all learned during the battle against William the Bastard. He had lost sight of that in the dark days. He would not do so again.

Once they had returned to the well-hidden valley where the rest of the Athanatoi were camped, Hereward looked out across the remnants of the once-mighty fighting force and felt a pang of regret. Tiberius sat by the fire, sucking the grease from a fowl bone. Ten years seemed to have passed since the last time Hereward had seen him. His face was drawn, his skin greying, his eyes hollow. When he looked up, he held the Mercian's gaze for a long moment and nodded before returning to the remains of his meal. No words needed to be said.

At dawn, the Immortals and the English broke camp and rode west. As they skirted the forests and crossed the grasslands, Hereward looked up and saw a pall of smoke hanging over the way ahead. Soon they reached what was left of a town. Fires still glowed among the ruined buildings, and bodies were scattered everywhere.

Further west, more smoke drifted.

Silence fell across the ranks as they rode on.

Along the road, town after town, village after village, had been laid to waste, a trail of destruction leading inexorably towards Constantinople.

Then, on the fourth day, they reached the high ground overlooking the Bosphorus and the Sea of Marmara. The dome of the Hagia Sophia glowed under the high sun and the city spread out beyond it in all its magnificence. And yet, as he sat up on his mount, Hereward could only see the vast army of Roussel de Bailleul, waiting to lay siege to the seat of an empire.

'So many,' Maximos said, shielding his eyes against the sun's glare. 'Against an army that is not worthy of the name. The emperor has let it wither away. What hope is there of holding back the Norman tide?'

'We have been here before,' Hereward said. 'The few can defeat the many, if there is fire in their hearts.' And yet these Romans were not the English. Could they be trusted to fight to the last for all they had?

As he watched the campfires belching black smoke into the air, and the sun glinting off the armour and the weapons, he could not help but think that a slaughter was coming to Constantinople, a bloody ending into which they would all be drawn.

# Chapter Forty-One

Fire roared up the vast wooden cross. Black smoke billowed to the heavens and swallowed the setting sun. Across the Bosphorus, the reek of pitch and charring swept towards Constantinople. Flames flickered to life on a second soaring cross, further to the south, and then on a third. The message was clear to everyone in the City of God who cared to look to the forces massing on its eastern flank. Though it was to many the centre of Christendom in the civilized world, Constantinople could no longer count upon the Divine to protect it.

On the eastern sea wall, a small knot of men and women looked in the direction of Roussel de Bailleul's army. Though the sprawling camp reported by the scouts lay out of view, none of them could any longer deny the brooding presence.

Alric felt his chest tighten as memories flooded him of that rain-lashed night when he looked out from the walls of Ely across the vast army of William the Bastard. But this time things were different. There seemed as many enemies on this side of the defences as there were staring them down. The English stood alone, surrounded on every side by those who wanted to destroy them.

'The walls of Constantinople have stood for years beyond measure.' Nikephoritzes glowered at the burning crosses.

'However large Roussel de Bailleul's army, they will not fall now. We can afford to bide our time.'

A lazy smile danced on Anna Dalassene's lips. Her eyes looked hazy from all the wine she had swallowed – she rarely seemed to be without a goblet in her hand, Alric noted – but her wits were always sharp. 'And you think the Norman will not have considered the strength of our defences when he decided to bring his army across the miles to our door? Do not be over-confident, Nikephoritzes.'

The eunuch grunted. He did not like being lectured on strategy by a woman. 'You have been absent from the court for many a day, Anna. Why have you decided to appear now, when our enemies threaten us?'

Anna flashed a look at the two women who accompanied her, Rowena and Ariadne, posing as her servants. 'There is little joy at court these days. Not when it is the hunting ground of Falkon Cephalas, who sees every man, woman and child as a threat against the emperor.'

Nikephoritzes flinched. Anna's voice was honeyed, but Alric knew the emperor's adviser took her words as a strike against his authority. He had appointed Falkon Cephalas. He approved the reign of terror that was being inflicted upon the city.

'Constantinople has always been a boiling cauldron, but there has never been such peace here,' Nikephoritzes said. 'Falkon does good work.'

'Falkon Cephalas is a stain upon the godly nature of this city,' Alric snapped, unable to contain himself any longer. Never had he felt such anger. He remembered his despair as he watched the bodies of those too young to fight swinging on the gibbets that had sprouted everywhere in Constantinople like the spring growth. 'We have heard much talk of Roussel de Bailleul believing himself to be the new King William, but Falkon is the Bastard's true heir. A murderer of children.'

Anna laughed silently, amused by this outburst. The eunuch was not used to hearing sharp words.

Nikephoritzes' eyes burned with rage. 'Who are you to speak so, monk?' he spat.

'Why, he is a man of God,' Anna said, her voice light but her words like knives. 'Every day he prays for the safe homecoming of my son Alexios, in return for a small payment to his monastery. I have found much strength in his devotions. When he sees men who defy the Lord's plan, he must speak out.'

'You will be the first monk to do so, I wager,' the eunuch grumbled. He turned back to the shimmering crosses. They seemed to be burning even brighter now that dusk was falling.

Alric felt that Anna had understated the case. The more he had seen of the miseries Falkon had inflicted, the more he felt that God was revealing Alric's own path. He must take a stand, even if it cost him his life. And once Nikephoritzes reported his comments back to Falkon that was a likely outcome. The cold-hearted dog would not tolerate such an outspoken enemy.

The monk knew his patron had brought him along as moral weight for her argument. Now he had spoken, she drew herself up, her moment chosen. 'Falkon is not God. He makes mistakes like any man. And he has made one that could cost us dear – the arrest of Wulfrun of the Varangian Guard.'

'Wulfrun is dead,' Nikephoritzes said without care.

'All Constantinople would know if that were true.'

'As good as. His execution is planned for dawn. There is nothing I can do for him.'

Anna's smile hardened. 'You have no power over your own dog.'

The eunuch's face became like stone. He would not meet the woman's eyes.

Sucking in a deep breath of the smoke-tinged air, Anna continued, 'You know I am loyal to the emperor, and like you I wish only for our empire to be as strong as it was in the days of our ancestors. I seek no personal gain here. But I fear for us all, for the emperor most of all, if Falkon has, as I believe, made a great error. Roussel de Bailleul has not yet revealed his plan, but there will be war, of that there can be no doubt. The Varangian

Guard will be at the forefront of that battle, and now they are without a leader. We cannot afford to lose a warrior of Wulfrun's skill. We need him, Nikephoritzes. You know that.'

The eunuch's lips tightened. 'Falkon Cephalas believes Wulfrun is a danger to the emperor. Until I learn otherwise, I choose to play no part in this.'

Alric could see that though the eunuch had his doubts, he would not lose face by wavering in front of strangers.

A faint whistle rang out from deep in the shadows. Few would have paid it any heed, but Alric knew it came from Salih ibn Ziyad, who had remained on watch in case any of Falkon's brown-cloaked soldiers approached. At Anna's nod, he eased back into the dark next to one of the towers. Night was coming down hard and the Keeper of the Flame had not yet lit the torches. Cloaked in the gloom, he watched as four figures appeared at the top of the stone steps. One he did not recognize, but this one had been badly beaten not so long ago. The second was a great oak of a man with broad shoulders and arms that could snap a spine. His skin was dark and leathery and his long hair the colour of steel. The monk thought he could see the mark of the Verini in his features, a fact confirmed when Ariadne's eyes widened and she backed away. She seemed as afraid of this man as of her own father. The boy, Justin Verinus, was there too, his face as blank as always, his eyes dead.

When he saw the fourth man, Alric felt rage burn in his chest. It was Ragener, the sea wolf who had tortured him. Unable to help himself, he lurched out of the shadows. When the ruined man recognized the monk, his eyes lit up with cruel glee.

Seeing Alric's rage, Anna held up a hand to command him to hold back. Fighting back his anger, he came to a halt, simmering with hatred.

'Karas Verinus. It is long since I have seen you in Constantinople,' Anna said. 'What brings you from your eastern home?'

When Karas ignored her, Alric saw a cold light flare in her eyes, but she held her tongue. 'I have risked all to bring news of great danger,' the tall man said, fixing his stare on the eunuch, 'aye, risked my life itself. The threat from that dog Roussel de Bailleul is greater than you could ever have imagined. Doom is coming, Nikephoritzes, for you, for the emperor, for all of us, and Constantinople itself. We must make ready before it is too late.' He shoved the beaten man forward so hard he almost fell to his knees. 'Speak, you.'

Through split lips, the man blurted, 'A new emperor has been proclaimed by Roussel de Bailleul. The Caesar, John Doukas. He stands now with our enemy's army, ready to seize the throne.'

'This cannot be!' Nikephoritzes blanched.

'I saw it with my own eyes.'

'He speaks the truth,' Karas growled. 'Roussel set us free to bring this message to you.'

The eunuch stared at him for a moment, his thoughts racing. Gripping the wall, he peered over the edge as if he were afraid he would plunge into an abyss. 'John Doukas did this of his own free will, or with a blade at his neck?'

'What matters it?' Karas snarled. 'There is now a rival emperor with a powerful claim to the throne. You know the dangers as well as I, Nikephoritzes – that unhappy citizens will rally to his call, that axes-for-hire will sweep in to swell the rebel army. That we will find other enemies joining with him . . . the Turks, perhaps.'

So pale was the eunuch that Alric thought he might faint dead away. 'We have no army of any note to defend us,' he breathed. 'What is left will be crushed in an instant.'

'We cannot waste another moment,' Karas urged. His voice was a low growl. 'I will tell all that I know of the enemy and his forces, and give what aid I can. But we must hurry to the emperor. Plans must be made. Now.'

'Yes, yes, you are right,' Nikephoritzes gabbled. He all but ran along the wall towards the steps. As the new arrivals followed, Ragener flashed a sly glance back at Alric.

Once they had gone, Anna glared towards the burning

crosses. 'Then the Athanatoi failed. Now we must pray that they survived their encounter with Roussel.'

'The people have suffered too many miseries,' Rowena said. 'Can we be certain they will support Michael?'

Anna shook her head. 'But it will be worse for all of us with John Doukas upon the throne, Roussel de Bailleul whispering in his ear, and Karas Verinus now worming his way into the rotten heart of it all.'

'My uncle would not be content to be the new emperor's general.' Ariadne looked close to tears. 'He has a plan in place, make no mistake, and he is more savage than my father.'

'Come,' Anna said, leading the way along the wall. 'There is much here to think on.' For the first time, Alric thought he heard a note of worry in her voice.

Salih was waiting for them at the foot of the steps, his face a mask. Ariadne slipped to his side. But barely had they plunged into the shadowed streets leading away from the wall when Alric noticed a hooded figure waiting ahead. As they neared, she pulled back her cowl. Salih hissed, his hand flying to the silver knife at his waist.

Juliana Nepa showed a brazen face, though Alric thought he glimpsed a spark of fear in her eyes. 'Take my life if you must,' she said, her voice defiant. 'I came here knowing full well that you might be quick to use your blade upon me. I am not afraid. But know this – if you do you will doom your friends.'

Anna reached out to stay Salih's hand. 'Speak,' she said.

'I seek to make a bargain,' Juliana replied, her eyes looking from one face to the next. 'There is no love lost between us, we all know that. But if we can put aside our hatreds, I offer you the chance to become allies—'

'Never,' Salih snarled.

'And together,' Juliana continued, ignoring him, 'we may yet survive this dark dawn.

# Chapter Forty-Two

The three burning crosses glowed a dull red against the night sky. Now that the pitch had seared away, the wind whipped the smouldering wood into a shower of sparks. Even miles distant on the banks of the Bosphorus, ashes floated in the air and the reek of charring lingered. Beyond the lapping on the shore and the creak of boats straining at their mooring ropes, all was still. The waters were black and scattered with shards of silver as the war-band crept along the river's edge.

Hereward cocked his head, listening. He nodded to Guthrinc, who passed the signal down the line of the English to where Maximos and Alexios took up the rear. A long glance over the muddy stretch told him they were alone. The fishermen had returned to their homes. None of the packs of Roussel de Bailleul's warriors searching for enemy scouts roamed nearby. With relief, he squelched on across the sludge. Their trek had been long and circuitous, but it had been worthwhile.

When they had left the Athanatoi hiding in a deep, secluded valley, they had known there was no possibility that the Immortals could reach Constantinople without coming under attack. But the English were ghosts on the land. Many hard lessons had been learned in the long years they had spent crawling over the sodden fens and through surging waterways to avoid William the Bastard's men. Of all the fighting men, only they had the skill to reach the city and bring back reinforcements. Yet still Hereward could not quite believe they had avoided all scrutiny. He had expected that at some point they would have to fight their way to the river. But here they were, swords still sheathed.

Where the fishing boats bobbed, Hereward splashed into the cold shallows. Guthrinc eased beside him. 'Five boats should do it,' the tall man murmured.

'The currents are treacherous, so I have heard. But they can be no worse than the fens. We row ahead, and we will be warm and dry in the city before dawn.'

Guthrinc glanced across the wide river to where the torches were flickering along the city walls. 'And then? What fighting men will the Romans bring together to save the Immortals now that they have let their army wither away? Will they doom Tiberius and his men?'

Hereward clenched his jaw. He feared the worst. The Immortals had borne their sacrifices like true warriors. They did not deserve to be abandoned.

'We will do what we can for them,' he replied, without yet knowing what. 'That is my vow.'

Before he could clamber into the nearest boat, a cry rose from the river's edge. Whirling, he saw Hengist dancing across the mudflats, his face chalky in the moonlight.

'Hush,' Guthrinc hissed, a finger to his lips.

But Hengist was too frightened to heed him. 'We are haunted,' he moaned. 'Haunted.'

Hereward grabbed him by the shoulders to calm him, but the madman writhed free and pointed across the foreshore to the waist-high yellow grass. Silhouetted against the starry sky, a shape was wading towards them. Wild, it looked, and brutish.

As Hereward squinted, unsure what he was seeing, Guthrinc roared like a wounded bear and raced towards the stalking figure.

'A ghost,' Hengist cried, clutching at his head.

Guthrinc crashed into the grass and swept the intruder up in his arms, pressing him to his chest as if he were trying to snap his spine. His roar swelled to jubilant laughter.

'Set me down, you jolt-headed bog-crawler,' the captive boomed, writhing in the big man's grip.

Hereward furrowed his brow at the familiar voice. 'Kraki?'

Unable to contain their rejoicing, the English surged forward as one. Once Guthrinc had lowered his friend to the ground, the warriors crowded in, slapping the Viking's back and cheering. Snarling, Kraki shook his fists in face after face, driving the exuberant men back.

'Do not paw me. I am not some Frankish whore,' he bawled.

'We thought you dead,' Sighard exclaimed.

'Then you had no faith. You are curs, every last one of you.' The Viking glowered, but Hereward knew him well enough to read the glimmer in his dark eyes.

The warriors parted as Hereward strode up. 'You are like an old dog who does not know when to die,' he said.

Kraki scowled. 'All has not gone well. They took my axe.'

'We will get you a new one, a sharper one. For now, we need to be away from here before our heads end up on Norman spikes.'

They clambered into the fishing boats and pushed off from the river bank, Hereward squatting in the prow to listen as Kraki told of his struggles since his capture by the Turks. As the tale settled on him, the Mercian felt a flame flicker deep in his head and he began to grin.

The Viking narrowed his eyes. 'What gold have you found in those words?'

Before Hereward could reply, Guthrinc grunted and pointed out across the black waters. In the distance, the ruddy glow of a fire-pot whisked across the swell. 'A boat,' he murmured. 'Someone who knows these currents better than we do.'

'Who would be out on the river at this hour?' Sighard asked, sweating at his oar.

'Someone up to no good,' Hereward replied. He watched the red glow sweep towards the western bank and the port of Boukoleon.

As the torches along the quayside drew nearer, he felt relief that the dangerous lands to the east were now behind them. His men could rest, fill their bellies and lick their wounds while he pressed for reinforcements for the Athanatoi. On dry land once more, the spear-brothers tied up the boats, their voices rising as they spoke of taverns and beds. But they fell into silence when an urgent whistle reached their ears. Hereward followed the sound to Maximos, who was crouching at the foot of a flight of stone steps. He had prowled along the quayside, curious as to why there had been no harbour men or wall guards to inspect the new arrivals. A body lay sprawled at his feet.

The Mercian could see that the man had died from a single sword thrust to the heart. From the fallen helm and newly painted shield, the victim seemed to be a soldier, though Hereward did not recognize the brown cloak and tunic.

'A fresh kill,' Maximos said, pressing the tips of his fingers against still-warm flesh.

Hereward slid Brainbiter from its sheath and looked up the steps. Blood dripped down the stone. Another body slumped at the top. Standing, Maximos drew his own sword and together they crept up the flight.

More corpses trailed away from the steps, their blood puddling on the flagstones. Hereward counted four in all. Beyond them, a figure waited in the shadows under an archway, a bloodstained double-edged sword held at his side.

As the Mercian raised Brainbiter in anticipation of a fight, the swordsman stepped forward into the circle of light beneath a hissing torch. It was Deda.

'It seems,' the knight said in a wry tone, 'that you were expected.'

# Chapter Forty-Three

Rosy dawn light flooded the courtyard. Fingers of shadow reached across the flagstones from the stone-faced ranks of the Varangian Guard to the splintered wooden block in the middle of the square. Crimson capes flapped in the cool breeze, a reminder of the blood that was to come.

As he stumbled out of the door from the Boukoleon palace, Wulfrun blinked in the first sunlight he had seen in days. He was pleased that his men showed no emotion. Even Ricbert, his aide and confidant for so many years, revealed none of the grim thoughts that must be rushing through his head.

Did his men accept the accusation that he was a traitor? Wulfrun could not believe it. Brothers in battle knew the true hearts of everyone they fought alongside.

Glancing at the block, he smiled tightly. He was more than aware of the bitter irony as he remembered dragging the hated Hereward to this spot to end his days. Perhaps this was God's judgement for holding the desire for vengeance in his heart for so long. His time in that dark cell had passed in a haze of pain. But he had not confessed to any of the false accusations put to him. Nor had he betrayed the Nepotes. He had long since decided that he would go to his death rather than see any harm come to Juliana. After a while, the torments had lessened.

Perhaps Falkon Cephalas realized he would never speak. Or perhaps someone had intervened on his behalf. At least he faced his execution with his body intact, his eyes still seeing. He could hold his head up and look death in the face.

Flanked by two guards, the commander trudged across the dusty stone to where his executioner waited. He nodded to Dorlof, the Rus, whose arms looked as though they could chop down an oak with a single stroke. That was good. The thought of a weaker swordsman taking five or six attempts to hack through his neck did not fill him with pleasure.

Turning his face to the sun, he closed his eyes and enjoyed the warmth for the last time. Birdsong filled his ears. Simple joys, the best in life.

'Wulfrun of the English. You know the charge against you?'

His eyes jerked open and he felt a surge of rage at the sound of that grating voice. But he would not show his feelings.

'Aye,' he boomed.

Falkon Cephalas showed an emotionless face too, a noble one, almost, and most definitely practised, Wulfrun thought. He had placed himself on a high pedestal and it seemed he had taken a liking to his new position. Nikephoritzes stood at his side, his eyes fierce and unreadable. Others from the court waited behind, all witnesses to a traitor brought low, as Falkon intended. They would spread the word far and wide. No one was beyond justice, not even the feared battle-leader Wulfrun of the Varangian Guard.

And behind them stood a row of Falkon's own guard, scar-faced rough fellows all, a travesty of the highly skilled and ordered team that Wulfrun commanded.

Falkon began to make a speech, something about treason and betrayal and dishonour. Wulfrun closed his ears. There was no need to hear those lies repeated. They were words for the polishing of Falkon's name, nothing more.

Marching up to the block, he looked Dorlof in the eye. The Rus nodded, showing his respect.

'Wait.'

The word rang out, an English voice. Wulfrun looked round and saw Alric pushing his way through the Guard. He must have been waiting behind them, perhaps hiding, until the captive was brought out to face his fate.

'This man is innocent of all crimes,' the monk announced, holding his arms wide. He strode in front of Falkon and met his eye, defying him. 'The only true crime here is one against God's will.'

Wulfrun glanced at Falkon and saw the fury rising in his face. What game was the monk playing? A few words, even godly ones, would not change the minds of the hard men gathered here. Instead, the churchman would only provoke retribution. Falkon Cephalas would never allow such a challenge to his authority. With his eyes, Wulfrun urged the monk to be silent, but Alric only raised his chin higher as he continued to speak.

'The Lord will damn all who would doom a good man, a brave man, one who has served the emperor loyally.'

'And you claim to speak for God, do you, monk? Blasphemy,' Falkon sneered. He glanced furtively at his men, a silent command. The leader of his guard dropped his hand to his hilt and stepped forward.

Wulfrun felt a surge of gratitude that this man, that any man, would speak out on his behalf under peril of death. The monk owed him nothing. Indeed, Wulfrun had shown little more than contempt for all the English who had sided with the man who had brought about his father's death. But he felt dismay, too. He could not bear to see the monk suffer Falkon Cephalas' vengeance.

'Enough,' he called.

Alric glanced back at him, his righteous anger at Falkon still glowing in his face. But then his features softened, and something that looked like relief flashed across them. Wulfrun realized the monk was looking past him, and turned.

In the doorway to the palace, a frail figure wavered. It was Godred, the true commander of the Varangian Guard and the man who had guided him with kind words ever since his arrival in Constantinople. Made haggard by the illness that had assailed him, Godred looked on the brink of death. His eyes were rheumy, his cheeks hollow; barely more than skin draped on bone, he shook with every agonizing step. Yet he had put on his helm, and his crimson cloak, and he bore the splintered shield upon his arm that had served him well in battle upon battle. Though he was a shadow of the feared warrior he had been, he wore the colours of the Guard with pride, and with good reason, Wulfrun knew. He felt a surge of long-stifled emotion. No man in Constantinople was more respected, not even the emperor. And he had come there, from his deathbed, for Wulfrun.

And he was not alone.

As Godred stumbled, about to fall, a figure darted out from the palace to take his arm. Juliana looked to her love, her eyes shining in the first light. Wulfrun's throat narrowed. She too had risked all to save him. All the doubts he had about her faded. But then his heart began to pound. Falkon would never let her leave alive. He did not want this.

'He is here,' Alric called, though to whom Wulfrun could not tell.

At the door to the palace, the emperor emerged, bleary-eyed at being woken at such an early hour. With sleep still heavy upon him, he looked even younger, Wulfrun thought, and a little bewildered. Behind him stepped Anna Dalassene, resplendent in a crimson dress embroidered with gold that sparkled in the dawn sun. Her lips twitched into a ghost of a smile, one that grew hard and triumphant when she locked eyes with Falkon Cephalas.

Wulfrun grinned, the first timc in many a day. The Roman bastard had been outmanoeuvred. There could be no other explanation. Anna and the Doukai had long been rivals, but here she was guiding the emperor she no doubt secretly despised. Michael was still raw and easily swayed. Anna must have known he would respect her age and wisdom when she begged him to come here, to this dismal place of slaughter, expressing no doubt a litany of fears about what was to take place.

A hush fell over the yard. Nikephoritzes gaped, puzzled. Falkon's face hardened.

Godred bowed to the emperor. 'Do you remember when I carried you on my shoulders as a boy?' he said, his face crinkling in a smile.

'I do, loyal Godred.' Michael's face lit up at his memories of the man who had shown him more kindness than any other in Constantinople.

'You have heard the words of the monk,' the old guardsman said, turning his attention to the assembled throng. His voice was little more than the rustle of autumn leaves, but so great was the hush that it carried across the square. 'The execution of Wulfrun will be a sin in the eyes of God. But hear me – where too is the wisdom in this course? Our enemies are at the gates. I have sworn an oath to serve the emperor in all things.' The old man lurched for a moment, his hand fluttering to his mouth, but Juliana held him steady. 'And I serve not just with my axe and my good right arm,' he continued, wheezing, 'but my counsel . . . a wisdom forged in battle. And I say that this foul act today threatens the doom of Constantinople, aye, and the emperor too. Wulfrun is the fire in the heart of the Varangian Guard. There is no better man to lead, no better man to defend the emperor unto the last. This is my judgement, and if you value all I have given here over the course of my miserable life, you will heed me now. End Wulfrun's days and you do not strike a blow for justice . . . you strike a blow against the emperor himself.'

Wulfrun failed to stifle a laugh. Falkon was scowling as if he was being stabbed with hot needles.

Michael raised his eyes to the lightening sky and strode to the bloodstained block. Bowing his head, Dorlof the executioner backed away. 'No man has ever given me better counsel, loyal Godred,' the emperor said. Nikephoritzes flinched. 'This day I have heard only words of great truth and power issue from your lips. Whatever crime Wulfrun of the English has been accused of, it is balanced by the sacrifices he has made, for me, for the empire.' Michael glanced at the captive and nodded his appreciation, then turned his gaze to Falkon. 'I pardon him. Set him free. The true threat is out there, beyond the walls. Let us waste no more hours on these matters.'

Wulfrun could scarcely believe what he had heard. A shudder of relief ran through him, but this business was not yet over. When he glanced at Falkon, he saw seething resentment there. That serpent would demand retribution for his humiliation.

The emperor himself took Godred's arm and led him back into the palace. Once they had gone, Juliana hurried over to Wulfrun. She was beaming, as relieved as he was that all had gone to plan. Wulfrun could see her fighting the urge to embrace him.

'I could not leave knowing you were in danger,' she told him.

'You have made my heart sing,' he said, 'but now it is you who are in danger. Flee, before Falkon digs his claws into you.'

Her eyes darted. Falkon was ranging along his line of cut-throats and rogues, gesticulating. 'Do not worry about me,' she murmured, her voice strained.

Ricbert marched up, one eyebrow cocked. 'What now for the sea of wine we had ready to mourn your passing?' he said, feigning a deep sigh.

'Take Juliana away from here,' Wulfrun said. 'Keep her out of the hands of Falkon's men.'

The aide nodded, and steered the woman towards the palace door. As she disappeared from sight, she flashed Wulfrun a smile that promised much. Aware of the threat to his own life, Alric hurried after her.

As relief flooded him, Wulfrun felt the last of his strength ebb. He sagged down to sit upon the executioner's block, sucking in a deep, juddering breath. As the sound of running feet passed by him, he lifted his weary head. The brown-cloaked rogues were racing towards the palace. Falkon demanded blood; nothing less would do.

# Chapter Forty-Four

Alric crashed through the palace door. His heart was pounding, his back slick with sweat. Praying and ministering to children, that was where his strength lay, not in confronting powerful men. But the hastily assembled plan had worked well. A life had been saved. He could ask for no more, except, perhaps, escaping with his own miserable head still on his shoulders.

The gloomy corridor echoed with the sound of footsteps as Ricbert and Juliana hurried ahead. The woman glanced back at him, offering a silent prayer of hope, and then the guardsman dragged her along a branching corridor.

Alric ran after them. Behind him, the door slammed open once more and Falkon's soldiers surged in pursuit, yelling at him to halt.

The monk did not dare look back. Sprinting on, he weaved a path through the labyrinthine corridors with the rogues closing on him by the moment. He imagined the fierce look in their eyes, the sharp edges of their swords as they prepared to run him through. They would not try to make a show of his execution, as they had with Wulfrun. They would not waste their time throwing him into a deep cell. He was less than worthless. His body would no doubt be tossed over the wall into the Marmara sea, a feast for the fishes, forgotten by all.

Finally, he glimpsed the door that led out to the front of the palace. A sleepy-eyed guard waited beside it. Wrenching it open, Alric tumbled out into the rosy sunlight. As he sprawled across the flagstones, he heard the jubilant cries of his pursuers rise up at his heels. But he felt only relief.

Rolling over on to his back, he drank in the startled expressions of Falkon's men as a row of warriors stepped in to confront them.

'Stay back or lose your heads, your choice,' Deda said, levelling his sword at the nearest rogue. Salih ibn Ziyad stood beside him, his cruel silver knife glinting. They were flanked by Guthrinc, Sighard, Hiroc the Three-fingered, Derman and six others of Hereward's men.

The soldiers' grins faded. Uneasy eyes searched those flinty faces and saw that these men meant business.

'Tell your master the monk escaped,' Salih said, as he prodded his knife towards another cut-throat. 'You will feel the edge of his tongue, no doubt, but you will live to fight another day.'

Alric felt a flood of relief. He had survived the part of the plan that he had dreaded most. A hand closed on his arm, and he looked into the face of the girl, Ariadne. 'You are as much a warrior as any other here,' she whispered, as she helped him to his feet.

With a curt nod, the one who seemed to be the leader of the soldiers turned and the others followed him back into the palace. Ariadne slipped in beside Salih, looking up at him with wide eyes. 'Your wisdom is great,' she murmured, 'and I am proud of you. This is the right path.'

'This day,' he replied, but the monk saw that his smile was fond. 'And now?'

'Now,' Deda said, 'we wait.'

But Alric knew he could not. He felt the weight of the warriors' stares upon him as he pushed past them and walked back into the palace. The stakes here were high and became higher by the moment. Doubt flooded him as he climbed the stone steps to the first floor, but he pushed it aside. He had faith.

The corridor stretched out before him, and he began to count the doors as he had been instructed. Ahead, he heard voices, one calm, one strained. Anna was leading Nikephoritzes to the destination. The eunuch shook his fist and clutched at his head and cursed, a man who could feel doom fast approaching. When Anna opened the door, she caught sight of the monk and smiled, leaving it open so he could slip in behind them.

The chamber was long, with tall windows that looked out on the azure sea. Bathed in the sweet scent of mullein flowers, two sweat-reeking earth-walkers stood in a shaft of low sunlight. Even stained with the filth of the road, Hereward looked like a great leader. His hand rested on the golden hilt of Brainbiter and his chin was raised. He looked Nikephoritzes in the eye, demanding the eunuch's attention. Beside him, Kraki glowered, refusing to show any respect.

'You bring me to these dogs?' Nikephoritzes exclaimed. 'The world is crumbling around our ears and you waste my hours with this?'

'We are not dogs,' Kraki spat. 'We are the ones who will save all your necks.'

Nikephoritzes snorted and turned back to the door.

'Heed them,' Anna told him. 'There may well be salvation here, if only you will listen.'

'You have a rival emperor waiting to take the throne and a vast army of the fiercest fighting men in Christendom,' Hereward said, his tone measured. 'Your own army is little more than mist. You will be overrun before you have even raised your swords. Hope for you, for the emperor, for Constantinople, is fading fast.'

'Doom is coming,' Kraki said, nodding. The Viking seemed to be enjoying himself.

Alric watched Nikephoritzes grit his teeth as a rage born of desperation built inside him. 'You are dogs, both.'

Hereward narrowed his eyes. 'Then heed the barking of these dogs. For here lies your last hope.'

# Chapter Forty-Five

The standard fluttered in the light breeze. Any man could see it was pristine, the golden double-headed eagle glistening against the red background, the wooden pole polished to a shimmer. Beneath it, warriors craned their necks up, their faces glowing with pride. Here was a fresh start, a chance for redemption. They would seize it, even if it cost them their lives.

In contrast to the standard, these fighting men had seen better days. Their once-gleaming armour was now dulled by the dirt of the road, dented, scratched and streaked with the brown of blood and rust. Beards and hair had grown wild. Yet they were rested now, their eyes shining with purpose, their horses fed and watered. The Immortals were ready for what would no doubt be their final battle.

Beyond the ranks, two men watched lips moving in silent prayer. For a long moment, they drank in the peaceful view, reflecting on what had been and the horrors of what was to come.

'These are not the warriors who rode out from Constantinople,' Tiberius said.

'Battle changes a man,' Hereward agreed. 'When you have seen a friend fall, when you have been soaked in the blood of a brother, the world can no longer touch you.'

'The emperor would be proud of them.' Tiberius nodded, pleased at what he was seeing. Hereward thought how the commander of the Immortals had changed too. The slaughter outside Amaseia had cut the legs out from under his arrogance, as it would have any war-leader's. In the end, he was responsible for every life lost that day.

'The standard?' the Roman continued. 'We have you to thank for choosing to bring it to us?'

'These fighting men have earned it. They are reborn.'

'They would make amends for their failings.' Tiberius cast a sideways glance. 'And I too.'

Hereward felt a pang of recognition. Sometimes he wondered if he would spend the rest of his days making amends for the failing of his younger self. 'Your courage will not go unnoticed. After this day, the Athanatoi will live on. Nikephoritzes has given his word. The Immortals will be at the heart of the new army he is building.'

Tiberius raised his eyes to the blue sky and smiled with pride.

Bands of cloud marched across the grasslands. The sun was high. It was almost time. 'Prepare your men,' Hereward said. 'I will gather the English.'

Beckoning to Guthrinc, the Mercian strode up the slope to the top of the ridge. At the summit, he shielded his eyes against the glare of the sun and looked out over the land rolling down to the blue-green sea glinting in the distance.

Word of the invaders had spread through the streets like the plague. Before he had taken the boat to the eastern shore, he had seen the dark expressions and heard the prayers. But though Nikephoritzes had tried to dampen talk of the rival emperor, word of that too had begun to make its way through the marketplaces. For many, those broken down by Falkon Cephalas, or crushed by near-starvation and rising prices, it seemed like hope. Nikephoritzes had been right to be worried.

Lowering his head, Hereward let his gaze trail back over the sprawling camp of Roussel de Bailleul. Banners flapped in the breeze over tents of crimson and amber and ochre. From numerous smouldering campfires, lines of smoke twirled up to the heavens. In their pens, the horses swished their tails, lazy in the heat. Hereward could see little other movement. Warriors dozed in the shade. Others squatted around the embers, or whittled with their long knives.

The warlord could afford to bide his time. Let worry gnaw away at his enemies. Let dissent rise behind the walls, and let Karas Verinus and the other vipers work to undermine the authority of those in power. He was clever, that Norman. When he finally chose to attack, the blow would come like a hammer.

'We have been seen,' Guthrinc said, pointing.

One man, probably the lookout, was pointing and shouting. Another raced to the horses.

'It matters little now,' Hereward replied. Raising his arms, he half turned and hailed his men. With their shields on their arms and spears in hand, they raced up the slope.

'Today we fight as we have never fought before,' the Mercian said, looking into each face in turn. He was proud to see no fear there. Still, he wished Kraki were there at their side. 'There are ten of them for every one of us. But we have the high ground. Let them come to us, and we will show them hell.'

At the foot of the slope, the Immortals were now all mounted. All eyes were on Tiberius as he sat high, his sword stabbing towards the sky. 'We are the Athanatoi, the ones who are without death,' he boomed, his voice carrying over the swaying grass to the top of the ridge. 'Never has that been more true. For even should your days end here, your names will live on for all time. A warrior who is remembered in the hearts of many can never die.'

Hereward nodded. Good words. For a moment, he watched Tiberius urge his mount up the incline, with Isaac Balsamon, the Boar, and the snake Lysas Petzeas close behind. Then the ground began to throb, as a multitude of hooves rumbled as one.

'Shield wall,' the Mercian commanded.

From the edge of the Norman camp, three scouts began to gallop towards the interlopers. Ignoring them, Hereward felt his blood begin to pump. His men dropped into formation, their shields slotting into place. Spears nestled in the crooks of arms, tips pointed down ready to thrust at anyone who dared venture near the wall. At his command, the English marched over the crest, each step in perfect time so that the wall held solid.

Within moments, the rattle of their mail-shirts was drowned out by the thunder of the Immortals. Over the lip of his shield, Hereward watched the scouts turn tail as the fear of God descended on them.

The camp erupted. As one, warriors raced for weapons and shields and armour. When he saw that frantic movement, Hereward thought of a disturbed ants' nest. He sensed Sighard tense beside him, as he took in those swarming numbers.

'We are strong,' Hereward said. 'We are ready.'

The Immortals swept down towards the camp in two lines. They had the upper hand, for now, but the Mercian imagined how the attack must look to those rallying Norman warriors: a handful of English sheltering behind a shield wall, and an unkempt Roman force, few in number. He thought he could hear the laughter even above the rumble of the hooves.

Roussel's army stormed out of the camp. The Athanatoi did not slow as they tore into the first wave. Swords hacked down. Horses reared up, their hooves like hammers. Warriors fell on every side. But the Normans were not fools. Only a madman would send a foot soldier against a mounted foe. Row upon row of bowmen nocked shafts and the air turned black with whining arrows. The Romans threw up their shields in time. The sound of bolts thumping into wood was like thunder. Some riders were unlucky or slow, the shafts skimming the edges of their shields and slamming into faces and chests. Horse after horse went down.

Tiberius' cry rang out. The Athanatoi wheeled as one,

storming back up the slope, ready for another turn. Bodies littered the edge of the camp, Normans and Romans both. The churned earth was already turning into a ruddy swamp.

Hereward blinked away the stinging sweat dripping from the edge of his helm. The Immortals were brave, of that there could be no doubt. But any man could see that this would soon turn into a slaughter. Even the high ground was not enough of an advantage.

'I have seen worse,' Guthrinc said at his side.

A few men laughed. Hereward grinned, but only for a moment. With a full-throated battle-cry, a horde stormed up the slope towards them, a great wave of steel poised to smash them into the ground. And at their head, the Mercian saw, was Drogo Vavasour. His face was contorted with righteous fury. Somehow he sensed that his hated enemy lurked behind that row of shields, and finally, after all the miles he had tracked across, he was determined to have his vengeance.

'Now would be a good time,' Guthrinc murmured as he eyed the wall of swords and axes hurtling towards them.

'Aye, now,' Hiroc muttered.

Hereward gritted his teeth. Had he wagered everything and lost?

But then Drogo and his men began to slow, and then stop. The Mercian grinned once more as he watched a shadow cross their faces. Their eyes looked up, over the shield wall and past the English.

Hengist begin to snicker. 'Death comes for us, and then it comes for them,' he sang in a reedy voice.

Drawing himself upright, Hereward glanced back up the slope. A roiling cloud rumbled along the length of the ridge.

The Turks had come.

# Chapter Forty-Six

The wave of Seljuk warriors crashed down the slope towards Roussel de Bailleul's camp. Like thunder booming overhead, a throat-rending battle-cry drowned out the din of war. Their cavalry rode as if hell was at their backs. Their bows were already in their hands, as if they had no need to guide their steeds. Snatching arrows from the quivers at their leather saddles, they nocked them. A black cloud of shafts whined down towards the rooted Norman army.

Over the ridge they swept, in a seemingly never-ending flood. The very ground seemed to shake. Swordsmen surged from the left and right flanks where they had been slowly building their might in the deep, hidden valleys.

Hereward watched, amazed. Never had he seen such numbers. This was not any army that he understood. There seemed to be no generals, no leaders of any kind, or perhaps there were a hundred separate leaders. But somehow this collection of disparate tribes came together as one.

His face twisting with fury, Drogo Vavasour lashed a hand in the air to drive his men back to the camp where there would, at least, be some safety in numbers. And not a moment too soon. The battle-serpents rained down. Arrows ripped through the ranks. A hundred Normans died in one moment, screaming.

Swords slashed. Heads flew like ripe fruit at harvest time. The blades hacked into shoulders, tore across spines. The fleeing warriors went down, the Turks trampling them underfoot as their shrieks spiralled up in even greater intensity.

Hereward grinned. The Normans had been too confident. Their scouts had been watching for attacks from the front, from Constantinople, not from the flanks where they knew no Roman forces waited.

'Now is our time, brothers!' the Mercian yelled. 'Never has the risk been greater, so keep your wits about you and that fire in your chests. But never has their been a chance for greater glory!'

The shield wall began to grind forward as the Seljuks flowed around it. Ahead, the camp descended into mayhem. Those hardened Normans, some of the fiercest fighting men in the world, scurried like rabbits in all directions, overwhelmed by the immensity of the force railed against them. Fear had been driven into their hearts.

A familiar battle-cry rang out – 'Blood and glory!' – and all the English heads snapped to the right. Grins leapt to lips. A cheer echoed. On the edge of the Turks raced Kraki, a new axe in his grasp. Black coals shone from the eyelets of his helm. His mouth was torn wide in an O of battle-lust. Beside him ran a Turk, laughing like a madman, as if he had never found such joy in his life. This could only be Suleiman, the commander of the band that had taken Kraki captive. The plan was working better than Hereward had ever dreamed it could when he and Kraki had been hatching it in that swaying boat washing back towards Constantinople. Only a bold move could provide any hope – and that was what he and Kraki had offered to Nikephoritzes: an alliance with the Turks. Hereward had feared that the cure might be worse than the disease, but that was a matter for the Romans. And when Emperor Michael had enthusiastically agreed to the plan, there was no going back.

Hereward stared over the lip of his shield, frowning. Already the Norman ranks were coming together in some order. Roussel de Bailleul was too experienced a war-leader to let his men dissolve into chaos. Over the heads of the swarming Turks the Mercian glimpsed the warlord raging along the edge of the camp, bellowing orders.

At his command, the archers turned their bows upon this new foe. Another cloud of shafts shrieked across the blue sky. Screams rang out as the arrows thumped into the marauding Seljuks by the dozen.

Hereward half glimpsed Tiberius leading the Immortals back down the slope to defend the flanks of the Turks, an unlikely alliance that he never thought he would live to see. But then his spear-brothers pressed the shield wall into the edge of the camp, and they were swallowed by the maelstrom of battling bodies. The sky itself seemed to darken. Friend and foe crashed against the shields and rolled away. The Mercian's ears ached from the screams of the dying and the roars of the victorious, and the butcher's yard sound of iron meeting flesh.

'Onwards,' he cried. 'Let nothing slow us.'

Now everything depended upon cutting a swathe into the very heart of their enemy.

As the shield wall pushed on, Hereward glimpsed Kraki in the thick of battle. The Viking was glowering – war was a serious business. His axe hooked the side of one man. Wrenching it free, Kraki swung it into the face of another. Both went down in a red mist.

The Turks were doing their work well, as had been agreed when Kraki had ridden into the lonely hills for his council with Suleiman. They were fierce fighters, seemingly unafraid as they hurled themselves in wave after wave at Roussel's lines.

On the edge of the camp, Hereward spotted a weakening of the Norman line. He felt his heart beat faster. That was all they needed. In the sweltering heat behind the shields, he hissed his command. The wall drove towards the place where he could see clear blue sky between the churning bodies. Every foot kept in time with the beat of Hiroc's barked 'Hi-ho, hi-ho'.

The Normans turned on them as they rammed their shields

into the line, trying to break through. An axe crashed against Sighard's shield. Wood splintered. A sword glanced off Guthrinc's helm, raising sparks.

Thrusting with his spear, the Mercian ripped at the legs of the warrior in front of him. As the man went down, howling in pain, Sighard stabbed, then Guthrinc. The iron tips struck like serpents and retreated just as quickly. Back the Normans were driven, and back. But still they fought, their axes raining down like a smith's hammers upon the shields. Hereward knew they would not be able to take such punishment for much longer.

'To the English!' The voice boomed out even above the deafening tumult.

Through the gap in the shields, Hereward glimpsed Suleiman ripping open faces and necks and chests with each arc of his sword. Still laughing, the Turkish commander locked eyes with Hereward and seemed pleased by what he saw. Raising his left arm, he snapped it towards the Norman line. Whooping and howling, his men leapt and danced on each side of the shield wall. Within moments, the spear-brothers' fierce allies had opened up the Norman defences.

'Now!' Hereward bellowed.

The shield wall smashed through into the camp. Once they were among the tents, the English broke ranks, scattering in all directions. One shaven-headed Norman bore down on Sighard. Sweat flying from his red hair, the young warrior whirled and rammed his spear under his foe's chin, deep into the skull. Without a second thought, he tore his weapon free and raced on.

Guthrinc jabbed his own spear into the chest of another roaming foe, oblivious of a black-bearded warrior racing to stab his sword into his unprotected back. But as the Norman neared his prey, Derman rose up as if from nowhere. His knife whisked once, twice, and Roussel's man fell away, clutching at the crimson shower gushing from his throat.

Into the camp they ran. Every spear-brother knew what was expected of him. Weaving among the billowing tents, the

Mercian found himself in surprising peace at the heart of the furious battle rolling around the perimeter. No enemy had followed them, and the spear-brothers could tear open the canvas flaps and peer into the tents unchallenged.

When a piercing whistle rang out, Hereward grinned. Sprinting in the direction of the sound, he found the rest of the English converging on a large amber tent. Herrig stood at the doorway, sweeping an arm to usher his leader inside.

Hereward tore open the flaps and stormed into the sultry interior. In the far corner John Doukas cowered, one arm thrown over his face. The English crowded into the entrance, grinning that they had found their prize. Striding across the tent, the Mercian levelled his blade at the Caesar.

'Where is your courage now, dog?' he growled. His thoughts burned with the memory of the Roman's arrogant expression as he prepared to betray them to Roussel de Bailleul in the palace at Amaseia.

'The Norman bastard forced me to denounce my emperor,' the Caesar whined, his voice cracking. 'Under threat of my life, he made me proclaim myself emperor, but I would never—'

'Still your lying tongue,' Hereward snarled, 'or I will cut it out. I only have to drag you back to Constantinople to face justice. It matters little if all the pieces are there.'

The Caesar worked his mouth silently, like a codfish. He could see this was no idle threat. Hereward flicked the tip of his sword up and the Roman jumped to his feet.

'I have gold,' John Doukas said. 'Once we are out of this camp, set me free and you will be well rewarded.'

'The emperor has more gold, and he will want to speak to you at length about this business.'

Dipping his head, the Caesar allowed himself to be herded out of the tent with the tip of the Mercian's sword twitching at the nape of his neck. Once outside, he ground to a halt. A row of Norman warriors waited. Blinking into the hot sun, Hereward looked into the eyes of Drogo Vavasour. Bewildered, John Doukas glanced along the row, unsure with whom to side.

'I thought I glimpsed you skulking into the camp like a whipped dog,' Drogo spat. He levelled his sword at the Mercian. 'Now my brother will be avenged.'

Grabbing the Caesar by the shoulder, Hereward thrust him into Guthrinc's hands. 'Get him away from here,' he whispered.

The Norman commander seemed to care little about the man who had been proclaimed emperor. That was good, Hereward thought. As he listened to Guthrinc dragging the Caesar away, he raised his own sword, ready to buy his friend time.

His men needed no order. As one, they rushed their enemies, spears thrusting. Drogo's men broke line, using their shields to bat away the iron tips so that they could lash out with their axes. The dance rolled out among the tents.

Hereward locked eyes with Vavasour. The Norman had hungered for this moment for years. He would not back down.

'You have left a trail of misery in your miserable life,' Drogo said. 'It must end now.'

'I am wiser now than the man who took your brother's head,' the Mercian replied, 'but still I would do it again. Good English folk suffered his torments. He deserved his punishment.'

Vavasour gritted his teeth, his anger burning hot. Lowering his shoulders, he narrowed his eyes and prepared to attack.

'But you would do well to learn a lesson here,' Hereward continued. 'Every man is the sum total of his days gone by. They shape us for better or worse. But do not let them live on in your heart, or they will poison you.'

Drogo spat. Barely had the mouthful of phlegm hit the dust than he lunged. Hereward was ready for him. Whipping up his sword, he parried the strike. A trail of sparks glittered.

A blood-lust seemed to descend upon Vavasour and he thundered in, swinging his sword to Hereward's neck, then low, to his side. Putting his shoulder behind his shield, the Mercian felt the storm of blows jolt deep into his bones. Even in the midst of his fury, Drogo's skill as a swordsman was clear.

'Once I have slain you here, and pissed on your leaking body,

I will hunt down your men and slaughter them one by one,' the Norman barked. 'And thus will all see the true legacy of Hereward of the English – death to everyone who crossed his path.'

The Mercian felt the flames of anger rise. His father was dead, his brother gone too. He had no personal hatred for Drogo, but he would not let days long gone claim him any more. Days yet to come were his for the taking.

His eyes narrowing as if he could sense his enemy's thoughts, Vavasour hacked down from the right as if he were felling an oak. Hereward easily blocked the stroke with his shield. He felt the throb of blood in his head turn to whispers, and without any doubt in his mind he summoned his devil. For too long it had been his enemy. Now he knew he had to make it friend. Hungry, it rushed into him, possessing him even as his vision closed in and all sounds of battle ebbed away. He saw a shadow cross Drogo's face as he sensed what was coming. Perhaps it was fear. Hereward did not care.

He would not be thwarted again.

Wrath powered his arm. Brainbiter became a blur, the gold hilt shimmering in the hot sun.

The world turned red.

# Chapter Forty-Seven

The head swung on a strip of skin. Though the eyes rolled up white, the body lurched around on drunken legs as if it refused to believe that it was dead. Glistening rubies trailing from his axe, Kraki whirled, ready for his next foe. But there was none.

For a moment he wavered, getting his bearings. Gradually the fog of battle began to lift. He had been lost in a frenzy of hacking and slicing for what seemed like an age. His right arm felt as heavy as one of the bibles the monks laboured over at Eoferwic. Every joint burned.

Looking down, he saw he was standing on a mound of bodies in the centre of a red bog, steaming in the midday heat. More corpses littered the ground from the edge of the camp to where the Turks howled as they routed the remnants of Roussel de Bailleul's army. Shielding his eyes against the glare, he watched a stream of horses sweep across the grassland towards the horizon. The Athanatoi were hounding those enemies who had already chosen to flee rather than face the judgement of the Seljuks.

'Ah, you make me weary, my friend.' The deep, honeyed voice, laced with humour, dragged his attention from the scene of carnage. 'Breathe deep. Enjoy the sun on your face.'

Suleiman sat on the grass, his sticky sword across his knees. A gash on his forehead trickled blood and his hair was matted, but he showed his white teeth in a broad grin.

With the back of his hand, Kraki wiped the stinging sweat from his eyes. 'I will rest when the battle is won.'

'You have done all you can, and more. To fight alongside you as a brother has made my heart sing. So much fire in your heart! Why, there must be Turkish blood flowing in your veins.' Suleiman looked across the battlefield and his brow furrowed. 'We have lost many good men this day. The Normans fought as hard as I feared. But the rewards are great, perhaps greater than I ever could have imagined,' he added, his voice brightening. He clapped his hands together and rubbed them, anticipating what was to come.

'For the emperor, there was much at stake. He would have paid any price to see Roussel de Bailleul defeated.'

'I am happy with my lot, my friend. I will not be greedy.' Closing his eyes, Suleiman turned his face to the sun. 'Only one thing remains, and then our work here is done.'

As Kraki rested on his axe, catching his breath, he glimpsed fighting among the tents. Squinting, he realized he was watching the English crushing a group of men who had been pursuing them. Heaving with all his might, Guthrinc lifted a wriggling foe up on the end of his spear. Sighard rammed his own weapon through another chest. But as he looked on, he realized Hereward was nowhere to be seen. His chest tightened and he began to fear the worst.

Racing into the camp, he found Guthrinc prodding his spear at the Caesar to urge him to walk towards the last line of tents. With a frown and a shake of his head, the English oak pointed back the way they had come. Kraki spat an epithet and ran on. Finally, the Viking felt a rush of relief as he caught sight of the Mercian standing at the entrance to a tent. Red, he was, slaked in blood from head to toe. His sword hung limply at his side.

Kraki slowed his step. As if in a dream, Hereward stood unmoving, staring at a crimson mass at his feet. Only when he neared did Kraki realize it had once been a man. Worried, the Viking peered into the Mercian's eyes, wondering if he would see the bleak stare that often haunted him after such slaughter. But for once, Hereward seemed at peace.

'The battle is all but over,' Kraki ventured, 'and we have won.'

Hereward nodded slowly. As he looked up, he seemed to be returning from some distant land. 'Nothing will ever wipe away the stain of our defeat at Ely. But for the first time since we left England, I see better days within our grasp.'

The Viking grunted to hear words that chimed with his own thoughts. 'Within our grasp, aye, but still not there. I will raise my mead cup only when I can sink my teeth into that promise.'

'A wise course.' The Mercian sheathed his sword, examining the mess at his feet as if seeing it for the first time. 'Drogo Vavasour chose his path. It was the wrong one. We yet live to walk our road and we will find our reward at the end of it, I know that in my heart . . . if we stay true, if we are prepared to fight for it, aye, and kill.'

'Constantinople is a city filled with folk who would stand in our way. Would you kill them all?'

The Mercian laughed without humour. 'If I must. We have passed our days bowing our heads to their rules. Now we make our own.'

Wiping the blood from his eyes, Hereward strode off towards the edge of the camp. Kraki followed. 'I am pleased you did not flee, brother,' the Mercian said without looking round.

'The road ahead is hard, but it is the right one.' Kraki felt Roussel de Bailleul's words rush back into his mind. The world he had left behind still called to him, but it was like the mist and filled only with perils. He would not weaken. With his axe, he would carve out a new world, and it would be a better one.

As they left the tents, Kraki watched a horde of whooping Turks stream towards Suleiman. As they washed away in search of victory celebrations, they left in their wake a kneeling figure, bloody and beaten, hands bound behind its back. Roussel de Bailleul looked up at his captor as if he had never known defeat.

'What now?' the Norman warlord said. 'You would turn me over to Emperor Michael and his running dogs so that my head can sit on a pike at the city walls?'

Swinging his arms wide, Suleiman grinned. 'My friend! We have feasted together. We have sung, and we have laughed. We are brothers in all but name.'

'Then you will set me free?'

The Turkish commander feigned a troubled expression. 'But how would that be true to our friendship? You would never forgive me if we parted ways without one of us filling our hands with gold.'

'Ah. The Romans are paying you well to deliver me to them.'

'They have paid me well to defeat you. They would open even more coffers to see you crawling before them, I wager.' Suleiman squatted so that he could look the other man in the eye.

Kraki watched a silent communication pass between the two men. They both smiled.

'My wife sits in Ancyra with more gold than she knows how to spend. A wise man might send a messenger to her with word on how she can rid herself of that burden,' Roussel said lightly.

Suleiman tapped his forehead. 'If only I had thought of that, brother. I will make it so. For now, my men will take you to my tent where you can tend to your wounds. We will feast on hot lamb together at sunset.' Folding his hands behind his back, the Turkish commander walked away. Without looking back, he called out, 'And next time choose your allies better, my friend. I might not have been so easily swayed if I had not seen you in the company of that savage dog Karas Verinus.'

'My thanks for the lesson, brother,' Roussel called. 'I will learn it well.'

Kraki turned up his nose. This was not England. They fought their battles in strange ways here in the east. As he turned to comment upon this to Hereward, he saw that the Mercian's hazy gaze was fixed across the glinting waters of the Bosphorus to the shining dome of the Hagia Sophia in the distance. His features had darkened.

'We have won a great victory here today, but the truth will out when we return to Constantinople,' Hereward said. 'Falkon Cephalas waits for us like a fat spider in its web. We still have a fight on our hands.'

# Chapter Forty-Eight

Through the window, the full moon silvered the rooftops of Constantinople. In the chamber, though, only a sea of shadow swelled. The ghost of a recently extinguished candle lingered in the air. After a moment, the beat of approaching footsteps broke the smothering silence. When the door creaked open, a blade of faint, flickering light hewed a path across the flagstones.

Silhouetted against the dim glow of a distant torch, Falkon Cephalas hovered on the threshold. A muttered curse rustled out, and he stepped into his room and fumbled for the candle he knew he had lit earlier that evening.

The door swung shut behind him, seemingly of its own accord.

Falkon cried out in shock and whirled. The room was too dark to see anything, certainly not the hand that clamped over his mouth, nor the arm across his chest that dragged him back towards the window.

Salih ibn Ziyad smiled, his spicy breath warming his captive's ear. 'Do not breathe a word,' he whispered. And to make his point, he raised the hand pressing against Falkon's chest. His silver knife glinted in the moonlight. From over the Roman's shoulder, Salih watched the white of the other man's eyes grow wider. Bringing his blade up, he pressed the tip against flesh, a touch too hard. Blood bubbled.

'Once, a long time ago, a boy wandered out of the desert, half dead from thirst,' Salih murmured, a dreamy cadence to his voice. 'A nobleman found him and took him to the court of the great and wise caliph. The boy could not remember his own name, nor that of his father, or where his home lay. All of his days gone by were lost in the mists. And so the waif was entrusted to the care of the caliph's greatest adviser, a man of much learning, who knew the movement of the stars, and the ways of beasts, and the herbs and spices that healed. A man, some at the court would whisper, who could summon devils and foretell what was to come, and kill with but a word.'

Salih pressed the tip of the knife deeper still. Falkon squirmed, his cry muffled by the hand.

'Over the years, the boy learned everything the adviser knew. And he became that man's blade, bringing doom to the caliph's enemies. He slit throats in alleys, and poured hot lead into the ears of sleeping merchants. He poisoned the emissaries of foreign powers. He became death.'

Every fibre of Falkon's body seemed to stiffen. Salih smiled.

'I know a thousand ways to kill a man,' he whispered, his lips almost brushing his captive's ear. 'Poisons without smell, or taste. Unguents that dissolve the flesh. Where to cut to bring a slow death, filled with agony. Where to slice to trap wits inside a body that will not move. Do you hear my words?'

The Roman tried to nod, though the blade at his throat bit with each movement. Salih pulled back his hand from the other man's mouth. His words had done their work. Falkon could not bring himself to utter even a sound.

'Fortune smiles upon you,' Salih continued. 'I have chosen not to end your miserable life this night. But do not rest easy. One day I will come for you, when you least expect it, when you feel all is well in the world and joy lies in your heart. There is no safe place for you. Unless you heed my words, now. Leave the English be. They are not your enemies, nor are they enemies of the man you profess to serve. Do this and you may yet live to see your limbs grow feeble.'

He pricked Falkon for a response. The Roman gave a curt nod.

'And one other thing: never again must you harm a child. Disobey this command and your fate will be filled with more agonies than you can ever imagine.' Salih gritted his teeth at the thought of all the young ones who had suffered at the Roman's hand, but he would show no emotion. 'Go now,' he said. 'Do not waste your breath calling for the guards. No trace of me will be found.'

Salih whisked the knife away. For a moment, Falkon hesitated, scarcely able to believe that he had survived. Then he wrenched open the door and bolted along the corridor without. The door swung gently shut behind him. For a moment, Salih frowned. He had learned to judge a man by the smell of him. Too sour, too sweet, both spoke of a dark heart. Falkon smelled of nothing at all.

'*A boy wandered out of the desert, half dead from thirst.*' The teasing voice floated out of the shadows.

Crooking a finger, Salih beckoned, and Ariadne stepped into a shaft of moonlight.

'Three times I have heard you speak of your days gone by, and each one has been different. Where does the truth lie?'

Salih only smiled.

Her thin face darkening, the girl glanced over her shoulder at the door she had closed. 'Will he heed you?'

'For now. His anger will rise once he thinks on this night, but a part of him will still fear. The game he plays will continue, of that I am certain. But he has made too many enemies, too quickly, not the least among the Varangian Guard. Yet he is a clever man. He will show some caution . . . at least until he feels he has the upper hand.'

Ariadne eased the door open a crack and peered out. All was quiet. The Roman had not raised the guards. Salih watched her with fondness. For so long he had dedicated his life to guiding

Meghigda, the queen of the Imazighen in Afrique. But this girl had just as many wounds in her heart as Meghigda, and as much courage too. She needed him, and his wisdom. He could not turn away from that call, for God revealed his plan in strange ways.

'A change has come over you,' Ariadne said in a quiet voice, as if this notion had suddenly leapt into her head.

'We all change. That is how it should be.'

'You have less anger in you. After Meghigda's death . . .'

'After Meghigda's death, I wanted vengeance,' he said, 'nothing more. But vengeance consumes the heart and leads a man away from the true path.'

Ariadne furrowed her brow, puzzled. 'Then we no longer hunt the Nepotes?'

'The Nepotes will destroy themselves, by degrees. That is the nature of their lust for power. God has opened my eyes.' Salih slipped out of the door and beckoned Ariadne to follow.

'And when do you plan to tell me of this true path?' she asked archly, one step behind him.

'When you have learned the wisdom of a still tongue.' She had fire in her heart – he liked that. But now she would need his protection more than ever. 'Greater threats than even Falkon Cephalas are blooming in Constantinople. War is coming, any fool can see that – a war outside the city walls, and one within too. We must be ready.'

Salih stepped down into the dark, and the girl followed.

# Chapter Forty-Nine

The fire roared up to the heavens. Billowing clouds of black smoke swept across the moon as a shower of sparks swirled across the Boukoleon palace. At the centre of the courtyard, the pyre painted an amber glow on the warriors' downcast faces. Their reverent silence accompanied the crackle and spit of the blazing logs. Godred of the Varangian Guard was going on his final foray.

Hereward looked along the ranks of mournful men. His head bowed, Wulfrun stood front and centre, still holding the brand with which he had lit the fire. That was both an honour and an act of the greatest respect, the Mercian knew. And with the loss of the one who had guided him, Wulfrun had now earned a burden that would crush a lesser man, the command of the emperor's elite force. Wulfrun looked weakened by his time in captivity. His shoulders sagged and bruises still puffed his cheeks. But once he was strong again, Falkon Cephalas would have to beware. He had made a powerful enemy.

Beside him stood Ricbert, his face like stone, and at the fringes some of the surviving Immortals, who had been invited to honour their victory in the battle against Roussel de Bailleul. Battle had wearied Tiberius. In the glare, he looked ten years older, the Mercian thought. But he held his head up with pride.

'So the Immortals get showered with glory and told they will be at the heart of this new army that Nikephoritzes is building. But what do we get for risking our necks? Nothing, as usual.' Kraki hawked up a mouthful of phlegm and spat it on the flagstones.

Hereward smiled to himself. 'Do not rush to judgement.'

The English kept their respectful vigil in one corner of the yard, but Hereward knew the Viking was right – the Romans cared little that they were there. But they would soon learn.

As the fire died down to glowing embers, the warriors broke up and drifted away. Wulfrun remained, though, his head still bowed in remembrance or prayer, his hands clasped in front of him.

Hereward watched Maximos and Alexios trail over. Both men, too, seemed changed. A smile ghosted Maximos' lips and there was a lightness to his step. In contrast, Alexios' shoulders sagged and his face was drawn.

'You have made your plans?' the Mercian said to the elder Roman.

Maximos nodded. 'I will bid my kin farewell . . .' He grimaced. 'That will not be an easy task. I foresee sharp tongues in my future, and scorn and tears and pleading. But then, at dawn, I will ride out of the Kharisios Gate, and my life, at last, will be my own.'

'You have earned your second chance,' Hereward said. 'Seize it with both hands.'

Alexios raised his eyes to the night sky, refusing to meet the gaze of any. Ever since he had returned to the city, he seemed to have a great weight upon him.

Guthrinc rested a heavy hand on the young Roman's shoulder. 'You look as if you need some wine inside you. Come – the tavern calls us.'

After a moment's reflection, Alexios nodded, a wan smile lighting his face. Hereward watched his spear-brothers troop away with Maximos and Alexios among them, pleased that their spirits were high after so much striving. But he could not join them. The true victory had still to be sealed.

For a while he waited, watching the burning shards blown by the night breeze. And when Wulfrun finally abandoned his watch, still he stood in the shadows, alone. But then he heard a door open and the sound of voices and he readied himself.

A group of nobles stepped out into the glow from the dying fire. Nikephoritzes led the way, his piercing stare fixed upon John Doukas. His head dipping, the Caesar would not meet the eunuch's accusing gaze. But he would escape punishment, Hereward guessed. He was of the emperor's blood, after all. Perhaps only banishment to his estate awaited him for his treason.

The nobles shuffled across the yard with a weary gait. Their discourse had dragged on for long hours, but the final outcome had never been in doubt. Hereward nodded. He could see from the grin on Suleiman's face that the Turk had got everything he had been promised. His voice was louder than most. 'And so we are all friends,' he boomed. The scowl on Nikephoritzes' face gave the lie to his words.

A woman walked at the rear. Anna Dalassene wielded more power than any other woman in the city, Hereward had come to realize, perhaps almost as much as Nikephoritzes. And she hungered for more. When she caught sight of the Mercian standing in the shadows, she nodded and came over. The men continued on their way, oblivious. They would soon regret making such errors, Hereward guessed.

'How tiresome these talks are,' she said with mock-weariness, 'but men love the sound of their own voices.'

Hereward glanced at Suleiman as the Turk clapped an arm across Nikephoritzes' shoulder. 'I think the emperor's decision will come back to bite him in the arse.'

Her face darkening, Anna glanced back at the knot of men as they disappeared into the feasting hall. 'I fear that you are right. What madness assailed him? To cede to the Seljuks all rights to the land they have conquered. The sultan of Damascus will reward Suleiman well. And we have given up a swathe of our empire without a fight, and for what . . . because we had no army of note that could defeat a Norman upstart.' For once her mask slipped away and Hereward glimpsed a face of stone. 'It will not end here. The Turks will demand more and more. Michael has invited them into his hall, but they carry knives behind their backs.'

'This will weaken the emperor further.'

'But at what cost?' Her features softened, and a sly smile crept on to her lips. 'Still, there is sun after every storm.' Fixing her gaze upon Hereward, she narrowed her eyes and silently urged him to ask the question that he had been waiting so long to utter.

'It is done?' he said.

'The gold you took from the carts in Roussel's camp is part payment,' she replied. 'The remainder will come from my coffers, as we agreed. I will be your patron. The Varangian Guard will accept you and your men into their ranks.'

Hereward felt his heart surge. Finally, after all the striving, they had clawed their way out of the mire. But he knew there would be a price to pay.

'What do you ask?' he said.

Anna pursed her lips as if deep in thought, but he knew she had long since decided her side of the bargain. 'After the ceremony, you will give your oath to the emperor, as is right, but you will also work for me. Juliana Nepa has Wulfrun, and I will have you.'

Hereward nodded. He had expected no less.

'This will be difficult for you, a great leader of men.'

'You will have my sword, but not my soul. Honour above all, that is my code. I will not betray that.'

Anna stroked her lips with her slender index finger. 'You will tell your men where your loyalties lie?'

'They do not need to know.'

'You must care greatly for them, to spare them this burden.'

'My burden,' he growled, 'and mine alone.'

'Then let us see what the days yet to come hold,' she said, pleased with her deal. Her smile gave him no comfort. She moved away into the smoke drifting from the pyre. Her voice floated back. 'Be ready to use your sword, Hereward of the English. You will need it.'

# Chapter Fifty

'You are a coward and a traitor!'

The amphora shattered against the wall a hand's breadth from Maximos' head. Juliana bared her small white teeth. Her cheeks were flushed, her eyes flecked with tears of rage. Behind her, their mother Simonis flexed her fingers as if she wanted to throttle the life from her son's neck. In his chair in the corner of the chamber in the house of Nepotes, Kalamdios twitched and jerked. His eyes rolled wildly and spittle flew from his mouth as his mewling spiralled up.

Maximos forced his winning grin, knowing it would do little good. He had expected dismay when he told his kin that he was leaving – leaving Constantinople, leaving them all to stew in their own endlessly bubbling pot of plots and deceit. But he had not been prepared for this explosion of rage.

Another amphora with an ornately painted image of Apollo thundered towards him, one that had belonged to his grandfather. Jerking aside, he batted it away with his hand.

'When I was lost in Afrique, you did well enough without me,' Maximos protested.

'We held faith in your returning,' Simonis snarled. 'All that we have planned, all of it, over these long years . . . you were always at the heart of it. You would have been emperor.'

'And now you are nothing but a filthy rat, scurrying away in search of carrion,' Juliana spat.

Simonis jabbed a finger at her son. 'You have been around those English too long. They have corrupted your mind. They do not want power, only wine and women and fighting.'

Maximos shrugged, then regretted it. He decided not to reveal his fondness for that same road. 'You risked all to aid Wulfrun when his life was in peril,' he said instead.

'But I did not choose between him and kin.'

With a deep sigh, Maximos held out his hands. 'My decision has been made. Will you not wish me well?'

'Go,' Simonis replied, her voice wintry. 'And I pray that I never lay eyes upon you again.'

Maximos felt a pang in his heart. But he knew his choice was the right one. He could not be a slave to his kin's hungers any longer. 'Where is Leo?' he asked, drained of all emotion.

'When he heard you speak with your treacherous tongue, he fled this house. You have broken his heart,' Juliana said, cutting him as hard as she could.

Maximos winced. Of all of them, Leo was the one he would miss the most. 'I will return, one day,' he said, 'and then perhaps you will look on me with kindness once more—'

'Leave this house,' Simonis ordered.

With a sigh and a nod, Maximos strode out of the chamber. He could feel the weight of their resentful stares upon his back. As he picked up the sack filled with the few possessions he was taking with him, he hoped they would find it in their hearts to forgive him. But he knew them too well.

Once he was outside in the warm night, he felt his mood lighten, a little. The burden that had crushed him for so long was lifting. Ahead lay new towns, new folk who did not know him, and a chance to make amends for the miseries he had inflicted over the years. Ahead lay hope.

As he set off for the Kharisios Gate, he found Leo sitting against the wall of a house, his head in his hands. Relief flooded him. At the least, he could say goodbye. He felt a touch of regret when he saw that the boy nursed the sword he had given him when he was teaching him how to fight. They had been close. Of all of them, Leo would miss him the most.

'Why must you go?' the boy demanded without looking up. His voice was low and hard.

'When you are grown, you will understand. There are worlds beyond Constantinople, and this web we Nepotes weave for ourselves.'

'You have no love for your own kin?'

'I love you more than ever!' Maximos was taken aback that Leo could think such a thing. Squatting in front of the boy, he made his voice low and warm. 'I must find my own destiny, and it is not here in Constantinople.'

Leo shook his head, incredulous. 'You are grown. Why do you speak like a child? We are the Nepotes. We work for each other. One wins, we all win.'

Maximos felt his heart sink as he heard the words of his mother and father quoted back at him. His head swam with a sudden vision of Leo's days yet to come, a life made up of deceit and murder in pursuit of power, until all the innocence in his heart had been wiped away.

'There is another way,' he tried to explain. 'Your mother and sister . . . they see only one path in life, all our wants and wishes set aside in a constant struggle to gain the throne—'

'And then we will be content, for all others will have to bow their heads to us.'

'No! Even were you to gain such a thing, after long battles and much suffering, what seems like gold from a distance will only be clay when you hold it in your hand.'

'You are a jolt-head.' Leo glowered. 'You could be emperor, and you would throw it away.'

'Can you not hear what I am saying?' Maximos leaned forward, pushing his face into the boy's. 'Pay no heed to what your mother and sister tell you. What do *you* want, brother? What is your desire?' When Leo only looked away sullenly, he said soothingly, 'I would not have you suffer as I have. Your life would be filled with joy if only you would seek it out.'

'I ask you one more time,' the boy said in a small voice, 'do not leave.'

'I must.' Maximos held out a hand. After a moment's reluctance, Leo took it, allowing his brother to haul him to his feet. 'I hope you will pay heed to my words. If not now, if not this night, then when I am gone. Follow your own path.'

Maximos hugged the lad tight to his chest, and felt a pang of sadness when his brother remained stiff, his arms hanging limply at his side. 'And keep up your lessons with that blade,' he said with a grin, trying to raise the mood. 'You will be a great swordsman one day.'

Choking down his feelings, he told himself that it was only a brief parting and he would see his brother again one day. But as he walked away, he heard the sound of small feet hurrying behind him. He smiled, and had begun to turn to give the boy another hug when an agonizing pain burned in his side. In shock, he glanced down. A blade had burst from his belly. Blood pumped from the edges, soaking his tunic and streaming down his legs to puddle around his feet.

'My sister is right,' Leo hissed, wrenching the sword free. 'You have betrayed the Nepotes. You do not deserve to live.' The boy danced in front of him, his face twisted with righteous rage.

Maximos gaped, unable to accept what had happened. Pleading, questioning, he reached out his hands and saw they were stained red. His legs gave way and he sagged to his knees in the spreading pool. 'You have killed me?' he stuttered.

Leo leaned down and snarled into his face. 'My desire is to be emperor, brother. When you were missing, the throne was offered to me, and when you returned they snatched it away. But it will be mine. I will fight for it harder than you ever would. This blow is struck for the Nepotes, and I am proud to be one. I will never be a coward like you.'

The lad's pale face hovered for a moment. Maximos could

see no remorse there, only contempt. And then Leo spun on his heel and raced away into the night.

Maximos slumped down, his cheek pressing into his own hot blood. As the dark closed in, more visions flashed before his eyes. He could see the path of misery continuing for Leo, and for all the Nepotes who came after him, a path without honour. There was no end to it.

Footsteps echoed and a shadow loomed over him. Through the haze, Maximos squinted. A great hulk of a man was squatting in front of him. A low chuckle emerged. When the new arrival leaned in, the broad, leonine face of Karas Verinus hove into view.

'And another of the Nepotes dies in the filth of the street,' he gloated.

Maximos tried to spit an epithet, but only blood bubbled between his lips. For a moment, coughs racked his body, and when he looked back Karas was rocking on his heels, looking up at the stars.

'The heavens look down upon us and our battles,' the general mused. 'We must be as nothing to the angels watching o'er us. We strive, we fall, we rise, we fight again. For what?' He shrugged. 'For power, of course. It is the coin of our realm down here. We can do no other. Fight or die.'

Maximos shuddered. The night was hot, but he felt colder than he ever had in his life.

'And in the coming seasons there will be a hard-fought battle for the throne here in Constantinople,' Karas continued, looking down at his enemy. 'The emperor's days will soon be done, any fool can see that. And all those who hunger for that crown are moving into place. But now you will not be one of them.' He laughed, low and throaty.

As his head spun, Maximos heard the other man's words echoing as if from a long tunnel. He knew he should be feeling anger, but nothing burned in him. He had been hollowed out.

'You are weak, Maximos Nepos,' Karas said, his voice almost

too dim to hear. 'A strong man would bend his kin to his will. But you flee, likc a rabbit. And if you run, you die.'

And then Maximos sensed movement around him, and heard other, stranger sounds. At first he thought Karas' angels had come down to claim him. After a moment, he realized he was watching a man with ruined features and a boy with a face like the moon roaming around him, and they were making a sound like cattle lowing. Round and round they went, round and round, and he thought perhaps they were dancing, and singing in jubilation, singing that he was soon to be gone.

He thought of Arcadius, his childhood friend, whom he had murdered for the sake of his kin, and of Meghigda, the only woman he had ever loved, whom he might as well have murdered.

It seemed there was no escape from the plots and games even at the last.

Karas settled back to watch him die.

# Chapter Fifty-One

Dust motes floated in the shaft of pale dawn light. Shadows clustered hard against it as the line of warriors peered towards the sole, narrow window, high up on one glistening stone wall. The iron scent of blood hung in the air, and the vinegar reek of fear-sweat. Most of that dank chamber lay below ground, and the steady drip of water echoed all around. Chill and dark apart from that feeble promise of the rising sun, to the men there it was a grave in all but name.

'Death waits in silence.'

The voice boomed out of the gloom, low and hoarse. The warriors chanted the words back into the dark. A flint was struck, the sparks flaring. A torch sizzled into life. The shadows flew away, hungering at the backs of the row of naked spear-brothers.

Hereward blinked, squinting as his eyes adjusted to the amber glow. He was proud. Here was the moment for which they had fought for so long. Once he and his men emerged from this pit into the new day, they would be reborn as members of the Varangian Guard. Gold and glory would be within their grasp, finally.

'Death waits everywhere.'

Another torch roared alight. A mountain of a man lumbered

from the rear of the chamber into that sunbeam. Naked to the waist, his shoulders were as broad as an ox. A large, round belly hung over his leather belt. His head was shaven, his left eye milky where a jagged pink scar ran from temple to cheek. A gold ring glowed in one ear. No one there knew his name, but they had been told he would guide them to Death, and, if they were strong, back to the world again.

Hereward could sense Guthrinc to his left and Kraki to his right, but every man kept his eyes ahead, as they had been commanded. Somewhere Hengist began to whimper.

'Quiet,' their guide barked.

A stone table was swathed with shadows in one corner. From it the shaven-headed man fetched a golden bowl. The dark contents gleamed in the torchlight, and the Mercian breathed in that familiar scent of the battlefield.

'Here is the blood of the lion and the bull,' the guide intoned. Dipping two fingers into the gore, he walked along the line, painting an X on each man's forehead. 'You are marked,' he said. 'Death will see you now. Your old life will be gone.'

As he passed in front of him, the guide's good eye locked with Hereward's. Pupil and iris seemed all black, and the Mercian felt that this scarred man was looking deep into his skull, right through him, and out through the walls of that place.

Once he was done, the guide strode back to the stone table and fetched a wooden pail. Placing it on the beaten mud floor in front of him, he tugged aside the cloth hanging from his belt, grasped his cock with both hands and pissed into the bucket. The stream was long and strong and steaming.

After he was finished, he lifted the pail and carried it to the end of the line, pushing it against Sighard's lips. 'Drink,' he said. 'And soon you will fly beyond Midgard to the shores of the great black sea, and there you will be judged.' He had eaten the toadstools that gave a man wings. Many died when they swallowed that dangerous food. In the piss, though, it kept its power, but the chance of survival was greater, Hereward knew.

Down the line the guide moved with the pail, each warrior swigging back a mouthful of that hot, bitter drink. And then they waited.

Hereward felt his stomach churn and bile rise into his mouth. The sound of dripping became the beat of a war-drum. His vision twisted and he closed his eyes.

'You will meet a beast, or a bird, or a fish there,' the guide was saying, 'and when you return, if you return, you will paint it upon your shield.'

More words echoed, but Hereward could not understand them. He heard the thunder of wings, and then he was flying, up, out of that chamber, high over the world and away.

*

Along the shores of that black sea he walked. His father and his brother were not there to meet him, and for that he was thankful. But he was greeted by a squat, fierce Viking with a beard dyed the colour of blood. A raven sat upon his shoulder.

'This will be your sign,' the Viking growled.

Hereward felt convinced he had met this warrior before, but for the life of him he could not remember his name.

He walked on.

A woman waited for him, in a dress the colour of spring leaves. Smiling, she reached out her arms to welcome him, and he saw it was his wife, Turfrida. Taking him by the hand, she led him along the water's edge as she told him of many secret things. And then she cupped her hand, and whispered in his ear, and he saw his son, far, far across the whale road, in England. Hereward wanted to watch him longer, but Turfrida shook her head. He felt a great sadness, but when she kissed him on the cheek it passed.

And then he was flying again, and looking down upon himself seated on the ledge in Malakopea-below, staring into the dark where the devils danced.

The world held its breath.

*

Hot sun flooded the courtyard of the Boukoleon palace. The wind swept grey ashes from the pyre across the flagstones as the grave-priests silently collected the remnants of Godred's charred bones and slipped them into sacks.

Hereward barely gave them a second glance as he strode out into the light. His heart still swelled with all that he had seen and felt. Had it all been a dream, or a vision, or had he truly visited that place? One thing was certain: he felt changed by it.

Behind him, his spear-brothers cheered and slapped each other's backs, every one of them filled with a joy that they had not known for far too long. Hereward turned and looked at them, marvelling at their crimson capes, and their new gleaming helms and vambraces.

Guthrinc threw his arms around him and crushed him so hard he thought his ribs would snap. 'All that you promised you have delivered,' he said, his eyes narrowing as if he knew the doubts that had haunted Hereward for so long.

'Aye,' Kraki said, shaking his new Dane-axe. 'We are filthy rogues and thieves and murderers no more. We are the emperor's men!'

The English cheered once more.

Turning, Hereward glimpsed Alric standing on the other side of the courtyard. The monk was smiling, more at ease than the Mercian had seen him in a long time. Leaving his men to their euphoria, he strode over to his friend.

'I am pleased that you have finally gained your just reward,' Alric said once they had embraced.

'There are still battles to fight. At least now we will be well paid for it. And you,' he added, 'I am told you stood up to Falkon Cephalas.'

'It seems I am a warrior too, in my own way,' the monk replied with a shy smile. 'And there will be more battles there too, but I will not shirk from them.'

For a moment, Hereward thought he heard wings, and he raised his eyes to the blue sky, but there was nothing.

Alric furrowed his brow. 'What troubles you?'

'No troubles this day, monk. Today we feast and drink.' The Mercian paused. In his mind's eye, he glimpsed a boy playing on the edge of a vast forest. 'But I was thinking of England, and all we left behind.'

'We will never forget.'

'No. We will never forget. But no more will it haunt us.' Shaking off his reverie, he clapped an arm round Alric's shoulder. 'Now, come. There is a tavern waiting, and much wine to be swilled before the sun sets. And tomorrow, monk, tomorrow the fight for gold and glory begins in force.'

Across the courtyard they walked, to the band of spear-brothers. And the world held its breath.

# Chapter Fifty-Two

*England, All Hallows' Eve*

The rain had stopped not long after dawn. Though the black clouds had scudded away, in the trees it was as gloomy as dusk. Moisture dripped from the branches in a steady patter as the man dragged the boy by the hand. Around them, the sodden forest seemed to be holding its breath. No birds sang.

'Do not tarry,' Centwine the monk snapped. His exhortation hung in the dank air. 'There are great men to see you. We must not keep them waiting.' He cursed as his twisted spine threw his gait off and he almost stumbled over a gnarled root.

The boy had Danish blood, anyone could see that. His hair was blond, his skin pale, his eyes an icy blue. Though he had only seen three summers, he was tall for his age, and wilful. Scowling, he struggled to wrench his hand free. 'Let go.'

The monk only gripped tighter. 'Stop your struggling or I will teach you a lesson with this.' Baring his teeth, Centwine swung up his free hand.

'Do not strike him.'

Jolted, the monk whirled, searching for the source of the voice.

'Come to me.'

On her horse, the woman waited for the squat churchman to

locate her. A grey woollen cloak swathed her slender frame, the hood pulled low to hide her features. She felt calm now. The ride had been long and hard and dangerous. The three warriors who sat on their steeds at her back had guarded her well from the cut-throats and rogues stalking the wild areas. But her greatest fear had always been that she would arrive too late.

When the monk saw her, he glanced around, thinking of running. She imagined he encountered few strangers here, away from the main road to the abbey, and any that he did were probably up to no good. But he took in the warriors and their axes and knew it would be futile to run. Hauling the lad behind him, he eased forward as if he were approaching a cornered dog.

The woman slipped down from her mount and waited.

'Who are you?' the monk asked, narrowing his eyes.

In the depths of her hood, the woman smiled. 'I know of you, Centwine of Crowland Abbey. You are dragging this lad to Richard fitz Gilbert, who has ridden from Windsor with the other Norman bastards.'

The monk's eyes widened. 'How do you know this?'

'Ears hear and tongues wag. And I know what fitz Gilbert will do once he has this lad in his grasp. As do you.'

Centwine lowered his eyes. Though he could not see her face, the woman knew he could feel the weight of her judgement.

'You would sell an innocent soul for a bag of gold,' she continued, her words like pebbles falling on wood. 'I would think you would want to be away from here, to pray for forgiveness.'

Startled, the monk looked up. 'But the king's men—'

'Go. Or *my* men will see how fast you can run with an axe at your back. Richard fitz Gilbert will return to Windsor empty-handed this day.'

For a moment, Centwine hesitated, weighing whose wrath would burn hottest. Slowly his fingers slipped from the boy's wrist and he edged away.

'Go,' the woman commanded. Turning, the monk scrambled

through the dripping undergrowth until he was lost in the trees.

When there was only the patter of falling droplets to disturb the stillness, the woman threw back her hood. Her skin was as pale as snow, her hair black as raven wings. Dropping to her haunches, she cupped the puzzled boy's hands in her own cool fingers. 'You are safe now,' she murmured. 'I will take you far from here, where you can grow to be a man without fear of harm.'

'Who are you?' the boy asked.

'My name is Acha, of the Cymri. I knew your father. I stood beside him at the battle of Ely, when he fought to free the English from the rule of a cruel king.' She hesitated as the flood of memories threatened to drown her. Of the first time she met Hereward in frozen Eoferwic and of feelings as sharp as a new knife. Of the struggles and the hardship and the crushing disappointment of that final battle. And she thought of Kraki, the man who had loved her more than any other. His face floated in her mind, and the tenderness he kept hidden from all others, and she felt warmth flow deep into the heart of her. 'Your father is a great hero. All the stories they whisper of him in the taverns and by the home-fires are true. No man was braver.'

The boy stared at her with wide eyes. 'My father?'

'He waits across the water now, and one day he will return to save us all. Do you have a name?'

'Elstan.'

She shook her head. 'You are Hereward, son of Hereward. Know it well from this moment on. One day you will live up to all that that name means.'

'Hereward.' The lad let the word play on his lips for a moment. Then he craned his neck to look back into the trees. 'You have sent Centwine away. How will I find my way to the abbey?'

'You are done here now. No more chill cells, and thin gruel, and cold-hearted monks. You will have a new home, in the west.' She brushed his hair back from his forehead, seeing the mark of his father in his features. Smiling, she added, 'I have a child too. He is only a babe in arms, but he will be a brother to you. Come.'

Acha took the boy's hand and led him to her horse. Climbing up, she hauled him on to the animal's back and placed his arms around her waist. Her life had been hard, and at times bitter, but she felt her spirit soar that she had done this good work. This boy would have better days, and if all went to plan he would leave his mark upon the world.

The rain began falling once more. The pattering of droplets on leaves quickened, drowning out the snorts of the horses. Pulling up her hood, Acha leaned over her mount's neck and urged it on, into the trees, into the shadows, into the days yet to come.

# Author's Notes

Hereward was already moving into myth within living memory of his epic struggle with the invading Norman force after 1066. As they slipped into their twilight years, those who knew him, who fought alongside him, were spreading stories of a hero who seemed more than a man . . . not just a simple war-leader, but someone who had left his mark upon history in an almost supernatural way. These stories were circulating, and growing in the telling, over a time span in which many other real, historical figures would have quickly been forgotten. This tells us a great deal, not just about Hereward himself, but about the importance of what the English of that time thought he had achieved.

It also informs us about his death. There are plenty of theories about what happened to Hereward after the battle of Ely, but no record of the facts. But if we're sifting through sand, as we have to do when we examine the skimpy evidence from such a long time ago, we can be quite sure that he didn't die at Ely. If he had, that great death would have been part of those stories that began building soon after the defeat of the English rebels.

Academics are bound by evidence. Writers of historical fiction have huge advantages when it comes to playing 'what if . . .' – we can use what we know of human nature to make informed judgements. One of the theories is that Hereward received a payoff, a bribe perhaps, from the new King William, and retired to his new estate to live out his days in comfort. But would a man who was such a dangerous and wild force in his youth, and risked everything to lead a rebellion with no clear personal stake, go so quietly? Would the Hereward of Ely be bribed into silence? I suggest not.

We don't know for certain, of course, but we do know many English rebels fled the country, and many nobles too. After *Hereward: End of Days* it would have been easy for me to move on to new characters, a new story, perhaps a new era (and there are plans afoot for that), but I wanted to understand what it must have been like for those defeated heroes – men who had lost everything, family, friends and livelihood. A good many of the warriors did indeed head to Constantinople, to gain service in the Varangian Guard, or to work as mercenaries. A number became pirates in the Mediterranean, as was shown in *Hereward: Wolves of New Rome*, and then attempted to establish a New England to the north of the old Roman empire.

Things do not happen in isolation. One of the themes of these books is how what has gone continues to influence what is. But we also know that what happens in one place can ripple out across the globe. I wanted to show the big picture, geopolitics if you will: the world of the eleventh century, and what was happening elsewhere while England was simmering in defeat, and the links that bind it all together.

*Hereward: Wolves of New Rome* was a transition novel. I weighed the idea of starting the fourth Hereward book with all the spear-brothers already in Constantinople. But then I would have missed the opportunity to show the rough journey that many of the English rebels suffered, and those ties that connected old home to new.

But now, with this book, we have returned to the backdrop of real historical events. The campaign of the Norman adventurer Roussel de Bailleul, the rival emperor, the growing plots against Emperor Michael – all of this happened. And there are even greater battles, betrayals and machinations just over the horizon, all of it as gripping – and as important to the history of the world, and to England – as the struggle against William the Bastard (we just don't get taught much of it in our school history lessons).

Those who know their history of the Byzantine empire will understand that Anna Dalassene is a towering figure. We meet her for the first time in this book, because, as she rightly points out herein, she was in exile when Hereward and his men first arrived in Constantinople, and her sons were keeping a necessarily low political profile. But as you can guess from the end of this book, her story, and that of her son Alexios Comnenos, will continue.

And what of the new King William? What of England? There are stories aplenty to be told there. Should we examine what is happening in the old country under this strange new rule? Only time will tell.

James Wilde

## ABOUT THE AUTHOR

Born in the East Midlands, **James Wilde** read economic history at university and worked as a journalist before becoming a full-time writer. His debut novel, *Hereward*, was the first in a bestselling series that recounts the life of this near-forgotten hero. Despite travelling the world in search of adventure, James remains a Man of Mercia: he lives and writes in a house in the heart of a forest that his family has owned for several generations. To find out more, visit www.manofmercia.co.uk